Falcons

A Siege of Malta novel

Melvyn Fickling

The Book Conspiracy

Dedicated to Janice Alamanou with love

Acknowledgements

Many thanks are due to Gary and Carol Ashton for hosting my trip to Malta and for their continued interest in, and encouragement for, this project.

PART 1

AVVENTURA

Chapter 1

Saturday, 31 May 1941

The vomit spiralled down, reflecting glints of cool Mediterranean moonlight as it twisted past the rows of portholes and splattered unheard into the sea like the guano of a monstrous seabird. Bryan Hale spat the bitter vestiges of bile into the void. Wiping his mouth on his shirt sleeve, he raised his gaze to the imperious bulk of Gibraltar swinging away behind the ship. The flat top of *HMS Argus* blocked out the sky above his head, but the stars glistened with detached innocence above the Spanish coastline across the water to the north. The emerging moon lighted the carrier's passage to the hostile eyes that undoubtedly spied upon their departure.

Bryan contemplated the large wooden lifeboat creaking on its warps and squinted beyond its bulk to the inky waters, a fathomless cavern of invisible danger, a creeping threat that escalated with each thrust of the bows. The six Hurricanes lashed to the flight deck and the further six nestled in the hangar below made the *Argus* an irresistible target whose best defence was to pass through danger as quickly as her engines could carry her.

The bulk of another warship loomed behind the carrier, her bow wave peeling a seductive shimmer of foam from the water's dark surface as she slowly overhauled her charge. A lamp flashed across a signal as she passed to take up her position as a protective vanguard. Bryan craned his neck to see the second escort cutting across their wakes to take up the starboard station.

Bryan examined his hands. The tremor of previous months had stilled. The commitment to action with all its manifold perils had displaced the brooding fears and doubts that had dangled like hungry spiders around his hospital bed. He was going where the *Argus* would take him and the iron vessel's solidity lent rigidity to his purpose.

He walked carefully along the gangway, the slow shift and roll of the deck playing with his balance, until he came to the steps that led him down into the ship. Using the walls as support he moved along the corridor, past the open doors of cabins filled with murmuring voices to the one he'd left in a hurry a few minutes before. A face looked up from the lower bunk.

'Hello,' the man said, sitting up on his mattress. 'I've been assigned to share.'

'Bryan Hale.' Bryan clacked his tongue against the roof of his mouth. 'Sorry, I've been on deck feeding the fish. He extended a hand.

The other man shook the offered hand. 'Ben Stevens,' he said and reached under his pillow. He pulled out a bottle and held it up. 'Fancy a mouthwash?'

Bryan accepted, uncorked the bottle and took a swig. The warm, softness of dark rum scraped the sour aftertaste of stomach-acid from his tongue, spreading its heat down his gullet and quietening his unsettled stomach.

'Very appropriate,' he said, handing back the bottle.

Stevens smiled. 'I made a little detour to the galley after we sailed. It would be a shame to waste the chance to put our feet up for a day.'

'I wouldn't get too relaxed.' Bryan crossed the small cabin and unlatched the porthole, sniffing at the influx of air like a cautious cat. 'We've got the Spanish on our left, the Vichy French on our right and quite probably some Italians lurking about beneath us.'

'Well, I don't know that worrying will change anything.'

'Almost certainly not, but it doesn't hurt to know where the exits are.'

Sunday, 1 June 1941

The carrier steamed due east through the early morning light, Bryan and Ben leaned on the rail, allowing the fresh sea breeze to blow away the memory of the dank humidity below decks. Away on the port side and slightly ahead, their escorting destroyer ploughed a parallel path.

'I didn't see you at breakfast,' Ben flicked his cigarette butt over the side and it curved away with the wind.

'I couldn't see the point in breakfast. It never tastes as good on the way up.'

Ben smiled. 'This breakfast didn't really taste that good on the way down. Where have you been posted from?'

'I was on night-fighters over the winter, Spitfires before that. I spent the summer at Kenley.'

'You were in combat? What's your score?'

Bryan shrugged. 'I don't know. I don't worry about the score, I'm just glad I'm still at the crease.' He lit a cigarette behind cupped hands. 'Where were you?'

'I've been on Hurricanes out of Manston. I arrived there in December, so not much doing. I've flown a few sweeps over France, but I don't think I ever fired at anything worthwhile, and I'm fairly certain nothing worthwhile has ever fired back at me.'

'Christ! Look at that.' Bryan pointed at escorting warship.

The vessel's huge grey bulk leaned over in the water as it flared into a violent turn away from them, churning white foam away from its stern as its propellers strained against its inertia.

'What's he doing?' Ben's voice tightened with tension.

'I don't know, but it certainly doesn't look like good news,' Bryan answered.

The gangway dipped away under their feet as the aircraft carrier lurched into an opposite turn. Bracing his arms against the rail, Bryan kept his eyes locked on the destroyer. As it completed its about-face, several small objects ejected in pairs from its stern, arced a short parabola through the air and splashed into the sea.

'Shit,' Bryan hissed. 'They're depth-charging something.'

Moments later the surface bulged and split, spouting colossal founts of water skywards. Dull reverberations clanged through the carrier's hull, ringing the passage of vicious shockwaves as each fountain collapsed back into itself.

The Argus completed its ninety-degree turn and swung upright on its new southerly bearing. Something in the water to one side of the quelling disturbance snagged Bryan's vision. Two bubbling trails scored straight lines that reached out like ethereal fingers towards the carrier, rapidly gaining on the fleeing ship.

'Bloody hell,' Bryan blurted, 'torpedoes!'

Both men leaned further over the rail, straining to follow the missiles' progress. The tracks vanished into the foaming wake, reappeared, and skimmed alongside, overtaking the *Argus* on a slim but widening diagonal.

Horns blared as the second escort destroyer churned past them in the opposite direction, hurrying to add its ordnance to the counterattack.

'That was close!' Ben's voiced stretched with stress. 'What happens now?'

Bryan squinted against the reflections dancing on the brightening water. 'I suppose we can hope that Italian submarines don't hunt in pairs.'

The gangway tilted again as the carrier started a wide curve back to port and accelerated onto an easterly course. Behind them, and now receding in the distance, the two destroyers criss-crossed the same patch of sea, trailing tumultuous violence through its depths.

'I hope this doesn't spook the captain,' Bryan muttered.

'What do you mean?' The other man's face was drained pale.

'Rumour has it, last year they flew a dozen Hurricanes off this same tub. The ship wasn't anywhere near close enough and only four made it in to land.'

'You're joking.' Ben looked at him aghast.

Bryan scanned the sea with lingering suspicion. 'I can think of funnier things to joke about.'

****

As the shadows lengthened into sunset, the destroyers steamed back into their flanking positions. The two pilots remained on deck. Unwilling to descend into their cabin's steel embrace during the heat of the day, they now lingered to enjoy the cool evening air.

'Do you think they got him?' Ben asked, nodding at their escort.

'It's not something we need to worry about,' Bryan said. 'Submarines aren't fast enough to chase ships like these and if they're still stooging about when this little lot sails back to Gibraltar, then that's somebody else's problem.'

A moment's peaceful silence fell between the men, broken at length by the scratching illumination of a struck match as Bryan lit a cigarette.

'What do you know about Malta?' Ben asked.

'Well let's see… It's about the same size as the Isle of Wight, but hopefully a bit prettier. We're using it to annoy the Germans by sinking their supply convoys to Rommel and his African Rats, or whatever they're called. Mussolini is also annoyed because he's promised it to the Italian people as part of a grand Mediterranean empire. It's far too bloody close to enemy airfields on Sicily for its own good. Everyone, but everyone, believes fervently in God yet they all still drink goat milk. It's hot and sweaty all summer and pisses it down in winter, and the women are beautiful.'

Ben smiled. 'Sweet.'

Another pilot swayed unsteadily down the gangway towards them.

'Weather forecast is set fine for tomorrow,' he called as he approached. 'Briefing in the hangar at 05:00, first take off at 06:00.'

'I take it we'll be close enough by then?' Bryan asked as the man staggered past them.

'I expect we'll all find out before the day's end. No more than thirty pounds of personal kit and don't forget your Mae West.'

9

Bryan winked at his companion. 'A holiday in the sun. Just what the doctor ordered.'

Monday, 2 June 1941

Hale and Stevens clumped through the bulkhead door into the hangar. They wore full flying kit and carried canvas duffel bags stuffed with their belongings. Echoes of metal against metal clanged around the cavernous space. Thirty feet above them, the flight deck's underside hung with cables and pipes. Queued down the hangar's length, pooled in the green glow from electric lights, sat six Hurricanes, facing away from the elevating platform that stood ready at the end of the hangar to lift the aircraft up, one at a time, to the flight deck for take-off. Their squadron leader, Dennis Copeland, stood on the platform, ticking names from his clipboard as they congregated in front of him.

Bryan grabbed Ben's arm. 'Hang around at the back. We want one of these,' he said, inclining his head towards the aircraft lined up behind them.

'What? Why?'

Bryan arched an eyebrow. 'The man who takes off last has the most fuel.'

They shuffled up to the back of the group as Copeland called for silence. The squadron leader ran through the flight plan, handed out maps and detailed cruising speed for best fuel consumption.

'We'll fly as two sections. Red section will take the aircraft up top.' He walked across the front of the group touching each pilot on the shoulder. 'You are Red 2, Red 3, Red 4...' He walked around the back of the group. 'The other six will fly as Blue section and take the hangered aircraft. You are Blue Leader, Blue 2, Blue 3...'

Bryan grinned at his companion as they were assigned Blue 5 and 6.

Copeland returned to his place in front of the men. 'Surrender your personal kit to your mechanics. They will pack it into the ammunition boxes in the wings.' He paused and swept his gaze across the group. 'Given that you'll carry no ammunition, it's probably needless to say that we do *not* engage any hostile aircraft we might come across. Check over your aircraft carefully; there'll be nowhere to land for the next 450 miles. Good luck, gentlemen.'

The group dispersed. Bryan and Ben walked the length of the hangar to the last two Hurricanes in the queue. Bryan treated his companion to a farewell slap on the back, dropped his duffel bag under the wing and started his walk-round of the fighter.

The sand and earth coloured desert camouflage gave the squat aircraft a distinctly cavalier demeanour, although the factory-fresh smell of paint gave away its combat chastity. Examining the leading edge, Bryan's hand lingered on the red canvas patches doped over its gun-ports. He smiled for a moment in anticipation. Crouching below the wing, he surveyed the incongruous gaiety of the pastel-blue underside, pulling and pushing the aileron to check it moved freely. Ducking under the engine, he stroked the tumescent curve of the tropical air filter, peering at the grille for blockages. Emerging on the port side he walked to the tail, cuffed the rudder and wiggled the elevators, checking their motion countered each other closely.

He walked back to the wing as a mechanic arrived with his parachute. Bryan pulled on his flying helmet, shrugged the parachute onto his back and fastened the straps. He climbed onto the wing root and clambered into the cockpit. The mechanic followed him onto the wing and helped to strap him in. Bryan pushed the control column through its full range and kicked the rudder back and forth. The mechanic watched the control surfaces moving and nodded in answer to Bryan's unspoken question. Another mechanic finished loading the requisitioned ammunition boxes into the wings and jumped onto the starboard wing, hunkering down next to the open cockpit. All three men sat quietly in impassive contemplation, waiting.

The hull tilted slightly as the carrier adjusted its course into the wind, then the background hubbub of engine noise ascended a tone as the ship slipped into full-ahead. In counterpoint harmony with this lazy growl, the higher-pitched bark and roar of a Merlin engine sounded from the flight deck above their heads, joined by another and then layered with yet more. One engine note swelled to an angry snarl and the noise traversed the hanger, marking the first Hurricane's dash for liberation into the air.

Bryan waited and counted. As the fifth fighter tore down the deck, all exterior noise was drowned by the choking clatter of an engine clanking to life inside the hangar. Bryan raised his eyes to his rear-view mirror to see blue exhaust smoke hazing the air as the pilot of the furthest fighter gunned his engine to warm his oil. A few minutes later the second Hurricane chugged into life, as behind it, the first was elevated out of the hangar's gloom towards the brightening dawn sky and the flight deck.

The cacophony ascended as each Hurricane came to life. The mechanic with the starter trolley arrived, plugged into the engine and Bryan's Hurricane kicked into being. He ran at medium revs for a minute, watching with satisfaction as the oil temperature crept towards optimum. A jab on his shoulder brought his head round to see the mechanic's face close to his.

'Brakes off!' the man shouted through the din.

Bryan throttled back to idle and released the brakes. The two men jumped from the wings and set their chests against the tail-plane, pushing hard to overcome inertia and get the Hurricane moving backwards towards the lift. They paused, waiting for the elevator to complete another cycle, then heaved the Hurricane along in the queue.

At last it was Bryan's turn. Two more mechanics dashed in from either side and pushed against the wings, helping to bump the aircraft onto the platform.

A man from the tail slapped the fuselage to gain his attention, 'Brakes on,' he shouted and strode away from the plane.

The lift mechanism jolted into motion and Bryan ascended through the thickening smog of exhaust fumes, up and out into the fresh Mediterranean morning. The lift platform locked into the deck with a jolt and a seaman standing just beyond his starboard wingtip waved to attract Bryan's attention. Bryan nodded to him and the man held his hands above his head and rotated them around each other. Bryan pushed the throttles open and felt the stocky fighter straining against its brakes. The man continued the signal and Bryan gingerly added more revs. He sensed the brakes starting to slip.

'Come on,' he muttered under his breath, 'let me go or I'll go arse over tit.'

The seaman dropped to a crouch and stabbed his pointing finger down the deck.

Bryan released the brakes and pushed the throttle wide open, tapping the rudder to hold his line as the Hurricane bounded forwards. The tail lifted, gifting Bryan a view of the deck's end approaching quickly. He eased the stick back and the rumbling of wheels against metal ceased abruptly as tyres and deck parted company. The Hurricane yawed a degree into the wind and sank towards the water. Bryan's stomach lurched and he swallowed against a flutter of panic as he eased the stick back further. His fighter flirted with disaster, then caught a secure grip on the breeze and climbed slowly away from the waves, its engine coughing greasy exhaust fumes back along its pristine paintwork.

Bryan flew straight for a long moment waiting for his undercarriage to clunk home into the wings, enjoying his return to the air and the swell of half-forgotten pleasures it inflated in his chest. He scanned the sky and found the orbiting squadron coalescing a few thousand feet above him. Banking to follow their circuit, he set his nose to climb towards them.

Below, the carrier and its flanking destroyers sliced sparkling wakes across the swell. The shape of Ben's Hurricane emerged through the flight deck and Bryan watched it buck into forward motion and rush along the floating runway. It barrelled off the end of the flight deck and dipped towards the sea, like an awkward courtier delivering her first curtsy, then it too climbed away strongly.

'Good man,' Bryan muttered to himself, casting his eyes eastward into the sun's rising glare. 'We're in business.'

Bryan and Ben joined the assembling formation. Copeland circled them once in farewell over the ships that scribed their own arcs in the sea as they turned back towards Gibraltar, then struck out into the eye of the morning.

****

Bryan sat at the back of the formation as it droned on the seemingly never-ending flight east and then south-east. He resisted the ingrained urge to weave, rather trusting to luck in the serious game of fuel conservation. Out to his right, the distant coast of Tunisia had long since melted away, but on his left the bulk of Sicily had appeared and persisted as a menacing dark line intersecting a featureless vault of blue. Grimacing, he clenched his buttocks to persuade some blood to flow into his cramped legs. He glanced at his fuel gauge with a prickle of nerves in his stomach; the bloody place ought to be close by now.

'Flight Leader to all aircraft.' Copeland's voice jarred into his earphones. 'I think that's our new home dead ahead.'

Bryan squinted into the distance, struggling to discern where the sky gave way to the sea. Then he saw them; two sand-coloured shapes, small and insubstantial in the vast stretch of water, like autumn leaves floating beneath the summer sun. Malta, and its smaller sister Gozo looked tiny in their solitude.

Bryan glanced back at the endless bulk of the haze-laden Sicilian coast stretching away on the horizon an alarmingly short distance away, and whistled softly. 'Looks like this will be a barrel of laughs,' he muttered to himself.

The squadron dipped to lose altitude and the two brown patches acquired texture as the distance closed. The Hurricanes swooped over Gozo, then the channel that separated it from the main island. The waters sparkled with a surreal clarity and the waves drew coruscating lines of breakers against the rocks of the Maltese coast. Huddled villages, still and quiet in the sunshine, offered up white towers and golden domes to the heavens. All around them, like an interlocked jigsaw of sun-bleached stone, low walls divided the scrubby fields. Far ahead, in the belly of the main island, swathes of dust climbed into the air, rolling away across the landscape on the lazy breeze.

'Flight Leader to all aircraft. That's Ta'Qali airfield, where we are supposed to be landing. It looks like it's under attack. Climb with me and prepare to scatter if there's any trouble.'

The squadron eased into a southerly heading to bypass the airfield and its attackers. Bryan picked out the bomber formation and above them a small fighter escort. Suddenly, almost in one motion, the enemy shied away, like nervous dogs in an unfamiliar street. The bombers dived north for home and the fighters climbed away to the north-east.

Copeland brought the squadron round into a shallow orbit south of the airfield.

'Flight Leader to Ta'Qali Control. Seeking permission to land. Twelve Hurricanes. Can you take us?'

A few moments of static crackle disturbed the silence.

'Fighter Control here. Yes, when you're ready. It should be alright.'

The squadron dropped down in pairs to the dust-shrouded airfield, their propellers swirling vortexes in the smoke that drifted thickly from the many bomb craters smouldering across the station. Ground crew met them, grabbing wingtips and guiding the fighters over the rough ground out to the perimeter and into makeshift stone blast-pens, many unfinished, some blown apart.

****

Bryan shut down his Hurricane and climbed out of the cockpit on stiff legs. He jumped down from the wing where mechanics were removing panels to retrieve his kit, lit a crumpled cigarette and surveyed the field around him. Ragged piles of rubble dotted the spaces between surviving buildings. Scattered through these, bell-tents stood in small groups, their khaki canvas filmed with pale dust. Parties of men with spades swarmed around the fresh craters, hurling the fractured earth back into place. A hundred yards further along the perimeter, the skeleton of a burning Hurricane drooped and twisted in the heat of its own conflagration. Another, next to it, tilted painfully on a broken leg, its wingtip bent and crumpled against the ground.

'What the hell...' Ben arrived at his side.

'Yes,' Bryan murmured, 'you might be right.' He cast his eyes around the dry, flat-featured airfield. 'Look, there's the boss.' He gestured at Copeland striding across the field at the head of a knot of pilots. 'I suppose we'd better follow him.'

****

Dust drifted from their boots as the group of weary pilots trailed across the perimeter track to a low building set apart from the airfield. The earth-coloured stone on its front elevation bore shrapnel scars from nearby bomb-strikes and most windows were cracked or shattered. An orderly hurried out to meet them and dropped into a hushed conversation with the squadron leader.

Bryan squinted into the strengthening sunlight. 'I'd forgotten how sweaty this part of the world could be.'

'Forgotten?' Ben asked.

'I was stationed just outside Cairo in 1935, the last time we had to keep a close eye on our friend Mussolini.'

'Thirty-five?' Ben raised an eyebrow. 'How old *are* you?'

'Old enough to be worried about the odds of getting much older.'

Ben's retort died in his throat at the sound of Copeland's voice.

'The resident squadron is rotating out, but they're not leaving until tomorrow. So, there'll be a spot of overcrowding tonight. There are camp beds set up in the corridors, so you'll just have to make the best of it.'

'Typical,' Bryan tutted, 'I knew I should've booked a hotel.'

Chapter 2

Tuesday, 3 June 1941

Another figure shuffled past in the gloom, walking with stiff discomfort. Bryan's eyes flicked open. Further down the corridor, the man pushed through the latrine door. Bryan stared at the dark ceiling and waited. A gushing of liquid and a quiet groan broke the silence. A minute later, tendrils of stench slithered down the corridor, building to a nauseating miasma that cloyed like grease in his nostrils. Bryan clamped his lips firmly shut, struck a match and held it in front of his face to beat back the fetid gases.

After several minutes, the man walked back along the corridor with a less encumbered gait and Bryan shot him a glance.

'Sorry, mate,' the man whispered as he passed. 'Malta Dog, you have to take it for a walk about once an hour.'

The match guttered and died.

'If my dog smelled that bad, I'd shoot the poor bastard,' Bryan muttered.

Somewhere in the middle distance a stick of bombs rumbled their detonations through the humid night like distant summer thunder.

****

Bryan and Ben sat on a low wall adjoining the barrack block, pushing their breakfast of scrambled egg around their greasy mess tins.

'If it *is* dysentery, I'd like to know how to avoid it, to be frank,' Bryan said, eyeing the yellow stodge with suspicion.

'It's down to dodgy water, I reckon,' Ben speculated.

Bryan switched his scrutiny to the tepid, beige tea in his mug. 'Well, I certainly didn't sign up to get the shits.'

Engines kicked into life on the airfield and a bank of dust rose in harmony with the noise, blocking out their view of the runway. As they finished their breakfast, a section of three Hurricanes rose from the dust blanket, carving vortexes through its shroud. Three more sections followed at short intervals. The full squadron circled the airfield once and then struck out on an easterly course. The dust cloud rose higher, slowly surrendering its form to the gentle shredding of the breeze.

'They looked like the new Hurricanes. I wonder what the flap is?' Bryan mused.

'And I wonder who's flying them?' Ben said.

'Indeed. Come on, let's find Copeland.'

The two pilots took their utensils back to the mess and walked the short distance to the perimeter. They stopped and surveyed the aerodrome. Apart from a team of mechanics stripping the fighter destroyed in yesterday's raid, and the slowly rotting wrecks that had fallen victim to previous attacks, the main field was empty of aircraft.

The pair walked around the perimeter track until they came to a makeshift blast-pen in which two Hurricanes sat. One was running an engine test with an airman in the cockpit gunning the revs while another stood to one side of the fuselage, listening like a connoisseur at a concerto. A third airman leaned against the other plane's wing, watching his companions at work.

Bryan approached the idle man. 'Who's gone up in the new Hurricanes?' he shouted over the noise.

The mechanic drew himself upright. 'They posted the last squadron to Egypt, sir.' He cupped his hands around his mouth to be better heard. 'They're on their way to Alexandria.'

'What, in our aircraft?'

'Yes.' The airman nodded.

'What does that leave for us?'

'As of this morning, we've got four serviceable, sir.'

The air cracked to a loud metallic impact and the spinning propeller clanked to a sudden standstill, lurching the Hurricane viciously two feet to the right.

The mechanic glanced nervously at the now-silent fighter and chewed his lower lip. 'We've got *three* serviceable.'

Bryan looked from the airman's reddening face to the seized engine's battered and scratched cowling, his eyes lingering on the curl of smoke that twisted up from behind the propeller boss.

'Where's the readiness hut?' he asked quietly.

'Tent, sir.' The mechanic grimaced his discomfiture. 'It's a readiness tent, over by what's left of the hangars.'

Bryan and Ben strode across the airfield, sweat prickling their foreheads and spreading across the backs of their shirts.

'Imagine,' Bryan muttered, 'if that engine had seized on take-off. You'd have no chance.'

They entered the large bell-tent to find Copeland leaning over a trestle table scribbling into a notebook, a field telephone stood close by his feet.

He looked up from his writing. 'Yes, I know, Hale.' He held up a hand to forestall Bryan's question. 'There was nothing I could do to stop it. We're to use what we have until the next batch gets flown in. That'll be ten days, maybe.'

'What we *have*, at the very latest count, is three serviceable Hurricanes,' Bryan said.

'It's not as bad as it could be.' The squadron leader straightened and picked his notes up from the desk. 'There have been no Luftwaffe sorties for over a week, probably too busy supporting their infantry in Crete. In any event, they've left us to the Italians for now, and it seems they prefer bombing at night.'

Outside, air-raid sirens lifted their bitter, mechanical chorus to the skies. A frown creased Copeland's brow and he looked down at the telephone. A moment later the bell jangled and the squadron leader grabbed the handset.

'Hello…' He listened intently for a moment. 'If that's the case, then surely we should scramble?'

The first stick of bombs detonated at the airfield's far edge, their blast waves tugging at the canvas flaps.

'Christ!' Copeland dropped the handset. 'Take cover!'

The tent disgorged a knot of men, skidding in the dust and sprinting towards the slit trenches that slashed the ground at intervals around the perimeter. Bombs pounded across the field, coughing gouts of dry earth into the air. The noise redoubled as heavy anti-aircraft guns stationed around the aerodrome slung retaliatory explosions towards the heavens.

Bryan dropped into a trench, scraping skin from his elbows on the hard-baked earth. Ben fell in beside him followed by a tangle of airmen and ground crew.

Ben squinted up to where the AA shells blossomed a thickening pattern of grey blobs against the blue, and caught the small silhouettes of bombers amongst them.

'They're bloody high.' He raised his voice against the noise.

'They're bloody Italian,' Bryan shouted back, ducking his head to protect his face from the small chunks of concrete-hard earth that pattered down, in and around the trench. 'Safety first with that lot.'

'Why isn't anybody taking off?'

Bryan shook his head. 'They'll be back in Sicily boiling pasta for lunch before you could get any of our tractors to that altitude. At least there's bugger all left on the airfield for them to hit.'

A fresh stick of bombs walked over the perimeter somewhere to their left, crashing impotent destruction into the scrubby wasteland between the airfield and the barracks. The last explosion echoed away to leave the staccato bark of AA guns to beat their steady tattoo. This too subsided as the attackers drifted out of range.

Dust drifted down, settling across the huddled men as they waited, listening to the ringing in their ears and the babble of unintelligible shouting drifting across the field. The short blare of the all-clear siren released them into action and they helped each other clamber out of the trench.

Soldiers with shovels trotted through the sandy haze to throw their backs into re-filling craters. Something large burned in the distance, throwing out furiously tight coils of orange flame, the source of the excited voices.

'Hale.' Copeland appeared at Bryan's shoulder. 'As we've got next to no fighters, we don't really need a dozen pilots on readiness. But I would like to know something about the organisation on this island and what it can or can't do for us. Phoning me up ten seconds before the first bomb goes off won't get us anywhere.' He grimaced. 'So, tomorrow I want you and Stevens to visit the control rooms in Valletta. Have a chat with a few people, see if there are any trade secrets we need to be aware of.'

****

As dusk became night, the heat turned viscous, piling extra weight on Bryan's limbs and making his blood pulse like porridge through his restless leg muscles. He lay on his cot and read the chit written by the squadron leader listing their two names and requesting they be allowed to observe the work taking place in the control room. Flipping the paper over he studied the pencil-drawn map and directions from the bus-stop to the control centre. He sighed, tucked the chit into his shirt pocket and looked across at the man on the other cot in the room. Ben Stevens was leafing through an old *Daily Mirror*, seeking out the photographs to draw moustaches on the men's faces and exaggerate the natural endowments of the women with a red crayon.

Bomb blasts rumbled in the distance. Bryan guessed the target was Valletta and the harbours that skirted the capital.

'I can't fathom why we're hanging on to it,' Ben mused to the room in general. 'It seems an awfully small rock to get so worked up about. Is it to do with national pride or something?'

'It's to do with oil,' Bryan answered.

Ben propped himself up on his elbow and pursed his lips in thought. 'Where's the oil?'

'Where it's always been,' Bryan said, 'in the Middle East. And as long as we hold Egypt, we control those oilfields.'

'So why aren't we in Egypt?' Ben asked.

Bryan lit a cigarette. 'The Germans have a socking great army in North Africa, commanded by a nasty little man called Rommel. He's been told to capture Egypt.'

The frown deepened on Ben's forehead. 'So... why are *we* not in Egypt?'

'Well, Rommel gets his supplies in boats that sail from Italy to Tripoli. And Malta is smack in the middle of their shipping lanes.'

'Ah, I see.' Ben rolled onto his back to continue his editorial enhancement of his newspaper. 'You'd think they'd send us some aeroplanes, then.'

Wednesday, 4 June 1941

The two men watched the scratched and rusty bus lurch to a halt at the airfield gates.

Bryan climbed aboard, 'Valletta?' he asked.

The driver nodded and smiled with glee as he and Ben boarded. They sat on the stained leather seats, next to windows completely bereft of glass. The bus pulled off and jolted violently three times as the driver ascended the gears. The passengers blinked and squinted until the vehicle moved ahead of its own thick wake of dust.

The uneven road surface swayed their charabanc on its creaking suspension and they gripped their seats for support. Scrubby trees lined the road, each leaning away from the prevailing wind. Behind the trees, a low wall delineated the road, built from a jumble of sandstone blocks, bleached near-white by the sun and interlocking without the assistance of mortar. The hard edges of the walls were softened at intervals by large cacti; collections of flat, spiny, paddle-shaped appendages jumbled haphazardly on a single plant.

As they travelled east, they came to residential streets. Terraces of flat-roofed houses, some white, some golden yellow, with balustraded balconies. Many balconies overflowed with large pots of basil, the glossy green plants poking their fragrant leaves between the rounded balusters. Men stood outside shops wearing black suits and black hats. Women hurried along the pavements in hooded cloaks, the starched cloth forming an umbrella-like arch over their heads to ward off the sun's heat. A grizzled old man with goats trailing behind him paused his procession to watch the bus rattle past.

As they entered the outskirts of the island's capital, the intermittent bomb damage became denser and the character of the architecture changed. The industrial necessities of a port city stripped many buildings of their picturesque niceties, drawing them up instead like opposing sandstone cliffs between which the river of traffic was obliged to flow.

Abruptly the yellow bulk of barefaced warehouses dropped away on their right to reveal a view across Valletta's Grand Harbour to the domes and towers of churches dotted amongst the buildings on the opposite bank. Half a dozen fat barrage balloons lolled in the sky like corpulent, khaki war pigs exhausted by the unremitting conflict that swirled around their passive bulk. A warship berthed against the quay bristled with guns pointing skyward, as if to hold the balloons to their mundane duty.

The road narrowed towards a huge and ancient fortification, sitting squat and impassive in the strengthening sun. The road dived into a tunnel beneath this colossus, its sudden confines amplifying the clattering of the bus amidst the trapped fumes of smoking engines. Breaking out the other side into the re-dazzling sunlight, the driver pulled over to the edge of the quay wall.

'Valletta,' he called over his shoulder. 'Quarry Wharf,' he added by way of explanation as the two pilots stood to disembark.

Bryan paused by the driver and fished in his pocket for change. The driver shook his head and waved him off the bus. The door closed and the bus clattered away.

'Nice people,' Bryan muttered as the bus receded down the quay. He pulled the makeshift map from his pocket and looked around to get his bearings. 'This way I think.'

They climbed a sloping, dog-legged road, feeling the sweat prickling on their brows. A short, enclosed stairway took them into a courtyard surmounted by a large arch. At the courtyard's far end a double-doorway stood open, flanked by two armed infantrymen guarding whatever lay in its dim interior. Bryan led the way across the courtyard and presented the chit to one of the guards. The man read the paper and ducked inside to use a wall-hung telephone. The other guard eyed Bryan suspiciously and unslung his rifle, hefting it in his hands.

Bryan's thoughts chased back to a London street and the smoke curling from a bombed-out café.

'Flight Lieutenant Hale?' the voice derailed his memories.

'Yes?'

'I'm Sergeant Tanner.' The man handed back the chit. 'I can show you around, but we need to stay as quiet as possible. Follow me.'

The sergeant led them through the door. Bryan and the belligerent soldier exchanged sidelong glances before the gloom swallowed the pilots from view.

They walked along the dimly-lit stone corridor, its incline leading them deeper into the solid rock of the bony promontory that supported the city of Valletta. They walked past many doors; most were closed, but through others they caught glimpses of charts on walls, wireless sets on tables, soldiers seated at desks, bookshelves filled with files, bunks and lockers.

They reached a door marked RAF Operations. Sergeant Tanner placed a finger on his lips to emphasise the need for silence and, opening the door, ushered them onto a balcony overlooking a large room. Below them a huge oblong table bore a painted map. Almost half the map was taken up by the yellow bulk of Sicily and the tip of Italy's toe. Shockingly small by comparison, and separated from Sicily by a narrow channel of blue, sat the sister islands of Malta and Gozo. Half a dozen civilian women sat on stools around the table wearing headsets. To their right, the wall supported a blackboard showing available aircraft. Above them, the balcony held desks with telephones where two officers sat, peering at the map with detached boredom. Only two plot markers sat on the map, both over the coastal waters of Sicily. One of the women stretched across and moved one marker back over the land.

'It all seems quiet at the moment,' Tanner whispered. 'Those are probably single bombers on flight tests.'

'We got hit badly at Ta'Qali yesterday.' Bryan leaned close to the sergeant to make himself better heard. 'We got no warning at all.'

The sergeant nodded sadly. 'Our RDF station is on the other side of the island. Telephones went down for an hour. Sorry.'

'We're newly posted,' Bryan continued, 'what warning will we normally get?'

'Not enough.' The sergeant grimaced. 'So, once you're up, we generally send you south, away from the raid. That way you can get some altitude without being bounced, then we bring you back in to meet the bombers.'

Bryan raised an eyebrow. 'We'll engage the raiders over the island?'

The sergeant nodded.

Bryan gestured at the near-empty 'available' blackboard. 'Is it always as bad as this?'

'It gets better occasionally. But we've got nowhere to hide the aircraft, so the enemy always knows where they'll be.' He pointed at the map. 'They only have to fly sixty-odd miles to get here. At that range you could fly three sorties a night if you fancied it.'

****

The pilots emerged blinking into the sunshine.

'What now?' Ben asked.

'Well' – Bryan stood for a moment, hands on hips – 'I suppose we could gather some intelligence on the state of the bars.'

'Amen,' Ben breathed. 'Let's go.'

The two men wandered north, away from the quayside. The road curved lazily upwards, its incline lending a brutal weight to the sunshine beating at their backs. The harbour, its glittering water and the ships with their primed defences, slid away behind them as the hot ground beneath their feet straightened into the grid-like pattern of Valletta's street plan. They moved with relief into the shadows cast from the buildings on either side. A strip of vibrant blue sky topped this man-made sandstone gorge, and its narrow confines funnelled what breeze there was to kiss the men's glistening cheeks.

The street was crossed by another, and at this intersection the corner block lay partly collapsed into itself, the broken edges of the stones glowing incongruously golden with fresh, un-weathered surfaces. On the building diagonally opposite, the statue of a saint stood in a niche ten feet above their heads, holding out its hand in supplication and tilting an imploring visage to the heavens, as if shocked from its placid stoniness by the violence of the bomb-strike.

23

They continued north. Above them, the sandstone walls sprouted stone plinths on which enclosed balconies perched, first and second floor living space stolen from void above the road. The incline crested into another crossroads and another statue – the robed Virgin holding the Holy Child, her face serene and forgiving.

The men turned left and walked on. They passed cafés, but each contained only knots of dour old men nursing long-cold herbal teas.

'There has to somewhere that's got a bit more spice,' Bryan said. 'It is a port, after all.'

A large building caught his eye, a sign on its flat frontage declared it as the newspaper office. A couple stepped out of its arched entrance onto the pavement.

'Ah, a journalist,' Bryan muttered. 'He'll know.'

Bryan called out as he approached the man and spent a few moments absorbing the directions he was given. As the journalist turned to go, Bryan's eyes fell on his companion. She wore her long black hair loosely bunched and pinned away from her face. Her tanned skin crinkled at the edges of dark brown eyes as she waited for her friend to re-join her. She caught Bryan's gaze and the ghost of a smile flickered across her face. Then she turned and the pair walked off. Bryan watched her move across the dusty stone pavement with an easy, animal grace and felt the memories of dead feelings he'd intended to leave behind stir in his chest.

'Christ,' he muttered under his breath.

'I'm getting thirsty.' Ben's voice snapped the moment. 'Do we know where we're going now?'

'Yes,' Bryan said, 'Strait Street. Back this way.'

After taking a couple more doglegs at crossroads overseen by the blank-eyed stare of saints and martyrs, and walking down several narrow streets where Italian bombs had punched gaps into the terraced buildings, they arrived at Strait Street. A faint undercurrent of evaporating urine edged the air with vinegar and a man walked past them with the exaggerated nonchalance of the morning drunkard.

'Here we are,' Bryan murmured, looking at the pub signs sprouting from the walls down what was more an alley than a street. 'Let's try this one.'

They stumbled to a halt inside the tavern doors, the dimness inside robbing the vision from their sun-narrowed pupils. As their eyes adjusted, figures and furniture coalesced from the dissolving gloom and they moved to a free table by the shuttered window. A waitress followed their progress across the room and took their order for beer.

On the table next to theirs, three seamen sat, empty glasses littering their stained wooden tabletop. One man was engaged in a hissed conversation with one of two women at another table across the room. The girl listened to the sailor and shook her head, listened once more and shook her head again. Throughout this exchange the girl's companion examined her fingernails with an expression of resigned boredom that had long since flattened the sparkle of her young eyes. The sailor whispered something else. The girl relayed the information under her breath to her bored friend. She nodded once and both women stood to leave. Two of the sailors tipped the remains of their beer down their throats and hurried out after their business deal.

Bryan caught the remaining matelot's eye. 'Not enough entertainment to go around then?'

The man turned his stubbled face to Bryan and held up his left hand, brandishing a silver wedding ring. 'I have recently forsaken all others.' He smiled ruefully. 'No regrets.' He chewed at his lower lip for a moment.

'What sort of ship are you on?' Bryan asked.

'Not a ship, a boat,' the man said. 'A submarine, based across the harbour.'

Bryan's eyes widened. 'We had a brush with a submarine on the way out here, damn nearly got us. The navy gave *those* poor bastards a pounding.'

The submariner nodded. 'The water is too clear for submarines. Once they see you, it's hard to sneak away.'

Ben leaned over to interrupt. 'Is there anything to do around here, other than drink?' he asked.

'There are dances around and about the place on a Saturday night. Nowadays they wind things up before eleven o'clock so people can get away before the night raids start. There are a few British girls on the island, they generally turn up for a dance if they can. The other good place to meet them is the Mtarfa hospital.' The submariner treated them to a wry smile. 'Although since the Luftwaffe shipped out, not so many of you Brylcreem-boys are ending up there.'

****

Bryan and Ben stepped from the bar's gloom into the unrelenting glare of the afternoon sun. Flies dipped and wheeled around their faces, hungry for the fresh, salty sweat that budded and bloomed on their foreheads. They paused at the sound of hooves against stone, flattening themselves against the wall at the sight of an approaching cart.

A single white horse leaned into its harness; its lean flanks were serried by ribs that pushed their curves into its grey-tinged hide. Its head bobbed low against the weight of its load as it laboured up the slope. A red felt cap, stitched carefully to fit snugly over its ears, gave it the aspect of a horned beast and a red wool band fixed across its nose flashed like a battle wound.

The carriage it pulled stood taller that it was long. The driver perched on a narrow ledge directly behind the horse's emaciated rump. Behind him, under a delicate fringed canopy, sat a young girl in a satin wedding dress next to an older man in a black suit. Her face was tinged with sadness, his was lined with belligerent determination. Neither looked at the pilots as they rattled past on the clatter of the cart's iron-rimmed wheels.

Chapter 3

Friday, 13 June 1941

'What is that? A lucky mascot?' Ben nodded towards the shelf above Bryan's cot as he laced up his dust smirched desert boots.

Bryan paused in checking the connections on his oxygen mask and glanced up at the knitted pilot figure sitting atop the rough wooden ledge.

Bryan pulled a wan smile. 'He was a Christmas present from a lady I once knew. It's as easy to keep him as throw him away.'

'What was the lady's name?'

Bryan ignored the question. 'Come on, we're due on readiness in five minutes.'

They walked out into the waning afternoon sun, its fetid heat wafted into their faces on desultory breaths of breeze. They joined two other pilots at the readiness tent. Ben jumped into the card game that was already well underway. Bryan dropped his helmet onto a tattered deckchair and wandered away from the group, kicking at loose stones in the dusty soil as he meandered away from the tent. Looking up into the blue bow of the crystal-clear sky, he pushed away the reawakened ghosts that flapped unbidden around his heart and replaced their yammering with the cold, glassy desire for combat.

****

The hours trailed past. A bead of sweat blossomed on Bryan's forehead, trickled down around the end of his eyebrow, diverted along the toe of his crow's foot and delivered its salty sting into the corner of his eye.

'Damn,' Bryan muttered. He hauled himself out of his deckchair and stepped into the tent. 'When are we off readiness?'

The orderly at the desk checked his watch. 'A little over forty minutes.'

'Right,' Bryan said, 'we're taking off.'

The orderly's chair fell backwards as he jumped to his feet. 'You can't do that without an order from control, sir.'

Bryan ignored the man's exhortation. 'Come on, lads,' he said, 'let's go for a spin.'

The four pilots strode across the hard earth towards their dispersed Hurricanes. Ground crew, spotting their approach, hauled themselves out from the shade under the fighters' wings and plugged in starter batteries.

Bryan's Hurricane roared into life. Squinting against the dust-laden prop-wash, he pulled on his parachute, clambered onto the wing and replaced the airman who scrambled out of the cockpit.

Bryan gunned the engine, fishtailing the fighter out onto the landing strip and waited for Ben and the other two to form up behind him. Once all was ready, he pushed the throttle forward and his aeroplane clawed its way into the cooling air of the approaching evening.

Bryan swung the flight due south and climbed hard, watching the turmeric ground drop away as his altimeter ticked up. The cliffs of the south coast slid away underneath them and Bryan held the climb, exulting in the buffeting breeze that rattled through his open cockpit.

At 8,000 feet, Bryan pulled the formation into a wide climbing turn to head north, back to the mainland. They made landfall at Kalafrana, set on the mouth of Marsaxlokk Bay, and continued their climb across the island's rump. As Grand Harbour and the huddled roofs of Valletta shimmered out of the heat haze, the tone of static in Bryan's headphones compressed, presaging a transmission.

'Fighter Control to Falcon Leader. Who requested your scramble?'

'Hello, Fighter Control,' Bryan answered. 'I'm sorry Control, a misunderstanding, obviously.'

A long pause crackled with more static, then the controller's voice sounded again. 'We have twenty-plus bandits climbing away from the enemy coast. Vector zero-one-five to intercept.'

'Roger Control,' Bryan answered. 'There's a bit of luck.'

Veering starboard to correct their course, the four Hurricanes overflew Grand Harbour and headed out to sea.

The minutes ticked by and the sun sank lower in the west, painting tendrils of purple across the blue. Bryan squinted ahead, sweeping the sky for movement.

'Falcon Two to Falcon Leader,' Ben broke in, tension stretching his tone. 'I see something dead ahead and a fair bit above us.'

Bryan concentrated on that patch of sky and the small profiles of lumbering aircraft spattered the previously blank void.

'Thanks, Ben. I see them,' Bryan answered. 'Let's continue the climb. Watch out for escort aircraft.'

The engine droned its monotonous clamour into the cockpit and the approaching silhouettes grew larger as the Hurricanes clawed away their enemy's height advantage.

'They're breaking!' Ben's voice again.

The edges of the formation peeled into wide turns, dark motes dropping away beneath them. In less than a minute the whole gaggle of bombers completed an about-turn, their loads falling impotently to waste and exploding in the sea.

Bryan speculated for a moment on their altitude deficit, the progress of the setting sun and their proximity to the Sicilian coast, then made a decision. 'Falcon Leader here. Break-off. Return to base.'

****

Bryan taxied into a blast-pen beyond the perimeter, waited while the groundcrew arriving at his wingtips swivelled the aircraft to face across the field, shut down the engine and locked on the brakes. Leaving his parachute on the wing, he walked back towards the readiness tent through the rapidly failing light. The squadron leader stood at the tent's entrance watching his progress and ducked into the tent as he got closer. Bryan followed Copeland inside and found the officer sitting on the edge of the trestle desk.

'Sit down, Hale.' He gestured at the wooden chair in front of him. 'Exactly what do you think you're doing? The fighter controller is bloody furious.'

'We turned back a bombing raid before it got anywhere near the island.' Bryan lit a cigarette and blew the smoke down at his boots. 'So, I suppose the answer to your question is saving lives.'

'You can't take matters into your own hands. You know full well there's a system that must be respected.'

Bryan looked up at his commanding officer. 'With respect, the system scrambles us too late and then sends us in the opposite direction to gain height. By the time we get some altitude and head back, the bombers are over their target getting their job done. We need to be patrolling at the right height to intercept them over the sea. Just like my flight did today.'

Copeland leaned forward and jabbed a finger towards Bryan's chest. 'You were lucky the enemy made an appearance to validate your vigilante escapade, without that you'd be on a rocket right now.'

29

'Why?' Bryan held out his arms in supplication. 'Why are we making it so difficult for ourselves? Why are we sacrificing the homes and lives of people with a so-called system that doesn't work?'

'Because,' Copeland's voice dropped to a hiss, 'we're on a bloody knife edge. There are next to no supply ships making it through from either Gibraltar or Alexandria. Every single drop of fuel we burn takes us closer to running out.' He paused to allow the concept to sink in. 'And when we run out, we'll be forced to surrender this whole bloody island to the Italians. And you know what that will mean for our lads in Egypt.'

Bryan remained silent, dropping his cigarette on the floor and crushing its glowing tip under his heel.

'Yesterday,' the squadron leader continued, 'a submarine arrived from Alexandria loaded with tin cans of fuel. I'm told it carries enough to give us three- or four-days flying time with every trip it makes.'

Silence fell between the men and Copeland stood, laying his hand on Bryan's shoulder.

'I recognise your good intentions, Bryan. But we are truly in the shit. So please, no more freelance scrambles.'

Saturday, 14 June 1941

Bryan paused, bent at the waist, and watched the sweat drip away from his nose. It fell onto the lump of sandstone he'd just heaved into place on the wall of the half-built blast-pen. The moisture darkened the stone's surface for a moment, then the colour lightened, receding gradually to its own centre as it evaporated. Behind him, Maltese workmen dropped more stones from a donkey-drawn cart into a pile next to the wall.

'Bloody God-forsaken medieval hell-hole…' he muttered under his breath and heaved his shirtless back as straight as his protesting muscles would allow. Walking to the pile, he grabbed one end of a large rough-hewn block as Ben grabbed the other. The two men hefted the stone and tottered back to the wall, swinging it onto the top and shuffling it around to seat it steadily on top of its predecessors.

'We're like fish in a bloody barrel.' Bryan wiped the sweat from his temples. 'They know where we are, and they watch what we do.'

An airman walked past with a bucket of water and a ladle. Both men took a drink and splashed their grimy faces with the lukewarm water.

'At least we're not in artillery range.' Ben smiled. 'Always look on the bright side.'

The drone of aero engines interrupted their exchange and, shading their brows with outstretched palms, they watched a new squadron of Hurricanes circle the field, undercarriages dropped in readiness for landing. Here were the occupants for the new blast-pens they toiled over.

Bryan gazed beyond the arriving fighters, above them to the hazy clouds that edged the heavens over the island. 'Somewhere up there, in his nasty bulbous bi-plane, is a little Italian joker, counting these lads in and calling them out to his bomber bases, he muttered. 'How I'd love to wipe the grin off his face.'

****

Bryan stirred from the sweaty doze that counted for sleep in the humid, boxy barracks. He blinked at the dark ceiling in momentary confusion before the air raid siren penetrated his consciousness and pulled a groan from his chest. He rolled on his mattress, its rough cloth damp with his perspiration, and grabbed his shirt from the bedpost. The three other pilots stirred in the darkness around him.

'Let's get moving,' Bryan croaked past furry, dry teeth. 'No doubt they'll be throwing everything they've got at the new kites.'

Outside, the faintest of breezes tickled the sweat on their cheeks as they trailed across to the slit trenches and dropped into their fragile shelter, joining those already huddled there. Spotlights lanced into life around the airfield, swinging skywards to probe the vanishingly deep, cloudless Mediterranean night. Bryan watched their slow sweep across the ebony dome, the familiar chill of helpless vulnerability tickling at the nape of his neck.

One of the yellow beams swept past a small object, illuminating it brightly like a silver moth flashing through a shard of moonlight. The operators tracked back, searching for another taste of this tiny, hostile insect.

'There!' Bryan pointed as the light rediscovered its victim and followed its slow progress across the night. 'It's one of those three-engine Italian jobs. I bumped into some of those over Canterbury last year.'

As the men craned their necks past the edge of the trench, two more searchlights swung in ponderous arcs to latch onto the unlucky raider. The airmen flinched at the percussion banging through the hard ground as the nearest heavy anti-aircraft battery opened fire. Its strident bark was soon

31

interlayered with the yapping of smaller guns as all the defences roused from rest to meet the skyborne menace. Small flashes glittered in and around the searchlight beams, building a box of slashing shrapnel that swirled death and disfigurement into the dark.

'Their shells are fused too low,' Bryan muttered. 'He's going to get away with it.'

Black specks fell from the aircraft, slicing through the illumination and vanishing into the darkness between the beams. A whistling rose behind the beat of the guns, like the pipers of a demonic army, to be lost in the thudding explosions laid down by the pinned bomber and its gaggle of unseen companions, stitching a pattern of mayhem across Ta'Qali's runways.

The trenchful of airmen hunkered lower to the stony base of their shelter as the strikes meandered closer. One man's quaking voice staggered through the Lord's Prayer as detritus pattered around their heads. The final bomb roared its vehemence no more than fifty yards away and the last line of shaky benediction wavered from the praying man's mouth as the rumbling detonation rolled away through clouds of dust.

A crooked smile pulled at the corners of Bryan's mouth as he lifted his face back to the sky to hear the lumbering Italian bombers climbing away, chased blindly by the now-impotent AA fire. The memory of their fat, corpulent bodies wallowing through his gunfire in the grey Kentish sky sparked a tingle of urgent desire in his vitals.

'Forever and ever,' he echoed under his breath. 'Amen.'

Sunday, 15 June 1941

Copeland walked slowly across the airfield through the strengthening dawn light, his shoes scuffing up dust as he went. At his shoulder, Bryan sucked on a cigarette, his features crunched in concentration. Both men surveyed the destruction as they went. Several hurricanes lay lopsided like crippled seabirds, some smouldered from opened bellies, settling in on themselves as they decayed into the licking flames. Other fighters, though still whole, revealed rents and tears in their fabric as the men passed close by, presaging unknown internal damage, enough to make the plane unserviceable until checked over. The pair skirted a bomb crater, a thin pennant of white smoke curling up from its centre.

'How can we fight them if they only come at night,' Copeland said.

'Italians.' Bryan chewed on the word. 'I certainly wouldn't recommend stirring them up; they'll fight damned hard if they're cornered. But they tend to look for the' – he searched for the right words – 'least hazardous way of conducting their operations.'

'We need more anti-aircraft guns, more shells and more gunners,' Copeland's voice sizzled with his frustration. 'But nothing's coming through. It seems we really are stuck between the Italian devil and the deep blue bloody sea.'

'Well.' Bryan flicked away his cigarette butt and lit a fresh smoke. 'They know where we are, and they *will* keep coming back. But that means *we* know where *they* are going to be.'

Copeland frowned. 'What are you talking about, Hale?'

'We should put up a few fighters to meet them every night.'

Copeland barked a laugh. 'You're joking!'

'Think about it.' Bryan blew a stream of tobacco smoke through his nostrils. 'A standing patrol at night will never be a waste of fuel, because we're practically guaranteed a target will turn up, with the added bonus that they'll have no escorts.'

They walked on in silence past a collapsed slit trench. Three bodies lay on the ground under a tarpaulin and two medics laboured to recover a fourth from the slumped earth.

Copeland stared at the scene for a long moment, then cleared his throat. 'How do you propose to find a raider in the dark?'

Bryan gazed at the blocky lines of a Hurricane standing on the perimeter and pursed his lips. 'Well, in England we used a socking great Beaufighter with a magic box in the back and four cannons in its belly. Obviously here, things will be a bit more… Heath Robinson.'

'What do you have in mind?'

'Last night I watched the searchlights cone a bomber. The gunners were on it straight away, but they have to range and lead a target which is effectively coming to the end of its bomb-run and turning away for home. What shots they managed to get off were well below target. They might've punctured his tyres if they were lucky. Other than that, he got away scot-free. Things would be a lot easier in a fighter flying at the right altitude. Once the bandit is illuminated, the pilot simply has to drop in behind it and shoot it up the arse.'

Copeland grimaced. 'Isn't it bloody dangerous, flying through a bomber formation in the dark?'

Bryan glanced back over his shoulder. 'No more dangerous than sitting in a shitty little trench wondering where the next bomb will land.'

Copeland's nose wrinkled at the blunt reality. 'Alright,' he said. 'Let me put it up to the AOC.'

****

With men working to repair the runways and little chance of daylight incursions, Bryan slipped away from the airfield and jumped onto a transport heading to Grand Harbour. With shouted promises of a rendezvous to catch a lift home, Bryan dropped from the truck's tailgate on the approach road to the harbour on the northern side of Valletta.

The sun, climbing towards mid-morning, warmed his face as he walked the last sweeping curve in the road and the north harbour opened up before him. The far bank jostled with buildings that shimmered white and grey in the strengthening haze. The shore they massed against extruded a promontory, less crowded by construction, that still boasted scrubby gardens unsubdued by dry, barren sandstone. Along the edge, an ancient arched palisade rose from its waterborne reflection, like a palatial residence lifted from a desert oasis.

Sloping walls lined the road Bryan walked, set as if to defend against this supplanted Egyptian menace. He walked on, grateful for the beneficent shade thrown by these belligerent bastions. Across the glittering water, another edifice slid into view. Atop the promontory, set full-square on the rock, commanding the harbour waters that split around its seat, a palace or a fort from a different war, long past.

The road curved east and the sun's eye bored into his forehead, backlighting the bomb-damaged domes and broken spires of Valletta, at once exalting their time-worn solidity, but lighting their uncertain vulnerability against the power of this new age of siege machines that came at night with no respect for bastion or battlement.

The lilting chime of bells paused his step, its loosely frayed pattern soon overlain with a different sequence from another church, both joined by more until the entire city tinkled with the gentle calls to worship.

Bryan took a side road, grateful to escape into the shade between its towering walls, and moved into the city proper. Around him a sedate eddy of humanity emerged from battered wooden doors and flowed towards the nearest, loudest peal of the bells. Families mixed with couples, and they hailed greetings to ancient, solitary men in black jackets and grease-banded hats, all of them intent on giving thanks for what little they had and, as their reward, receive a morsel of holy sacrament.

Bryan stopped, allowing this stream of humanity to break around him, talking and calling in a language that tipped alien, meaningless words into his ears like the music of an unknown instrument. He lulled towards it, suddenly enticed by its boundless, unconditional compassion. Then the memories flashed: the sirens, the crowds cascading into the tube stations, the flinty self-preservation of the troglodyte shelterers in the shattered and burning London he'd left behind. He withdrew. He pulled himself back from the resonant ambience of simple, unquestioning joy.

He lit a cigarette and walked on, once more alone in the crowd.

Chapter 4

Tuesday, 24 June 1941

Bryan sat in the tiny mess room and regarded the lumps in his thin stew with deep suspicion. He bisected one with his spoon, exposing a russet interior flecked with white and grey fibres. He lifted a piece to his mouth and chewed it carefully. The substance tasted of salt and string, so he concluded it must be corned beef.

'Have you heard?' Ben sat down opposite him and smoothed out a copy of *The Times of Malta* on the table between them.

Bryan pushed away his bowl and pulled the page closer. The headline read '*Nazis Invade Russia.*'

'When did this happen?' he asked, scanning the article.

'Sunday,' Ben answered. 'That's the reason there haven't been any Germans over the island for the last month.'

'What is that little Austrian twerp up to?' Bryan's voice rang with his astonishment. 'He's got most of Europe in his pocket, Britain's no great danger to him and he had Stalin safely tied up in the non-aggression pact. Surely he should've left him there until he'd taken Egypt and got his hands on the oil.' He looked up into Ben's face. 'He's mad. This *actually* proves he's mad.'

Ben frowned. 'So, what does it mean for us?'

Bryan glanced down at the congealing remains of his lunch. 'Hopefully it will make pushing a convoy through from Gibraltar a lot less dangerous, so we might get something decent to eat.' He scratched at the stubble on his cheek. 'Having said that, the Germans still need to supply *their* blokes in Africa, so we're certainly a long way from being off the hook. But at least, for a while, it will be an all-Italian hook.'

'For a while?'

'This little adventure won't stop the German factories making aeroplanes. We can only hope the Russians soak them up for as long as possible.' Bryan jabbed a finger at the newspaper's masthead. 'Where did this come from?'

'The Maltese print it in Valletta,' Ben said. 'Remember? You collared a journalist for directions outside their offices. I understand they haven't missed an issue yet.'

Bryan nodded in mild appreciation. 'Commendable stuff.'

Saturday, 5 July 1941

Bryan and Ben walked through the mercifully cooling evening, drawn by the seedy allure of Strait Street.

'I would've thought fighting a war might have involved shooting at something,' Ben said, side-stepping out of the way of a drunken couple weaving in the opposite direction. 'I've sat on the toilet for more hours than I've sat in a Hurricane.'

'Don't knock it too much, my friend,' Bryan said. 'The Russians might just end this whole thing for us and we can get back to the important business of flying air shows at Biggin Hill.'

'Do you think so?'

Bryan stopped and looked at his companion. 'No,' he said flatly, his eyes refocussing on something over Ben's shoulder. 'Now, that looks interesting.'

Ben turned to follow Bryan's gaze. On the corner of an adjoining street sat a large square building. On the balcony that stretched over most of its frontage, a large banner proclaimed its name to be the 'Egyptian Queen' in lettering reminiscent of a wild west saloon. Beneath the balcony were three doors. Above the left-hand door, a sign indicated it led to the 'International Bar'. In the centre stood the shuttered entrance of a tobacconist's kiosk, closed for lack of stock. Running down either side of the third door, signs read 'Cabaret' and 'Variety', and the strains of a strident waltz drifted out onto the pavement.

'Let's take a look,' Bryan said.

The two men walked across the street, through the third door and up the stairs. At the top, they ducked through a beaded curtain into the muggy atmosphere of a function room packed with dancers, its atmosphere close and shot through with the acid tang of body odour. The eight-strong band all played battered brass instruments, gamely covering their lack of finesse with a thick layer enthusiasm. Their dark Maltese eyes followed the dancers as they whirled across the front of their low stage, glittering with pleasure at the abandon their halting music inspired.

The pair jostled through the press of bodies to the bar and Bryan caught the bartender's attention.

'Two beers, please.'

'No beer, sir.' The barman grimaced in apology. 'We're waiting for a delivery.'

'From the brewery?'

The barman shook his head. 'No, sir. From England.'

Bryan held the man's gaze, sensing an undercurrent of hostility. 'So, what can you offer us?'

'Wine,' the man answered.

'Excellent. Which kinds do you have?'

'Red.'

Bryan turned to Ben, intent on leaving. But his companion was deep in conversation with a local girl who laughed and smiled as she gazed into Ben's face. Bryan sighed and turned back to the barman.

'Two glasses of red, then.'

Bryan paid for the drinks and tapped his friend on the shoulder. Ben looked at the offered glass in mild confusion for a moment, then took it and resumed his conversation.

Bryan took a sip of the blood-warm liquid and grimaced as it dried out on his teeth.

'Not impressed with the local plonk?'

Bryan turned to the sound of the female British accent and looked into the light-blue eyes of its owner. Blonde hair framed a face flushed pink from the exertion of dancing and her cotton dress clung to her petite frame where sweat had spread in patches under her arms and around her neck.

'It's my first taste,' Bryan answered. 'I'm trying to find something about it to like.'

'It's safer to drink than the water.' The woman smiled. 'Which has to be a good thing.'

She stood on tip-toe and raised a hand to attract the barman.

'No, please,' Bryan said, 'let me get you a drink.'

'That's very kind. They've probably got some Pimms, now all the navy wives have been evacuated.' She pulled a sodden lock of hair away from her eyelid, 'Would you mind if I met you on the balcony? I'm absolutely melting.'

Bryan bought the drink and wormed his way through the dancers to the door that led to the balcony. Once outside, he handed the woman her glass.

'Thank you... er...'

'Bryan Hale. Based in Ta'Qali. I only shipped in a month ago.'

She shook his offered hand. 'Katie Starling.'

'That's an interesting surname. Does it mean you're fond of birds?'

Katie snorted a laugh. 'No. They terrify me, especially pigeons. Would you believe I've never visited Trafalgar Square because of the pigeons?'

Bryan leaned on the balcony rail and swirled the wine in his glass. 'Me and that barman didn't seem to hit it off.'

Katie took a sip of her drink. 'Well, there are two trains of thought amongst the Maltese. Most of them feel more British than the King. But there are some who think they'd be better off under the Italians. The way they see it, it's our fault that they're running out of all the things that make life bearable, while their nearest neighbour is delivering bombs every night instead of meat and drink every week.'

'Things will probably get better soon,' Bryan said, 'what with the Germans out of the way for a while.' He lit two cigarettes and handed one to Katie.

'Thank you.' She took a gentle pull of smoke. 'It needs to happen quickly, though. Did you know they have a 'surrender date' calculated? That's the day that the food and fuel is expected to run out. It gets pushed back if a ship or a submarine gets through, but the clock is always ticking.'

Inside, the trumpet player delivered a lavishly off-key flourish and Katie giggled at the absurdity.

Bryan smiled at her good nature. 'Is this the best place in town?' he asked.

'It's probably not the best.' The band staggered to a finale, paused for a moment and then launched into a ragged foxtrot. The noise dragged another smile onto Katie's face. 'But I like it. There are several bands that rotate around the city. Some are better than others. You'll hear them all eventually.'

'Well.' Bryan held out a hand. 'Would you like to attempt a dance to this?'

'How could I refuse such a brave man?' She took his hand and they went back inside to the crowded dancefloor.

****

The bus jolted along the road back towards Ta'Qali.

'You could've warned me.' Ben broke the strained silence that had descended between the two men.

Bryan sat with his arms folded, gazing into the thickening darkness through the unglazed window frame next to his seat. 'Did it not occur to you that she was getting rather too friendly, a bit too quickly?'

Ben's head sunk into his hands and he groaned. 'Everyone was watching me. More to the point, all the nice girls were watching me. My reputation is ruined.'

'Don't talk nonsense.' Bryan ruffled his companion's hair. 'None of the nice girls even noticed you were there. And now you've done the reconnaissance, you'll be able to spot the prostitutes on our next sortie.'

Ben straightened his back and smoothed his hair back into place. 'Who was that girl you were dancing with? She was sweet.'

'A nurse, works up in the hospital at Mtarfa. Not my type really.'

'Get away!' Ben said. 'She's lovely.'

'So she might be.'

'I saw the way she looked at you.' A smile crept over Ben's face. 'She was getting quite dewy.'

Bryan stared silently into the night as the air-raid sirens around Valletta began wailing their mournful warning.

Thursday, 10 July 1941

The air inside the bell-tent pressed on Bryan with a still, stifling heat, swilling in and out of his lungs like thin soup. He pulled himself out of his chair and stepped outside. The slow-baked heat of the canvas interior gave way to the fiery blast of the incalescent sun. Bryan glanced at the dispersed fighters, their outlines blurred and wavering in a heat haze. Riggers moved like shape-shifting wraiths around them, their bronzed torsos blending into their khaki shorts, making them appear as creatures of sand. He raised his gaze to the fathomless blue dome. It remained steadfastly empty of enemy planes, leaving him empty of purpose. A fly buzzed in front of his eyes and landed on his nose. He brushed it away and returned to his seat in the tent.

'I left Scotland to come here,' he announced to no-one in particular. 'I bet it's raining cats and dogs in Edinburgh.'

The squadron leader stuck his head through the entrance. 'Hale. I need to have a word. Would you come with me, please?'

Bryan hauled himself out of his chair again, pulled the fabric of his sweat-dampened shorts away from his buttocks, and followed his commanding officer back out into the sun. The two men strolled out towards the perimeter.

'I've got word back from HQ,' Copeland began, 'they think your night sorties might be a good idea. They just need to be convinced by the technicalities.'

'The technicalities?'

'Yes.' Copeland stopped and faced him. 'They want to know how you'll make it work.'

'Me?' Bryan gasped. 'I haven't put much thought into it.'

'Well.' Copeland placed a hand on his shoulder. 'You'd better start thinking. They're expecting you to turn up at HQ with a plan, tomorrow at midday.'

Friday, 11 July 1941

The airfield truck dropped Bryan off at the end of Scots Street. As it roared off behind him, he glanced down at his sweat-stained shirt and shorts, and scratched at the stubble on his cheek. He looked the way he felt, beaten down by heat and forced inactivity, with only the flies and the fleas to battle against.

He glanced at his watch and walked up the narrow street. Ahead of him, the starched presence of two military police guards marked out his destination. Negotiating his way past them brought him into the lobby of RAF HQ where an orderly sat at a polished desk, the wall behind him hung with the Union Flag and an RAF ensign. Bryan walked across the bare flagstones to the desk, the sudden cool of the airy stone chamber drying the sweat between his shoulder blades.

'Flight Lieutenant Bryan Hale,' he said. 'I've come to see the AOC.'

The orderly squinted at his appointment book, found the required validation and stood up.

'Follow me, please.'

Bryan fell in behind the man, walking down a corridor lined with portraits of grand old RAF and RFC officers bedecked in braided dress uniforms. The orderly paused at a polished oak door, knocked twice and twisted the handle.

'Flight Lieutenant Hale to see you, sir.'

Bryan entered the room and heard the door click shut behind him. The office held another, larger polished desk behind which sat the man in command of Malta's air defence. Bryan snapped to attention, silently regretting his tattered appearance.

'Sit down, Hale.' The officer indicated a chair in front of his desk. 'My name's Lloyd.'

Bryan took the seat and waited.

'I've read through your file, Hale. Very impressive.' He flicked through the papers resting on his blotter. 'Kenley in the summer. Night-fighters in the winter.' He looked up and his flint-sharp eyes, set slightly too close together, latched onto Bryan's. 'It mentions operational tiredness,' he said. 'What's the story?'

Bryan felt the sweat reimpose its dampness down his back, but he held the other man's gaze. 'Two or three really bad things happened very close together. It knocked me sideways for a while.'

The older man's eyes bored through the silence that fell on the room, gauging the mettle of the pilot sitting before him. He closed the file and leaned back in his chair.

'So, how do you intend to carry out night interceptions over Malta?'

'It won't be easy, sir.' Bryan scratched at his stubble. 'They tried putting Hurricanes up at night over England with patchy results. Without electronic detection onboard, you need to be talked onto the target until you're close enough to get a visual contact. But, if the searchlights can hold onto a bandit, and we're close enough when that happens, I reckon we should be able to do some damage.'

The older man nodded.

'Having said that,' Bryan continued, 'being at the same altitude as a bomber stream over their target is as dangerous for the interceptor as it is the raider. So, we need to hit them as they make landfall, and again as they leave. We'll need a few dedicated searchlights in a grouping on the southern end of the island and a few more on the coast well north of Valletta. We need to make sure the gunners on the ground know that anything coned in those particular lights belongs to us.'

Lloyd nodded. 'Anything else?'

'Yes.' Bryan leaned forward as he warmed to his subject. 'We'll need to be in position at least two-thousand feet above the bombers as they arrive, two Hurricanes circling over each nest of searchlights. We have to be waiting for them. Which means allocating the fuel for what is essentially a standing patrol.'

The older man nodded. 'Is that all?'

'No.' Bryan shook his head. 'Our planes must be exclusive to us. No-one else flies them; an engine failure in the dark would be very difficult to survive.' A smile crept across his face. 'And I want them painted black.'

Lloyd mirrored Bryan's smile. 'Alright, Hale. Leave it with me, I'll let you know.'

Chapter 5

Wednesday, 16 July 1941

As Bryan and Ben walked along the perimeter track, a sluggish breeze buoyed the dust kicked around their boots. It was strong enough to cool the sweat on their faces, but too weak to completely dry their slick skin. They walked past the skeletal remains of a bomb-wrecked fighter. A skinny rigger tinkered with the blackened engine, searching for useful morsels like a starving scavenger picking at a bonier corpse.

Further along, the cobalt blue of a welding torch flashed from beneath a Hurricane's wing. The two men veered over to the craft and watched the fitter fixing clasps to the airframe, waiting until he paused in his work.

'What are *they* for?' Bryan asked.

The fitter flicked up his welding mask and blinked in the sunlight. 'Bombs, sir,' he said rubbing his eye with a thumb, 'twenty-five pounders. It's for a trial.'

The two pilots continued along the track, the crackle and sputter of the welding torch receding behind them.

'Bombs on a Hurricane?' Ben mused. 'What's that all about?'

'Lloyd was originally a bomber boy,' Bryan answered. 'I reckon he'd fit a bomb-rack to his wife if he could.'

Ben laughed. 'But twenty-five pounders? That's hardly enough to open a packet of biscuits.'

Bryan shot his companion a sideways glance. 'That's not really the important thing here. Think about it – a month ago, we got bollocked for taking off without permission in case we were wasting fuel. Now it looks like they're planning to send intruders across the water into Sicily.'

Ben's brow furrowed and he said nothing.

Bryan dropped his voice a tone. 'So, it's fairly obvious there's a supply convoy planned very soon.'

Ben's expression smoothed with his enlightenment. 'Crikey! You should be a spy.'

'Frankly,' Bryan muttered, 'you should pay more attention to your surroundings.'

The squeak of an un-oiled bicycle made them pause and turn. An orderly pedalled towards them, straining against the drag of almost-flat tyres.

'Mr Hale, sir!' he called. 'The squadron leader wants to see you as soon as.'

****

Bryan knocked once on the door of the storeroom that Copeland had requisitioned to serve as a makeshift office, and pushed into its cluttered interior. The squadron leader, sitting behind a desk built from tea chests and planks, looked up and smiled.

'I have what you might consider as good news.' He gestured Bryan to sit.

Bryan lowered himself onto the stool in front of the desk and waited.

Copeland picked up a memo and squinted at the typed text. 'Air Vice Marshal Lloyd has seen fit to approve your idea. As a result, you're required to form the Malta Night-Fighter Unit, codename 'Pipistrelle', and prepare for operations to commence within the week.' Copeland paused and looked at Bryan from under barred eyebrows. 'You are to choose eight Hurricanes from those on station at Ta'Qali and these will be reserved for night-fighting purposes alone. Pilot volunteers will be assigned and limited training flights will commence as soon as possible. Once formed, the MNFU will be barracked away from the airfield at Mdina.'

Bryan craned his neck in an attempt to glimpse the text. 'Does it mention black paint at all?'

****

Bryan and Ben strode into Strait Street as the dusk quickened in the Mediterranean sky.

'Isn't flying around in the dark a bit dangerous?' Ben's face carried a worried scowl.

'Yes, but you get to choose who you shoot at and hardly anybody gets to shoot back. Plus, we'll be barracked away from the airfield. No more stinking latrines and shitty slit trenches. And' – he slapped his comrade on the back – 'you get to sleep during the day. Very continental.'

'Well, alright,' Ben mumbled. 'I'll volunteer for your stupid squadron. But it's against my better judgement.'

'As if you've *got* any better judgement. Come on. The Egyptian Queen awaits.' Bryan caught his companion's shirt sleeve and pulled him towards the dance hall. 'You can tell your enterprising acquaintance that she's not the only one who's going to be working nights.'

45

Thursday, 17 July 1941

Bryan chewed on his lower lip in concentration as he guided his paint-loaded brush along the tight fabric, carefully cutting around the red, white and blue roundel on the Hurricane's fuselage. The black paint shone wetly for a few moments, then its surface dulled and crackled as the brutal heat dried it too quickly.

'Squadron Leader Hale?' A woman's voice behind him broke his concentration.

Bryan tilted his chin up and cocked his head to the sound. The velvet tone underpinning the words stiffened the hair follicles on his neck and dropped an iciness into his vitals.

'That's probably an exaggeration.' He turned to face the speaker and a shock thrilled through his scalp. For a moment he stared, confused by the familiarity of a woman he didn't know. Something in the dark eyes, something about the loosely bound black hair…

'My name is Jacobella Azzopardi. I'm from *The Times of Malta.*' She held out her hand.

Bryan dropped his brush into the paint and set the pot on the ground. He wiped his palm on his shorts and shook her hand. The smooth warmth of her skin caused his grip to linger half-a-second too long.

'I've come to interview you,' she added.

'You're a journalist?' Realisation finally tumbled, pushed by a memory: 'Ah! I saw you in Valletta outside the newspaper offices, with… a man.'

She smiled. '*He* is the journalist. I'm his assistant. Today he is ill, so they sent me instead.'

'Malta Dog?' Bryan grimaced in sympathy. 'There's a lot of it about.'

Jacobella blinked once in silent affirmation but said nothing.

'Yes. Sorry.' Bryan gestured towards the mess building outside the perimeter track. 'Shall we find some shade?'

They walked across the dusty field together, Bryan mumbling some complimentary things about the newspaper, '–*impressive production standards*–' and the city in which it was based, '–*wonderful statues, surprisingly beautiful*–'. Jacobella remained silent at his side. From the corner of his eye he caught the sway of her skirt as she walked and the dusky dryness of the skin at her throat. A bead of sweat trickled from his temple to his jaw.

They entered the mess and sat at a table in the corner of the small room.

'I suppose there are rules?' Bryan asked. 'Censorship and the like.'

'Well' – Jacobella opened her notebook and examined the point of her pencil – 'it would be foolish to go to press with numbers and details, but we assume that anything we print about the general situation is already common knowledge to the Italians.'

Bryan's eyes widened. 'Spies?'

'Technically.' She pursed her lips. 'But it's mostly family connections. For our part we try to give the people some good news about their defenders whenever we can. For instance…' She scribbled something in block capitals and held up the notebook. 'My headline.'

Bryan squinted at the page. '*Battle of Britain Hero Arrives to Direct New Night-Fighter Force.*' He felt his cheeks flush with rising blood. 'Well, I suppose some of that is true.'

She smiled and placed the notebook back on the table. 'So, tell me your story.'

****

The pair stood outside Ta'Qali's entrance waiting for the bus. Bryan's eyes danced on and off Jacobella's face, unable to resist indulging in the furtive glances, but wary of her catching his gaze.

'I hardly knew Malta existed until I landed here last month,' he said, finally finding refuge by looking at his feet.

She smiled wistfully. 'It's a beautiful place to live. Even now, in between the bombing, it lays like a lamb in the sun. I wish it didn't have to be destroyed.'

Bryan looked up and caught the glistening in her eyes. 'It's not hopeless. Not yet. We're here to help you.'

She nodded. 'Some of my friends wash clothes for the soldiers in the coastal battery. It's a small way of saying thank you. May I help you in the same way?'

The grinding of gears heralded the approaching bus.

'There's no need,' Bryan stammered. 'I wouldn't want to impose.'

The bus pulled up and its windowless door flapped open.

Jacobella reached out and touched his arm. 'Bring it to the office if you change your mind. Thank you for your story.' She climbed on and the bus rattled away in a billowing curl of yellow dust.

Friday, 18 July 1941

A crescent moon hung in the clear ebony sky like the lop-sided smile of a lunatic and the island lay quiet beneath its manic glare. The Italians were late – but it was unlikely they'd stay at home. Four dark figures stood in the wan light, three of them listening to the fourth.

'So, for us, the easiest parts of a daylight combat sortie have just become the hardest parts of flying at night; taking off and landing in the dark are now the biggest threats to your long life and continued happiness.' Bryan looked around the three faces that gazed back at him in the gloom. 'We'll eventually be a ten-man squadron with eight Hurricanes. But tonight, it's just us, testing whether it's possible to get off this airfield and back again in one piece.'

The other pilots shifted uneasily under his words.

'We take off and fly in pairs,' Bryan continued. 'Everyone keeps their tail light on. Keep your leader's light in vision during all manoeuvres and we should be able to avoid collisions.

'The runway lights will be illuminated briefly. Don't waste time while they are; they'll draw any hostile aircraft like moths to a candle. Get up and get away quickly. My section will fly south, the other pair flies west. Tonight is a familiarisation flight. Check and memorise the landmarks you'll need to recognise on your journey home, then fly out over the sea, ten minutes maximum, and make your way back.

'When you're back in the circuit, call up control and they'll telephone the field to illuminate the runway so you can land. Again, make it snappy.' He looked again from face to face. 'Right. Let's see if we can make this work.'

The pilots trudged out to their aircraft that sat gaunt and black in the still air. Engines coughed into life and an aircraftman at each wingtip guided them as they taxied to the end of the landing strip. Lights along each edge of the runway flared into incandescence and one pair of Hurricanes, then a second, roared across the field, clawing into the air. As the last plane rose away from the ground, the lights choked off and darkness smothered the landscape once more. One pair of tail lights climbed steadily south, the other pair curved away towards the western coast.

Saturday, 19 July 1941

'What if that girl is there again?' Ben asked.

'Of course she'll be there. She works there,' Bryan said.

'What if she remembers me? What if she chats me up again?'

'I don't think that remembering faces is a skill that has much practical use in her profession,' Bryan said. 'Just keep your head down and only accept dances from nice girls.' Bryan cocked his head. 'Listen.' The faint strains of a clarinet snaked through the cooling dusk, stitching together its melody with devilish proficiency. 'The band sounds a lot better this time.'

They strode up Strait Street and took the side turning to the Egyptian Queen. Bryan glanced at the couples chatting on the balcony before ducking through the door, climbing the stairs two at a time and sweeping the beaded curtain aside.

The dance hall's dim lighting emphasised the enforced intimacy of the small space and, beneath the rippling pall of cigarette smoke, couples slow-danced their grim realities away with eyes closed, momentarily safe against the warmth of another's fragile body. The two men wriggled through the dancers to the bar. A blackboard propped on a shelf announced the continuing lack of beer.

Bryan leaned towards a barman. 'Whisky?'

The man nodded and went to retrieve the bottle.

'Two,' Bryan called after him. 'Make them large.'

As he waited for the drinks, he felt someone's gaze penetrating his space. He looked along the bar to see Katie standing with a couple. Her face glowed with a smile when she met Bryan's eyes.

The drinks arrived and Bryan fumbled for the change to pay. He handed one of the whiskies to Ben who clinked glasses with him and drifted away into the dancers. Bryan turned back in Katie's direction just as she arrived at his side.

'Hello,' she said. 'I looked for you last Saturday, but you weren't here.'

'No.' Bryan looked into her blue eyes, then followed the line of her nose down to the pout of disappointment on her lips, waiting to feel a spark that didn't come. 'It's been a busy week.'

A smile of triumph banished her sulk. 'I wondered if it might be you!'

'If who might be me?'

'The article in *The Times of Malta*, yesterday.' She closed her eyes for a moment, as if visualising the words. 'Battle of Britain ace to lead fight against night raiders.' Her eyelids fluttered open again, her gaze flicking between Bryan's eyes, searching for a lie. 'It is you, isn't it?'

Bryan looked down into his glass and swirled the amber liquid. 'I may have something to do with it, yes.'

Her face dropped into sudden seriousness. 'My friends must meet you.' She beckoned to the couple she'd been standing with and they weaved towards her through the drinkers at the bar.

'This is Steph,' Katie announced, 'she works with me.'

The girl bobbed her head, sending a tremor through her auburn ringlets.

'And this is Al,' Katie continued. 'He's in the navy.'

Bryan recognised the submariner he'd met in the bar on his first trip to Valletta.

'Wait here, chaps,' Katie cooed, 'we need the powder room.'

The two girls went off to the toilets. Bryan sipped his drink and regarded the sailor. 'Al?' he said, eyebrow raised.

'It sounds better than Albert,' the other man said.

Bryan nodded at the man's left hand and the naked fingers wrapped around his glass. 'What happened to that brand-new wedding ring?'

Albert's cheeks reddened. 'We lost a boat a couple of weeks ago. Thirty men sent to the bottom. No signs of what happened, except radio silence. It spooked me; I knew most of them. I'd watched them read their letters from home, from wives and girlfriends. It brought home how easy it had been to say 'until death do us part' thinking that it would be a reasonably long time before Death collected on the deal.

'The Med is no place for submarines, it's too clear and too shallow. It made me realise there's plenty of room for regret, and in a sunken sub it's likely you'll have plenty of time to think about it.' He looked over Bryan's shoulder. 'You won't say anything?'

Bryan turned to follow his gaze and saw the two girls making their way back across the room. The band of freckles across Steph's nose and the bobbing of her curls made her look too young to be in a dance hall.

'It's really none of my business, Bertie,' Bryan said. 'You'd just better hope she doesn't fall in love with you.'

Bryan threw back the rest of his whisky and put the empty glass on the bar. As Katie arrived, he whisked her straight into a quick step, careening across the flow of dancers, flashing a smile at Albert as he went.

****

Bryan and Katie walked out onto the pavement. The evening, although still warm, was several degrees cooler than the dance hall.

'Come on,' she said, 'it's not far to the northside. There's a public garden there that overlooks Marsamxett Harbour. Let's see if we can catch a sea breeze.'

They followed the narrowing Strait Street back south-west until they came to the ancient armoury's bluff walls. They skirted the base of the blank-faced building and entered Hastings Gardens.

Bryan glanced upwards. 'The Italians might be on their way already,' he murmured.

'Katie glanced at her watch. 'No, it's still early. Come on, let's walk a while.'

The dark blue sky began its descent towards black as they took a path that followed the tended beds along the narrow strip of the public gardens. They reached the bastion that curtailed the gardens at their northern end, stood for a moment to enjoy the cooling breeze that flowed up its sloping walls, then walked to the gate, past a huge empty plinth and out onto the road, heading back into the city.

'Your friend seems very nice.' Bryan said.

Katie nodded. 'I do worry for her, though. We have to deal with some frightful things at the hospital and she's such a sensitive girl.' She stopped and put her hands on her hips in mock admonishment. 'Anyway, you shouldn't be talking about other girls when you're promenading with me.'

'Habib!'

The call came from the buildings lining the road. Bryan twisted on his heel to find its source.

Jacobella stood on one of the balconies, taking wet washing from a basket and draping it over the railing.

Bryan gazed up at her and she waved, smiling as she worked.

'Doesn't that mean Darling?' Katie's voice had hardened.

'I'm not sure,' Bryan mumbled. 'I think it can also mean Friend.'

He watched Jacobella moving back and forth, the smile never leaving her face.

'Goodnight then, Bryan.'

Bryan turned to see Katie walking away, back the way they had come. He watched her in some confusion for a few moments, but did not follow.

He looked back to the balcony, but it was empty. He scratched his cheek and lit a cigarette, his eyes still on the railing and its dripping clothes.

'Habib,' he muttered to himself.

Sunday, 20 July 1941

Albert Chandler roused from his shallow slumber and lay, eyes closed, listening to the gentle breathing beside him. He pulled himself up to lean on his elbow and gazed at the girl sleeping by his side. She lay with her back to him, her breasts gathered in her folded arms and her knees drawn up. Her auburn ringlets lay tangled across her cheek, exposing an elfish ear, like a white seashell laying on dark, wet sand. Her shoulders, rising and falling with each breath, were scattered with freckles that lessened as his eyes moved down her back to where her buttocks rose unblemished. He placed his hand on her hip and traced the dipping curve of her waist, up onto her side and back to her shoulder. He leaned over and kissed her neck, the taste of her still keen on his lips.

Rising, he dressed quickly, his eyes lingering on his lover as he moved quietly around the room, collecting his clothes. When he was ready to go, he checked the change pocket of his shorts. The hard circle of his wedding ring was still there. He searched his heart for remorse, and found none. Closing the door softly behind him, he descended the stairs and slipped out into the pre-dawn air. Without glancing back, he followed the alley downhill, towards the harbour and the sea.

****

The sun dipped towards the western horizon, tingeing the island's humped back with a sanguine shade. Sailors stood and waited under the ancient arched walkway of Lazzaretto while the water lapped a languorous rhythm against the wall at their feet. A preternatural silence lay over the men. Their talk stilled as they arrived at the designated time in twos and threes, joining their comrades in the descending dusk. Their coming together instilled an introspection, triggered by the impending transition they must make. Albert fished out his wedding ring and put it back on his finger.

A short distance away from the wall, the water's surface puckered and swirled in portent, then a metal snout broke the surface, like an awakening sea monster. The conning tower emerged behind it and between them they dragged the hull above the water. The bright cobalt vessel, settled into equilibrium, gleaming wetly in the dying light as it shed cascades of water from its decks and bridge. U-Class submarine, *Ulric*, had emerged from its daytime hiding place, loaded and ready to hunt.

Shore crews hauled on the mooring ropes, inching the craft closer until a gangplank banged into place and was secured on the deck. Thirty-one men hefted small duffel-bags of belongings onto their backs and shuffled towards the gangway.

Albert crossed from the shore to the submarine. As soon as his boots hit the deck, he became alive to the thrum of pumps working in the body of the craft, and his legs braced to manage the fluid instability common to all vessels that float. As he waited for his turn to climb the ladder to the bridge and the open hatch, he looked out over Valletta. Bells rang to call the Catholic faithful to evening mass where they would bolster enough courage to face the bombs that would almost certainly fall from the midnight sky. Most would have their prayers answered, but some would reap the realities of their fragile faith before the sun rose again.

Chapter 6

Monday, 21 July 1941

Bryan leaned against the building on the street's shady side, a duffel-bag of shirts and underwear hanging from his shoulder. The dusty limestone façade radiated the day's heat onto the back of his neck, an act of inanimate spite in the already oppressive atmosphere of St Paul Street. Bryan glanced down the thoroughfare that dipped away towards the end of Valletta's peninsular and the entrance to the harbours. Halfway down, fresh gaps in the tall terraces left their detritus of blocky rubble piled across the pavements. He placed a cigarette between his dry lips and settled his gaze on the arched entrance to the newspaper's offices.

The work day was drawing to a close. People trailed in and out for many minutes as the heat pressed down on him and his resolve began to crumble like the wall against which he slumped. Then the thrill of recognition straightened his back as the woman he waited for emerged from the shadows of the lobby.

'Miss Azzopardi,' he called, 'hello!'

She turned to the sound of his voice and crossed the road. 'Mr Hale. Bonswa! So, you've decided to let me help.' She took the canvas duffel bag from him.

Bryan smiled. 'It seemed churlish not to. Can I buy you a drink or something?'

'Thank you, but no. I have to get home.'

Bryan took the canvas bag back from her. 'Then let me walk with you.'

They walked up St Paul into the open square of Castille Place. Veering right, they dog-legged onto the road that took them past the armoury.

Jacobella threw him a sidelong glance. 'I think you should know, it's Mrs Azzopardi. I'm married.'

Bryan held his gaze to the front and swallowed hard. 'He's a very lucky man.'

A wistful smile stole across Jacobella's lips. 'Do you think so? Mikiel doesn't say much about the way he feels. It just seems like we've been together forever, and that's all there is, or ever will be.'

'Does he work on the island?'

'No, he's in the navy.'

Bryan risked a look at his companion. Her face had become drawn with introspection. 'It must be difficult,' he said, 'with him being away so much.'

'Not really,' she said. 'He would often go away before the war, before he joined the navy.' She let out a short sigh. 'Even then, I was never sure he'd come back to me. But it always made me glad when he did. So we carried on, and then we had Lučija.' She looked up and her eyes flashed with pride. 'Lučija, my beautiful, naughty daughter. Because of her, I know I can survive anything.'

They walked without talking for a while, the first cultivated beds of Hastings Gardens lined the pavement to their side.

'I'm sorry about Saturday night.' Jacobella broke the silence. 'I didn't mean to upset your girlfriend.'

Bryan blushed. 'No, Katie's nothing more than a dance partner. I hardly know her.'

Jacobella smiled at his discomfiture. 'She's a very pretty lady.'

Bryan shook his head. 'Blondes aren't really my thing.'

They walked on along the road and Bryan recognised the imposing bulk of the statue-less plinth marking the gardens' northern end. They drew to a halt and she took the washing bag from his shoulder.

'Come around for your laundry whenever you like,' she said. 'I live behind the blue door over there. I'll leave it in the hallway. Now, I must hurry. My mother-in-law is looking after Lučija and she can be difficult if I'm late. Goodnight… Bryan, isn't it?'

'Yes, it is.' He fought the urge to lean towards her, rocking on the balls of his feet with the effort. 'Goodnight.'

He watched her cross the road and open the chipped wooden door. She vanished inside without looking back.

Wednesday, 23 July 1941

Merlin engines coughed blue smoke into the fetid air and swirled vortices of gritty dust across the field. As one burst into life, another choked and died, creating a perpetual canon of mechanical music.

Bryan walked down to the field and spotted Copeland, arms folded and a handkerchief tied across his face, surveying the activity around him. Squinting against the storm of dust, Bryan approached him.

'What's the flap?' He raised his voice against the noise.

Copeland nodded a greeting. 'Oil checks,' he answered. 'Would you believe they haven't even been doing oil checks?' He shook his head sadly. 'We sent up two Hurricanes yesterday to chase away a reconnaissance, one of them seized solid just after take-off. The lad tried to glide it down into a field, but there's not enough space between those bloody boundary walls. He ploughed straight into one and broke his neck.'

The men walked back towards the mess building. Copeland pulled the handkerchief down from his nose.

'We're putting up standing patrols from dawn tomorrow. I don't want to lose anyone else to sloppiness.'

'Standing patrols over what?' Bryan asked.

'There's a convoy getting very close,' Copeland said. 'They sent a decoy formation waddling out of Alexandria a couple of days ago. The Italians fell for it, and while they're distracted, the navy has taken the chance to scoot a few ships across from Gibraltar. They should be here late tomorrow.'

'Good news,' Bryan said.

Copeland slapped him on the back. 'For you, it's great news. Once the fuel is unloaded, Pipistrelle Squadron will go operational.'

The two men stepped into the mess building.

'I received orders yesterday evening that you and your pilots are to move to dedicated quarters. Wait here.' Copeland ducked into his office and emerged a moment later with a slip of paper. 'It's a mile or so west from here, in Mdina.' He paused and scanned the document. 'A place called Xara Palace.'

****

'Do you reckon it's anything like Crystal Palace?'

Bryan looked at Ben, trying to gauge his intent. 'I would imagine not.'

'More like Buckingham Palace, then?'

'Why don't we just wait until we get there?'

The truck ground on along the road, swaying from side to side in the ruts and potholes, climbing steadily between the scrubby fields and tumble-down stone walls which eventually gave way to familiar limestone facades as they entered Mdina. The transport crossed a bridge that spanned a wide, dry ditch and led to an ornately decorated gate that gave access to a walled section of the town. Once through the gate, the truck crawled along the constricted thoroughfare, took a sharp right down the narrow gap between precipitous walls and, with a final crash of gears, staggered to a halt. Ben unhooked the tailgate and all ten pilots on the truck dismounted into the flagstone courtyard of Xara Palace, dragging their kit-bags with them.

'Strewth,' Bryan breathed, 'this is more my style.'

The main entrance filled one edge of the courtyard, its large central doorway set in a shallow porch. Above the door, three large windows sat between four faux columns built onto the façade and the central window boasted a balustered balcony atop the porch roof. On the courtyard's right side, three wide arches gave access to a covered walkway, its roof providing a wide balcony for another wing of the building.

The truck choked back to life. The driver regarded the group of pilots for a moment. 'Lucky bastards,' he muttered and started a laborious three-point turn, churning heavy black smoke from the exhaust.

Bryan tried the main door and it opened under his grip. The men trailed into the cool cavern of the entrance hall, dropped their bags in a corner and split up to explore their new lodgings.

Bryan and Ben walked up a stone staircase that lifted them to a long corridor, heavy oak doors punctuated the walls and a richly patterned red runner bisected its length. At the far end, another unlocked door led them onto a wide roof terrace, protected from both sun and rain by a tiled canopy supported on a sturdy wooden framework. Both men stopped in their stride.

The palace sat in the walled town's eastern district, atop a ridge that dropped away steeply towards Ta'Qali. The balcony faced east and gave a clear view of the aerodrome, and beyond it, across the island's width, to where the sprawl of Valletta and Sliema lay glimmering like mercury under an ethereal mirage of shimmering heat haze.

'This would be an ideal place to build a bar,' Ben said.

Bryan nodded, still enraptured by the view. 'Yes,' he murmured, 'it would be rude not to.'

Thursday, 24 July 1941

Bryan roused in the early afternoon from the deepest sleep he'd enjoyed since he'd mounted the gangplank at Gibraltar. A sense of purpose had evicted the constant nag of vulnerability that had clung to him at the mess in Ta'Qali. The tools he needed to strike out at the enemy were slowly assembling, and the final, vital elements were drawing close; petrol, the life blood of his aircraft, and ammunition, its teeth and claws, were lodged in the bellies of a convoy of fat merchant ships, wallowing like milk cows towards the island.

He crossed the room on muscles that felt tauter, with senses that shone sharper. He splashed lukewarm water onto his face from the bowl on the dresser, snapped out his razor and scraped the stubble of several days from his sweat-oiled skin. A concern for his appearance had re-acquired a proto-ritual gravity, an elemental expression of respect for the warriors he would soon be seeking to kill.

He brushed his teeth and gargled, swallowing the fouled water with a grimace. He dressed quickly in a shirt and shorts, and tightly laced his oil-stained desert boots. He left the room, strode along the corridor and almost danced down the staircase, the importance of the day layering his movements with a barely-restrained impatience.

He walked past the open door to the dining room from which drifted the murmured conversation of a knot of pilots taking a late lunch. Bryan's guts were too tight with expectation to allow space for eating, his mind too focused to engage in small talk. He strode out through the front door and across the courtyard towards the battered RAF truck, parked up against the wall. Bryan opened the passenger door and swung up onto the worn leather seat.

'Ta'Qali,' he said.

'Fuel restrictions, sir,' the driver answered. 'I'm not supposed to move with less than four passengers.'

Bryan swivelled his head to look at the airman. 'Drive me to Ta'Qali.'

'Yes, sir.' The man fumbled with the keys, the ignition coughed and the engine fired.

The truck sidled across the town, through the gate and bumped off down the hill towards the airfield. As they lost elevation, the landscape flattened and the horizon dipped away. Robbed of his bird's-eye view of the aerodrome, Bryan scanned the bright sky for movement. There, dead ahead of them, dark against the deep blue backdrop, four shapes rose from the ground, tightened their formation and banked into a climb, heading due north. The patrols were up; the convoy was close.

The truck pulled through the airfield gates and Bryan jumped down as it shuddered to a halt. A patina of dust from the take-off hung in the air as he loped down towards the readiness tent.

A different section of four Hurricanes buzzed the airfield and climbed away into a landing circuit. Bryan squinted at their wings as they passed overhead. Doped red canvas still covered the ports of their unfired guns so the convoy couldn't be under any kind of concerted attack. Grinning with satisfaction he ducked into the tent to find Copeland in flying kit chatting with an orderly.

'This is more like it,' Bryan said. 'Have you been up yet?'

Copeland's eyes shone bright with the purpose of action. 'I took the first patrol, and I'm up on the next one.'

'Anything doing?'

Copeland shook his head. 'A flight of aircraft shadowed us for a bit, but they decided to go home in the end. Probably didn't fancy their chances getting past the escort screen.'

'How far away are the ships?'

'The convoy's bang on schedule. It should be in the harbour well before nightfall.'

Bryan left the tent amid the roar of the landing patrol, their wings flattening out on a cushion of warm air that dropped the craft delicately onto the hard-baked ground. Bryan walked out to the perimeter. Hurricanes stood in their blast-pens with airmen re-filling fuel tanks from metal cans, the fumes blurring their features as they concentrated on getting every drop home.

The sharp tang of aviation fuel tingled into Bryan's nostrils and the grinding cacophony of taxiing fighters embattled his hearing. He stood for long minutes amongst the swarm of noise and motion, allowing the tingle of adrenalin to swell and glow all the way down to his fingertips.

Copeland's flight taxied out and swung onto the runway as Bryan strode back towards the airfield's gate. He stood at the bus stop and watched the four sand-coloured fighters rise from the field and swing north, towards the sea and the ships that brought the island a chance of survival.

The rumble of aero-engines receded and was overlain with the pneumatic rattling of the approaching bus. It slewed to halt and Bryan jumped aboard.

'It's a good day,' he said to the driver.

'Yes, my friend,' the driver said. 'Always good day on Malta.'

****

The bus clanked to a halt on Quarry Wharf. Bryan alighted and walked east along the northern edge of Grand Harbour. The low growl of truck

59

engines rolled across the water from the harbour's south side as preparations continued to receive the incoming vessels.

The road rose before him, narrowed between two walls and crested next to a wide bastion that supported a heavy anti-aircraft gun. A semi-circular bulwark of sand bags surrounded the gun, casting shade over its lounging crew.

Beyond this emplacement the road commanded a panoramic view of the harbour entrance and the staggered breakwaters. Along the pavement small groups of islanders gathered, leaning on the wall and squinting out to sea. Children played around the legs of adults who chatted in hushed tones of excitement. Bryan found a space, leaned on the wall and lit a cigarette. The westering sun stretched the edge of their shadows along the ground as they waited.

A shape, no more substantial than a shadow, creased the haze on the horizon. For long moments, its apparent lack of motion belied its solidity, then it burst through the heat rumpled air. A grey warship, thrusting up a sparkling bow wave, coalesced in the distance, surging towards the harbour. Behind it, the haze creased again and again as a knot of cargo vessels pushed through the veil of hope and steamed into solid reality.

Ragged cheers broke out along the sea wall as more people arrived to swell the numbers gathered there. The islanders moved with the fluid grace of a congregation, their short pilgrimage measured in yards from their battered homes in the capital's shattered streets, their purpose to bear witness to the miracle of temporary salvation.

Bryan glanced at his watch; it was close to five o'clock and the newspaper offices would be closing. He walked through the increasing flow of people back up a narrow alley and turned left onto the long drag of St Paul Street. The news of the convoy broke like a wave ahead of him, pasting smiles of relief to the faces of those that passed him on their way to the harbour. Bryan scanned the faces, hoping that Jacobella might be amongst them.

He plodded up the increasing incline through the lessening throng of strangers, his breath growing ragged with the exertion. The gradient flattened as he arrived at the newspaper offices to find the doors locked. His spirits sagged; he'd missed her and his contrived hope to walk and talk with her was dashed.

He set off alone, across the square, towards the gardens so he could pick up his clothes from her hallway. His pace slackened to a stroll and his racing thoughts levelled out. 'She's married,' he muttered to himself, 'and you've got work to do.'

A flight of four Hurricanes, probably Copeland's, flew low over the city towards Ta'Qali in the west, and Bryan quickened his pace towards Valletta's north shore.

****

Bryan arrived at the plinth and scanned the empty balcony and the blank, lightless window behind it. With a sigh of resignation, he crossed the road and opened the latch on the blue door. It opened into a dim windowless hallway. Along one side, two doors stood closed, each painted the same blue, each peeling and flaking to expose a lighter undercoat. A rusty bicycle hung from nails on the opposite wall and beneath it stood a rough wooden chest. His canvas bag was nowhere to be seen. He opened the wooden chest to reveal only boots and shoes jumbled around a pair of ancient umbrellas.

Frowning he crossed to the doors. A small brass bracket secured to the doorframe on the right held a handwritten card bearing the word *Azzopardi*. Bryan hesitated for a moment, then knocked. The clump of footsteps crossed the floor above his head and grew louder as they descended the stairs behind the door. A bolt drew back and the door opened.

Jacobella, wearing a stained canvas apron over a sage-green dress, wisps of black hair escaping from her hairband, smiled in greeting.

'I'm so sorry to disturb you.' Bryan felt his face flush in her presence. 'I was looking for the washing.'

'It's in my kitchen.'

She started up the stairs. Bryan stood mute, his eyes drawn to her movement.

Halfway up, she paused and turned. 'You're welcome to come in.'

Bryan moved to follow her. Jacobella reached the top and slipped out of sight. Bryan, still only halfway up, found himself looking into the face of a small girl. She stared down at him with implacable disapproval, her hair and eyes mirroring Jacobella's in their darkness. Bryan slowed his progress and pulled what he hoped was a reassuring smile.

'Lucija,' her mother called, 'come and finish your food.'

The child dashed away as Bryan reached the top of the stairs. The apartment was simply furnished and uncluttered, the unadorned limestone walls lent a cool ambience to the air. Bryan walked through the living space

61

to the kitchen. The little girl clambered onto a chair at the plain wooden table, picked up her spoon and dipped it into her bowl. Her glare flashed back onto Bryan from under a frown, annoyed by her mother's wielding of authority in front of a stranger. Jacobella, her back to him, opened the shutters, letting more light wash into the room. She stooped into the corner of the kitchen and brought Bryan's kitbag across to him.

'Would you like some soup?' She stood and waited; hands folded in front of her.

'Well, yes please,' Bryan said. 'As long as you have enough.'

'Sit down,' she said, reaching to retrieve another bowl.

Bryan put his bag onto the floor and pulled out a chair opposite Lučija, easing himself down into the seat. The girl's eyes bored into him as she slurped soup from her spoon.

'It's mostly potatoes,' Jacobella said, 'with lots of basil.'

Underneath the table, Lučija's sandals kicked against Bryan's knees in a steady rhythm as she swung her feet backwards and forwards, one after the other.

Jacobella put a bowl of soup and a plate in front of Bryan, then went to fetch a spoon. Half a slice of rough bread sat on the plate, and Lučija's eyes dropped from Bryan to the bread. Bryan put his index finger on the plate's edge and pushed it slowly across the table to come to rest next to the child's bowl. Lučija glanced back at Bryan, then grabbed the crust. Under the table the kicking stopped.

Jacobella handed Bryan the spoon and placed a small bowl of rock salt by his hand. She'd noticed his gesture. 'That was kind of you,' she said. Sitting down, she leaned towards her daughter. 'What do you say?'

Lučija's eyes remained locked on the bread in her hands. 'Grazzi,' she mumbled.

Bryan tasted the soup and sprinkled some salt over its surface. 'Thank you for the washing. I can't tell you how much I'm looking forward to clean underwear.'

Jacobella smiled silently, her eyes flitting back to watch her daughter eating.

'I still feel a bit awkward,' he continued. 'I can't help thinking your husband wouldn't approve.'

Jacobella tucked a strand of hair behind her ear and cocked her head, considering his statement. 'Someone does his washing on the ship,' she said. 'We all deserve clean underwear.'

'Do you know where his ship is serving?' Bryan asked.

'In the Atlantic, last I heard. He'll be hating that; he can't stand being cold.'

Quiet fell on the room, padded out with the contentment delivered by the warm food. Bryan scraped the last of the liquid from the bottom of his bowl and broke the silence. 'I've been told you decided to print your scurrilous headline about me.'

Jacobella breathed a short laugh. 'I wrote that on my pad to break the ice so you'd be at ease with my questions. But after you told me your story, I realised it was wholly appropriate.'

Bryan looked into her dark brown eyes. 'I didn't tell you my full story.'

Jacobella picked up the empty bowls and carried them to the draining board. 'I wrote a short article about aeroplanes. You'll need to find someone with more spare time if you want to dictate your memoirs.'

'I thought my story was all but over,' Bryan continued. 'But it's not finished; it's not complete.'

Jacobella turned and leaned against the sink. 'Life will always go on,' she said.

'I'd stopped believing that,' Bryan said, 'until I saw you.'

Jacobella turned her back to him and opened the tap. The pipe rattled for a moment before the water sputtered into the sink and she rinsed a bowl under its dribbling flow.

'You hardly know me, Mr Hale.'

Bryan flinched at the use of his surname.

'And in any event,' she continued, 'you know I'm married.' She paused, placing a second cleaned bowl carefully onto the draining board. 'And... I love my husband.'

Bryan's shoulders slumped and he pressed a hand to his forehead. 'I'm sorry...' he muttered, '...being stupid...'

Jacobella turned to regard him with a level gaze, drying her hands on her apron. 'But I'd be proud to be your friend.'

Bryan looked up into her eyes. They held a steady resolve that was softened by a deeper tenderness. He nodded. 'Alright. Yes.'

Chapter 7

Friday, 25 July 1941

Bryan pulled a clean shirt from his locker and pressed it to his nose. Inhaling deeply through the fabric, he picked up the scent-echo of Jacobella's kitchen and the implication of her own sultry redolence. He blinked back the fantasy, and plucked open the buttons on the empty shirt, enjoying the glide of crisp fabric over the skin of his arm. As he dressed, his focus shifted; the airfield was now stocked with aviation fuel from the unloading merchant ships and Pipistrelle Squadron would rise against the night raids for the first time tonight.

Fully dressed, Bryan grabbed his flying helmet and cigarettes, then left his room. He breezed down the corridor and descended the staircase. In the lobby, three other pilots waited, Ben amongst them. As Bryan strode towards the door, the other men dropped in behind him, heading for the truck that waited to take them to Ta'Qali.

****

Two pairs of Hurricanes slinked out of the safety of their stone blast-pens into the cooling darkness of the near-deserted airfield. The new moon cut a curved sliver from the heavens, like the sickly smile of a preternatural predator hiding amongst a glittering blanket of galaxies. Its meagre gleam did nothing to separate the night-fighters' silhouettes from the darkness of their nocturnal intent.

Bryan led them along the perimeter towards the runway, his canopy open, his head swinging from side to side, taking guidance from the riggers that walked alongside, one at each wingtip. At the runway's end, the two men spun the fighter through ninety degrees, like cart horses at a mill-wheel, and beckoned Bryan forward to make space for Ben's aircraft to park behind him.

Bryan throttled back, held his mask over his mouth and pressed transmit. 'Pipistrelle Leader to Control. We are in position and ready to take off. Listening out.'

Bryan let the mask drop and tilted his face to regard the stars. His breath caught in his throat as a memory from a north London midnight pushed into his head – *"We mustn't forget the beautiful things, Bryan. We mustn't forget the things that bring us joy."*

A surge of nausea welled in his throat and the wings of nascent panic flapped at his ears. He pushed against his tightened straps in an involuntary spasm to escape the cramped confines of the cockpit.

'Fighter Control to Pipistrelle Leader.' The grating metallic voice in his ears stilled Bryan's tightening muscles. 'You are clear to take off. Good luck.'

The flare path flashed into life and the two airmen retreated from their positions. The sudden glare blasted the demons away from his shoulders and Bryan, freed into action, slid his canopy closed, pushed the throttle forward and squeezed the brakes off. The fighter surged ahead, its tail lifting like expectation. Moments later the rumble of tyres on hard ground ceased and the aircraft clambered into the night sky. Bryan steadied his breath and looked into his rear-view mirror. He caught the back-lit silhouette of Ben's plane behind him, before the lights extinguished and the runway plunged back to blackness.

Bryan banked east, climbing for the coast north of Sliema and the searchlight battery assigned to their patrol. Down on his starboard side, the flarepath at Ta'Qali flashed into life once more and two black shapes scuttled along the slab of light that slanted over the mustard-hued ground, dragging long shadows beside them. The second flight of night-fighters gained the air, bound for the island's southern tip, and darkness once more consumed the airfield.

Italian bombers habitually flew past the island far to the east, then swung round and made landfall on the southern coast, overflying and bombing their targets on the northerly course that would take them home.

Bryan glanced into the blackness behind him, trusting Ben was close behind, and pushed the guard away from his firing button. The smooth movement under his thumb sent a short thrill of pleasure up his arm, settling his resolve. Ahead, the reflective ripple of waves against the landmass described the seafront of Sliema. Bryan flew out to sea for a few moments then switched to transmit.

'Pipistrelle Leader to Fighter Control. We are on station. Orbiting now.'

The wireless hissed static into his ears. 'Thank you, Pipistrelle Leader. We'll alert your searchlight crew.'

Bryan lounged into a gentle bank, pulling a wide circle that lapped over Sliema, then curved out over the sea again, spiralling higher with each orbit.

'Ben?' Bryan's voice was flat and calm. 'Are you still there?'

'Bang on your tail light.' Concentration tautened Ben's words.

Bryan continued the lazy circle, levelling out the climb at 16,000 feet, and the minutes ticked by.

Sudden static burst into his earphones. 'Fighter Control to all Pipistrelle aircraft. We have thirty-plus bandits, south of the island, wheeling north. Angels fifteen. Landfall over Kalafrana in five minutes. Suspect they're lining up for Grand Harbour.'

Bryan eased his nose up, adding altitude to get above the oncoming raiders, but stayed in the leisurely orbit, circling over the sea and waiting. In the distance, at the island's southernmost tip, searchlight beams climbed into the void, their yellow fingers groping around for their lumbering enemies.

Below the fighters circling Sliema, their own searchlights flashed into being and angled south-east to sweep above Grand Harbour. Bryan sidled their orbit south to bring them landward of the harbour, planning to follow the raiders over their target and out over the coast.

Sudden glare clamped around the Hurricane's cockpit, stealing his vision for long seconds. Blinking against the dazzle he squinted at his instruments and pulled into a violent jink. The searchlight stayed with him and a second beam swung across to intercept his zig-zagging attempt at escape.

'Bastards!' Bryan's cry squeezed out through clenched jaws.

A concussion hammered the air behind his head, knocking his senses into darkness…

Bryan groped back through his blurred vision, confused at a spinning world that pressed him into his seat.

'Shit,' he mumbled into his mask.

Kicking the rudder to kill the spin, he pushed the stick forward, pointing the nose directly down. The horizon tilted up past his windshield and gun flashes lit up the decks of the warships that were firing at him. Bryan snarled like a cornered cat, took a gasp of breath and rammed the throttle fully open. He pulled hard on the stick, his cheeks sagged with the g-forces and his vision edged towards grey. Darkness engulfed the cockpit as the fighter flattened out into horizontal flight and outran the searchlights.

Bryan swallowed hard against the nausea rising in his throat, blinking to re-focus on his instruments. He'd lost over half his altitude; the enemy was now hopelessly far above him. A line of flashes to his left snagged at his attention, a similar cascade erupted on his right side as bomb loads pounded into Valletta and its harbours. Bryan's eyes snapped to his compass; he was flying due north – under the bombing raid. Something slashed the air on his starboard side like a whip-crack and his wing lifted with the compression. Gritting his teeth against his naked helplessness, Bryan pulled at the stick, steepening the bank of his aircraft to curve away from the bomber stream. Beneath his dipped wing, the dark cityscape sparkled with detonations, the carpet of glinting illuminations crept north like deadly phosphorescence in the flowing tide of the attack.

Bryan levelled out and flew unseeing into the dark. He pushed his goggles up onto his forehead, pinched the bridge of his nose between thumb and forefinger, and closed his eyes like a penitent in a confessional. He drew in a deep breath and pressed transmit.

'Pipistrelle Leader to Fighter Control. Request flare-path for landing. I think I have flak-damage. Suggest you have a fire crew stand by.'

Saturday, 26 July 1941

The RAF truck bumped and rolled down the hill towards Ta'Qali, Bryan and Ben rocked in harmonic sympathy, like swaying marionettes on the bench in the back.

'I still don't understand why didn't you bail out,' Ben said.

'Because I didn't want to put a socking great engine through somebody's roof.'

'It would've been safer for you.'

Bryan cast a sideways glance at his companion. 'We didn't come here to be safe.' He lit a cigarette and watched the smoke curl out the back of the crawling truck to hang in the still afternoon air. 'You say you didn't get any contact at all?'

'Nothing. I didn't see a bloody thing,' Ben said, 'except you, wallowing about, lit up like a bloody fairy on a Christmas tree. I thought you'd bought it.' He grimaced with chagrin. 'I'm afraid I backed off when the flak came up, so I suppose I might've missed something. After that, all I saw were the explosions on the ground.'

'Right' – Bryan flicked his cigarette over the tailgate – 'tonight we orbit over the sea outside the harbour, out of the way of the navy's gunners.'

'Aren't we supposed to stop the Italians from bombing the navy?' Ben asked.

'With only four fighters in the air?' Bryan shook his head. 'No. Night-fighting is largely about revenge.'

The truck grumbled through the airfield gate and wheezed to a stop. Ben and Bryan jumped down and walked out across the hard earth.

'There she is.' Bryan pointed to a black Hurricane sitting between the airstrip and the perimeter, sagging like an injured bird.

They walked across to the fighter. Two fitters stood on stepladders either side of the naked engine, stripping out its vitals like skinny hyenas tearing at a near-dead behemoth. The Hurricane's back was broken forward of the tail and the fuselage drooped onto the earth, rucking and creasing the fabric that held the two parts together. Around the break, and aft over the tail-plane, there were holes and rents torn by the spattering shrapnel of a flak shell.

'I must've brought her down a bit hard,' Bryan said.

'The flak that broke the camel's back,' Ben smirked at his own joke.

A pair of armourers arrived to strip out the unfired guns and their ammunition, and the two pilots left them to their tasks, walking away towards the tatty group of tents that passed for the airfield's nerve-centre, and the long wait for the sun to dip into dusk.

****

Bryan eyed his instruments more out of habit that necessity. The waxing moon's strengthening light defined the island's rocky edge and highlighted the splash of the low waves that broke against it. Circling a good mile north of Grand Harbour's entrance he regarded the finger of land that bisected it and the dark mass of the capital's ancient buildings that huddled there, exposed in the naked moonlight to the inevitable cascade of explosives that must be approaching in the pregnant bellies of labouring Italian bombers.

The engine's level drone counted the passage of time and Bryan blinked drying eyes against its soporific persuasion. The wireless remained stubbornly silent and the island's searchlights slumbered in the still-peaceful darkness. Bryan banked the orbit seaward, the horizontal horizon wheeled slowly across his windshield, the demarcation of sea and sky marked by a subtle change in the dark purple livery of the Mediterranean night. Something tiny moved away from that line, joined by other movements to either side.

'Pipistrelle Leader to Pipistrelle Two.' Bryan's curiosity coloured his voice. 'I'm going a bit further out to sea. Stay close.'

Bryan glanced into his mirror to see the dark bulk of Ben's Hurricane locked in position behind him on his starboard side, its bobbing on the turbulence of his slipstream the only thing that defined its autonomy from the night. Bryan's eyes dropped back to the horizon and he relaxed his pupils until the shimmering specks reappeared, each one followed by a suggestion of agitation on the water's surface, a dark blue anomaly of torpid luminescence.

'Pipistrelle Leader to Fighter Control. There's a flotilla of small boats heading towards Grand Harbour. Are you expecting anything?'

'Hello, Pipistrelle Leader, checking with the navy now, stand by.' The wireless dropped to crackling inactivity.

As Bryan closed on them, the small boats grew more distinct, their positions locked in his vision by the lengthening disturbance of their wakes, like spindly digits of menace stretching across the open water towards the harbour and the half-disgorged merchant ships that wallowed there.

'Fighter Control to Pipistrelle Leader. No such arrival is expected. Harbour defences have been alerted. Good work. Thank you.'

Bryan overflew the speeding vessels and curved around behind them in a wide arc. All along the shore on either side of the harbour entrance, searchlights flickered into life, reaching skyward for a moment before swinging down to probe across the water. One by one the approaching craft breached into the questing fingers of light, running on straight down the stark corridors of illumination, lacking the leeway to take evasive action. Speculative machine-gun fire sparkled along the coastline; gunners centred at the harbour were quickly joined by emplacements along the neighbouring seafronts. The flash of artillery blossomed from the dark coast and a crop of explosions fountained ahead of and amongst the flotilla. One boat spiralled away from a detonation, circling as it slowed.

As the survivors ploughed on, light anti-aircraft batteries pulled their elevation down to horizontal and a fearsome weave of tracer stitched in layered tendrils across the dark water, washing over and around their lighted targets. Exploding torpedoes erupted in their firing tubes, tearing three vessels to flotsam in quick succession. Others belched sheets of flame, careering onwards with no control. One vessel on the flank of the attack veered away, its sleek bows cutting a tight curve through the sea, cascading a sparkling wash into the yellow beams of light that clung to it, denying the crew the refuge of darkness. Tracers hosed after it, peeling chunks of debris from its retreating stern, tipping it prow-up to bob like a monstrous fishing float.

A plume of water rose like a spindly crystal from a torpedo strike on the breakwater that narrowed the harbour entrance, followed by a corpulent splash as part of the structure collapsed.

Bryan tightened his orbit and scanned the scene below. No boat that remained afloat was making headway. Disabled vessels wallowed everywhere, pinned like specimens by merciless searchlight crews and taking bursts of fire that foamed the sea around them until they lurched, rolled and slid away beneath the water.

Sunday, 27 July 1941

Katie woke with a start; hands gripped her shoulder, shaking her roughly.

'They're invading!'

The hissed urgency in the voice cut through the last vestige of slumber and charged a thrill of adrenalin into her muscles. She blinked against her blurred vision and Stephanie's gaunt face swam into focus.

'Listen,' the other girl croaked. 'They're coming.'

The crackle and thump of gunfire drifted across the island through the still night air.

'Get dressed,' Katie said, an undercurrent of fear frayed her voice. 'There'll be casualties. We'll be needed.'

The two women bustled about the dorm room under the dim light of a single ancient lightbulb that dangled from a dust encrusted cable in the centre of the ceiling.

'What are we supposed to do?' Stephanie's voice creaked with strain. 'What if they come in shooting?'

'They won't,' Katie said with a conviction she didn't quite feel. 'It's a hospital, there are conventions.' She grabbed her friend and placed firm hands on her shoulders. 'The only people we have to care about are the ones who need our help. We can deal with the others later.' Stephanie nodded once, though her eyes still flashed with fear.

'Good.' Katie released her grip. 'Let's get on with it.'

They left the dormitory room and skittered down the corridor towards the stairs. Katie slowed her pace and tilted her head.

'Listen,' she hissed, 'the guns have stopped.'

They descended the stairs and pushed through the doors into the main hospital reception. The window blinds lightened with the onset of dawn and Stephanie moved to open them. Katie noticed a doctor seated at the reception desk, engaged in a hushed telephone conversation. She moved closer to listen.

'– you say it's over? There are no more?' He glanced up and flashed Katie a reassuring smile, then hunched over the phone again. 'How many casualties? I see. Thank you.'

The doctor dropped the handset back into the cradle and turned to Katie. 'The Italians sent some boats to attack the harbour. Apparently, they were torn to pieces. So far, they've pulled one survivor out of the water. They're on their way with him now. He's suffered burns. Can you make ready?'

Katie nodded and hurried to the ward. Working quietly to avoid disturbing the still-sleeping patients, she pulled a screen around an empty bed. Then she visited the store room, returning with fresh bandages, Vaseline and tannic jelly. When all was set, she walked back to the reception where she found Stephanie perched on a stool, wringing her hands with worry.

'It's not an invasion,' Katie reassured her friend. 'It was a sneak attack on the harbour. They're bringing us an injured Italian sailor.'

Both nurses settled down to wait.

After a while the earthy grind of a truck's engine approached, rattling the windows as it pulled to a halt outside. The engine coughed into silence, its noise supplanted by a reedy, high-pitched wail. A man in army uniform opened the hospital door and held it back. Two more soldiers shuffled through carrying someone on a stretcher. The casualty's screams filled the lobby.

'This way, please.' Katie pointed to the ward door and walked alongside the stretcher as the soldiers carried it through.

The young Italian man clenched his jaw against his own cries, staring at Katie with feral panic in his eyes. With an act of will, he compressed his screams into rasping gasps of breath, squeezing his eyes shut with the effort. His face, although streaked in oil and sweat, was uninjured, but from the neck down, his whole left side was blackened and burnt. Katie held her breath against the tangy odour of engine oil underlaid with the stink of seared flesh. With a sickening start she realised that what she took to be the burnt fabric of shirt and trousers flapping over the edge of the stretcher was in fact the disengaged skin of a naked man.

Awakening patients hauled themselves up in their beds to stare, pale-faced, at the injured apparition of youth brought before them.

At the bed, the soldiers held the stretcher level with the mattress. Katie braced under the man's neck and undamaged right shoulder, Stephanie grabbed the man's boots, and they hoisted him onto the cotton sheets. Katie noticed the canvas of the stretcher came away from the man's back with patches of skin adhering to it, like crackling on a roasting dish.

The soldiers moved away quickly, glad to have passed their noisy burden on to somebody else, anxious to get back into the fresh air away from the cloying smell of burnt hair and skin.

Katie caught Stephanie's eye; her friend's face was drawn into a mask of appalled horror. She stood at the foot of the bed motionless and imploring.

'Go and get the doctor,' Katie said quietly. 'Go!'

Stephanie hurried away and Katie swallowed hard against the awful smell that clung inside her nostrils. She reached down and took the man's right hand in hers. His eyelids opened and his gasping redoubled. His eyes locked onto hers, a frightened realisation crept across his features and he squeezed her hand with the strength of desperation.

'Shhh…' Katie could think of nothing else to say. 'Shhh…'

The doctor arrived carrying a small bottle and a syringe. Katie held the man's gaze and gripped his hand while the doctor injected the liquid from the bottle into the young man's upper arm, stepped back and waited.

The terror and pain she saw in the sailor's eyes softened and dwindled. It shrunk back to a strange unfocussed introspection, drifting away from his agony. He blinked against the drift and re-focussed on her face for a long moment, a lover's smile playing across his lips. Then the grip in his fingers grew slack and his eyes lost their purchase upon her face, grew distant and faded to opacity. Katie laid the dead man's hand against his thigh and walked away.

****

Bryan stood near Valletta's most seaward tip, allowing the breeze to cool the heat of the climbing sun. The swell swished and runnelled up and over the outcrop's rocky edge, like the quiet breathing of a sleeping lover. Behind him the blank walls of Fort St Elmo rose, squat and implacable, their ancient demeanour debauched by the anti-aircraft guns angled skyward from the courtyard they protected.

This bulbous headland formed the western edge of Valletta's Grand Harbour entrance, and afforded a view of the now-serene killing zone of the previous night. Bryan leaned to look over the sea wall. Fragments of wood and cloth sprinkled the swell, lodging in the rocks only to be liberated by the next wave and bobbing a few feet to their next temporary landfall. The wet stones shimmered with a kingfisher hue, slicked with spilled diesel fuel. Thicker patches of engine oil undulated languorously on the water and clung tenaciously wherever they washed up.

Bryan glanced at his watch; it was well past 11 o'clock. He hefted his kit-bag onto his shoulder and walked back along the harbour front. Carpets of shell casings littered the sand-bagged gun emplacements ranged along the sea wall, their scratched brass gleaming in the sunshine. The gunners' eyes also glinted; it was a light that Bryan recognised and he dropped his gaze to avoid it.

He walked easily, sticking to the water's edge, as long as he could, glad for the breeze that tickled his skin. Eventually he swung his track north to traverse the city. An old man sat on his doorstep and watched him pass, his face placid, but his eyes haunted. Bryan's half-smile of greeting brought no response.

Bryan doglegged through the grid-like road system to reach the city's obverse harbour overlooked by the now-familiar gardens that led him to the stretch of buildings that contained Jacobella's home. He sat on the steps at the base of the empty plinth, placed his bag next to him, leaned back against the warm stone and allowed his eyes to close. The sunlight shone red through his eyelids, and sleep crept up and stole him away.

****

'Good afternoon.'

The voice roused him and he turned to see Jacobella sitting beside him, Lučija perched on her lap, both looking at him, both smiling.

'Good Lord.' Bryan pulled himself out of his slouch. 'I must've dozed off.'

'We're just back from church,' Jacobella said. 'Is that where you've been?'

Bryan shook his head. 'No. My father is a vicar. I was required to attend church far more often than is good for one person.'

'A vicar?' She chewed the word. 'In England?' Jacobella tilted her head. 'How romantic.'

Bryan regarded her for a long moment. 'Is it? Well, if you say so.' He shifted his weight on numb buttocks. 'I came to make sure you were alright, after last night' – he glanced sheepishly at the bag – 'and to bring you some more washing.'

She nodded, pulling the bag up against her thigh. 'Last night was very noisy, but it's always noisy this close to the harbour. At least there were no bombs.' Concern wrinkled her brow. 'Do you know what happened?'

Bryan looked down at his hands clasped in his lap. 'Somebody in Sicily thought it would be a good idea to send a fleet of little boats to attack a harbour where the defences are expecting a full-scale invasion. It was a massacre.'

Jacobella looked away across the gardens to where the bastion dropped down to the waters of Marsamxett Harbour. The distant murmur of waves counted like heartbeats. 'Why did you come to Malta, Bryan?'

Bryan studied her profile. 'I was sent here.'

She turned, catching his eye. 'I have the impression you chose it.'

A faint smile crept over Bryan's lips. 'Maybe.' He returned his unfocussed gaze to his hands. She waited, watching his face.

'Someone in England asked me to stop fighting. When I couldn't do that, she suggested I should hurry up and die so that she could move on. I thought it might be pleasant to get a bit of sunshine while I was about it.'

Jacobella laid a hand on his arm. 'I hope you don't die.'

Bryan glanced down at her tanned fingers resting on his skin. 'As it turned out, she didn't wait for it to happen. She upped and moved on anyway.'

'Is this the part of your story you missed out?' she asked.

Bryan scratched at the stubble on his cheek. 'I think it's one of the parts I might like to forget.'

Jacobella lifted her daughter back onto the ground and grasped the kitbag. 'I'll do these this evening.'

'I don't want to impose,' Bryan began.

She held up a hand to silence him. 'I want you to impose.'

He swivelled on the stone step to watch her cross the road to her door. This time she turned and smiled before she went in.

Chapter 8

Tuesday, 5 August 1941

'You want me to believe there's nothing in it?' Ben walked shoulder-to-shoulder with Bryan through the thickening dusk towards the operations tent.

'I don't care what you believe,' Bryan said. 'She does a bit of washing for me, that's all.'

'We have a laundry room at Xara. I used it myself yesterday.'

Bryan remained silent.

'So' – Ben smirked – 'what else is she cleaning?'

Bryan wheeled on his heel and shoved Ben hard on the shoulder, sending him sprawling onto the ground.

'She's a married woman. Beautiful, yes. Desirable, yes. But, in the end, married.'

Ben dragged himself back to his feet, brushing the dust from his clothes. 'I'm sorry,' he said. 'I'm just having a laugh.'

'Well it isn't bloody funny.'

****

The precise routine of take-off and the cradling confines of his cockpit cooled Bryan's temper as he dropped into patrol orbit outside the harbour entrance. He glanced into his mirror to see his wingman sitting behind his starboard wing, the nearly-full moon transforming his spinning propeller into a shimmering disc. Ben's words had struck a nerve he had not realised was so painfully exposed.

Bryan pulled his nose up a degree to gain more altitude, suspecting the moonlight's ghostly pallor might drive enemy intruders higher. He looked down at the island glowing a faint ochre under the moon's radiance. It was a bomber's moon, but it was a night-fighter's moon too.

'Fighter Control to Pipistrelle aircraft.' The metallic voice of the wireless buzzed into Bryan's earphones. 'One dozen bandits approaching, heading due north. Estimate they will overfly Luqa, Marsamxett Harbour and Sliema. Angels sixteen, repeat, angels sixteen.'

Bryan glanced at his altimeter and smiled in satisfaction; his flight was 1,000 feet above the raiders' approach. He levelled out, tightened his orbit and scanned the sky to the south, waiting.

In the distance, the southern searchlight battery beamed up pillars of light to penetrate the night, scratching away at the black dome, sweeping the blackness in search of enemy machines. A sudden jewel glowed at the top of one beam, glittering with reflected light. Two more searchlights angled in to bind the victim with illumination. From above the pinned bomber, a stream of tracer hosed around and across it, followed by a second burst from a different angle. The bomber nosed over and dived towards the ground, the searchlights flattening to follow it down like gleeful spectators.

Moments later a cluster of explosions blossomed in the centre of the island's girth, across the shallow basin that contained Ta'Qali's sister airfield.

'Stand by, Ben,' Bryan intoned, 'they're getting close.'

Searchlights flickered into life and slashed around over the capital's harbour like saplings in a stiff breeze and AA batteries sent up a box barrage blanketing the southern approach to the docks. Bryan squinted across the brightness of the searching beams, willing them to find a target. Then a cold certainty hit him.

'Ben!' urgency stretched his voice. 'They won't be over the harbour, not now they're empty. Follow me.'

Bryan pulled out of their orbit and pushed his throttle forward into a shallow dive, following the coast north-west and straining his eyes to pick up any movement. Turbulence from propeller wash bumped the underside of his aircraft and he swung onto a northerly course, a grin of triumph creeping across his face. '*Where are you?*' he muttered to himself.

An undulation in the night's fabric caught his eye. He let his pupils relax, looking through, rather than at, the anomaly. The blurred motion resolved into three ghostly discs; propellers reflecting the lunar glow.

'Ben, are you still there?'

'On your tail, Leader.'

'We've got one cold. Ahead and to starboard. Follow me in. Break left.'

Bryan banked slightly to lead his target and pressed his firing button. The trio of ethereal, shimmering circles drifted into his bullet stream and flashing strikes defined the lumbering bulk of the target. Then he flashed past above the bomber. Hauling away to port to avoid his wingman's fire that flashed motes of light across his rear-view mirror, he pulled a wide circle, dragging his compass back onto a northerly bearing.

Ahead, the Italian bomber illuminated itself with a fire that coursed over its port engine, licking banners of flame into its slipstream. The craft flew on for long moments, then the wing folded upwards and the fuselage rolled over into a spiralling dive towards the sea.

Saturday, 9 August 1941

Bryan left his room, walked down the corridor and pushed his way through the door onto the balcony. The light waned towards dusk and the panoramic view of the island softened around the edges as the sky transitioned from bright blue to a velvet purple.

'So, what do you think?' Ben slapped his hand on the newly constructed bar set against the back wall.

'Very nice.' Bryan crossed to sit next to him. 'Where did the wood come from?'

'We found some floorboards in a room that no-one was using.'

Bryan nodded at the bottles on the shelf behind the bar. 'The wine and the whisky?'

'They came from the cellar.'

'I thought that cellar was padlocked.'

Ben screwed up his face in chagrin. 'It was.' His features brightened. 'But the beer is legitimate. The first production run since the convoy docked. The delivery man was very proud of it.'

Ben skipped behind the bar and poured two beers from green bottles. 'It should be a good night,' he said, pushing one glass across to Bryan. 'Most of the pilots from Ta'Qali and Luqa are coming, some girls from the control room said they'd be here, and the nurses.'

Bryan paused with his glass halfway to his lips. 'Nurses?'

'From Mtarfa hospital.' Ben swigged his beer. 'I thought you knew them.'

A group of pilots arrived and Ben busied himself serving their drinks. Bryan stood up and drifted away along the balcony to lean on the railing and watch the darkness swallow the landscape. The mounting hubbub of conversation washed over him, but the sharp chirps and clicks of nocturnal insects cut through like a percussive counterpoint.

'Hello.'

Bryan turned his head to see Katie leaning on the railing next to him, a glass of wine in her hand.

'It's lovely place you have here' – a mischievous smile lit her eyes – 'and now it seems we're practically neighbours.'

'Thank you.' He returned his gaze to the darkening landscape. 'It's a shame I have to share it with so many erks.'

Katie giggled, then pulled herself upright. 'I'd like to apologise, for the other week, after the dance. I never meant to upset your girlfriend.'

Bryan's head sagged slightly. 'She's not my girlfriend. In fact, she's married. She wrote that article in the paper. That's how she recognised me.'

'Oh.' Katie leaned back on the railing, her elbow touching his. 'How is that going, the fight against the night raiders?'

'We've got a few of them.' Bryan lit two cigarettes and handed one to his companion. 'But not enough to make a difference.' He sighed. 'Half my planes will be up tonight while the ground crews work through the day to make the other half fly well enough to go up tomorrow.'

'We all do the job we're given as best as we can,' she said quietly.

Bryan scanned the crowd at the bar. 'Where's your friend?'

'Steph?' Katie took a draw on her cigarette. 'Oh, she's mooning to herself in our dormitory. She misses her sailor. He's out there somewhere in his submarine.' She nodded in the direction of the harbour and the sea.

'What do you make of him?' Bryan asked

Katie screwed her mouth up. 'I think he's a bit shady,' she said, 'but I suppose it takes a certain kind of man to get into little metal tube and sail it about under the water.'

Out to the east, around the harbour, searchlight beams stabbed into the sky and the rumble of anti-aircraft fire rolled across the landscape. The knot of people at the bar moved over to the railing, like theatre-goers returning to a show after an intermission.

Katie looked at them and tutted. 'I'd love to look around your palace.' The mischievous smile reappeared. 'Why don't you give me a tour?'

They dropped their cigarettes over the balcony and Bryan led the way down the corridor to the main staircase. They descended to the entrance hall and walked through to the inner courtyard. The courtyard doors stood open, allowing a breeze to filter into the building, and they stepped through to look up at the bat-flecked panel of stars framed by the enclosing walls.

They circled back to the entrance lobby and started up the stairs.

'It's all very lovely,' Bryan said, 'but I hardly spend any time here, except for sleeping and eating.'

They reached the top of the stairs and walked down the corridor towards the balcony.

'Where do you sleep?' Katie asked.

'It's just along here,' Bryan gestured down the corridor.

Katie dashed ahead of him. 'This one?' She pushed open a door and entered the room.

'Yes,' Bryan spluttered, 'Katie, stop it.'

He followed her into his room to find her standing at its centre, casting her eyes around the decoration.

'What a lovely bedroom,' she said. 'Close the door.'

'Katie, please don't.' His voice was barely above a whisper.

She undid the buttons of her blouse and shucked it off her shoulders. 'Don't make me do this with the door open.'

Bryan closed the door, turning the key in its lock with trembling fingers.

Tuesday, 12 August 1941

The water flowed smoothly around the submarine's prow as it crawled slowly towards its harbour approach. Albert Chandler stood to the port side of the foredeck, two other men stood with him, one on the starboard side and one facing forward. They scanned the water intently, each holding a sub-machine gun; the submarine's last-ditch defence against un-swept mines.

The sandy smudge of Malta's coastline grew closer. The sun, gaining in heat as it climbed to mid-morning, and the concentration of his task, sent rivulets of sweat trickling down Albert's back. He re-braced his legs and stared into the crystal-clear depths.

'Machine-gun party, stand down.' The shouted order came from the conning tower as the vessel drew close to the harbour. More men climbed through the hatch and clambered down the tower to the deck, stretching their backs and breathing deeply of the sea breeze. As U-Ulric nudged through the harbour's mouth, the collapsed breakwater drew a hubbub of speculative chatter amongst the men.

The submarine sailed past the entrance to Grand Harbour, around the tip of Valletta's promontory and into Marsamxett Harbour on the city's north flank. The men on the deck formed a line down the vessel's starboard side as it pulled into Lazzaretto Creek and approached its docking space.

The man next to Albert grunted. 'Why is there no-one ever waiting for us?'

Albert's smile creased his oil begrimed face. 'There's one I know is waiting for me.'

****

Bryan kicked the tyre on the Hurricane. 'Bloody useless tractor!' he shouted at the impassive black aircraft.

'Are you alright?' Ben wandered across from the next blast-pen, hands in his pockets, chewing on a matchstick.

Bryan turned on him. 'I won't be alright when this thing falls apart and drops out of the sky. Look at this!' He pointed at a propeller blade that differed in colour from the other two.

Ben squinted at it for a moment. 'It's a replacement blade. So what?'

Bryan's eyes bulged with outrage. 'Some bloke made this down at the docks.' He shook his head in despair. 'Some bloke' – his voice dropped to a hiss – 'some Maltese bloke, made this down at the docks with a hammer and an anvil.'

Ben tapped it with his knuckles. 'I'm sure it will be alright.'

'Oh!' Bryan raised his eyebrows. 'And what good is your blithe confidence to me when it flies off in mid-air and I've got nothing to crash land on except piles of fucking rocks?'

Bryan's shoulder sagged with the weight of his disgust. He walked to the back of the blast-pen and sat down on the pebble strewn ground, his back against the hard rock wall. He rummaged in his pockets for a cigarette, lit it, and blew a stream of smoke through his nostrils.

'Honestly, Ben' – his voice returned to a conversational tone – 'if we'd defended Britain last summer the way we're defending Malta now, Hitler would have his feet up on a desk in Whitehall and we'd be speaking German in Messerschmitt cockpits on the Eastern Front.'

'It's not that bad, is it?' Ben asked. 'We *are* holding them off.'

Bryan shook his head. 'They haven't come for us yet, not properly. Not like they did in France.'

'But you're talking about the Germans,' Ben said. 'And like you said, they're in Russia.'

Bryan looked up into Ben's eyes. 'Don't think they won't be coming back. They may come from Sicily or they may come from Africa, but they will come. They *can't* let us stand in their way much longer.'

The dusk gathered around them and the breeze cooled their cheeks.

'Did I see Katie leaving your room on Sunday morning?' Ben asked.

'No,' Bryan answered. He stared at his boots for a moment and narrowed his eyes. 'Yes,' he said, then hauled himself back to his feet. 'Come on. Let's see if we can find a mug of tea before I have to fly this bloody death-trap into the dark.'

Saturday, 16 August 1941

The golden sparkle of the beer in his hand layered comfortably on top of the whiskies he'd drunk before leaving Xara. The strains and tensions melted from his shoulders and his desperate exhaustion mellowed into warm fatigue, like the proto-pleasurable tiredness at the end of a day of hard physical labour. Katie stood next to him at the bar, not touching him, perfectly at ease with herself, implicitly with him, but fully self-possessed. His eyes lingered on the smooth skin of her cheek and the wisp of blonde hair that rested there. Then his gaze dropped along her neck, over the modest rise of her breast and down to her cocked hips and smooth, un-stockinged legs. Her foot tapped the wooden floor in time with the drummer and, with this visual reminder, the music flooded back into his consciousness. He looked up towards the stage and smiled in pleasure as the flood of melody washed over him. He turned to share the feeling with Ben, but his friend was engrossed in a conversation with Stephanie. He watched as Ben placed his hand on the woman's shoulder and leaned close to her ear so she could better hear what he was saying.

'Hey, you!'

A weight struck Bryan from behind, sending him lurching into Katie, cascading the remains of his beer down her dress. Bryan pulled himself upright in time to see the punch connect with Ben's head, sending him reeling into the dancing couples. Adrenalin crystallised Bryan's vision and he grasped the assailant from behind, pinning his arms to his sides. The man shouted something at Ben's prone figure and the band ground to a discordant halt.

'Shut up, Bertie,' Bryan hissed through gritted teeth. 'I'm getting you out of here before we all get bloody arrested.'

He man-handled Albert away from the bar. 'Stay here,' he mouthed at Ben, then in his cheeriest voice said, 'I'm very sorry – everything's under control – slight misunderstanding,' as he guided his captive to the door, through the beaded curtain and down the stairs to the street. Bryan released his grip and Albert spun around to face him.

'What do you think you're doing?' Bryan held his voice level, but his anger prickled the hair follicles on his neck. 'The bloody MPs will have you in the blockhouse if the owner reports this. What's wrong with you?'

'Your mate was trespassing,' Albert snarled, 'what would you do?'

'Trespassing?' Bryan's brow wrinkled in disbelief.

'That girl is mine.'

Bryan looked into the other man's eyes and shook his head. 'She's not yours, Bertie. Nobody in that group is anybody's.' He jabbed a finger into the other man's chest. 'Except you. You have a wife.'

The clack of heels sounded on the pavement behind Bryan. Albert looked over Bryan's shoulder and his face softened to a half-smile.

Bryan's voice dropped to a whisper and he leaned closer to the other man. 'You live this thing out with the girl any way you choose, but do not' – he paused until Albert's eyes met his again – '*do not* touch my friend ever again.'

Albert pushed past him and Bryan watched the matelot and Stephanie walk away down the street, his arm around the girl's waist and her head resting on his shoulder.

Katie emerged from the dance hall's door and followed his gaze. 'Don't blame her,' she said, 'you can't choose the people that move you.'

Bryan looked at her and smiled sadly. 'Where's Ben?' He changed the subject. 'Is he alright.'

'He's fine. He's back at the bar, surrounded by sympathetic ladies. Me, on the other hand' – she held out her arms and looked down at her beer-soaked dress – 'I really can't stay out like this. I smell like a drunken tramp.'

'Oh, Lord. I'm sorry.' He looked at his watch. 'The transport won't run for well over an hour.'

'There's a taxi-driver I know nearby,' she said, 'he's generally helpful to nurses.'

She linked her arm through Bryan's and led him along the street.

'I thought taxis had been banned,' Bryan said.

'This man has connections.' She tapped her finger to her nose. 'I'm sure he would've got some petrol from the convoy.'

After a short walk, they came to a façade of houses bisected by a small yard in which stood a car covered with a canvas tarpaulin.

'Wait here.'

Katie squeezed past the car and knocked on the door at the yard's end. The door creaked open and a short conversation followed. The door swung closed and Katie shimmied back past the car and gave Bryan a thumbs-up. Moments later a middle-aged Maltese man bustled out, hauled off the tarpaulin and reversed the car out onto the road.

Bryan caught the look of faint disappointment on the man's face in the rear-view mirror as he climbed into the back seat next to Katie.

'Hospital?' the driver asked.

'No,' Katie said, 'Xara Palace.'

She placed her hand on Bryan's thigh and absently moved her thumb back and forth.

'Katie?' Bryan mumbled.

'Yes, dear?

'How do you know what a drunken tramp smells like?'

Chapter 9

Friday, 5 September

Ben shifted his weight on the creaking cot. 'This isn't a bed, it's a bloody rack,' he moaned. 'I wish they'd let us know when they're not coming. I've got a bloody palace I could be sleeping in.'

Bryan lay staring at the canvas ceiling. 'No-one else is complaining.'

The tent contained four army camp-beds. The other two supported robustly snoring pilots, their faces sagging like death, with drool pooling on the canvas beneath their chins.

Ben lifted his head, winced at the crick in his neck and wrinkled his nose at the sleeping men. 'I give up,' he said, swinging his legs off the bed and sitting up.

An orderly pushed his head around the tent flaps, framed by the lightening, pre-dawn sky. 'Sorry, chaps,' he whispered, 'control have picked up a strange contact. They want a couple of fighters to investigate.'

'That sounds like us, then,' Bryan said.

He hauled himself off the bed and ducked through the tent's entrance. Ben caught up with him, limping slightly on a stiff leg.

Bryan slapped him on the shoulder and pointed at the breaking dawn on the horizon. 'Flying in daylight,' he exclaimed. 'This'll be just like the old days.'

****

Bryan eased his Hurricane into the air and pulled the canopy closed. Out of habit, he set a westerly course for Grand Harbour. He glanced into his mirror to check Ben was safely off the ground and pressed transmit. 'Pipistrelle Leader to Control. Airborne and listening out.'

'Good morning, Pipistrelle Leader. We have a small formation running in from due south, unusually low, angels five. Good luck.'

The nascent sunrise pushed the purple eastern sky into tones of blue as Bryan swung south and pushed the throttle forward. Towns and villages flashed below, blocky projections of the sand-coloured terrain from which they'd sprung. He pulled into a shallow bank to curve around the perimeter of Luqa airfield to avoid any misunderstandings, and barrelled on towards the south coast.

Puffs of dust erupted in the distance, and Bryan scoured the sky above them, finally pinpointing a group of three bombers wheeling away from the small aerodrome at Hal-Far.

'Three bandits, twelve o'clock, Ben. Do you see them?'

'Got them.'

'Good. Tally-ho!'

Bryan closed on the formation as they headed back out to sea, and thumbed the safety catch off the firing button.

The Italians saw their danger and the bombers splayed out of formation. Bryan stuck with the middle aircraft, catching up as it lumbered across the large bay that bit a chunk from the island's southern coastline. Below, two seaplanes bobbed at their moorings and Bofors guns stationed nearby opened fire as hunter and quarry roared overhead. Bryan squeezed out a short burst of fire that slashed across the port engine, punching holes in the wing, before he flashed over his target and hauled into a tight turn to re-engage.

The bomber headed due west, out to sea, running ahead of speculative bursts of fire that streaked out from awakened coastal emplacements, and trailing a thin ribbon of smoke from its damaged engine. Bryan climbed up onto the Italian's starboard quarter and shadowed the big aircraft. When the shore-fire ceased, he stooped into a dive, drilling a long burst of fire in and around the starboard engine, drawing tongues of flame from under its cowling. The big aircraft slowed and sank through the air, descending quickly, then flattened out to belly-land on the water.

Bryan circled and watched. The bomber tipped towards the weight of its three engines, raising the tail slowly into the air. Hatches opened and four men scrambled out. A dinghy inflated and the figures climbed into it, paddling away from the sinking aircraft.

Bryan circled the tiny yellow craft, his thumb caressing the fire button like a lover's tease. Then he levelled out and headed back towards the dun, rocky coastline to seek out his wingman. Behind him, the sun's shimmering disc broached the horizon like the dazzling light of divine revelation.

Friday, 12 September 1941

Stephanie walked next to Albert along the northern most edge of Marsamxett Harbour. A few hundred yards ahead, a truck chugged over the bridge from Manoel Island and its submarine docking bays, belching black exhaust smoke as it accelerated away from them, heading inland.

'When will you be back?' she asked.

'Three weeks, maybe a bit longer.' He shrugged. 'Or sooner if we run out of torpedoes. You know I can't promise anything.' The anticipation of sailing scratched a harsh edge onto his voice.

She looked up into his face. 'May I promise *you* something?'

Albert stopped and placed his hands on her shoulders. 'No.' He bent and kissed her forehead. 'I'll come to see you when I get back. I have to go. I haven't yet packed my kit.'

He stroked her cheek with the back of his fingers and strode away towards the bridge. Stephanie watched him go, a dull ache wrapped its tendrils around her guts and she bit her lip to hold back the tears.

Thursday, 18 September 1941

Albert awoke under the implacable weight of oppressive heat laced with the cloying odour of sweating cabbage and excrement. The boat's altered trim had dragged him from his fitful slumber and he shot an enquiring glance at a nearby sailor who simply jabbed a finger upwards. They were surfacing to recharge their batteries; it must be night-time.

Albert squeezed himself out of his hammock and shimmied along the smooth metal curve of a stowed torpedo. Although *U-Ulric* had encountered a few enemy vessels, they had all been northbound, and the skipper was not inclined to waste torpedoes on empty merchantmen. Albert wriggled his way towards the vessel's centre, drawn by the anticipation of the blast of fresh air that would flow through the hatch when it opened.

The hull levelled out as the bow breached the surface and the vessel rocked languorously in the grip of the swell. The conning tower hatch clanged open and salt-tanged air flooded through the submarine like the breath of salvation. Look-outs clambered up the ladder to watch for danger, and the men assigned to cook, opened tins of soup to be heated.

Albert wolfed down some soup with a couple of stale biscuits, then went on duty, relieving another crew member to eat and sleep.

The boat cruised at best surface speed, taking the chance to make headway, and Albert enjoyed the flow of cool night air circulating around him. Someone descended the conning tower ladder and spoke to the captain. The hull's thrumming ceased as the engines throttled back to idle.

The captain unhooked a pair of binoculars from the bulkhead and climbed the ladder to disappear through the hatch.

The silence left behind spawned a rising tension, the air-flow now felt chill, the sea outside once again became a theatre of danger. After long moments, the look-outs and the captain climbed down into the hull and the hatch was carefully closed and sealed.

'Ships sighted. Dive to periscope depth. Ahead, slow.' The captain's voice was calm and level.

Men immediately bent to their tasks, their movements unhurried in the cramped space in which they worked. The boat was brought beneath the surface and trimmed to run steady. Once satisfied his craft lay as he wanted it, the captain raised the periscope and rested his brow on the padded viewer, softly calling course changes to his helmsman as he drew the submarine closer to its quarry.

Word of 'battle stations' passed through the boat and a tense quiet tautened the air as the submarine slid through the water like a hunting shark.

'Two vessels,' the captain announced in a steady voice, 'steaming south, without escort it seems. Prepare to fire, all tubes.'

Again, men slipped into calm motion to enable the torpedoes, pre-loaded in the tubes since their departure from Lazzaretto, for firing. Water hissed through valves as the firing tubes flooded and wary eyes checked pressure gauges.

The captain called a final course adjustment, waited for a dozen heartbeats, then: 'Fire torpedoes one and two.'

The hull shuddered almost imperceptibly as two torpedoes kicked away from the boat, powering through the water towards the ploughing hulls of the Italian ships. But tension remained tight in the air; there were still two dice to roll and the captain stayed intent at the viewfinder.

'Stand by.' Again, the skipping beats. 'Fire torpedoes three and four.'

Once more, the percussive ripple rang through the boat's metal fabric as the missiles ran away. Tension drained into expectation that was shot through with hope. Men waited with heads cocked and eyes unfocused.

Two booms pulsed the length of the hull and the men's faces split into relieved smiles. The arrival of a third shockwave prompted a burst of hushed chatter.

'Steady everyone.' The captain turned from the periscope and glanced from man to man. 'We've hit them both. But let's stay careful in case there's an escort I haven't seen.'

He returned his attention to the viewfinder as the submarine crawled in a wide arc around its damaged victims.

'They're alone.' The captain pulled down the periscope and called orders along the boat. 'Surface! Let's finish them off. Gun crew and machine-gun party on deck at the double!'

The hull lurched once more towards the Mediterranean night air as Albert moved to the armoury locker and waited his turn to collect a sten-gun. Behind him, the hatch clanged open and he joined the men waiting to climb the conning tower ladder. Five men ascended before him, the captain and another officer followed him up.

Albert came out into the cool night air, standing for a moment while the men in front of him clambered down the exterior ladder to the deck. Shouts and calls drifted over the water, mingling from hundreds of throats to become a cacophony of human fear and panic. They were troop ships; they'd hit upon a convoy running reinforcements into Africa.

Albert pulled himself over the parapet and climbed down to where the calm water lapped against the dark, cobalt hull. The officer dropped a canvas bag of full magazines that hit the walkway behind Albert with a clang, then he lowered an ammunition box on a line to the three-man gun crew. As these men bustled about preparing the 3-inch deck gun, Albert gazed out over the scene before him, rimed in ghostly silver from the near-full moon. One ship was down at the stern, its prow already lifting clear of the water, the other was rolling to port. From both vessels, figures cascaded into the water. Around the stricken ships, the sea's surface rippled and splashed with flailing arms, scrabbling to escape the wallowing hulks that loomed over them.

'Open fire!'

The bark of the deck gun was followed by a flashing explosion on the side of the nearest ship, just above the waterline. The cries of panic redoubled.

'You men!'

Albert turned see the captain shouting at him through cupped hands.

'Keep the swimmers away from the boat!'

Albert exchanged a fleeting glance with his two companions, unshouldered his sten-gun and pushed off the safety catch. Forty yards away, the strongest swimmers were making good headway towards the submarine, one called out something in German.

Another shell boomed away from the deck gun, its clanging detonation bursting close to the first.

'Keep them away from the boat!' The captain's yell came again. 'Get on with it!'

The man on Albert's right squeezed out a burst of fire that stitched fountains of water around the foremost swimmer's head. The soldier pulled up, his face aghast, and began kicking away from the submarine. A second burst of fire slashed a plume of blood and bone from his forehead and he sank back out of sight under the dark water.

Albert swallowed hard and squeezed his trigger. Through squinted eyes he fired chop after chop of bullets at anything that moved in the water, blinding himself to the consequences he wrought. When his gun stopped firing, he dropped the empty magazine over the side and reached into the bag behind him for a replacement; he needed the noise of his gun to block out the screams and cries of so much hopeless, floundering humanity.

A deep, throaty moan reverberated into the night and, with the sound of metal grating on buckling metal, one of the ships slid under, stern first. Within a few moments the other completed its roll, baring its keel to the bright moonlight.

'Cease fire!' the captain called. 'Come aboard. We dive in three minutes.'

The gun-crew hauled the deck-gun to face forwards and worked to secure the weapon as Albert climbed the ladder on the conning tower, cordite scraping in his throat and murder pricking at his conscience.

Tuesday, 7 October 1941

'It makes no sense.' Bryan slumped into the chair in front of the trestle-desk. He gesticulated towards the tent's entrance and the airfield beyond. 'We're flying 1930s aircraft in a modern war, and now you want me to take my fighters on a bombing mission?'

Copeland shrugged. 'It's come straight down from the AOC. There's nothing to be done about it. We've tested the bomb-racks and they work adequately. I can't argue with Lloyd.' Copeland leaned forward. 'The fact of the matter is, he lost the last of his Blenheims last week and he's getting a bit twitchy that nothing's getting bombed.' A wan smile curved his lips. 'Except us.'

Bryan lit a cigarette. 'I'm more than happy to fly to Sicily, if you've got fuel enough to take me there. But for heaven's sake, let me intercept the bombers as they're forming up. Let me do some real damage.'

Copeland looked into Bryan's face. 'HQ has ruled that out. They think if we start knocking them down at the Sicilian coast, they'll put more resources into bombing our airfields.'

'So, we can't hit them for fear of them hitting back?'

'You, more than most, know how close the bombers came to wiping out English airfields last summer. We can't afford that happening here.'

Bryan shook his head in slow amazement. 'Are we trying to win this war?'

'We, that is you and me' – Copeland's voice was held low and steady – 'have to keep Malta open for naval operations for as long as we can. Nothing else matters.'

'Valletta doesn't matter?'

'No.'

'Sliema doesn't matter?'

'No. The needs of the navy take precedent.' Copeland leaned back in his chair. 'Six of your aircraft have been fitted with racks. Get your pilots back to the field by midnight; you fly in the early hours.'

Bryan stood and trailed out of the tent.

'Shiny-arsed bastards,' he muttered to himself.

Wednesday, 8 October 1941

Bryan flew low over the glittering, black water, his engine humming contentedly at a comfortable cruising speed. The moon, a few days past full, draped its gossamer light over the Mediterranean, drawing a dull gleam even from his Hurricane's black-painted wing. He flew with a fighter behind each of his wings. Away to his left, three more Hurricanes flew in a similar V formation. Bryan scanned the star-speckled dome of the cloudless sky; this was a night for hunting bombers. A night wasted, along with the fuel.

A solid dark bar drew a ragged edge across the horizon and a faint twinkling added itself to the coat-tails of the darkness.

'Pipistrelle Leader to Pipistrelle aircraft, loosen up, land-ho! It looks like they've left their lights on. This could be easier than we thought. Stick close to the coast, one run only, then home.'

'Pipistrelle 'B' flight, peeling off now. See you later.'

Bryan glanced across to see the three black shapes of the other formation bank away to head west along the darkened hinterland. He led his flight over the narrowing stretch of water towards a coastal town dead ahead.

The line of a breakwater stood stark in the moonlight, sheltering half-a-dozen fishing boats moored together in a huddled group. Bryan squeezed out a burst of fire that slashed across the breakwater and through the tethered vessels. Banking hard over the rising rooftops, he led the way east, scanning the ground for something to attack.

The coast curved away from the town into a sickle-shaped bay a couple of miles wide. The sweep of its arc ended with a squat, circular building. Bryan banked to follow the coastline's outward sweep, pulling the bomb-release toggle as the red-and-white-painted tower loomed under his propeller. He pulled up into a shallow climb, glancing in the rear-view mirror to catch small explosions straddling the building and his wingmen diving in to drop their ordnance onto the headland.

'Bloody firecrackers,' he muttered to himself.

Levelling out, he skipped westwards, just seaward of the rocky shoreline along the edge of another sickle-shaped bay. A movement in the air ahead caught his eye. He throttled back a touch and the shape resolved into a small float plane, banking away to evade him. Bryan tilted into the same bank and opened fire. Hits danced over the defenceless enemy aircraft. One of the large floats detached from its underside, sending it spinning around the remaining float down into the sea.

Hauling up over a beach, Bryan barrelled low over a headland, squirting short bursts of fire at anything that looked like a workshop or a factory. His guns rattled into silence and he searched in his rear-view mirror for his wingmen.

The headland's opposite beach flashed by beneath him and the open sea stretched away to the lightening eastern horizon.

'Pipistrelle 'A' flight, form up on me. Let's go home.'

Two dark shapes settled in behind his wings and he pulled a long, slow turn to the south-west for the run home to Malta.

****

On the top of *Ulric's* conning tower, the look-outs cocked their heads at the sound of engines. They scanned the purple dawn to find the aircraft and swung their binoculars up to examine them.

'Hurricanes,' one muttered to the other. 'What are they doing roping about at this time in the morning?'

His companion shrugged and went back to scanning the horizon.

Above their heads a hand-stitched pirate flag flapped from the short mast, two new white bars adorning its corner, as the submarine ran in towards the harbour entrance.

Chapter 10

Saturday, 11 October 1941

Katie helped the old man out of bed and into the chair by its side. She stuck a thermometer under his tongue and took his pulse. Smiling with reassurance, she checked the mercury and stroked the man's papery cheek. He stared back at her in unconcerned confusion.

Katie stooped to peel away his soiled bedclothes, bundling the clean parts over the stains to hold in the smell. Footsteps attracted her attention and she glanced up as Stephanie drifted into the ward and stood by the door.

'Steph!' Katie called, beckoning her across. 'Hold this open, please.'

She handed her friend a pillowcase and rammed the sheets inside it. Stephanie gazed into the space above Katie's shoulder.

'Are you alright?' Katie asked.

Stephanie nodded vacantly. 'Yes. Thank you.'

Katie narrowed her eyes and studied her friend's face.

'Come with me.' She grabbed Stephanie's arm and propelled her along the corridor to the laundry room. Closing the door, she shook the dirty sheets into the basin and opened the tap. As water trickled over the washing she turned to her friend.

'Now, what's wrong?' she asked. 'Is it something to do with Al?'

Steph's eyes dropped. 'Well, yes,' she murmured.

'What's he done?' Katie's voice hardened.

'We were together last night.'

Katie's eyebrows raised with her unspoken question.

'Oh, no,' Stephanie said, 'we've done it before, and he knows I wanted to do it again. I want to make him happy because I love him.' She paused, biting her lower lip. 'But last night it was like he didn't care whether I wanted to or not.'

Katie put her hands on her friend's shoulders. 'Did he do anything you didn't want him to do?'

Stephanie put her hand to her mouth and nodded once, tears welling into her eyes and spilling down her cheeks.

****

Bryan leaned on the railings of the Xara Palace balcony looking out across the darkened landscape. Nothing moved, no searchlights swept the sky, silence kept its private council over the island. He swilled a large whisky around his glass and considered Katie's story.

'So, what do you want me to do about it?' he asked.

'At the very least, you could have a word with him,' Katie said.

'Well' – Bryan pulled a face – 'it's not like she's my daughter.'

'No that's true' – Katie's voice rose a tone – 'but it *is* like she's my friend.'

'Come on, Katie. She's a grown-up woman. What did she know about the man before she got involved with him?'

Katie grabbed Bryan's arm and pulled him around to face her. 'What did *you* know about *me*?' Her eyebrows raised to emphasise her point. 'Al let you throw him out of a dance hall once, maybe he'll listen to you about this. I can't have her used like' – she struggled for words – 'an object.'

'Alright.' Bryan nodded. 'The next time I bump into him I'll-'

'She's seeing him tomorrow afternoon,' Katie interrupted, 'after work at four. They generally meet in The International Bar under the Egyptian Queen. You could probably bump into him there.'

Sunday, 12 October 1941

Bryan wandered along Strait Street and glanced at his watch; nearly three-thirty. He dropped his cigarette onto the ground, crushed it under his boot and walked slowly towards the corner of Theatre Street where the door to The International stood open. Resolved, he headed for the entrance and ducked into the gloomy space.

At once he spotted Albert sitting alone, brooding over the dregs of his drink. Bryan walked to the bar, bought two beers and carried them over to the table.

'Hello, Bertie.' Bryan put the drinks down on the table and pulled up a chair.

Albert swilled the remains of the old drink and took a gulp from the fresh one. 'Thank you. To what do I owe the pleasure?'

'Let's just say the friend of a mutual friend thought you were acting a bit strange.' Bryan took a sip of his beer. 'I'll hazard a guess it's got something to do with your last trip?'

Albert looked up at him. Mild surprise passed across his features, but he said nothing.

Bryan lit a cigarette and placed the open packet on the table between them. 'Unless of course, it's all a big operational secret.'

Albert took a cigarette from the pack and leaned towards Bryan's lighted match, puffing his smoke into glowing life. 'There's no secret about what we do. We sneak up on ships and sink them.'

'So, what was so different this time?'

Albert pinched the bridge of his nose and rolled his cigarette around between the fingers of his other hand. Bryan watched the other man in silence, waiting for him to reach a decision.

After a long moment, Albert spoke.

'This time it was two unescorted troop ships. They must've missed their rendezvous along the way somewhere. Anyway, they were sitting ducks. We hit them both with torpedoes and surfaced to finish them off with the deck gun.'

Bryan nodded and waited.

'I've never watched people dying before. I've never seen people so helpless.'

'I see.' Bryan crushed his cigarette out in the ashtray. 'Do you think that's any reason to be beastly to your girlfriend?'

Albert looked up, his eyes narrowing.

'Listen to me,' Bryan continued, 'you know I could blow the lid off this whole affair simply by telling her you're married. She's a sweet, principled girl and I guarantee she'd never want to see you again.'

'Why should you care about any of this?' Albert's voice held an edge of menace.

Bryan leaned back in his chair. 'I'm not sure I do care very much, Bertie. But I do know she loves you. Perhaps things will turn out so she never needs to know the truth. Either way, at some point in the future, her heart *will* get broken because of you. I think you should treat her with a bit more kindness until that day comes along.'

A prickly silence descended between the two men, broken after a few moments by a woman's voice.

'Hello, Al.' Stephanie walked up to the table. 'Sorry I'm a bit late.' She turned to Bryan. 'It's good to see you two have made up.'

'Isn't it?' Bryan stood. 'I'm sorry, I was just leaving.' He drained the remains of his beer. 'Have a lovely evening, you two.' He walked to the door without looking back.

Outside, the warm air embraced him, but tension still bunched in his nerves and the beer's bitterness rankled at the back of his throat.

Tuesday, 21 October 1941

Bryan sat in the passenger seat as the transport crawled down the hillside from Mdina to Ta'Qali. Ribbons of dust unfurled in the middle distance, each birthing a speeding fighter, expelling them from the murky airfield into the clean afternoon air where they climbed away north-west along the island's spine.

The truck lumbered onto the station and Bryan jumped out as it stopped. He shaded his eyes with his palm and watched a flight of three Hurricanes join the circuit for landing. The coverings on their gun-ports were intact; this was no combat action. He lit a cigarette and wandered around the perimeter, skirting the billowing dust clouds thrown up by the landing fighters. He came to a blast-pen where a black Hurricane sat, stripped of its cowling, a fitter on a step ladder engrossed with its innards and humming to himself.

'What's the flap?' Bryan called up to him.

The man jumped at the disturbance. 'Oh! Hello, sir.'

'Is there a convoy coming in?' Bryan asked.

'There's a rumour of a navy battle group, sir. Big ships. Cruisers and destroyers. Permanent posting, or so I've heard.'

Bryan scratched at his cheek. 'Any of our kites need a flight test?'

The young fitter smiled. 'There's always one needing something, sir. Perhaps you ought to check with the chief.'

Bryan wandered off in search of the crew chief.

****

'So, what am I watching for?' Bryan pulled on his flying helmet and fastened the chin-strap.

'Intermittent drops in the oil pressure,' the fitter explained. 'We've checked the pipes and found nothing, so we exchanged the gauge. Run her hard for a bit and see what happens.'

Bryan climbed into the black aircraft and started the engine, watching as the pressure gauge climbed normally. He taxied out along the perimeter, waited for control's permission, then powered along the landing strip and into the waiting grip of the air.

He climbed away on a westerly course to avoid the flight paths of the convoy patrol, overflew the hospital nestled on its hill at Mtarfa, and cruised out to the western coastline. Nosing out over the water, he climbed to an altitude sufficient for a safe bail-out, then pushed the throttles up to the gate. The engine had the bronchial edge common to all Malta's aircraft, but the oil pressure remained steady.

The coast streamed by in a series of bays and coves. Bryan throttled back as he reached the rocky ridge that Malta wore like a headpiece, and banked right to skim through the channel that separated her and her sister island.

The open sea lay before him, and there in the distance, moving like dark portent, a fan of four dark-grey warships sliced through the ethereal blue that supported their pugnacious bulk. Copeland had hinted that the naval stakes were raising, and now here came the players.

Thursday, 23 October 1941

Bryan stepped from the bus and paused. Across the harbour, spaced along a mile of its ragged dockside, lay the four bristling warships, bright white ensigns stirring languidly at their sterns, guns along their flanks elevated towards the hostile sky.

Bryan hefted his bag of washing higher onto his shoulder and set off across Valletta towards the opposite bank. He had plenty of time, Jacobella would still be at work, so he wandered into Hastings Gardens and leaned on the wall overlooking Marsamxett Harbour. Movements drew his eye to a submarine moored low in the water next to the wall of the ancient waterside building that skirted the edge of Manoel Island. Men carried boxes across gangplanks, stacking them on the deck to await stowage. Bryan eyed the sleek vessel from stem to stern with an appraising eye. It was required, like him, to sneak up unseen and deal out murder; only the scale of the ensuing destruction set them apart.

He walked away from the bastion wall, crossing the narrow strip of gardens towards Jacobella's house. He reached the statue-less plinth and dropped his bag onto the stone steps. Fumbling in his pocket for his cigarettes, he glanced across the road and froze. A man stood on Jacobella's balcony. His short black hair framed a dark, tanned face. He stood barefoot, wearing a plain bathrobe, and leaned on the balcony rail, staring absently across the gardens towards the harbour. The balcony door swung inwards and Lučija appeared. The man crouched down, picked her up and returned his gaze to the horizon. Lučija looked directly into Bryan's eyes and a smile broke across her face. She waved to him, gurgling with pleasure.

'Christ,' Bryan muttered, dipping his head and turning his back to the building. He went through a pantomime of searching for something in his pockets, then reached down for his bag. Swinging it purposefully onto his shoulder, he strode back the way he had come.

Saturday, 25 October 1941

Katie pushed her hips down and forward against Bryan's climax, gathering his urgent abandon into her warmth. Both her palms pressed his chest, transfixing him under her desire, her nails pricking indents into skin that ran slick with sweat. She felt his muscles unknot and relax, and she rocked her pelvis gently to enjoy the last of his receding hardness. He slipped from her, and she rolled off his body to lay by his side, propped up on an elbow, looking into his face. She laid a hand back on his chest, absently stroking her thumb against the rise and fall of his breastbone.

'You have something on your mind,' she said.

Bryan pulled his head back to better focus on her face. 'What makes you say that?'

She glanced towards his naked belly, then back to his eyes. 'You took a bit more persuading to join in than usual. You're distracted.'

Bryan returned his gaze to the ceiling. 'Everything's changed. Now those warships are here. It's all different.'

'Surely it's better?'

'I don't think so. The ships will draw heavier bombing raids onto the harbour, with all that brings for the people who live and work nearby. And whatever you think about our friend Bertie, those submarines are taking out a lot of merchant ships. Once those loss reports hit the right desk, the Germans will be back, and they'll be set on doing the job properly.' He sighed. 'Perhaps it's inevitable, perhaps it's necessary, but it's certainly not going to be better.'

She looked into his eyes, a wisp of suspicion on her face, then a smile crept over her features and her hand moved slowly down his body. 'Well, we'd better not waste the spare time we have left.'

Sunday, 9 November 1941

Ta'Qali buzzed with an optimistic undercurrent of the same ambience lately bestowed by the arrival of supplies. But today it was because ships had steamed out of the harbour instead of limping into it. At dusk the day before, the navy battle group had slipped away in the gloom. Rumours circulated of radio intercepts suggesting a large supply convoy escorted by Italian warships was making a break for Tripoli.

Bryan wandered along the perimeter from blast-pen to blast-pen, casting an eye over each of his black-painted fighters, trying to suppress the coiling spring of tension in his guts with banal, routine activity. The grinning faces of shirtless ground-crew irritated him, and the condition of his battered night-fighters was lost to the distraction of his craving. He retreated from the company of airmen, away from the bustle of maintenance and servicing, away towards the solitude of the bus stop where his nauseous frustration mellowed into expectation.

****

Bryan stepped from the bus and swept the harbour with a quick glance. The absence of the navy sent a furtive thrill down his spine. He paused, breathing deeply and steadily, even now resisting the pull of what he knew he shouldn't be doing. His resolve melted; it was just to see her face, that was all, just to see her face. He walked across the empty city, its people locked from sight, bowed in the rictus of morning prayer.

Striding along Windmill Street, he came to the battered blue door. He hesitated for a heartbeat, then opened it and entered the hallway. Cooking smells extruded from the gap under Jacobella's door, lacing the air with indiscriminate welcome. He reached up and knocked. Footsteps creaked down the stairs and the door opened.

Bryan looked into the old woman's sun-creased face, suspended for a moment in space, dangling over the chasm of his own misjudgement. He felt a frown crease his forehead; the contraction mirrored the narrowing eyes that regarded him with growing suspicion from the entrance.

'Bine,' Lučija blurted from her perch on the top stair. She pointed at him to reinforce the identification. 'Bine.'

'I'm really sorry,' Bryan stammered, 'I think there's been a mistake.'

He turned and left, closing the street door with exaggerated care. He leaned against the peeling paint and looked at his watch. Too early; Mass was barely over. He hurried away from the door, back down Windmill Street, wrestling with embarrassment and disbelief. He ducked around the corner into Mint Street, paused and lit a cigarette, shaking his head at his own stupidity.

Mint Street dropped away before him, its stepped pavements gleaming dull and smooth, reflecting the passage of uncountable shoes, before it reared up again, seaward, towards the imposing dome of the Carmelite church. Halfway down the slope a loose group of figures drifted out of a side road and climbed the hill towards him. All were dressed for church and now Mass had finished they were heading home.

At the back of the knot of people, he recognised her face, the twist of her hair, the way she carried her head and the flow of her walk. He stood and waited, helpless to avoid whatever might happen.

A smile flashed into her eyes when she saw him. The other people flowed past and she stopped, a step below him, looking up into his face.

'Hello, Bryan. It's lovely to see you.'

'I'm so sorry,' Bryan said, 'I knocked on your door.'

A flash of concern darkened her brow, but then she relaxed. 'So, you met my mother-in-law.' Her smile returned. 'What did she say?'

'Nothing.' Bryan grimaced. 'I ran away before she had a chance.'

Jacobella laughed. 'I thought you were braver than that.' She touched his arm. 'Let's walk for a while.'

She turned to retrace her steps down the incline. Bryan fell in beside her and they cut through the side alley onto Bakery Street.

'I did come a while ago, but I saw your husband was home,' he explained, 'so I thought it was best to fade away.'

'Yes.' She smiled ruefully. 'He asked many questions on that night.'

'Oh, God,' Bryan croaked, 'and now I've dropped you in it again.'

She shook her head. 'It is neither illegal nor immoral to have friends.'

They came to a church, its doors still open.

'Let's sit for a while.'

They stepped into the cool interior and Bryan looked around. Heavily decorated columns and arches supported a multi-domed ceiling, each dome forming its own hemisphere that displayed richly-painted scenes on multiple panels. Statues looked down at him from niches, some with eyes of pity and forgiveness, others with wrath and admonishment, some painted in bright livery, others clothed only in the silent, honey-coloured stone from which they were wrought. Bryan's gaze fell to the main altar where seven silver candle-sticks supported long waxen candles that pointed their bloodless fingers heavenwards. The altar stood in front of a wall that held a brilliant golden disc that brooded over the space like the impassive eye of an uncaring god.

Jacobella dipped her head briefly towards the altar and slid onto a pew. Bryan lowered himself next to her.

'So' – she regarded him from under dark eyebrows – 'you've come without any dirty shirts.'

Bryan glanced at the nearest statue-saint. It stared back with dead eyes, hands raised in supplication, its head haloed with the ultimate truths for which it was martyred.

'I heard the navy had sailed and' – he looked back into her still eyes – 'I wanted to see you.'

Her gaze remained steady but she said nothing.

'I know what it looks like,' Bryan said. 'But then, maybe it *is* what it looks like.'

Jacobella blinked and dropped her gaze. She shook her head, an almost imperceptible movement. 'It can't ever be what it looks like,' she said. 'I can only be your friend.'

Bryan bowed his head. 'Of course,' he said quietly. 'I'm being foolish again.'

She reached across, placed a finger underneath his chin and lifted his face up to look into his eyes. 'I think of you every day, Bryan, with both happiness and sadness.' She pulled a wry smile. 'But I'm married.'

Bryan's eyes stung with nascent tears. 'What can I do?'

She released his chin. 'Why don't you come here for mass on Sundays? We can sit together.'

Bryan's eyes flitted over the face he longed to touch. A tear escaped to run down his cheek. 'Yes,' he said quietly. 'We can sit together.'

****

Searchlights flicked on and their yellow beams climbed into the night around Grand Harbour, like monstrous altar candles seeking to illuminate the lost souls of the approaching bomber crews. Bryan watched the lights waver and wobble, while curving a course around them, sliding from his orbiting position over the sea, making landfall at Sliema and heading for the landward end of Valletta before hooking around to drop into a parallel course to the bombers. The explosive flashes of bomb strikes in and amongst the eastern docks suggested his timing was perfect.

A sudden glare illuminated his propeller disc, flaring brightness against his night-vision. His rising curse died in his throat as the searchlight tracked away from him and settled on a hunchbacked, tri-motor Italian bomber barely one hundred yards away on his starboard side. The harsh light bathed the enemy's desert camouflage without mercy, like an Arabian sun scorching a camel hide, making it a vibrant honey-coloured mote in the blackness of the Maltese midnight.

Bryan grunted with satisfaction, hauled back the throttle and kicked his rudder. The nose of his Hurricane slewed to the right and he thumbed the firing button. Bullets coned into the blocky fuselage above the wing-root, scything through the aircraft's skin into the cockpit. Bryan curved in behind the bomber, walking his bullet-stream out along the wing to the port engine, his body vibrating to the tuneless choir of his machine-guns' rattle. The engine flared out licks of startling orange that wriggled their hellish fingers, groping into life, strengthening, growing, then belching into a writhing conflagration, a righteous flame searing atop the candle, burning in affirmation of the only revenge that Bryan could take for what he could not have.

The guns clamoured to a halt, their passion spent, and Bryan banked away from the light and the fury, the burning terror and the blistering death, to fly into the cool, eye-salving darkness and look for home.

Chapter 11

Monday, 10 November 1941

Bryan and Ben sauntered along the corridor and through the doors onto the roof terrace. Ben ducked behind the bar and pulled out a whisky bottle and two glasses.

'I heard the navy have been spreading a bit of mayhem,' he said. 'Someone told me they've sunk a whole convoy; a dozen merchantmen and three of their escort destroyers. Caused a proper mess.'

Bryan accepted a glass and took a sip of the amber liquid. 'What I wouldn't give for a cube of ice,' he muttered.

The two men sat at a table near the railing, facing out over the night-shrouded island.

Ben raised his glass. 'To the navy, then,' he proposed.

Bryan levelled his gaze at the younger man. 'It's all very well and good,' he said, 'but the whole thing is completely arse about face.'

Ben lowered his glass to the table and frowned into the silence. 'I don't understand,' he said at last.

Searchlights unfurled into the dark and scratched away at the sky around the distant harbours. Bryan cocked an eyebrow towards them.

'Pipistrelle had three serviceable aircraft tonight,' he said. 'All of them are up.' He lit a cigarette and blew a stream of smoke into the still air. 'Copeland has barely twice that number to put up against whatever might come along during the day tomorrow. We're completely unable to defend the Maltese as it is. We need Spitfires, lots of them. And until they get here, we could do without a navy battle group swaggering about all over the Med beating the crap out of Rommel's convoys.'

Dull rumbling rolled over the island as anti-aircraft batteries opened up on the east coast, joined in counterpoint by the lower staccato roar of cascading bombloads stitching their paths through the docks.

Ben swivelled his head to gaze across at the twinkling violence on the horizon. 'Sounds like a big raid,' he said.

'Of course it is.' Bryan drained his whisky. 'The navy have pissed Rommel off, Rommel has a direct line to The Fuhrer, Hitler sticks the toe of his jackboot up El Duce's behind, he in turn roasts some fat wing commander and, lo and behold, fifty-odd bombers arrive to slaughter Maltese civilians.'

He flicked his cigarette into space, its burning end scribing an orange arc through the darkness. 'And I've got three Hurricanes to fight back.'

Saturday, 15 November 1941

The band at the Egyptian Queen squeezed out the last notes of a waltz and tripped immediately into a quickstep, the conductor grinning as the couples on the floor struggled with the transition. At the bar, Katie sipped a tonic water and regarded Bryan's impassive face.

'I hate to admit as much, but it appears you were right,' she said.

Bryan raised an eyebrow.

'The Germans,' she clarified. 'Albert got back into harbour yesterday. He told Steph they'd been warned about German submarines moving into the Mediterranean. Nothing definite yet, but even so.'

'There were rumours at the airfield about a sinking,' Bryan said. 'Some say it was an aircraft carrier.'

'Don't fret.' She smiled. 'Submarines can't hurt you in your aeroplane. Surely it's the navy's problem.'

'On the face of it, yes. But I do like eating, and my aeroplane needs petrol. If the Germans really have sent U-Boats…'

Katie screwed up her face. 'How did we get into such a mess?' She looked up into his eyes. 'What will happen now?'

Bryan took her in his arms. Her musky warmth fired an impulse and he squeezed her tightly to his chest. 'I have no idea,' he said, 'so let's just dance.'

They whirled out into the crowded hall, Bryan enjoying the feel of Katie's body pressed against him; the movement of her hips across his body as they changed direction stirred the embers of desire in the pit of his stomach. When she was this close, she filled his consciousness with her warm curves, her tingling scent and her carefree, lilting voice. Her eyes flashed with a mischief that he didn't seek to control or admonish and, when the night's dancing finished, he knew her lips would move over his shuddering skin with lascivious intent and her shameless purpose would tear him away from danger and privation for a long, delirious moment of sweet consummation.

Yet she was the wrong woman. When she was out of his sight, she also left his mind. Other hooks tugged at his heart. Their implacable sharpness snagged at him now, calling him to a place that he had no means to be. He breathed in the scent of Katie's pinned blonde hair pressing against his chin and felt a rush of empathy; he gave too little for what he took.

Something triggered her senses and Katie twisted her head up to look at him. She bared her teeth in a carnivorous smile and winked at him. Bryan felt a familiar tumescence buzz in his loins, squeezed her closer to him and carried on dancing.

Sunday, 16 November 1941

Bryan stepped from the bus onto Quarry Wharf. The vehicle pulled away, leaving him standing alone by the harbour wall. Sliding past him through the smooth, still waters of Grand Harbour a British cruiser made its way towards its berth further west. Bryan's gaze drifted beyond its stern to the breakwaters to see the other warships of the battle group steaming towards the port.

He hung his head, averting his eyes from the flotilla that bore Jacobella's husband back to fill her bed. But the snags in his heart still tugged, and he followed their pull. Through Victoria Gate and left, labouring up the steps into the city to join the Catholic faithful bustling along the dusty streets to Mass.

Within ten minutes he stood on the street outside St Augustine Church. Latecomers hurried past him as he walked slowly through the door and paused to let his eyes adjust. There, in the rear pew, she sat alone. Her back arched and her neck held straight, resolute and beautiful. He stood immobile, his heart leaping like a hooked fish on a grassy riverbank, scorched by the burning sun of its new reality. If she saw him, he would be lost.

'Sinjur?' a voice hissed by his side. Bryan turned to see an old man dressed in black, gesturing at the pew with his brow arched in encouragement.

'No,' Bryan whispered, 'I'm sorry.' He threw a worried glance at Jacobella's back and lowered his voice further. 'It's... it's the wrong church.'

Forced into action by the danger of being noticed, Bryan squirmed past his inquisitor and stumbled back onto the street. Behind him, the man closed the door with a grind of wood against wood and the clank of a metal latch.

Wednesday, 3 December 1941

A full moon hung over the island, its face dappled by scudding banks of cloud. Watery moonlight filtered between the open tent flaps, drawing a silvery outline across the toe of Bryan's flying boot.

An orderly ducked through the opening. 'Control have an RDF contact stooging up and down the coast. They want someone to take a look.'

Bryan hauled himself to his feet. 'I'll go.'

Once outside the tent, Bryan trotted through the cool night air to his Hurricane. Lounging ground crew pulled themselves into sluggish activity, helping him settle in his cockpit, connecting the starter and firing up the Merlin that coughed and spluttered into life before settling into a lazy growl. Bryan taxied with a shadowy figure guiding each wingtip until the fighter swung onto the end of the runway. The men backed away, waved and retreated. Bryan gave them a moment to get clear and pushed the throttle forward. The Hurricane surged down the hard-packed strip and lifted into the air. A banner of curling dust detached from its tail and rolled across the airfield, writhing like an incandescent silver snake in the impassive lunar glow.

'Pipistrelle One to Control.' Bryan's voice sounded mechanical against the labouring roar of his climbing aircraft. 'Can you give me a heading, please?'

'Hello, Pipistrelle One. Heading zero-seven-zero, angels five. Your bandit is a mile seaward from Grand Harbour and circling. He's been there too long for mine-laying; it's probably a reconnaissance flight.'

Bryan eased his rate of climb and banked onto the course. The darkened ground flowed away beneath him and the walls that divided the fields reflected the dim light from their dirty sandstone, jumping into relief like a net cast over the landscape. Fields gave way to the smudged ochre reflections of towns, becoming denser and coalescing into one as the glittering waters of the twin harbours rolled into view.

Bryan flew over Marsamxett Harbour to avoid disquieting the navy gunners on the brooding silhouettes of warships in Grand Harbour, immobilised and hostile at the end of their heavy anchor chains. Between him and the warships stretched Valletta, its profile crenelated with spires, domes and bastions, its ancient, crumbling façade enclosing frail and precious flesh. His engine rippled its noise against their walls.

Bryan scanned the emptiness ahead of him as he crossed the coast. 'Pipistrelle One to Control. Vector, please.'

'Hello Pipistrelle One, we have you. Vector due north, bandit is turning for another run.'

Bryan banked onto the new course and put the Hurricane into a shallow dive, to increase airspeed and stay below the intruder, keeping it between him and the light-source. A glinting reflection snagged his attention and he curved towards it, straining his eyes to fathom a shape. Another glint and he had it; a silhouette of barely darker opacity blocking the insipid lunar reflection. He dropped in below the aircraft and throttled forward to close the gap.

Bryan squinted hard at the indistinct shape that shimmered through the blackness. It didn't look like any Italian plane he'd seen. Its twin-engines and rounded nose looked strange, but familiar; he crept closer and thumbed the transmit button.

'Pipistrelle One to Control. Are you certain there are no stray friendlies around?'

Light burst from the intruder's belly, sending a chain of glowing tracers curling down towards Bryan, flashing over his cockpit like a lizard's angry, darting tongue. He jinked sharply away from the stream of fire, slamming the joystick right and then left. The intruder slewed away and accelerated towards a bank of cloud. As its fuselage tipped, the movement added solidity to its outline and the white edges framing a black cross flashed in the moonlight before the intruder was swallowed into the fluffy gloom.

'Control to Pipistrelle One. We've double-checked. No friendly aircraft expected. Repeat: No friendly aircraft expected.'

Thursday, 4 December 1941

Bryan sat in front of Copeland's desk, a cigarette clamped firmly between his teeth.

Copeland leaned forward on his elbows. 'Are you *absolutely* certain?'

Bryan's eyes flashed. 'It was a bloody Junkers 88. There's no doubt about it.'

Copeland regarded him in silence for a moment, then bent his head to scribble something on a sheet of paper.

'We're fucked,' Bryan said. 'Write that in your report.'

Copeland wrote on in silence.

'There are U-Boats in the Med and the Luftwaffe is back on Sicily,' Bryan continued. 'It's as good as over.'

Copeland sighed. 'You saw one German aircraft, Bryan. There's nothing to say they're back in any strength.'

'The vultures are there,' Bryan said in a quiet voice, 'I can feel it.' He leaned forward in his chair. 'If Kenley and Biggin Hill had been in the same mess last summer as Ta'Qali and Luqa are now, we would've deserved an invasion. Unless we get more fighters, proper fighters, that's what will happen here.'

Copeland shook his head. 'The navy will deter any invasion.'

Bryan slumped back in his chair. 'The navy can't do that without air cover. We *need* Spitfires.'

The other man laid his pen on the blotter with exaggerated, deliberate care. 'We've *asked* for Spitfires. They're reluctant to move any away from Britain.'

'Can't they see we need them?'

Copeland cleared his throat and looked down. 'They believe the deficiency lies with the pilots rather than the planes. They feel we should be trying harder with the resources we have to hand.'

Bryan stared at his commanding officer for a moment, blinking in disbelief. Then he stood up and walked to the door. Pausing halfway through the doorway he looked back into Copeland's face. 'We're here to save these people. We deserve to get the tools we need to do the job.'

The door clicked shut behind him.

Saturday, 6 December 1941

Bryan and Katie sat at a table in the International, waiting for the Egyptian Queen to open its doors.

'Did they give any details?' Bryan asked.

Katie shook her head. 'There was a brief mayday call early on Thursday. Nothing's been heard since, so *Ulric* is assumed lost at sea.' She looked into his eyes. 'No survivors expected.'

'How is Stephanie taking it?'

'Hysterically.' Katie frowned at the memory of her friend's distress. 'She'd built up such a story in her head about the way things would be after the war. She hasn't only lost a boyfriend; she's lost her perfect future.'

Bryan looked down into his drink and remained quiet.

'The doctor gave her something to help her sleep,' Katie continued. 'She was quiet when I left her.'

Air raid sirens raised their mournful voices outside, vibrating their invidious chorus through the early evening air.

'No dancing tonight,' Katie said. She reached across to squeeze Bryan's hand. 'Let's go back to the palace. I could do with some cheering up.'

PART 2

RESISTENZA

Chapter 12

Monday, 8 December 1941

Limpid sunlight filtered through the haze, bringing the slightest breath of warmth to the cool morning air. Bryan moved between the blast-pens, pausing at each black-painted Hurricane to hear a report on its airworthiness from the maintenance chief. The news was better than normal; half-a-dozen aircraft expected to be serviceable by nightfall.

The sputtering chatter of a service motorbike drew his attention. The machine chuntered through the gates and headed for the cluster of tents that served as the airfield administration. The rider dismounted and stepped into one of the tents. Bryan lit a cigarette and kept an eye on the tent's entrance, curious about the dispatch rider's mission. After a minute or two an orderly emerged, walking quickly. He stopped to talk to two fitters on the perimeter track, before striding off. The two fitters exchanged a few words and split up, each moving in different directions with their news; a rumour mill was starting to grind.

Bryan sucked the last of the smoke from his cigarette, dropped the butt into the dust and set off towards the administration tents. A small knot of anxiety gnawed at the base of his throat and he quickened his steps to cover the last few yards.

Ducking through the tent flaps, Bryan saw the intelligence officer sitting at his trestle table, staring unfocussed into the middle distance, his pallor ashen.

'What's happened?' Bryan asked.

The man swivelled his head to look at Bryan, his Adam's apple bobbed like a frightened animal.

'The American fleet has been sunk,' he said in tones stifled by the weight of the words.

'By the Germans?' Bryan sat down heavily on the chair in front of the table. 'Where?'

'No.' The officer shook his head, his voice still lowered. 'By the Japanese, in Hawaii.'

Bryan whistled through his teeth. 'That's everyone then. It's another world war.'

****

Darkness lay like an inadequate consolation over the island. The night-fighter pilots hunched together in the readiness tent, smoking quietly.

'But what does it mean?' Ben broke the silence. 'Does it make things worse... or better?'

Bryan sat with his elbows on his knees, twiddling his thumbs. 'In the long term?' he said, 'it makes the future a lot brighter. Our American friends will undoubtedly be forced to declare war on Germany and Italy as well as Japan. And I can't imagine a war that America could fail to win once it gets its factories rejigged and its call-up papers printed. So, in five or six years we should see the whole thing come to a shiny, victorious end.'

'What about us?' Ben said. 'What about now?'

Bryan pulled a wan smile. 'Well, it makes it all the more urgent for Rommel to break through in Egypt and secure the oilfields, which adds value to every packing case of supplies that gets lost on the way to Africa, which makes it all the more important that Malta is annihilated as quickly as possible.'

An orderly ducked through the tent flaps. 'Large raid, sixty-plus, crossing the Sicilian coast. Immediate scramble.'

Bryan sprung to his feet, 'Let's go, lads. Let's give them all the hell that we've got left.'

Thursday, 18 December 1941

Bryan and Ben leaned on the railings overlooking Grand Harbour. The scurrying of ratings preparing the vessels for imminent departure animated the warships that lay in view. Barrage balloons drifted over their pachydermal hulks in the teasing breeze, like shimmering puffer fish languishing at the end of their tether lines. A small patrol boat plied past the larger vessels, heading towards the breakwaters, its wake kissing the riveted iron sides of the battleships that dwarfed it.

Bryan's stomach churned with an undercurrent of jealous bile as thoughts of a sailor's farewell to his wife forced their way into his head.

'This must've been a wonderful place before the war,' Ben mused. 'Imagine taking a sailboat out and exploring the coast, dragging some lines behind you to see what you could catch.'

'I suppose that would be one way to get away from the flies and the dust.' Bryan pushed away from the rail and sauntered off along the pavement. Ben squinted across the water for a moment, then followed him.

They walked along the harbour's side, towards its mouth, ascending between the bastions where an anti-aircraft gun sat in its protective circle of sun-bleached sandbags. A soldier sat on the outside, with his back against the bags. He was absorbed with intense concentration over a tin object that gleamed dully as he moved it in his left hand whilst trimming a ribbon of metal from it with wire-cutters he wielded with his right. The two pilots paused to watch him as he placed his creation on the ground, picked an empty bully beef tin from the pile beside him and began carving a shape from its side.

'What are you making?' Bryan asked.

The soldier looked up, taking the interruption as an opportunity to suck the blood away from a cut on his knuckle. 'It's supposed to be a toy truck,' he said, talking around his finger. 'It's coming up to Christmas and the poor little buggers around here have got nothing to look forward to. Our commander suggested we make what we could for them.' He smiled wryly, examining his cut. 'Pity the poor little blighter that gets this one.'

Bryan and Ben walked on. The breeze stiffened as their elevation increased, swirling sandstone grit and flakes of old paint around their ankles.

'It doesn't feel like Christmas, does it?' Ben muttered. 'Peace on earth... goodwill...' He paused and pointed into the water below. 'Look! A seal.'

As they watched, the returning patrol boat diverted its course towards the black shape. As it drew closer, a seaman emerged from the wheelhouse and picked up a boathook from the deck.

'I don't think it's a seal,' Bryan said.

The sailor prodded at the object and, gaining purchase with the hook, hauled it upwards. As it rolled and broke the surface, the two onlookers could make out the stained yellow fabric of an RAF Mae West. The wearer's head sagged back towards the water, his fleshless face upturned towards the sky, his tongue-less mouth agape. The sailor signalled to the wheelhouse and the boat pulled away at a steady pace, the man bracing the boathook against the dead weight that splashed alongside them as they headed across the harbour in search of a slipway.

Saturday, 20 December 1941

Katie's skin pressed warm against Bryan's body. She lay with her shoulder lodged in his armpit and her chin resting against his collar-bone. Her palm lay flat on his belly, lifting and falling with his steady breathing.

'There's been a call for volunteers for a re-posting,' she said. 'Steph and I have put our names forward.'

'A re-posting?' Bryan grunted. 'To where?'

'Who knows?' Katie rolled onto her back and gazed at the ceiling. 'To the farthest reaches of the Empire,' she added with a wistful flourish in her voice.

A heavy silence descended between them.

Katie pulled herself up to sit on the edge of the bed, stretching out a leg to hook her knickers from the floor with her big toe. 'It's around about now a girl might expect some display of emotion from the man she's leaving behind.'

Bryan let his eyes wander across the sculptured skin of Katie's shoulders and slip down the sinuous canal that marked her spine. She stood up and pulled her underwear over the smooth curve of her buttocks.

'To be honest,' Bryan said quietly, 'there's a girl I left behind in England, she's been on my mind a lot – more than I expected.'

Katie bent to pick up her bra and turned on him. 'Don't begin a sentence with "to be honest" and finish it with a lie.' A wry smile spread over her face. 'There's a girl alright, but she's somewhere on this island.' She scooped her breasts into their cups and pulled the straps up over her shoulders. 'You've been with me only because you can't be with her.'

Bryan felt his face redden as he watched her squeeze her feet into her stiletto shoes. 'I'm sorry, Katie,' he muttered. 'I've been a complete heel. I've taken advantage of you.'

Katie pulled her dress off the chairback, dropped it over her head and wriggled it down over her body. Her face emerged from the fabric and she gazed at him with a flat look. 'Taken advantage?' She raised an eyebrow. 'I'll tell you what you've taken.'

She went to her handbag on the dresser and unzipped a small side-pocket. Fishing out a simple band of gold, she turned back towards him and slipped it onto her ring finger.

'You've taken everything I promised not to give away. But do you know what really breaks my heart?'

The colour drained from Bryan's face. 'Please, don't,' he muttered, 'please stop it.'

Katie ignored him. 'I *wanted* you to take it, I *wanted* you to have me. I needed to feel alive amongst all this shit and death, and I used you as the tool to get that feeling.' She slumped into the chair, suddenly spent. 'And together, in that bed, we each betrayed the ones we really love.' She looked up into his eyes, weary resignation relaxing her features. 'What does that make us, Bryan?' She shook her head with short, sorrowful movements. 'What does that make us?'

Bryan sat up in the bed, pulling the sheets up over his waist. He hung his head. 'Christ, Katie. You have a husband…'

'Yes. I have a husband.' She bit her lip for a moment. 'I don't know if I'll ever get back to him, and if I do, I don't know if he'll be there to meet me. If he is, part of me hopes he's been kind to himself, indulged in life without losing me from his heart. In this noxious bloody madness of war and killing, surely sanctity can be stretched a little.' She picked up her handbag and clutched it to her chest. 'It seems lives are cheap.' She stood and shrugged, a sad smile curling her lips. 'So what price fidelity?'

She walked to the door and grasped the handle. She paused with her back to him and her shoulders sagged. 'I might not have had all of you, Bryan. But I had all the bits I needed.'

The door closed behind her and Bryan sank back onto his pillow.

Sunday, 21 December 1941

Bryan rummaged through his kit-bag, felt the soft, knitted weave of the object he sought, and pulled the pilot figure into the light. He brushed lint from the doll's blue tunic and ran his thumb down the yellow stitches that mimicked golden buttons and echoed the shock of blond hair on the figure's knitted head. The remembered chill of a London Christmas sent the ghost of a shiver across his shoulders. He pushed the doll into his tunic pocket and hurried out the door. Today he had the courage to face a Catholic Mass.

****

His resolve wavered as he stepped from the bus onto the harbour-side. Across the blue-grey water, lolling vaguely at their moorings, sat two cruisers. Both leaned awkwardly towards a rent in their bows. Those dark holes, with ragged edges from which sea-water ebbed and flowed, witnessed

115

mine strikes. Tug-boats flustered around one of the ships, beginning her transfer to a repair dock further down the harbour, nudging and pulling her into slow, painful motion.

The sound of a klaxon split the air, and Bryan's gaze shifted to the harbour mouth through which a seemingly undamaged destroyer sidled. The navy was back, this time battered and bloodied, and fewer in number.

Bryan turned his back on the wounded vessels and started up the hill into Valletta.

****

The doors to St Augustine Church stood open. Bryan skirted the rubble scree from a bombed-out building, crossed the road and stepped over the threshold. He slowed his pace, allowing his eyes to make terms with the gloom, then smiled in recognition; Jacobella sat on the back pew, exactly where he'd last seen her. He inclined his head briefly towards the altar and slid onto the worn wooden seat next to her.

For a moment she stayed impassive, eyes closed and head bowed. He traced the line of her profile with his gaze, waiting for her prayer to end. She stirred, suddenly alert to his presence, and looked up. Surprise flashed across her face, but it only lived a fleeting moment on the shadow of her deeper distress. Her red-rimmed eyes were stamped with the passage of tears and she grasped a damp handkerchief to her chin. Still, from behind all this, the warmth of a smile softened her features.

'Hello, Bryan,' she whispered. 'I was worried something might have happened to you.'

Bryan leaned towards her, resisting the pressing urge to embrace her. 'What's wrong?' he asked in a low voice. 'What's happened?'

Jacobella held a finger to her lips. 'Shush.' The ghost of the smile flashed again in sad reassurance and she turned to face the altar.

The doors clunked shut behind them and the service began.

Bryan took his cue from Jacobella, standing when she did, following her back down to the pew when she sat, bowing his head while she and those around them recited responses he did not know, using words he did not understand. Often, he stole a glance at her face, her smooth serenity an easy match for the alabaster Madonna that gazed untroubled from a gold-encrusted niche above them, her fidelity a flawless equal to the martyred saints in the paintings on the walls. All the time, the creeping half-knowledge of her misery's source tugged at his conscience, begging unanswerable questions about his intentions, questions that he pushed aside because even here, even in a house of Catholic righteousness, his desire smouldered like a penance.

****

The service drew to a close, the doors opened behind them and the congregation shuffled past, back out to their besieged and broken city. Bryan sat in respectful silence and waited, glancing occasionally at Jacobella, whose eyes were once again closed.

The church emptied and she straightened her back and opened her eyes. '*HMS Neptune* has been sunk.' Jacobella's voice was low, but steady.

'*Neptune?*' Bryan guessed, but needed to hear.

'Mikiel's ship.'

Bryan looked down at his feet, scared at what his face might reveal. 'What happened?' he asked.

'They sailed straight into a minefield. Several mines exploded and the ship capsized. They tell me it happened very quickly.'

Bryan stayed silent, clenching his muscles against the need to take her in his arms and comfort her, to give some release to the subsumed grief that burned behind her eyes.

'I have said my prayers today.' She looked up at the Madonna, her face momentarily matching the statue's beatific half-smile. 'Our Lady is the Star of the Sea. She will save him, if he can be saved, or comfort him if he is lost.' A tear pushed from the corner of her eye, trickled down her cheek, curved along the line of her jaw before dropping onto the prayer book she clutched in her lap.

'What will you do?' Bryan whispered.

She wiped the tear's wet track from her face. 'I am a wife and a mother.' She regarded Bryan through tear-softened eyes. 'I will go home, look after my daughter, and wait for my husband to come home.'

Bryan stood and offered his hand. 'May I walk with you?'

She nodded, allowed him to help her up, and they left the church side by side.

They walked the dog-leg in silence, slowing down to labour up the final gradient of Mint Street. Instead of turning towards her house, Jacobella gestured ahead; they crossed the road and entered Hastings Gardens.

'I can ask at the airfield,' Bryan ventured, 'see if anyone has any contacts, try to get some news.'

'By all means,' she said.

They reached the bastion's edge and paused, looking out across the harbour to the arched waterside walkway where a group of figures manhandled a small rowing boat into the water. One of their number stepped into the rocking vessel, sitting in its centre, and his companions passed him a pair of oars. He pushed off and heaved at the water, leaning back with the effort of powering the tiny vessel out into the harbour.

'But there is little to know that wasn't seen from the other ships,' she concluded.

Bryan reached into his pocket and retrieved the knitted figure. 'I thought Lućija might like this for a Christmas present.' He held out the doll.

'It's you?' She took it from him.

'I believe that was the intention.'

She tucked the toy into her jacket. 'Thank you. I'm sure I have some coloured paper to wrap it.' A frown rumpled her brow. 'It will be a strange Christmas.'

The incipient buzz of engines filtered into the air and Bryan glanced beyond Jacobella towards the harbour's entrance. Four single-engine aircraft approached from the sea, barely one hundred feet above the water. They bucked over the headland and their leader dipped into a shallow dive. Lurid orange flashes sparkled along the edge of his wings and the calm water of the harbour erupted into a viciously cascading patch of roiling foam that spiralled around and then slashed through the rowing boat.

Jacobella's cry was drowned in the cacophony of engine noise as the assailant's wingman cruised past the bastion, yards from where the couple stood. The yellow-nosed cowling bled into a mottled grey and green fuselage that bore a large black cross. Instinctively Bryan threw protective arms around Jacobella as the German fighter's slipstream washed over them like the breath of a malevolent giant.

'Are you alright?' Bryan's voice raised to combat the receding roar of the German fighters. Jacobella said nothing. Bryan followed her wide-eyed gaze across the water. There, in the middle of the harbour, amongst the splintered remains of painted wood, an object floated like a broken bundle of ripped rags in the centre of an expanding slick of bright red blood.

Bryan grasped her chin and turned her face towards him, connecting his eyes to hers. 'Go to Lućija and get under some shelter,' he said. 'I have to get back to Mdina.'

Jacobella nodded stiffly and ran towards her house as a second flight of four Messerschmitts barrelled in over the breakwater. Bryan watched them fan out and head inland, then sprinted away into the streets of Valletta.

Chapter 13

Monday, 22 December 1941

Bryan trotted through the shredded remains of the admin tents, grimacing at the speckling of blood stains turning black on the khaki cloth.

'Christ,' he muttered. A fitter strode past him. 'Where's the intelligence officer, and where's Copeland?' he called after the man's back.

The fitter spun in his stride and pointed. 'Storage buildings, outside the perimeter track.'

Bryan redoubled his pace, squinting against the roiling dust thrown up from a section of Hurricanes scurrying across the field and climbing skyward. He headed towards two small, block-built huts on the airfield edge, not much bigger than bike-sheds. As he approached up the incline, he saw that camouflage netting had been strung between them and in its shade huddled a group of pilots in flying gear. The intelligence officer sat behind his trestle, its closest legs jacked up with rocks against the uneven ground; a level desk, an enforced normality.

Bryan arrived under the netting and wormed his way through the press of airmen.

'Where's Copeland?' he demanded. 'I want to take my flight up.'

The intelligence officer paused in his scribbling and looked up. 'I have as many pilots as I need at the moment, Mr Hale.' He nodded at the knot of men at Bryan's back. 'It's probably best if you go and rest up somewhere. I'm sure they'll be coming back tonight.'

Bryan turned at the sound of a murmured commotion. His eyes followed a pilot's pointed finger. High above the field, a 109 jinked across the sky, its yellow nose etching a jarring zig-zag across the gentle blue-grey dome. Behind it, a Hurricane wallowed in the opposite rhythm, snapping off bursts of fire as its target swung past its nose. From above, two more yellow motes curved across the scene, two more 109s. The stooping fighters slashed past the Hurricane, raking it with a moment's maelstrom, tipping it into a spinning spiral with gouts of flame tracing its arc towards the ground.

Muscles bunching with the need for action, Bryan pushed his way out from the crowd and loped back towards the perimeter, staying low and keeping his eye on the pair of Messerschmitts that now circled the airbase at a leisurely distance. Skittering down the slope, another engine note intruded, the coughing clatter of a Merlin throttling back in a landing approach. A swell of alarm filled his craw as the Hurricane wobbled towards the runway, its gear locked and its flaps down.

With the immutable sweep of inevitability, the German fighters banked around their circuit, levelling out behind their floundering target like wolves at a calving. With the danger sensed late, the Hurricane's wheels unlocked and lifted, and the engine note rose to a panicked scream. The fighter's nose angled upwards and flew through a diagonal storm of ordnance. Cannon shells barked through the air, knocking shards out of stricken wings and ploughing gouges from the runway below, their impact on the hardened earth sending thudding vibrations into Bryan's heels. The Hurricane sagged in the air like a deflating balloon and dropped fifty feet to the ground, bounced once with a broken back and separated into two pieces that spun to a halt amidst desultory flames.

The Messerschmitts climbed away, lines of tracer fire from the ground waving behind their tails as they clawed back into their circuit. Bryan ran, his feet pounding along the perimeter track, suddenly exposed, soft and weak, his heart lurching as the Germans banked for another run. The enemy planes tipped into their turn, displaying their top-sides like courting birds, flashing the large black crosses atop their wings and the bright yellow plumage of their tails.

Panting hard, Bryan swerved into the first blast-pen he came to, slid under the aircraft's wing and rolled with his momentum until he hit the far wall. Metal slashed through the air above him like the ripping of canvas, overlain with the eggshell crunch of the disintegrating Perspex canopy on the Hurricane, and resolved by the explosive clatter of cannon-shells against the far wall spitting fragments to spatter back against the fuselage. A moment of calm, then the 109 zoomed over the pen with a concussive shock of compressed slipstream and a blinding swirl of choking dust.

'Shit,' Bryan muttered. Spitting grit-mired saliva onto his chin, he dragged himself into a sitting position. Rubbing his trembling thigh muscles, he surveyed the black Hurricane's shattered cockpit and perforated engine cowling. 'Shit.'

Christmas Eve, 1941

Bryan and Ben sat out on the roof balcony at Xara watching the twirling dance of fighters scribing spirals in the sky above a small gaggle of bombers that cascaded bomb loads across the southern docks of Grand Harbour. At this distance the aircraft were nothing but grains against the haze, and the bombs just a frisson of flecks that darkened the space through which they fell. But to one who knew the manner of such things, this diminutive display was a puppet-show of oblivion.

One of the circling dots sparked with light, then flared more brightly, climbing higher at the unseeing behest of its burning pilot before curving into a parabola that decayed into a long, flaming spiral towards the sea.

'We're getting hammered,' Bryan said. 'Sending Hurricanes up against 109s, it's tantamount to murder. I'm surprised we can't hear them laughing from here.'

Ben looked at his watch. 'What time do we need to get to readiness?'

'We don't,' Bryan said. 'Every single one of our planes has picked up at least a dozen holes from strafing or shrapnel. I've declared them all unsafe to fly.'

'Can you get away with that?' Ben asked.

'We'll see.' Bryan scratched at his chin. 'They won't come over tonight, anyway. Say what you will about the Germans, they do like a Christmas truce.'

Smoke rose in slow coils from the docks, the bombers vanished north, their escorts dived away from their combats to follow them and Bryan squinted into the failing light to count the returnees to Ta'Qali. Three small shapes, descending as they flew inland, approached the airfield and dropped towards the landing strip. Bryan shook his head at the futility.

'I was talking with the caretaker,' Ben said. 'He's a local chap. Seems quite nice.'

'Uh-huh.' Bryan gazed at the returning fighters until they fell below the horizon and merged with the mottled landscape.

'He listens to Italian radio,' Ben continued. 'He says they were talking about that cruiser that was sunk.'

Bryan's head swivelled to face him. '*The Neptune*?'

'Yes, I think that was the one.'

'What about it?' Bryan's voice held an edge of tension.

'It seems an Italian patrol boat came across a drifting raft with thirty blokes inside,' Ben said. 'Apparently they'd all died, except one.'

Bryan turned his gaze back towards Valletta. Far out to sea, a bank of dark clouds piled over themselves, conquered the horizon, then rallied to advance on the island.

Christmas Day, 1941

Bryan awoke with a start, at once alert and wary of a strange throbbing noise in his room. It took a moment to identify it as the low thrum of heavy rain on the flat roof. Pulling himself out of bed, he dressed quickly, scratched the fur from his teeth and tongue with a threadbare toothbrush, spat the foul yellow goo into the basin and swilled his mouth with dust-filmed water from the glass at his bedside. He grabbed a blanket from the bed and draped it over his shoulders against the uncommon chill in the air.

Outside his room, the sound of carolling drifted up the stairs from the dining room, off-key and masculine. He smiled; it was Christmas Day. It had slipped his mind. He pulled the blanket closer around his neck and moved along the corridor, away from the singing, towards the roof terrace.

He paused at the door and squinted through the glass. The wooden roof shingles weren't fully watertight and leaks dripped water in many places, pooling into puddles on the floor. But the promise of the rain's freshness drew him out. Stepping onto the balcony, he sucked in the sweet, cool air like it was ripe fruit. The landscape beyond the railings leapt out in sharper contrast; the wet sandstone glowed like mustard, the dusty, tired soil took on a fecund, hazel hue and the paddle-cacti accented the scene with vibrant, dripping greens, like clusters of emeralds strewn across the land by a profligate giant.

Bryan dodged the streaming leaks and leaned over the bar, reaching under it in search of something to drink. His fingers found a bottle – whisky, nearly half-full. He pulled the cork with his teeth and took a swig. Grimacing against the burning in his empty stomach, he weaved through the cascades to find a dry spot by the railings. In the distance, where the land met the sea, lay Valletta, a battered city full of faithful citizens who, even now, knelt in supplication, giving thanks for what they had, no matter how much they had already sacrificed. He took another deep draft of the fiery liquor. Somewhere in that charnel house was a small girl, sitting in her mother's arms, clutching a knitted toy, who couldn't yet know just how much she had been required to lose.

Sunday, 28 December 1941

Bryan leaned against a tree at the edge of Hastings Gardens. The position gave him a view down Mint Street and Jacobella's route home from church. He rubbed his cheeks with both hands in an attempt to scrub away his tiredness. He checked the sky above and behind, as if he was in a cockpit, the menace of the marauding 109s pricking away at his peace of mind. Nothing moved in the grey dome that sat over the island except the wispy remnants of rain clouds hurrying to catch up with the retreating rainstorms. The familiar flow of released congregations lapped into the street and Bryan felt his stomach muscles tense as he searched for the familiar figure.

Jacobella appeared amongst the crowd, her head inclined downwards, her progress up the steep incline slow. As the people around her filtered away into doorways and up side streets, he saw that Lučija walked next to her mother, hand in hand.

Eventually the pair reached the top of the hill and crossed the road to where Bryan waited. Lučija beamed a smile and held up the knitted airman for him to inspect.

Bryan mirrored her smile. 'He's a handsome chap,' he said. 'Is he a pilot?'

Lučija descended into sudden shyness, cuddling the doll close to her chest.

Bryan switched his gaze to Jacobella. 'How are you?' It was the fewest words he could use to pose the largest of questions.

She looked over his shoulder, scanning the horizon. 'Come inside for a while,' she said, 'it's safer indoors for the little one.'

The trio walked the short distance along the side of the gardens and entered the house. Jacobella lifted her daughter onto the couch, kissed her forehead, and walked through to the kitchen. Bryan followed her and stood in awkward silence. She lit the stove and lifted a saucepan onto the flame.

'Sit down.' She spoke without turning. 'Will you eat with us? My cousin had to kill a goat when it broke a leg. He gave us some of the meat for our Christmas table. I've made some stew with the last of it.'

'Yes, thank you.' Bryan looked for a moment at the back of her head. Her dark hair, dulled through lack of washing, hung limp in a simple ponytail. He sat down at the table. 'How are you? He repeated the question.

'I was told what they said on the radio.' She lifted the saucepan's lid and stirred the contents slowly. 'There were more than seven hundred men on that ship, and now there's only one left alive.' She replaced the lid and put the spoon down on the draining board, finally turning to face him, her eyes glistening with moisture. 'That's too many wives and mothers all clinging onto the same, single hope,' she said quietly. 'Today, with Lučija in my arms, I committed Mikiel to Our Lady with a silent prayer. He's at peace now.'

Bryan shifted uneasily on his chair. 'I don't know what to do.'

Jacobella smiled and wiped a tear from her cheek. 'You're doing it.' She retrieved three plates from a cupboard and sat down opposite him. 'My family is the world to me. But it's important to have a friend who knows about the world. You make a difference, Bryan. That's all you need to do.'

Bryan felt his cheeks redden. 'How is Lučija?'

Jacobella glanced through the door to ensure her daughter was occupied. 'She is used to her father not being around. She knows something is wrong, but she can't tease it out from all the other things that are wrong in this poor old city.' Her face brightened slightly. 'She certainly loves that doll.'

The saucepan lid rattled in resonance with the bubbling stew and Jacobella rose to stir it. Breathing in the heady aroma of cooking meat, he moved his fingers on the wooden table, worn smooth by the hands of strangers, and gazed at the stone walls, darkened by the passage of other bodies.

'It's ready,' Jacobella said, 'let's eat.'

New Year's Eve, 1941

Bryan looked at the three figures hunched in the darkness under the camouflage netting. Huddled in flying jackets against the night's chill, they smoked cigarettes in cupped hands. The breeze mounted upon itself, then dropped to rise again, its antics presaging more rain. The men's murmuring voices laid a mellifluous undertone to the intermittent flap and crack of the netting above their heads.

Bryan glanced at his watch; five minutes to midnight. He drew in a breath to announce the approach of the new year, but paused as a low rumbling intruded into the night. Thunder? No, it swelled rather than faded.

'Listen,' he hissed, silencing the hushed conversation.

The growling grew in volume, evolving into the beating clamour of unsynchronised engines. Bryan leapt to his feet and stepped out from under the netting. The light from the near-full moon dusted the airfield like icing sugar, and through its weak gleam a twin-engine raider bore down, fast and

125

low, bomb doors open. It streaked the length of the runway and objects tumbled from its belly. Two bounced and skittered along the ground, the others burst with bright orange violence, stitching a procession of explosions in the wake of the speeding aircraft.

Bryan dropped to a crouch as blast waves plucked at his clothes, shielding his eyes with an arm. 'Junkers 88,' he called over his shoulder. 'The bastard came in too low for RDF.'

The engine note dropped a tone as the raider banked away. Bryan pulled himself upright and the three pilots joined him outside the shelter.

'Should we get after him?' one suggested.

Bryan shook his head. 'The runway's full of new holes and there are unexploded bombs out there somewhere.' The engine noise swelled again. 'And he's coming back.'

Bryan herded the men under cover as the German bomber made another pass, raking the Hurricanes in the perimeter blast-pens with machine-gun fire from its nose and ventral guns.

'Damn it!' Bryan raged with frustration. 'Where's the bloody AA?'

The bomber banked around again, the engine noise rising to a bellow as it made another firing pass. Shouts drifted on the breeze from the blast-pens, small arms popped and crackled in futile defiance.

Bryan stood rigid, breathing heavily through his nose. The bomber came around for another pass and he growled through gritted teeth. The rattle of the German guns tore once more through the night, suddenly joined by the thump-thump of a Bofors gun on the other side of the field. Tracers whirled into the air, sweeping wide of the raider's wing and spiralling in its wake as the pilot jammed his throttles wide open to run for home.

The thumping stopped and the engines receded to a gentle buzz. Shouts and cries of pain echoed from the perimeter and flames flickered from a burning fighter.

'Happy new year, gentlemen,' Bryan muttered. 'Welcome to 1942.'

The netting above his head flapped violently with a stiffening breeze and large drops of rain splashed onto the ground, dotting the earth with dark circles.

New Year's Day, 1942

The windows and doors of the palace rattled quietly in rhythm with the gusting winds that lashed the rain onto the bastion walls of Mdina. Bryan stood at a window in the dining room, watching the gale push slicks of water around the panes. Behind him, Copeland sat hunched over a tin mug.

'I've had enough of sitting around waiting for the Luftwaffe to call the shots,' Bryan said. 'It costs money and lives to get those bloody fighters over here and then we leave them standing around so the Germans can send over a single aircraft to stitch them all up.'

'It's not as if we can hide where we are,' Copeland said, stirring his tepid tea.

Bryan turned to face the other man. 'I agree. So we need to be in the air. We need to run standing patrols.'

Copeland shook his head. 'You know why we can't do that. We need to preserve our fuel stocks. If we're prudent we might have enough to last us until June, maybe July.'

Bryan sat down on the other side of the table. 'There's no point in conserving fuel so we can trickle Hurricanes into the sky to get shot to pieces.' He lowered his voice. 'How many pilots did you lose in day-fighting in the week before Christmas?'

Copeland regarded him across the table with a level gaze. 'Over half our strength.'

'And how do the rest of them feel about that, sitting in obsolete fighters fitted with half the number of pea-shooters they should carry, waiting for state-of-the-art Messerschmitts to come over and shoot whacking great cannon-shells up their arses?'

Copeland stayed silent.

'We need Spitfires,' Bryan said. 'It's as simple as that.' He stood up and paced back to the window. 'And while we're waiting for them, we should use the fuel we have to meet the enemy in the air, on our terms.'

Copeland pushed his chair away from the table and stood up. 'Let me see if I can talk to someone,' he said. 'I can't promise anything, Hale, but I will try.'

Sunday, 4 January 1942

Bryan stood beneath the tree at the top of Mint Street, waiting. The rain had eased off to a fine mist that swirled in the fitful breeze like the gossamer smoke from empyrean fires. He saw Jacobella and Lučija trudging up the hill and went to meet them.

'Hello,' he called out as he approached.

Mother and child looked up, both smiled.

'I hope it's alright.' Bryan said. 'I don't want to become a nuisance.'

'No. It's lovely to see you.' Jacobella's smile was weary but genuine.

'Bine,' Lučija said to herself.

'I'm afraid I have no goat,' Jacobella said. 'In fact, I don't really have anything.'

'That's alright.' Bryan patted his satchel. 'I've brought some bully beef.'

They hurried through the damp air and into the house, wiping the sheen of rain from cheeks and eyelids. Bryan placed the tin of beef on the kitchen table. Jacobella whisked it onto the draining board and bore down on the lid with a can opener. The thick aroma of preserved meat drifted across the room as Jacobella spooned the contents into a pan, chopping it up with the spoon.

Abruptly she stopped working and swallowed hard. She dropped the spoon and ducked her head into the sink, retching loudly. Strings of saliva hung from her lips as she convulsed in pain, vomiting nothing from an empty stomach.

Bryan moved to her side. 'Are you alright? What's wrong?'

Jacobella coughed and spat. 'Mother of God!' she hissed through clenched teeth as another spasm gripped her and lurched her body forward.

Lučija ran into the kitchen and hugged onto her mother's leg, her face darkened with concern.

'What can I do?' Bryan lifted Jacobella's hair away from the bile pooling in the sink.

'Nothing!' Jacobella's voice was a ragged rasp. She coughed and spat again. 'There's nothing you can do.' Her voice softened. 'It's morning sickness. I'm pregnant.'

Bryan's hand still held her hair, his knuckles resting against her smooth, cool skin. The unfamiliar proximity and the intimacy it suggested filled him with a lumpen awkwardness and the words he searched for died in his throat.

Chapter 14

Thursday, 22 January 1942

Copeland walked towards the blast-pens, Bryan moved at his side, a flying helmet hanging from his hand. The rainstorms had abated over the last two days and most of the puddles of standing water had drained away. The two men skirted patches of glistening mud as they made their way around the perimeter.

'You'll have to trust me, Hale,' Copeland said, 'there are things happening that I can't talk about.' They arrived at a pen containing one of the black Hurricanes. 'We have to take this thing one step at a time.' He put a hand on Bryan's shoulder. 'This is the first step.'

Bryan eyed the aircraft with suspicion. 'What the hell are those?'

Underneath the wings, outboard from the undercarriage, two cylinders hung from brackets.

'Extra fuel tanks.' Copeland smiled. 'These give you the range to mount a proper intruder mission into Sicily and meet the bombers on their home territory.'

Bryan's eyes narrowed. 'Do they work?'

Copeland shrugged. 'Let me know when you've finished your test flight. Make sure you switch back and forth a few times. Put them through their paces properly.'

Copeland walked away and groundcrew bustled around the fighter, preparing it for flight. Bryan pulled his flying helmet over his scalp and climbed onto the wing.

****

Bryan took off from Ta'Qali, feeling the sag of extra weight in the fuel tanks on his wings, and pulled into a shallow climb to the south.

'Pipistrelle One to Control. Airborne on flight test. Listening out.'

A brief acknowledgement rattled back, ending in background static that hissed in his ears as he overflew the rocky coastline and banked out over the sea.

Checking he had sufficient altitude for a bail-out, Bryan flicked the fuel taps over. The engine coughed, missed a beat and roared back to life.

Bryan smiled to himself. 'Well, well. It looks like we're off to Sicily.'

Sunday, 25 January 1942

'It really is time you moved somewhere safer,' Bryan said. 'The weather will start getting better and they'll come back again and again.'

Jacobella sat on her couch, Lučija perched on her lap, snoozing against her breast. She stayed silent.

'There's every likelihood they'll flatten Valletta completely before they're done,' he pleaded. 'Listen to me, I'm speaking as your friend.'

She looked up. 'It's my home,' she said quietly. 'It's as far from the docks as a building can be, and' – she gestured at the wall with her free hand – 'it's made of rock.'

'Your husband would agree with me.'

Jacobella's eyes widened slightly. 'My husband isn't here.'

Bryan flushed red at his clumsiness and stepped out onto the balcony to escape his discomfort. Aircraft noise snapped his attention to the sky. Passing over the buildings of Sliema a gaggle of Hurricanes laboured in a battle-climb out to sea, off to give air cover to a ship movement. He watched their progress until another scratchy motion in the blue-grey heavens drew his eye. Far above, a dozen dark silhouettes curved down towards the British formation, embroidering an angry edge to the buzzing engine noise, then overlaying its drone with the hammering of cannon fire. The Messerschmitts flashed through the formation, leaving flares of flame in their wake. Three Hurricanes sagged from the formation, trailing black and white streamers of smoke and fumes. Below them, the Germans flattened out and, riding their blistering speed, streaked inland to seek out targets on the ground. Over the sea that swallowed their aircraft, two pilots drifted down under creamy-white parachute canopies.

Bryan ducked back into the room. 'I'm sorry,' he said, hoping it would be enough. 'I have to go.'

Jacobella looked up, nodded faintly and returned her gaze to her sleeping child.

****

The quarter-moon hung behind emaciated clouds and their frayed drapery diffused and softened its thin light. Bryan's awareness grew as his vision adjusted. The black expanse below him became a subtle undulation of watery darkness, the impenetrable blank dome over his head revealed the slow scudding of tattered cirrus, and the horizon solidified into the caliginous bar of the Sicilian coast.

He lofted the nose of his Hurricane slightly to better define the shoreline's profile as he made landfall. Glancing at the map taped to his thigh, he made his best guess at his location, marked it with a pencil, noted the time and set a due-north bearing. Mindful of detection, he sank his craft closer to the ghostly trees and fields that rolled away below him, swathed in the ethereal cobwebs of the incorporeal lunar light.

Bryan looked around, resting his eyes from the dim instrument lights, allowing them to relax once more. A sense of preternatural calm descended on him; the extra fuel he carried made time his ally. He eased the throttle back, damping the growl of the engine closer to a purr, a sound that better suited the maverick danger he carried into the enemy sky. A near-blind tiger on the prowl, yet still possessed of tiger's claws.

Bryan checked his watch and ran a quick mental calculation; he was at least forty miles inland on the large island's rump, which put him over open ground in the middle of a cluster of five enemy airfields marked on his map by red dots. He tweaked the throttle forward and dropped into a shallow bank to starboard that led him into a wide, slow orbit. He let his helmeted head sag back onto the cushioned rest and held his unfocussed gaze out over his lowered wing, fishing for minnows of light in a sea of ebony anonymity.

On his third circuit, a stubby, silvery speck appeared on the ground away to the south. Keeping his eyes locked on this fragile scintillation, he banked out of his orbit to curve back down-country and investigate.

As the miles rolled away, the transient gleam acquired the rigidity of a hooded searchlight beam raked along what was almost certainly a runway. Keeping a cautious distance, Bryan dropped into a wide circle around the anomaly, seeking some confirmation for his suspicion.

A shape moved across the beam at one end and was reabsorbed by the darkness. Bryan circled, intent, his expectation rising. Moments later, from the other end of the bar of illumination, rising steadily into the void, two navigation lights scribed ascending lines through the night before blinking out.

Bryan looped back to the other end of the enemy airfield, counting away the seconds under his breath. '...twenty-eight, twenty-nine, thirty...'

Another pair of lights climbed away from the beam and extinguished.

Bryan thumbed his safety catch to fire and restarted the count. 'One, two, three...' He dropped into a figure-of-eight pattern to eat away the seconds.

131

'…twelve, thirteen, fourteen…' Banking around he lined up with the beam and began his approach. '…twenty-three, twenty-four, twenty-five…' The searchlight station passed under his nose, its finger of light bisecting the darkness ahead. '…twenty-nine, thirty.'

A black shape lifted into the air at the end of the light-path, bracketed by navigation lights that nestled neatly into the edges of Bryan's windshield. He jabbed his thumb onto the firing button and his aircraft rattled with recoil, tracers flashing and bouncing in the night.

A blinding yellow flash, an instinctive pull on the stick, engine screaming, the concussion of an exploding bomb-load somewhere too close behind, a flirtation with a stall, adjust, recover, buoyancy, flight, speed and escape.

Bryan glanced into his mirror with dazzled pupils. The landscape around the airfield erupted with anti-aircraft guns pumping anger and vengeance into the space he no longer occupied.

Friday, 30 January 1942

Knuckles rapped on the wood, paused, then repeated their urgent summons. Bryan lifted his head from his pillow and glared across the room at the door. Champing against the dryness in his mouth, he fumbled on the bedside table for his watch and squinted at its face. 'Christ,' he muttered to himself and swung off the mattress. 'This had better be a bloody emergency,' he called as he strode across the room. Opening the door, he stood staring blankly at Squadron Leader Copeland. 'What?' he asked quietly.

'There's a meeting in half-an-hour,' Copeland said. 'I've requisitioned the mess.'

Bryan blinked. 'It's a dining room.'

'Whatever it's called, there's a meeting there in thirty minutes, all flight leaders are required to attend. Embry is on his way.'

'Who is Embry, and is he not aware that I work nights?'

'It's Group Captain Embry' – annoyance stretched Copeland's tone – 'and I'm fairly certain he doesn't give a toss about your nocturnal habits. Wake up, Hale, and see to it that you're not late.'

Copeland strode off down the corridor and Bryan swung the door closed. 'Shiny-arsed bastards,' he breathed and tottered towards his dressing table.

****

Twenty-five minutes later, Bryan sauntered into the dining room. Chairs, arranged in rows, were filled with pilots, many from the other aerodromes, some that he did not recognise. He found an empty seat in the back row and sat down.

Moments later Copeland entered with the group captain and everyone rose to attention. Waving them to be seated, Copeland introduced the other officer and stepped back to allow him to speak.

'Good morning, gentlemen,' Embry began, 'I've been sent from London to take a look at the way things work out here.'

As the man spoke, Bryan examined his face, vaguely handsome with brown eyes shining from under dark eyebrows and a downturned mouth unaccustomed to mirth.

'I've visited control HQ in Valletta and inspected all the airfields,' the group captain continued. 'It's obvious you've been tasked with a difficult job under less than ideal circumstances.'

A polite murmur of agreement rippled around the room.

'I understand that scarcity of fuel is a major limiting factor. However, the complaint I've heard time and again from pilots is the state of the aircraft you have been issued.' A faint smile displaced his lips. 'The Hurricane is a fine aeroplane and I've enjoyed flying it myself in the past. But I think its time in the sun is coming to an end.

'Uniquely, in your predicament, it comes down to simple mathematics. It takes fifteen minutes for the enemy to fly from Sicily to Malta. In that time, a Hurricane can climb to fifteen thousand feet – barely enough to reach the bombers, and always well below their escort. It's intolerable that you should be expected to operate at this constant disadvantage.' He paused and looked around the upturned faces. 'Especially as the Spitfire Mark V can climb to twenty-five thousand feet in the same time span. Consequently, I will be recommending that Spitfires be assigned to Malta as soon as operationally possible.'

Sunday, 1 February 1942

Bryan dropped from the back of the transport and trudged down the slope towards Ta'Qali's perimeter track. The metallic ring of shovels and the murmur of labouring voices drifted through the deepening gloom from parties of soldiers filling in the afternoon's bomb craters. An engine choked into life and dropped into a rough, rhythmic chug as the aerodrome's last surviving roller crept out from its camouflaged blast-pen and trundled out to flatten the scars on the landing strip.

Ben jogged up to Bryan's shoulder and matched his stride. 'Where do you slip off to every Sunday afternoon? Are you still getting your washing done somewhere?'

Bryan threw his companion a sideways glance. In the dying light the young man's bones pressed against his gaunt skin, throwing unnatural shadows across his face. His eyes were submerged in pools of shade, as if his skull sought to escape its fleshly sheath.

'Her name's Jacobella. She lives in Valletta.'

Ben barked a laugh. 'Has she replaced Katie, now?'

'No,' Bryan's tone was measured, 'Katie was' – he cast around for the right phrase – 'a dancing partner. Jacobella is a friend.'

'Until she isn't.' Ben smirked. 'Anyway, how do you manage to get away from the aerodrome every Sunday?'

They arrived at the readiness station and ducked under the netting.

'I told them I'd converted to Catholicism,' Bryan answered.

'Isn't that dangerous?' Ben asked.

'What? Becoming a Catholic, or lying about it?'

'Both.'

'No.' Bryan slapped a folded map into the other man's chest. 'Flying a clapped-out Hurricane across the sea to look for German airfields… that's dangerous.'

Saturday, 14 February 1942

The truck crept slowly through Mdina Gate then the engine roared as it lurched down the narrow road towards the aerodrome, the driver anxious to fulfil his responsibilities in the narrowing gap between air raids and strafing fighters.

Bryan sat in the passenger seat, bracing bony knees against the door and the dash, wincing with every jolt and rattle. Smoke from a recent raid laid a pall over the airfield, mirrored in the distant background by thicker sooty columns curling away from Valletta. Anxiety pricked for a moment in his heart, then it was subsumed under the blanket of weariness that shrouded his shoulders.

The truck lumbered through the airfield gates and Bryan clambered out. He scanned the sky with wary caution as he hurried along the perimeter to get maintenance reports from his ground crews. He slowed his pace as he came to the first pen. Two airmen busied themselves covering the black fuselage with sand-coloured paint, slapping it on with busy, careless strokes.

Bryan diverted up the slope, heading towards the stone buildings that bracketed the makeshift administration centre of the aerodrome. As he approached, Copeland turned to greet him.

'Good afternoon,' he said, smiling.

'Why are you taking my fighters?' Bryan arrived under the netting, breathless from hurrying up the slope. 'I can barely put up a brace every night as it is.'

'I'm not taking your fighters, Hale.' Copeland placed a reassuring hand on his shoulder. 'I'm disbanding Pipistrelle Squadron altogether.'

'What?' Bryan cocked his head in disbelief.

'Your chaps are reverting to daytime ops.' Copeland handed him the folded order. 'You really ought to be heading back to England, given how long you've been plugging away here. But I want you in my flight. If we ever get some Spitfires, I want you to be around to use one.' Copeland eyed him dispassionately. 'As long as you agree to stay?'

'Yes, sir,' Bryan stuttered. 'Thank you.'

'I'll need you available from dawn on Monday.' Copeland treated him to a mischievous wink. 'So tomorrow might be your last chance to go to church for a while.'

Sunday, 15 February 1942

The little girl slipped away from Jacobella's hand and skipped up the stepped pavement towards Hastings Gardens.

'Lučija!' her mother called. 'Come back. You must stay close to me.'

'I'll catch her.' Bryan loped up the steps in pursuit.

Lučija peeped around a tree, saw Bryan coming for her and squealed in mock terror, running deeper into the gardens and ducking behind a bush.

Bryan stopped by the tree, hands on hips, searching for some sign of the child.

Jacobella arrived by his side breathing heavily. 'Lučija! Come to me, darling, we can't play now.'

The lilt of childish laughter drifted back through the gardens. Lučija was heading back towards the house, dodging ahead of her guardians and revelling in her cleverness. 'Ommi,' she called and laughed skipping ahead once more.

'Such a naughty child,' Jacobella muttered.

'It can't do any harm,' Bryan chided, 'it's just a bit of fun.'

The path forked around a raised bed and Bryan took the parallel track to Jacobella, spreading out to corral the playful child towards her front door.

A low noise nibbled at the still air and Bryan felt the hackles rise on his neck. He scanned the sky, hunting for a physical presence to which he could pin the sound. Approaching from the north, buzzing low over Sliema, the glint of canopies, like dragonfly cyclopes, riding the crest of their own swelling roar.

'Run!' he shouted. 'They're bombing the submarines!' Sprinting down the path he combed the bushes and trees with darting glances. 'Where is she?'

Jacobella called out in Maltese, fighting to restrain the panic rising in her voice. The two of them ran together out from the gardens. Bryan veered to one side of the empty limestone plinth and twisted his head in time to register Lučija standing with her shoulders against the backside of the massive, pale block, her face shedding the pleasure at her game of hide-and-seek and crumpling into the first realisations of fear. On the other side of the plinth, Jacobella also turned, skittering to a halt, her mouth opened in shocked relief. A shadow flashed across her face as the German bomber roared over, barely one hundred feet above them.

The air around Bryan's head rippled into corrugations of force that hooked into his shoulder, lifted him from the ground and spun him away like a gyroscope. Objects coursed by his head, tearing the fabric of the air like a rotted cotton sheet, and the clang and chime of impacting shrapnel rang from the front of the stone pedestal. Slammed into the ground under the rolling wave of blast, Bryan lay limp, dazed with shock at the sudden violence. He lifted his head, blinking against the grit in his eyes and the throb of concussion in his temples. Lučija stood transfixed against the stone, quaking with fear, but safe from the blast. On the other side, Jacobella lay prone, her hips jerking in an unnatural rhythm.

Bryan dragged himself to his feet, testing his bones as he hauled his weight upright. He stepped across the scene on unsteady legs, holding up his hand to Lučija. 'Stay there.' His voice sounded distant against the buzzing chimes that dogged his hearing. He dropped to his knees next to

Jacobella and gently turned her now still body. Blood pooled on the ground.

'You've been hit,' he spoke directly into Jacobella's dust-grimed face. 'Where have you been hit?'

She opened her eyes, spilling tears onto her cheeks. 'No.' She sobbed, choking on her misery. 'I haven't been hit.'

Bryan lifted her gently to her feet and brushed the tears from her cheeks. 'I don't understand.'

Her eyes burned into his, boiling with her pain. 'I haven't been hit,' she repeated.

Bryan looked down in confusion. In the blood that glistened on the hard ground, something moved, something small and pale flexed in the congealing puddle of red.

'Jesus Christ,' he breathed, pulling Jacobella's face into his chest. 'Oh, God.'

Her voice keened a sorrowful accompaniment to the agony that fractured her heart, broken by the wracking sobs that squeezed from her chest.

Bryan moved her away towards her door, beckoning Lučija to follow them. Behind the plinth, black smoke rolled out from the gardens, gathering in the air over the road like a shroud, and the booming drumbeat of anti-aircraft batteries entrenched around Sliema rolled across the water.

Bryan felt Jacobella taking more of her weight on strengthening legs as they pushed through the door and up the stairs. Bryan helped her onto a chair in the kitchen and crouched down in front of her, searching her eyes that brimmed with tears.

Jacobella avoided his gaze and blinked the tears onto her cheeks. She looked down and grabbed the folds of her skirt, pulling the cloth over the blood stains that marked the garment's front. Only then did she look into Bryan's eyes and nod gently over his shoulder.

Bryan swivelled his head to see Lučija standing behind him, her complexion whitened with dust through which her own tears streaked their path. Her body shivered; this slight movement amplified by quakes that cycled across her shoulders every few seconds.

Jacobella patted her lap. 'Bring her to me.' Her voice was quiet in the room's stillness.

Bryan stood, took a single stride and gathered the child into his arms. He stood for a moment clutching the warm bundle, struggling to separate a sudden rush of love from his sorrow. He passed the girl gently to her mother. The contact unlocked a wellspring in Lućija and she buried her head into Jacobella's breast. The quaking of her shoulders amplified into wracking sobs of fear and bewilderment.

Bryan stood back, aware of the moisture on his own cheeks. He yearned to embrace the fragile, damaged people clinging together on the chair in front of him. Yet he stood still, watching them through the hard-paned window of his alien presence in their lives. He turned, wiped away his tears and slipped out onto the balcony.

Across the harbour, fires belched out coils of smoke from Manoel Island and the ancient fortress that bestrode it. Some strikes bled backwards onto the southern shore of Sliema, several buildings there had crumpled into rubble. In Hastings Gardens, thirty yards north of the monument plinth, trees angled away from the fetid, steaming crater of a single bomb strike. It was so far away from its intended target that it had to be a hang-up; a fault in the mechanical system that clung onto that one bomb, finally allowing it to slide away from its couplings long moments after the release lever was pulled and the rest of the load plummeted down onto the other side of Marsamxett Harbour. Had it fallen away just one second earlier it would've struck the bastion, exploding without harm, wreaking only meaningless damage on the impassive face of the immutable curved stones.

Yet the crater was in the gardens. It hissed its fumes into the air and the baby was gone.

****

Bryan sat and watched Lućija play. The knitted pilot in her left hand spoke with the full-body movements unique to dolls. A dirt-grimed wooden figure in her right hand, an artist's figurine bereft of its stand and missing a foot, listened to the cloth man's words, the whole discourse silent outside of the child's imagination, kept secret there from the confusions of the world. From the next room the soft splashes of water drifted in as Jacobella washed away the blood using cold water and rags.

A low rumble of explosions penetrated the air, an attack on Grand Harbour on the other side of the city. Lućija paused in her private pantomime and looked around, the seeds of panic lighting her eyes. Jacobella's disembodied voice rose softly into a song, a Maltese lullaby lilting gentle defiance against the bombs. Lućija tilted her head to listen, her eyes softening as she was drawn to join in with her mother's music as the first raindrops tapped against the window.

****

The hammering rain eased, relenting as abruptly as it had commenced. The storm front's dark belt rolled north with blind malevolence towards Sicily, chasing the long-departed bombers across the sea. Bryan slipped from the blue doorway and paused, shivering in the newly-cooled air. Rivulets of rainwater ran past his feet to gurgle away down the slope of Windmill Street. He glanced across the road, but the patch of blood by the plinth was gone, deliquesced by the dispassionate deluge.

He hurried away, skirting the edge of the gardens and dropping back into the city. The evening closed in; the hour, the raids and the rain made finding any transport unlikely. His footsteps went unheard on the deserted streets. He passed bars closed for lack of liquor and shops boarded up through lack of stock. Bombed out buildings punctuated the streets with incongruous gaps in their vertiginous facades. He walked past one bombsite, its debris still impinging on the pavement. A buried miasma of putrescence, revived by the moisture permeating the rubble, reached up to invade his nostrils with its sickly breath. He hurried by under the suspicious gaze of an emaciated cat that perched atop the stones, its fur still spiky from the drenching rain, its green eyes sullen and flat, void of any expectation of pity.

He trudged on, alone with his hollowed heart, heading out from the broken city on the long walk back to Mdina.

Chapter 15

Saturday, 7 March 1942

The sun climbed into the eastern sky, wavering in the haze that laid a silver filter over the Mediterranean azure. A knot of pilots stood on the perimeter track; a pall of cigarette smoke reflected the tension in their hushed conversations. To one side of the nervous group, Bryan stood with the squadron leader.

'Any idea when?' he asked.

Copeland shook his head. 'Strict radio silence. They'll get here when they do.'

Bryan lit a cigarette and scanned the horizon, hoping the 109s would stay at home this morning.

Army fatigue parties, reinforced by Maltese workmen, laboured to repair blast-pens and build new ones. The grind of stone on stone and the clink of hammers drifted across the field accompanied by the dust kicked up by their labours.

The intelligence officer sauntered across and murmured something into Copeland's ear. The squadron leader nodded and turned to Bryan. 'RDF have picked up a trace. They're coming,' he muttered.

The minutes crawled by, then the ragged teeth of engines gnawed away at the edge of the silence. The noise swelled and its bringers appeared in the sky. They circled the airfield and dropped into land in five flights of three aircraft, their long sleek noses raised in haughty indignation as they fishtailed away from the landing strip and onto the perimeter amongst gales of prop-washed dust.

Bryan and the squadron leader walked to the blast-pens as the first of the new arrivals shut off its engine and the propeller windmilled to a halt. Copeland greeted the pilot as he clambered down from the port wing and the two men drifted away, talking. Bryan stood alone and gazed at the aircraft in front of him.

He stepped forward and placed his hand on the wingtip, his eyes tracing its curving ellipse like the hungry gaze of a lover follows the swell of a thigh. He walked around to the leading edge where two red patches covered the machine-gun ports and, inboard of them, the strident shape of a 20mm cannon jutted with phallic aggression from a wing that bulged to contain it.

He ducked between the propeller blades and traced the line of the tropical dust filter set beneath the still-ticking engine cowling. It looked like a bemused mouth set below the fighter's nose, giving the aircraft the demeanour of a cat that has smelled something unpleasant.

Ground crew gathered around the aircraft and Bryan regarded the men, smiling.

'Spitfires,' he said, his voice bright with triumph. 'Now they'll be sorry.'

Sunday, 8 March 1942

Bryan watched Jacobella open the confessional door and step inside. A twinge of empathy ached across his chest, but loss also lodged in his heart. If a man can lose what he has never possessed, then surely, he had lost Jacobella. She would never have eyes that could recognise the fire she had lit, much less come to embrace it for the warmth that it offered. First, tied by the fidelity of marriage. Then, dismantled by grief at her husband's death. Now, distraught with guilt for losing the life her man had left behind inside her.

Lučija jabbed his ribs with her elbow as she shifted her position on the pew next to him. He looked down into a face contorted with the agonies of boredom and smiled at her enforced discomfort.

'Ommi,' she whined.

'Shush.' Bryan put his finger to his lips. 'Mummy's saying sorry to God,' he whispered into her uncomprehending visage. 'Although I think it's God who should be saying sorry to her.'

****

The trio trudged up Mint Street and took the right turn along the edge of the gardens. Bryan stopped, unwilling to revisit the scene of the trauma.

'I can't stay,' he said. 'I should be helping the ground crews get the new planes ready.' He tried a smile, but he knew it failed to convey anything he was feeling. He let the smile fall away. 'I just wanted to see you.' It sounded just as lame as it always had, but it was the whole, indivisible truth.

Jacobella reached out and squeezed his arm. 'Thank you.' It was nothing. But there was nothing more.

Bryan reached into his pocket and pulled out two small bars of fruit and nut chocolate.

'I brought these for you and Lučija,' he said. 'They're full of weevils.' He grimaced. 'But if you melt them in hot water, you can skim the insects off the top and drink what's left.' He handed the bars to Lucija who eyed the wrappers hungrily. 'It will still taste quite nice.'

Bryan said his goodbyes and walked back down the hill with frustration and failure perched on his shoulders.

Monday, 9 March 1942

Bryan's ears popped as the altimeter ticked up. The narrow confines of the Spitfire's cockpit held him with a tight and comforting familiarity. The Perspex bubble of his cockpit's hood, polished to perfection by his grinning groundcrew, allowed him to freely sweep the space above him as the sky deepened to a crystalline clarity around the climbing aircraft. He glanced into the mirror at the seven Spitfires strung out behind him; Ben was tucked in over his starboard wing, with three further combat pairs stepped up to his rear.

The wireless crackled into life. 'Fighter Control to Falcon Leader, we have an incoming raid approaching the coast north of Sliema at angels sixteen. Vector three-four-zero.'

A thrill of exhilaration ran over Bryan's scalp; his intercepting fighters were above their intended target for the first time. 'Falcon Leader here. Understood. Thank you.'

Bryan adjusted his course and watched his train of Spitfires follow the manoeuvre. Then he scanned the space ahead of his wings, looking for his enemy. A line of grey shapes revealed themselves against the darker sea, large aircraft in pulses of V formations, smaller escorting planes weaving a sinuous pattern above them.

'Falcon Leader here, bandits at 10 o'clock low. JU88s with 109 escorts.' A grin creased Bryan's face. 'Tally-ho, gentlemen, tally-ho.'

Bryan flipped his Spitfire onto its back and pulled it into a diving turn to intercept the raiders' course. A ripple of uncertainty twitched through the bomber formation and aircraft on the edges slid away from his line of attack. Some of the escorting fighters turned towards his dive, some curved away, seeking space to get onto his tail.

Bryan gritted his teeth as three German fighters flashed over his head, their silhouettes decorated by sparkling gun flashes, then he jammed his own firing button. The diving Spitfire bucked with recoil as his twin cannons barked explosive shells across the void. Their smoky trails dipped and wobbled, passing either side of a bomber's tail-plane as it flashed across his front.

Pulling hard on the stick he curved away from the bombers, following the course chosen by the circling escorts. Turning inside his expected target, with speed enhanced by his dive, he clamped his jaw against the grey shadows that invaded the periphery of his vision.

A blocky, squared-off tail appeared at the top of his canopy, its yellow paint failing to beautify its brutish outline. Bryan held the turn, drawing the 109 down the windscreen, inching it closer to his gun-sights. The dark shape reached the sights, travelled into them and edged out of the bottom. Bryan thumbed a short burst that curved down, flashing past the nose of his adversary. The other pilot grasped the danger of his predicament, reversed his turn and dived towards the ground.

Bryan wrenched his fighter around to follow, cursing as the engine misfired. A Spitfire roared over his canopy as he dived away; Ben had been thrown by the sudden change of direction, his propeller ripped the air dangerously close as he sped by.

Bryan focussed again on his target, now well ahead and diving inland, difficult to discern against the dun patchwork of bare fields. He pushed the throttle through the gate and ate away his opponent's advantage. A glance in the mirror showed only Ben's fighter circling to find him; no German aircraft sullied the sky behind his tail.

Flashing low over roads and houses, Bryan closed on the jinking 109 and squeezed out a short burst of cannon-fire. Hits peppered on the wing of his quarry, erupting with vicious orange flashes close to the fuselage. The wing snapped, folding upwards like a desperate gesture of surrender, sending the aircraft spinning along the axis of its engine, dipping ferociously downwards to plough a short furrow across the ochre earth before clattering into a low wall, cascading stones and dust through the air.

Bryan pulled up and banked away to port. The twin citadels of Mtarfa and Mdina swept past his windshield and he realised his kill had hit the ground less than two miles from Ta'Qali aerodrome.

****

Bryan and Ben trotted away from the blast-pens as ground crew moved back and forth with smooth resolution, manhandling four-gallon cans to refuel the fighters.

'We've got about half-an-hour before anyone misses us,' Bryan said. 'Let's see if we can get a trophy.'

Ben tapped him on the shoulder and pointed at a battered bicycle leaning against the stone rampart of one of the pens.

'Perfect, let's go.'

Moments later the two pilots wobbled along the perimeter track, Ben sitting astride the saddle and Bryan standing in the pedals, heading for the station gate and the open road to the valley that skirted Mtarfa. A thin coil of black smoke served as their course marker, and when Bryan judged the road had got them as near as it could, they abandoned the bike and clambered over the walls of the intervening fields.

The acrid scent of burning aviation fuel drifted by on the breeze, stinging their nostrils like pepper as it passed. The faint crackle of flames was cut by a stranger sound; a high-pitched, whining snarl, laden with desperate aggression. They reached the last wall and looked over into the field.

The Messerschmitt had ploughed a hole through the perpendicular stone boundary. The impact had crushed its nose and peeled the yellow cowling from the engine which now lay bare, flames dancing gently around its blackened metal. One wing languished separate and broken amongst the shattered stones, the other, folded and torn, stuck vertically from the fuselage like a blue-grey headstone.

The pilot, ejected by the same force that crushed the engine, lay a few yards ahead of his machine. Around him, a pack of three feral dogs stood in a lurid Mexican standoff, intermittently lunging at the body, biting and tearing at his exposed flesh, all the time snarling with distrustful fury at their competitors, their eyes full of fear and hunger.

The larger of the animals pounced on the dead man's head, ripping a chunk from his cheek and wolfing it down in one swallow. Emboldened by the taste of blood, it surged forward, barking at its retreating fellows, to stand over the body, hackles raised and teeth bared.

'What do we do?' Ben's voiced trembled with disgust.

The grinding growl of an army truck stuttered to a standstill behind them. Bryan turned to see soldiers alight from the vehicle and begin their clambering journey across the walls towards the crash site.

'We wait for the army,' he said.

The big dog took another lump of stringy flesh from the dead man's face as the other two starving curs circled, whining their frustration, looking for an opening.

The first soldier arrived at Bryan's shoulder and took in the scene.

'Fucking hell,' he breathed in disbelief.

The man unslung his rifle, settled the butt onto his khaki-clad shoulder and cocked the bolt. His single shot cracked through the still air. The dog's head snapped away from the dead man, erupting with a plume of blood and shattered bone as the bullet stretched its jerking body out on the ground. The other two strays scampered away, clearing the far wall in a single bound.

'Nice shot,' Bryan murmured.

The soldier lowered the rifle. 'Nothing to it,' he answered. 'I bloody hate dogs.'

Saturday, 21 March 1942

Bryan gazed across the aerodrome. The urgent need to fill craters had trumped the standard caution of the black-out, and across the flat expanse of Ta'Qali's runways the flickering oil lamps around which men had worked through the night, wielding shovels and barrows, could still be seen in the strengthening sunlight.

'Good morning, Hale.' Copeland appeared at his shoulder.

'Morning, sir,' Bryan said. 'What sort of bloody mess is this?'

'The sort you get when sixty-odd bombers turn up for a visit.'

Bryan glanced out to the eastern horizon where the ascending sun hardened the silhouette of Valletta and Grand Harbour. 'Perhaps they've decided it's time to finish us off. Let's hope they think last night did the job.'

'There's a convoy steaming in from Alexandria,' Copeland said. 'If we can hang on… If the ships can get here…'

Bryan smiled. 'Malta,' he said, 'one big Hobson's choice.'

The sun's yellow disc slinked higher, casting its slanting tendrils across the airfield and shortening the long shadows of the figures that toiled there. Bryan walked around the perimeter towards the Spitfires dispersed in and around the blast-pens. A knot of airmen sat around a small kerosene burner sipping from steaming mugs.

'Tea, sir?' One of them stood as he approached, holding out a full mug.

Bryan's reply was cut short by the sudden snarl of engines and he turned to see a trio of 109s streaking across the far side of the field and curving away as shapes dropped from beneath their wings. The working parties on the runways threw themselves flat as the bombs burst around them. Bofors guns opened fire, snaking tracer in querulous spirals after the retreating fighters. The noise resurged as a second wave of 109s ripped across the field from a different angle, releasing more black canisters to drop into the confusion below. The alerted Bofors crew swung onto the new target, pumping shells across the attackers' path. The outermost fighter collided with the stream of shells, shedding lumps from wing and body. It staggered out of formation, curving away from the airfield, still harried by ground fire and steadily losing height. The stricken craft's companions banked in the opposite direction, zooming away for the coast and safety.

'Get these Spitfires started up,' Bryan howled against the receding noise. 'Let's get them off the ground.'

'Too late.' The airman still held the mug of tea in his outstretched hand.

Bryan followed his gaze to the northern horizon where the clear morning azure was infected by dozens of tiny dark shapes heading towards them at altitude in wave after wave. The slow metallic grinding of air-raid klaxons wound into motion around the field, rising quickly to a mournful, cavernous howl.

'Shit,' Bryan muttered, then spun on his heel. 'Under cover!' he bawled. 'Get away from the aircraft.'

Mugs clattered onto the ground, splashing steaming tea onto the hard soil. Boots clattered and shouts rang out as the distant drone of engines swelled behind the advancing silhouettes, an ominous harbinger of the forces of explosive destruction creeping across the morning sky.

Bryan scanned the runways, discarded tools lay scattered around the half-filled craters, their erstwhile wielders sprinting away, legs pounding to get distance between them and the impending maelstrom.

The ground reverberated with dull, thudding reports as the heavy anti-aircraft guns around the aerodrome lobbed shells into the bombers' flightpath, peppering the space with puffs of black smoke that drifted sideways in the breeze.

Bryan ran up the slope, away from the blast-pens, to the rows of slit trenches that slashed thin sanctuaries in the hard ground. He loped past two already full of huddled airmen, skidded to a halt and dropped into the end of the third. As his boots hit the hard-packed soil, the first whistle of falling ordnance cut through the increasing tumult of drumming engines.

The whistle crashed into a detonation that rolled into the next and the next, generating a percussive tattoo of rolling cacophony that pulsated a rhythmic throb of blast waves across the top of the trench. Bryan gaped his mouth to protect his bulging eardrums from the suck and blow of the air around his head, curling his body down into the insulating security of the earth. The impacts pounded in swathes across the aerodrome, separating into individual explosive concussions as they crept closer. Smatterings of gritty soil mixed with sharp shards of bedrock cascaded onto the sheltering men and Bryan tensed his muscles against the expectation of a direct hit, his mind draining to a blank at the prospect of a single bright moment of crushing oblivion.

The marching annihilation stepped over his refuge and advanced up the slope, losing its cohesion and degenerating into ragged and sporadic blasts that eventually surrendered to silence. As the ringing in Bryan's ears receded, the jerking motions of the shoulder pressed against him became synchronised with sound as the airman's hysterical sobs penetrated the fug of concussion.

Bryan stood upright and searched the sky. The bombers had gone, their retreat marked only by the occasional glint of sunlight on Perspex high in the sky as they banked away out to sea. He climbed out of the trench, squinting against the rolling barrage of dust that drifted across the aerodrome. Through its obfuscating blanket, the burning flares of fierce fires pricked at his eyes. As the dust unfurled its grip, the damage to Ta'Qali became apparent. Flames licked from the hulks of vehicles and aircraft dotted around the perimeter track. A conflagration raged from a fuel store out at the aerodrome's edge. But Bryan's critical gaze focussed on the runways; pitted with dozens of craters, many overlapping, Ta'Qali looked unusable.

****

Dusk crept over the shattered aerodrome and Bryan slumped against the rough stone next to the tail of a Spitfire. Two more smaller raids had sent him and the ground crews scuttling for cover and the intermittent detonation of delayed action bombs tore new holes in the runway and frayed everyone's nerves.

Copeland arrived and hunkered down next to him. Both men watched as the oil lamps stuttered back into life, illuminating the men that shovelled and tamped the splintered earth.

'It'll be a week before this place is fixed,' Copeland muttered.

'If they're stupid enough to leave us alone to fix it,' Bryan said.

An extravagant grinding of gears caught their attention. Both men stood and sidled out of the blast-pen. A large truck lumbered through the station gates, its hooded headlights sweeping a dim arc on the ground as it pulled up and parked. A second truck swung in next to it, followed by several more. Figures tumbled out from the vehicles and formed into ranks. Shouts of command and admonishment rang out followed by a brief silence. One more order, bawled louder than the others, and the ranks broke up, fanned out and trotted towards the runway.

'Well, I'll be blowed,' Bryan said. 'The army's come to lend a hand.'

Sunday, 22 March 1942

Bryan pushed through the door of Xara Palace and headed for the dining room. With thoughts of food, the background rankle of hunger that he'd learned to ignore elbowed its way back into his consciousness. A thick and gamey odour hung over the pots on the serving table. Despite its cloying unpleasantness it roused his saliva to flow.

'What's this?' Bryan asked.

The orderly lifted the lid from the pot. 'We think it's rabbit.'

Bryan nodded, wrinkling his nose against the pungent aroma rising with the steam.

The man ladled a portion of stew into a bowl and handed him a small slice of dark-coloured bread. Bryan saw Copeland at a table, gnawing on the crust of his bread, and went to sit opposite him. Bryan dipped his own slice in the stew, breaking up the slick of yellow grease that floated on its surface.

Copeland's jaw worked like a dog chewing a shoe. 'The army's done a bloody marvellous job,' he said around his food. 'A couple of small raids slowed them down, but not by much. Their CO reckons we should be in business at first light tomorrow. Which is just as well.'

Bryan took a spoonful of the stew, grimacing at its salty sourness.

'The convoy's late,' Copeland continued, 'so instead of arriving in the dark tonight they'll be steaming in tomorrow morning. We'll be flying cover

over them for as long as we're needed.' He smiled at Bryan. 'Get your flight to readiness before dawn, you'll take second patrol.'

Bryan nodded, picking a thread of gristle out of his teeth. 'I hope they've brought some bully beef.'

Chapter 16

Monday, 23 March 1942

Bryan taxied his fighter along the perimeter, an airman lending a guiding hand on each wingtip. He cast a suspicious gaze along the runway as he approached its end. The patchwork of varying shades attested to its recent damage, but it appeared flat and solid. Copeland's flight sat waiting, so the squadron leader obviously had no qualms about the repair work. Nevertheless, Bryan pulled his straps a notch tighter as insurance against the Spitfire's narrow undercarriage. Swinging onto the runway he waited for Ben to settle in behind him.

Copeland's voice buzzed into his earphones. 'Falcon Leader to Control. We're ready to take off. Listening out.'

'Hello, Falcon Leader. You're clear to go. Bring 'em home lads, we're nearly out of cigarettes here. Control out.'

Copeland and his wingman surged forward. Bryan waved his attendant airmen away and gunned the engine. His Spitfire accelerated along the strip, jolting and banging over occasional pot holes like a Bentley on an unfamiliar country track. His tail lifted and the weight on his tyres reduced until the rumbling ceased and he climbed away from the field.

Ben settled in behind his starboard wing and Bryan pulled them both in behind Copeland's flight, taking an east-by-south course to head out towards the sea and the approaching convoy. Their track took them over the southern side of Grand Harbour where hazy smoke still rose from the previous days' blitz. Over his port wing, Valletta stretched away on the water's north side. Crumpled wrecks of buildings serrated the city's profile, like piles of broken crockery, and smouldering fires lent their own smoky layer to the murky mist that settled over the water. Barrage balloons swayed in the stiff breeze, ascending slowly on their cables to meet the tribulations of the new day, bucking lazily like tethered whales. The sun, very low on the horizon ahead, still lacked the force to dazzle, its outline shimmering through the hazy morning air.

The minutes crawled by and Bryan's eyes watered for squinting into the limpid light. A shape disrupted the horizon and he wiped away the moisture to focus on the anomaly. One shape became many and they resolved into a group of vessels in the distance.

Bryan thumbed transmit. 'Falcon Three to Falcon Leader, I think I see several ships ahead, on the port quarter.'

'Thank you, Falcon Three. That looks like our convoy, alright.'

Four merchant ships ploughed deep wakes in the choppy sea as they raced for the refuge of their destination. A tight ring of destroyers sailed around them and, further out, cruisers carved curving S-shapes through the waves.

Naturally wary of naval gunnery, Copeland adjusted their course to pass south of the convoy, outside its tight defensive screen, then looped around behind it and cruised away to the north.

'Loosen up, Falcon aircraft. Keep alert.'

Relieved to have the rapidly strengthening sunshine away to one side, Bryan scanned the sky for anything on its way south from Sicily whilst keeping a wary mirror-eye on the receding convoy. Within moments, Bryan saw what he was looking for; many black motes popped into being against the deep blue backdrop of the Mediterranean dawn.

Copeland saw them too. 'Bandits dead ahead, thirty-plus, bombers and escort.'

The four Spitfires cruised on, climbing slightly, as the enemy formation approached a bit to their port side. The bombers, accounting for two-thirds of the armada, travelled in two distinct groups of different aircraft. Their escort sat high above them, weaving lazily to avoid outrunning their charges. Copeland levelled out, higher than the bombers but below the fighters.

'Falcon Leader to Falcon aircraft. One pass through the bombers then break hard. Watch your tail, those are 109s up there. Good luck. Tally ho!'

Copeland pulled into a long bank to port and dived towards the bombers, dragging his wingman with him. Bryan waited for a second or two, then followed him down with Ben in his wake.

The Italian planes glowed pale ochre in the sparkling sunlight that shone from behind the undetected interceptors. Bryan watched the two Spitfires ahead of him skim over the first formation. The blocky fuselage of a bomber sprouted a plume of fire from its port engine and sank out of formation. Bryan chose another sandy-coloured body from the wallowing shoal of attackers and opened fire. His cannons jolted streaks of white smoke that passed above and below his target. He held the firing button and pulled the stick to sweep his shells at the next bomber in the formation and saw fragments burst away from its tail as it slid past his windscreen.

Bryan barrelled out of the Italian formation into empty sky. He pulled into a hard, starboard turn, searching the void above him through blurring vision for the retribution that must be falling towards him. Three shapes flashed by in quick succession, breaking into a fan of whirling adversaries. Bryan held his own turn to follow the fighter on the right of the trio, hoping Ben was still behind him to lessen the odds by attacking one of the others. Out of the right side of his canopy, Bryan became dimly aware of clusters of anti-aircraft shells exploding in the sky and plumes of water blossoming from the sea, before the jinking tail of his quarry descended from the top of his windscreen, dragging his concentration back to the physics of aerial battle. He needed the bulk of the 109 to pass through the gunsight to place his shot into its path. The swastikaed tail edged lower and Bryan's thumb hovered over the firing button. He glanced in his mirror as a black shape swung into view, flashes lighting its cowling.

'Shit.' Bryan reversed the direction of his turn. His target whipped away out of sight and his blood pounded through his forehead with the change in g-force. He clenched his jaw against the pain as his vision muted to red, fighting to hold the turn for as long as his faculties allowed, then he straightened into a shallow zoom, searching the sky with recovering eyesight. There was nothing near him. He wallowed back and forth to check his blind spots; he was alone.

'Falcon Leader here, regroup over convoy. Disengage and regroup.'

Copeland's voice startled him and he searched the horizon for the ships. The smudging stain of dispersing AA smoke lent him a clue and he banked towards it. Away to the east, receding into the distance, the bomber formations ploughed homewards with the 109s zig-zagging behind them, deterring pursuit.

Three familiar shapes circled on the edge of the convoy, Bryan altered course to join them.

****

Airmen buzzed around the aircraft as they landed, toting petrol cans and ammunition belts, unlocking panels and checking flight surfaces. Bryan sat on a rock by a slit trench, sucking on a cigarette and teasing the tangles from his greasy hair with oil-grimed fingers. The Spitfires being refreshed for more battle sat in a tight group just off the runway. Bryan fretted about the target this would gift to a strafing attacker. He glanced to the eastern horizon, hoping no Luftwaffe's attacks would penetrate as far as Ta'Qali. He pulled back his cuff and checked his watch, it was barely nine o'clock in the morning.

'Hale!' Copeland called out as he strode towards the Spitfires. 'Look lively. I need a wingman.'

Bryan flicked his cigarette butt away over his shoulder and trotted down towards his commander, pulling on his flying helmet as he went.

Copeland stood quizzing a crew chief about the fighters' readiness. As Bryan arrived, he turned to him, fastening his own chin strap as he spoke.

'Take this one.' He nodded his head towards the nearest Spitfire. 'Some of the ships are approaching Grand Harbour. They want something over them to watch them in.' He winked and trotted round to the next fighter in the line.

Bryan pulled on the parachute harness that hung from the wing and clambered up to settle in the cockpit. Men scurried under the fuselage and shouts of warning rang out before the two Spitfires coughed into life and taxied out onto the runway.

Bryan cocked his head to one side to watch Copeland's aircraft around the upward-pointing bulk of his own engine cowling. Seeing his leader surge away, he waited for a count of three and eased his own throttle forwards to hoist his fighter into the air and settle behind his flight leader.

The cross-country flight was short, and they were still climbing as they crossed Marsamxett Harbour with Valletta on their starboard wing. Bryan glanced down to find the finger of open space that was Hastings Gardens, relieved to see Windmill Street stood intact.

The pair of Spitfires flashed out over the sea and banked to starboard around the mouth of Grand Harbour. About half-a-mile from the breakwaters, a cargo ship sailed towards sanctuary shadowed by destroyer. A mile behind her, another merchantman with similar close support laboured towards land.

A flicker of movement caught Bryan's eye; screaming along at wave-top level and hugging the coast, a yellow-nosed fighter poured a stream of fire along the deck of the first cargo ship, vaulted over her masts and veered away due north, sprinting for home, followed by a furious stream of tracer from the destroyer's guns. Copeland banked away to give chase and Bryan

153

banked in the opposite direction to circle the vessels and guard against more hit-and-run attacks.

The first pair of ships cruised through the breakwaters and Bryan overflew them. The bastions of Valletta's southern flank rippled with movement as the gathered residents of the battered city waved arms and flags to greet the supply ships.

Bryan banked around the harbour showing his blue underside and flashing its roundels as he swept over the crowds and headed out to sea to cover the other cargo ship's approach.

Wednesday, 25 March 1942

A grey blanket of low cloud smothered the island and the surrounding sea, processing unbroken to the north-west and confining the defending aircraft to their pens on the ground. The distant drone of high-level engines came and went as small groups of raiders bombed through the clouds, chancing their best guess at where the harbour and its cargo-bearing vessels might lay.

Bryan stood gazing across the runways, shoulders hunched against the stiff breeze and the ambience of chilly gloom that the cloud cover cast across the field.

Copeland strode along the perimeter past him. 'Fancy a jaunt?' he called. 'I'm taking a truck across to Grand Harbour to see if I can track down some spares. I might try to divert something for the mess as well.'

Bryan cast another glance at the gelatinous clouds and hurried after the squadron leader.

Copeland climbed into a battered RAF truck and Bryan swung into the passenger seat beside him. The engine started with a bronchial cough and the truck lurched away through the gates.

'Only two of the four made it through, then?' Bryan asked.

'There's a third anchored off Marsaxlokk,' Copeland replied. 'It's taken damage to its engine rooms. So, Lord knows what they plan to do with her. The fourth was sunk by dive-bombers fifty miles out.'

'It's not a good enough score, is it?'

Copeland shrugged. 'It's a high price. But at least half of the supplies are safe. We'll take a look from the north side and try to work out which docks they're using for unloading.'

The truck jolted into Valletta and turned onto Lascaris Wharf. They drove past two destroyers docked against the wall. Once beyond the grey bulk of the warships, their view of the harbour opened out and Copeland slowed down and pulled over.

'What on earth is happening?' he breathed.

'Sweet Fanny Adams, by the looks of things,' Bryan muttered, reaching inside his jacket for his cigarettes.

The two merchant vessels sat anchored in line astern in the centre of Grand Harbour. They both sat low in the water, still bearing the full weight of their cargoes. No boats moved around them and no one worked on their decks. The ships looked abandoned.

'What madness is this?' Copeland's voice resonated with shock and disbelief. 'Where are the bloody stevedores?'

He crashed the truck into reverse, pulled a ragged three-point turn and roared back the way they had come.

****

Copeland sat at the trestle desk, the intelligence officer stood to one side looking down at his shoes and Bryan sat on the hard, wooden chair in front of the desk, rolling a cigarette around in his fingertips as he listened to the telephone conversation.

'Well whose responsibility is it?' Copeland's brow furrowed with his frustration. 'I flew cover for those ships as they came in. That was two days ago, and I'd bet my grandmother's life that not a single stick has been unloaded from them.'

He listened to the voice on the other end of the line, his expression growing darker by the second.

'That's as maybe, but here's what *you* don't understand.' Copeland switched the handset to his other ear and jabbed a paper on the desk with his finger as he spoke. 'My intelligence officer has just given me a weather report which predicts clearing skies tomorrow. Sixty miles away there are hundreds of German aircraft, with practically unlimited supplies of bombs, whose commanders are probably reading a similar weather report. And' – his voice dropped a tone – 'I have five serviceable Spitfires to send up against them.' Copeland listened in silence to the reply, the distant voice spilling unintelligibly from the receiver like the buzz of an unconcerned insect.

'Five,' he repeated, 'because the spares I need are still on those ships.'

The buzzing insect returned, but Copeland held the handset away from his head, gave it a final sidelong look of contempt and dropped it into its cradle.

'Apparently one of the ships is full of ammunition; if it blows, it will destroy large parts of Valletta and the docks,' he said. 'Best get an early night, gentlemen. It's going to be a busy day tomorrow.'

Thursday, 26 March 1942

A group of twelve pilots stood or sat between the small stone buildings that served as their readiness station. The milky dawn back-lit the clouds' moribund grey and the minutes ticked into hours under their obfuscating protection, accompanied by the fidgeting and coughs of the men smoking nervously under the sagging camouflage netting.

At last, the edges of the grey blanket frayed and alabaster shafts of light punctured the pearly ceiling. Bryan glanced at his watch; twenty minutes to ten. He turned to gaze at the telephone sitting in its cradle. The orderly at the table followed his look and jumped as the bell jangled into life. The man recovered himself and snatched the handset up halfway through the second ring. Bryan watched him and wondered idly why orderlies always nodded in silence as they listened to disembodied instructions.

The man let the handset drop away from his ear, clutching it protectively to his chest as he took a deep breath. 'Large raid building over Sicily. Scramble, all aircraft.'

Bryan loped down the slope after Copeland, Ben and two other pilots trotted with him. The reserve pilots watched them go, a nauseous mix of envy and relief jumbled in their faces.

Engines barked into life ahead of the running men, swirling grit into the air as they arrived at their fighters. They pulled on parachute packs and clambered into cockpits. Minutes later, they taxied onto the runway and, one by one, clawed their way into the air, banking south-east to gain altitude down the island's backbone.

The clouds tore and tattered like sullied snow melting on a corrugated roof, exposing long fingers of pale blue sky between their receding edges as they lost their form to the wind. The Spitfires climbed through the remnants and Bryan looked down behind his starboard wing, evaluating a movement against the dun landscape.

'Falcon Three to Falcon Leader,' he called, 'Hurricanes climbing to join us from Hal Far. I count six.'

The friendly fighters lagged below as the Spitfire formation soared across Marsaxlokk Bay, its waters empty of vessels. They skirted the point and flew out over the sea. Banking north, they held their climb and skirted the coast. The Hurricanes cut inside them and climbed onto their landward side as the accreted formation overflew the lonely, anchored merchant ship.

'Fighter Control to Falcon and Horseshoe aircraft, Sixty-plus bandits north of Gozo, angels twelve, heading towards Grand Harbour. Good luck.'

The Hurricanes levelled out, but the Spitfires continued slightly nose-up, seeking to reduce their disadvantage against higher escort fighters. Banking around the bulging bay-notched heel of the island, they dropped into a north-west vector along the straight cliff-edged coast, heading towards the mouth of the harbours. As they flew past the breakwaters, Bryan glanced left, over the rugged outlines of the pugnacious Hurricanes running alongside, down the harbour's narrow length and its docks. He caught a fleeting glimpse of barges and small boats flocking around the cargo ships sitting squat in the centre of the channel, nets on cranes swinging over the water, a snapshot of desperate activity, then the angle closed and he turned away to focus on the sky ahead where tiny shapes were gathering like flies over a carcass.

'Falcon Leader to Falcon Aircraft, bandits dead ahead. Avoid the escort as long as you can, we need to stop the bombers. Individual targets. Tally-ho!'

The insectoid swarm separated into three formations, a heavier mass of twin-engine bombers bore down on the docks with a group of single-engine aircraft close on their starboard side, and more escorts high above on their port quarter.

Bryan eased his nose down towards the oncoming bombers, eased off his safety catch and watched the black shapes expand into the predatory silhouettes of Junkers 88s. Slightly below him, ahead and on either side of his nose, Hurricanes flashed into the enemy formation spraying un-aimed tracer fire through the ranks of raiders. Aircraft bucked to evade the storm, one rearing into Bryan's flightpath, huge and alien. An instinctive stab on the firing button put one or two shells through the wing that flashed over his canopy, reverberating the Perspex with a vicious bang as the Spitfire wallowed through the cyclonic vortex of the larger craft's slipstream.

Clear of the bombers, Bryan hauled into a left turn, craning his neck to check for hostile escorts. Over the harbour, the explosive puffs of the anti-aircraft barrage colonised the void with drifting smoke. Black canisters detached from the bombers cascading towards the water and its milling small craft, while the smaller enemy planes dropped from the sky, one by one.

Bryan watched bewildered for a moment before the machines' crooked, bent-wing profile registered. 'Stukas,' he mumbled to himself.

He kicked on a touch more rudder and side-slipped down to get closer to the dive-bombers, gritting his teeth as he dipped his nose into the thick of the barrage. A Stuka, ahead of him, dropped nose-down towards the ships. Bryan eased back on his throttle, dropped into a shallower dive and wallowed back and forth, setting his jaw against the random explosions that peppered his path. A concussion hit the underside of his fuselage as the Stuka's bomb-load detonated below. Bryan eased back another notch, muscles tensed against blast or collision.

Wide and dark-green with creased wings, its blocky fixed undercarriage poking down like old-man's trousers, the Stuka pulled up right in front of him, filling his windshield. A round, pale face, open-mouthed in shock and fear peered at him from the rear of the canopy as the gunner fumbled to bring his barrel to bear, then everything dissolved into unfocussed blur under the vibration of the Spitfire's twin cannons. The dive-bomber yawed sideways under the impacts, flipped over and dropped away towards the water.

Bryan rammed the throttle forward, careening over the docks through the columns of swirling smoke that rose from shattered machines and burning barges. A JU88 careered across his front, a Hurricane close on its tail. The bomber flew through a sudden column of tracer spiralling up from a moored destroyer. Flame belched from the raider's fuselage and it dropped away. The Hurricane banked starboard, dragging its wingtip through the stream of bullets, shedding fragments of wing panelling as it curved away. Bryan pulled an opposite turn, standing his fighter on its port wing, sliding past the spout of ordnance unscathed and accelerating out towards the sea.

Crashing into clear air and crossing the coast, Bryan scanned the sky above. The main bomber force had wheeled out to sea and was heading north in regrouped formations. He held his turn to start a pursuit, climbing towards the receding raiders. Immediately a pair of 109s, from the group circling high above the bombers, dropped into a dive towards him, flashing over him without firing. Bryan pulled into a sharp bank to follow them, obliged to cover his own tail. The Germans zoomed up into a curving climb, using the speed from their dive to recoup their altitude. Bryan completed his circle and climbed once more towards the distant bombers. Two more 109s dropped from the high defensive gaggle, sweeping past him at speed. Once again, Bryan pulled into a defensive turn, faithfully performing his steps in this predictable, cagey dance. But this time he watched the 109s curve away while he continued south, down the coast, making his escape from this dangerous game of cat-and-mouse.

Banking over the cliffs and striking inland he looked out over his wing to the broiling, fiery chaos that engulfed the docks, mirrored by leaping flames that spouted along the southern wharfs of Valletta and from several vessels moored against them. He closed his weary eyes against the destruction for a moment, but its colour still burned through his eyelids.

****

Bryan leaned his elbows on the railing of Xara's roof terrace and gazed out towards Valletta. The sunset in the west, dropping into the sea behind Mdina, was matched and now outstripped by the crimson glow that settled in the east over Grand Harbour and the surrounding area. An ominous shard of brightness sat in the middle of the vibrant red dome, flickering with dread portent like an angry dragon's tongue.

The door opened, and Ben elbowed his way through carrying two steaming mugs.

'Last of the tea,' he said. 'I thought you'd appreciate the wet.'

Bryan grunted acknowledgement and reached out for the proffered mug. The movement caused the stink of his own rancid sweat to sting his nostrils.

Ben pulled up a chair next to him. 'How many did you fly today?'

'Three,' Bryan murmured. 'You?'

'Only two.' Ben took a sip of his tea. 'Bloody air filter packed up. I was lucky to get it down in one piece.'

They gazed in silence at the blazing harbour for a long moment.

'Does this mean we've lost?' Ben asked.

'Unless you count starving to death as some sort of moral victory.'

159

'Do you think we'll surrender, then?'

Bryan swigged his tea, his face lost for a moment in the tendrils of steam. 'No,' he said. 'You don't hang onto a bloody empire by surrendering. And, if this war is about anything, it's about that.'

Chapter 17

Sunday, 29 March 1942

Bryan stood on the edge of the wharf with Valletta at his back. Smoke swirled and drifted above his head, drying his teeth and grating in his throat. The two merchant ships and the destroyers that had been their shepherds lay sunken in the shallow water, wavelets lapping through their gunwales, their superstructures blasted, like abandoned buildings in a ghost town. Across the water, smouldering warehouses in the docks wheezed thin trails of soot that rose to thicken the overcast. A small wooden boat traversed the water, the sound of its stuttering outboard echoed from the bastion walls and clattered back on itself. It approached the closest cargo ship and a man onboard stood to survey the larger vessel with binoculars. Bryan watched its progress until it was lost from sight behind the sunken hulk.

An old man walked slowly towards him along the wharf from the seaward end. His long coat hung loose on his diminished frame, the dirt-grimed fabric flapped over stained trousers and a filthy white shirt. His gait was slow and careful, like a man who had lost his walking stick, or denied he ever needed one. He shuffled closer and stopped, standing shoulder to shoulder with Bryan. The old man lifted his chin and surveyed the ruined harbour with watery eyes.

'These are terrible times, my friend.' His voice rattled with a bronchial undertone. 'Today is the first Sunday I have not been to church.'

Bryan pulled out his cigarettes. The man accepted his offer and Bryan cupped a lighted match before the old man's face. He drew deeply on the smoke and two short coughs wracked his chest like explosive exhalations from a dusty cave. He looked at the cigarette between his fingers as a pawnbroker looks at someone else's heirloom.

'Because God has turned his back on us...' His voice trailed off as he swept his gaze across the devastation. 'The British should go home,' he said, then looked into Bryan's face and smiled. '*You* should go home, young man. Without God on our side we're lost. You shouldn't waste your life on us.'

'You want us to leave Malta to the Germans and the Italians?' Bryan lit a smoke for himself as the man considered the question with pursed lips.

'Perhaps it would be better to let them in rather than oblige them to kick down the door.' The man took another draw on his cigarette, holding the smoke for a few seconds before wheezing it out from between his yellowed teeth. 'What good is Malta when Malta is no more?'

Somewhere across the harbour a wall collapsed with a distant rushing sound, like a breaking wave heard from the top of a cliff.

'They destroyed my house.' The man spoke as if he was delivering the news to himself, attempting to absorb the enormity of his loss by a deliberate repetition of his new reality.

'Where will you go?' Bryan asked.

The old man flicked his cigarette out into the water. 'Maybe I should go to church,' he said. 'Perhaps God will turn his face back to me.' He squeezed Bryan's shoulder in farewell as he shuffled away behind him.

The boat emerged from behind the sunken vessel, navigating carefully around its stern. The man on the deck lowered his binoculars, turned to his companion and pointed at some detail on the wrecked ship. Bryan flicked his cigarette in an arc to land next to the old man's and together they floated with the tide.

Bryan crossed the road, heading up the slope into the city. The narrow lane funnelled the smoky haze from smouldering docks. Gaps in the tall façade framed the collapsed walls that sat now as heaps of rubble that splayed out across the road, forcing him to clamber over their broken stones.

Bryan trudged across the city's peninsula. Further north, away from the harbour, the density of destruction reduced, but still he passed a dozen or more families searching through the wreckage of their homes to salvage the debris of their lives. They paused in their labour to watch him stumble through the ragged scree that duned across his path.

He came to the corner of Bakery Street, bastioned by the bulk of Saint Augustine Church. The lilting sound of the singing congregation seeped through the closed doors. He listened for a moment, then walked on, dog-legging onto Mint Street and climbing the hill to Hastings Gardens. A half-guilty rush of relief swelled his chest as he arrived on Windmill Street to find its buildings undamaged. He sauntered along the edge of the gardens, grateful for the fresher air looping in from the waters of Marsamxett. The empty plinth stood solid and resolute and Bryan approached to sit and rest on its steps.

Something stood at its base, a flash of blue against the pale, carved limestone. Bryan crouched on his haunches to better see a small earthenware pot. A bunch of borage stems filled the container, their bewhiskered stems exploding into a tiny constellation of blue-starred flowers. A small label, cut from brown packing paper was secured around the pot's neck with white string. Bryan tipped the label with his fingertip so it caught the light. In a thin handwritten script was the single word "Qalbi".

Bryan lowered himself to sit on the step, the little pot to one side of his scuffed and dusty boot, and lit a cigarette. The ghost of the old man passed through his mind's eye as the tobacco smoke swirled away across the courtyard. Bryan hoped he'd found his solace, then wondered how close that was to a prayer.

'Hello Bryan.'

Jacobella's voice broke his reverie and he jumped to his feet, embarrassed to be caught slouching next to the tiny memorial.

'I'm so pleased you're both safe.' He brushed the dust from the seat of his trousers and crossed the road.

'Come in for a while,' she said, opening the door. 'I have some mint leaves, I can make some tea'.

Lučija clattered up the stairs ahead of them. Bryan followed Jacobella, trying not to watch her hips sway on the steps and failing to resist the temptation. At the top, she moved through to the kitchen, humming faintly under her breath, a hymn that she had so recently been singing. Lučija ran to her room and returned with the knitted airman under her arm. She clambered onto a chair at the kitchen table and sat the doll on the smooth wooden surface, leaning it against the pepper pot. She beamed a smile at Bryan, as if to share a clever secret, then her smile faded as she toyed with the figure's knitted feet and slipped away into the child-sanctuary of imagination.

Bryan moved across to the draining board where Jacobella worked. 'Thursday must've been a trial,' he said.

Jacobella picked small green leaves from their spindly stems and the fresh smell of mint pervaded the room as she rubbed them between thumb and finger, dropping some into a small saucepan of soup and the rest into another pot filled with water that was just beginning to waft with steam.

'It was hell,' she said, then tutted and crossed herself with the hand that clutched the leaves. 'They evacuated the south side.' She turned to regard him over her shoulder for a moment and her brow creased at the memory. 'A ship full of explosives was on fire. They said it could destroy half of

Valletta.' She turned again and this time a smile of genuine warmth lit her eyes. 'The gardens were full of families. I opened my door to let the children come in and sleep under shelter.' A shadow flitted across her face, dimming her smile as she went back to her task.

Bryan stood, uncertain. 'Are you' – he groped for a different word and failed – 'alright?' He winced at his awkwardness.

The water boiled in the saucepan and Jacobella turned off the stove. 'My heart will go on,' she said quietly, pouring the yellow-tinged water into three small cups. She handed one to Bryan. 'The priest told us that the Governor is making a broadcast. Can you find it for us?'

Bryan went into the living room and knelt by the small table that held the polished wooden wireless set. He clicked it on and swept the tuner dial. The laboured voice of Malta's Governor emerged from the mess of static.

'*...a grievous disappointment. We could not watch the burning of one of the ships without the deepest emotion...*'

Jacobella brought a bowl of soup and some mint tea to the table for Lučija. She offered nothing to Bryan and he noticed she had nothing for herself.

'*...Malta has suffered much and has been called upon to endure much...*'

Bryan moved to sit at the table opposite Jacobella. Lučija sat between them blowing her soup cool and dipping her spoon.

'*...but in the interests of Malta itself, of our Empire, and of the most righteous cause for which we are fighting, I call on you to endure still further and to continue to show the same courage which has won the admiration of the world.*'

The broadcast ended, to be replaced with light classical music.

Bryan stood up and switched the wireless off. 'He reminds me of Winston,' he mused. 'It used to annoy me, listening to that old oaf grumbling on about resistance and sacrifice.' He lit a cigarette. 'But I don't suppose they can speak the real truth. And it would help nothing if they did.'

'So, what is the real truth?' she asked.

He sat down at the table. 'The truth is there to see in the ruins of Valletta. The truth is you have nothing to eat and there are sunken ships in the harbour packed with food that's going to rot under the water. The truth is the Germans are intent on destroying everything on this island, no matter about anyone's courageous endurance.' He glanced at Lučija scraping the last of the thin soup from her bowl. 'I'm sorry,' he mumbled, 'it's not my place...'

'Were you flying against them?' Jacobella asked, leaning her elbows on the table and resting her chin on her hands.

Bryan nodded silently.

'What was it like?'

He pulled a bleak smile. 'The harbour was like a cobweb made of bullets, planes and shrapnel.' He dropped his cigarette into the dregs of his mint tea where it hissed angrily for an instant. 'I was lucky enough to fly through the gaps.'

'God protected you.'

Bryan shook his head once. 'I don't believe that.'

Jacobella reached out a hand and touched his forearm. 'That's the very reason why He is doing it.'

Wednesday, 1 April 1942

Bryan eyed his instruments with suspicion. The oil temperature was slightly high. He listened to the engine's tone, straining to pick out any irregularity. There was nothing untoward, so he returned his attention to holding his position behind Copeland's starboard wing. He flew as number two in a vic of three Spitfires climbing away towards the island's southern tip, clawing for altitude to intercept a small incoming force.

'Fighter Control to Falcon Leader, bandits are fast-moving. Vector three-four-zero. Buster.'

The small formation banked over the landward edge of Marsaxlokk Bay, setting course for Grand Harbour, black gouts of smoke coughing from their exhausts as they pushed their throttles through the gate to get maximum speed.

The landscape rolled away beneath them, punctuated with clusters of buildings hunched along the roadsides. Bryan's gaze swept the horizon as the interceptors levelled out, barrelling north-west. The thin fingers of the three creeks that penetrated the southern shore to form the docks crept into view. Then, across Grand Harbour, flashes and mushrooming smoke clouds peppered the capital's central belt, dozens of explosions stippled the cityscape beneath a sky beset with shell bursts.

The Spitfires hammered towards the unseen raiders, flashing over the harbour and across the city. Bryan's chest lurched as he saw the slender strip of Hastings Gardens obscured by dust and smoke from nearby bomb strikes. Bile squeezed into his throat and his shoulders tightened with a quiet fury.

The curling smoke from fresher detonations rose from Manoel Island, with even younger siblings climbing out of collapsing buildings across Sliema. Finally, the enemy became visible; fewer than a dozen tiny nebulous shapes, already out to sea and racing northwards.

'Falcon Leader to Falcon Aircraft, disengage, we've missed them.'

Bryan pushed the heel of his hand against the throttle that was already hard against the stops, and locked his eyes on the dark silhouettes that hovered in the hazy seam between the sea and the sky. The other two Spitfires fell back on his port side.

'Falcon Leader to Falcon Two, disengage and reform.'

Bryan gritted his teeth and pulled his wireless cable from its socket. The backdrop of static hiss in his ears dropped into a flat silence around which the roar of his straining engine clamoured at his skull.

The silhouettes ahead grew, sprouting twin engines on thin wings. They drew together in a tighter formation and one or two speculative lashes of tracer fire spiralled back towards him.

The engine coughed like an angry bull, snapping Bryan out of his transfixion. He hauled back the throttle and dipped the nose below the thickening stream of defensive fire, diving and banking around to point his aircraft back at the dark bar of Malta's eastern coastline. His seat thrummed in sympathetic resonance to the engine's rough vibration. He glanced at the oil temperature needle nudging the high end of its scale and eased the throttle back a notch further. With his Spitfire flirting with the stall, he scanned the sky above and behind, a sick fear crawling across his skin, the dread feeling common to the lame or the wounded traversing a predator's territory.

Relief tingled through his fingers as the wave-edged coastline slipped beneath his ailing fighter. Suddenly remembering, he fumbled for his wireless cord and pushed the plug home.

'-are you receiving?' A pause filled with swirling static, then: 'Fighter Control to Falcon Two, are you receiving?

Bryan pushed transmit. 'Falcon Two here, faulty wireless and poorly engine. I'm on my way home.'

****

Bryan banked gingerly onto the circuit and straightened up to land. The vibrations ascended to clanking jolts and black smoke streamed from the exhaust as the Spitfire cushioned down towards the hard-packed soil. The wheels touched and the engine seized in ghastly symbiosis and Bryan braked gently, veering off the landing strip as he slowed.

He shut down the engine and closed the fuel taps. Pulling his straps free, he banged back the canopy and squirmed out of the cockpit. Thick white smoke seeped from beneath the cowling and he hurried down the wing root, jumped to the ground and lurched away from the aircraft, his parachute pack banging against the back of his legs as he moved.

Once at a safe distance he shrugged the parachute pack onto the ground and watched the ground crews sprinting in to save his machine from the developing engine fire.

'Faulty wireless, my arse.'

Bryan turned to see Copeland, his face berry-red with ire.

'You disobeyed my direct order and went on a personal vendetta.' Copeland emphasised the last two words with finger jabs to Bryan's chest. 'What are you going to do if she *has* been killed?'

Bryan's eyes widened slightly in surprise.

'Everyone knows, Hale.' He gestured at the anonymous airmen struggling with the crippled plane. 'Everyone.'

Bryan pulled off his helmet and fumbled inside his jacket, searching for cigarettes.

'Answer me,' Copeland persisted. 'Are you going to stop defending everyone else when she's dead? And what help will it be to any of them if you get killed? I've got no use for dead heroes. By all means, kill yourself if you think it will make her love you. But bring my Spitfire back in one piece first and do yourself in some other way.'

A chill silence fell between the men. Copeland gazed at the smoking aeroplane, the anger receding from his face. Bryan gave up his search for a smoke and stared at the patch of ground in front of his boots.

'Go back to Mdina, Bryan.' Copeland's voice had softened. 'I've got more pilots than planes. I don't need you to fly again this afternoon.'

****

The beginnings of dusk crept across the fields with the stealthy tread of a seasoned hunter. The wailing klaxons of dive-bombers and the flat crunch of high explosives filtered from Grand Harbour across those same fields to the roof terrace at Xara. Salvaged ammunition from the sunken merchantmen, hand-delivered directly to the harbour's defences, provided a particularly vicious umbrella over the docks. Above this dome of drifting wisps, streams of flashing tracer lashed in sinuous curves, occasionally sparking a vibrant orange ball that dropped away from the dogfight like fruit from the strangest of trees.

Bryan watched the raid, his chest hollow of emotion, like a man beaten by thugs in full view of careless passers-by, knowing he couldn't stop the pain and unsure if he possessed the strength to endure it.

The door clicked open and Ben appeared at his shoulder.

'The squadron leader has taken you off the roster,' he said.

'I thought he might.' Bryan sighed. 'That makes me the spare prick at the wedding.'

'I'm not sure what I should do now.'

Bryan frowned. 'What do you mean?'

'I'm *your* wingman.'

Bryan looked into the younger man's face, the thin flesh on his cheek bones reddening at his declaration of allegiance. 'You have to do what you're told, Ben. That's the way it works.' He turned his gaze back to the combats in the distance. 'But, thank you,' he added, 'that means a lot.'

Friday, 3 April 1942

'Mrs Azzopardi,' Bryan said. 'I believe she's the assistant to a journalist here. Is she at work today?'

The receptionist regarded him with naked suspicion as she picked up her telephone and dialled a short number. She turned away from him as she spoke in Maltese into the handset, then turned back to face him, her mistrust undiminished.

'Who is it?' she asked.

'Azzopardi,' Bryan replied, 'I'm looking for Mrs Azzopardi.'

'No, no.' The receptionist jabbed her finger at him. 'Who *is* it?'

'Oh, Bryan. My name is Bryan.'

The receptionist raised an eyebrow at him, then turned away to deliver the information into the telephone. That done she dropped the handset into its cradle.

'You is wait,' she said and bent to the papers on her desk.

A minute later a door opened and Jacobella leaned into the room.

'I'm sorry to disturb you at work,' Bryan said. 'I wondered if you had such a thing as a lunch break?'

Jacobella smiled and nodded. 'Give me a few minutes,' she said and ducked back through the door.

Bryan felt the renewed hostility of the receptionist's disapproving gaze and chose to sidle onto the street, outside of its range.

St Paul Street dipped away to the city's north-eastern tip and bore the ravages wrought by the bombing raids on the harbour close by. By contrast, the flat, sandstone frontage of the newspaper offices stood indifferent to the rapacity of war; its survival was totemic, perhaps divinely guaranteed.

Jacobella skipped down the steps to where Bryan waited and they walked the short distance to Castille Place and turned into Barracca Gardens. As they walked under the archway, Jacobella pulled a copy of the newspaper from her bag and handed it to Bryan.

'You must be very proud,' she said.

Bryan unrolled the paper and read the headline out loud: '*Twenty-seven raiders downed – No RAF loss.*' He handed the paper back. 'I'm afraid I had to watch that one from the ground,' he said. 'I've been taken off flying duties for a while.'

A smile lighted Jacobella's face. 'That's a good thing, isn't it?'

Bryan shrugged. 'In any event, it makes me an unproductive mouth that needs feeding. So, I'm fairly certain they'll ship me off the island as soon as they get the chance. I wanted to tell you so you wouldn't think badly of me if I suddenly vanished.'

They walked through the small paved gardens to the wall overlooking the Saints' Bastion. To their left, the breakwater jutted from the fortress on the harbour's far side, gun barrels poking skywards through camouflaged netting. To their right, the wrecked docks extended inland, a twisted tangle of broken cranes and crumpled buildings, overlain with a thin smoke-haze from smouldering wood. The sunken ships wallowed like the bloated corpses of Fin whales, small boats dotted around them, risking the same fate to pluck anything usable from inside their bellies.

Jacobella regarded the devastation for a moment, then turned to face him. 'This whole thing is a complete disaster,' she said quietly. 'But life's been better for having you in it.' A rueful smile curled her lips. 'Even as a small part.'

Chapter 18

Friday, 17 April 1942

Bryan sat on an empty petrol can, gazing across the airfield. He pulled out his cigarettes, grimaced at the last three smokes it held and put the pack back in his pocket with its contents intact. The growl of Merlin engines dragged his eyes to the sky and he watched a flight of three Spitfires swooping in to land. He knew Copeland sat in one of the machines, so he stood and trailed after the fighters as they taxied to their pens, pressing a handkerchief to his face to ward off the swathes of dust kicked up by the aeroplanes.

He waited as the engines rattled into silence and groundcrews began re-arming and refuelling the aircraft. After a few minutes, Copeland strode out from one of the pens.

'Sir?' Bryan pulled himself into the semblance of attention as the squadron leader walked towards him. 'Can we speak for a moment? I've been grounded for over two weeks-'

'Walk with me, Hale.' Copeland cut him short.

Bryan fell in beside him, the need for nicotine tightening a band around his forehead.

'I revisited your records,' he continued when they were beyond any eavesdropping. 'It seems you have come seriously un-glued before.'

Bryan gave in and pulled out a cigarette, lighting it and drawing heavily on the smoke.

'My crewman was all but disembowelled,' he answered. He took another drag on the tobacco, causing the cigarette's tip to crackle and flare bright orange. 'I had to walk through his innards to get off my Beaufighter. It's true, it disturbed my sleep for a little while. But I got over it.'

Copeland gave him a sideways look, evaluating the steel in the other man's eyes. 'Alright,' he said, 'I'll put you back on the roster when the new Spits come in.'

'We're getting more Spitfires?' Relief flooded Bryan's features. 'That's unexpected.'

'Well, the navy made it clear there'd be no convoys without air cover for the harbours. The Governor made it clear, to Winston, that if we didn't get more convoys he could expect Malta to surrender in the not too distant future. Churchill then leans on Roosevelt, and Roosevelt lends us a carrier that happened to be on the right side of the Atlantic.'

Brian sucked the last of the smoke from his cigarette butt. 'How many, and when?'

'Fifty to eighty is what I was told, but I'm loathe to count chickens. They're loading now, so it will be a few days.' Copeland laid a hand on Bryan's shoulder. 'You continue your rest until they get here. I'll need pilots with experience to get through this.'

Bryan nodded his thanks, took a lingering look at the Spitfires at the perimeter and walked away towards the station gate.

****

A smell of stale fat greeted Bryan as he walked into Xara's dining room with Ben. The cook stood behind the serving table, his face red from either heat or embarrassment. He scooped some broth into two bowls and handed them to the pilots.

'What's in this?' Bryan asked.

'Nothing much,' the man said, handing them half-slices of grey bread.

They sat down at a table and Bryan swirled a spoon around in the liquid, searching for something solid. 'No wonder I've got the shits,' he muttered.

'Have you seen this?' Ben pulled a folded copy of *The Times of Malta* from his top pocket. 'The King has awarded Malta The George Cross.'

Bryan slurped some of the warm liquid from his spoon and grimaced. 'One each? For everyone?' he asked.

Ben frowned and scanned the copy. 'Just the one, I think. Awarded to the actual island itself.'

'How very gracious of His Majesty. Where's he going to pin it?'

'Come on, Bryan. The Maltese deserve this.'

Bryan dropped his spoon into the bowl. 'What the Maltese deserve is a government with the ability to organise a piss-up in a brewery.' He tore his bread into small chunks and dropped them into his broth. 'Or more precisely, an unloading in a harbour.'

Ben folded the paper and stuffed it back into his pocket. 'I'm sure it'll come right in the end,' he said.

Monday, 20 April 1942

Bryan opened the door of his room to investigate the noise outside. A commotion of moving bodies came up the stairs and a pilot hurried along the corridor leading from the stairwell.

'What's up?' Bryan asked him as he passed.

'The RDF stations have called a large formation coming in from the west,' he said, squeezing past. 'It's the Spitfires.'

Bryan retreated into his room and shovelled his feet into his shoes. He grabbed his jacket and dived back out the door, heading towards the stairs. He trotted down the steps into a hubbub of excited chatter. Copeland was picking the men to take the first transport. Bryan looked at him with eyebrows raised and Copeland nodded.

Bryan squirmed through the crush and out of the door, Ben ducked through with him. In the courtyard, under the glimmering dawn light, a battered blue truck stood with its engine idling. Bereft of its canvas, the open back was filling with pilots. Bryan and Ben accepted helping hands and clambered onto the vehicle, elbowing out a space to stand and hanging their hands from the crossbars that had supported the erstwhile covering.

Copeland emerged and climbed into the passenger seat. The truck revved and jolted out of the courtyard, along the narrow dog-legging lane that led from the palace, between the churches and convent walls and out through the Mdina Gate to the open road that dropped from the high ground into the depression that gave its space to Ta'Qali airfield.

The northern sky was speckled with aircraft, flying down the island's spine like swifts arriving on a spring breeze. The sight drew a ragged cheer from the men jolting around in the back of the truck as it bounced and rolled over the pot-holed road.

The mitigating swarm of fighters curved gracefully into a circuit of the aerodrome and groups of three detached, one after the other, to swoop towards the landing strip. Bryan counted the circling machines. They numbered four squadrons at best; the lower end of Copeland's expectations, but enough to make a difference.

The truck rolled onto the airfield and shuddered to a halt. The rolling wave of engine noise from taxiing Spitfires enveloped the men as they tumbled off the transport and stood in a loose group, watching the arrivals. The truck growled off behind them to collect more airmen from Mdina and Bryan weaved through the throng to find Copeland at its front.

The last pair of fighters flared out and settled on the runway and the noise diminished as the propellers of previously landed aircraft clunked into stillness. Bryan squinted through the haze of dust at the bright new Spitfires lined up either side of the runway, their pilots climbing out of their cockpits and chatting as they pulled off their parachute packs.

'They can't stay there like that,' Bryan hissed. 'The bloody Germans have got RDF as well, you know.'

Copeland looked confused for a second, then realisation drained through his features. 'Fuck,' he muttered, 'you're right.' He turned to the men behind him. 'Two groups,' he yelled, 'one with Hale, one with me. Let's get these planes shifted!'

The men ran towards the nearest fighters. Bryan jumped up onto the wing and leaned into the cockpit to release the brakes. Stumbling back to the ground, he ducked under the wing and pushed his weight against the leading edge. Men shouldered in next to him and the fighter moved slowly backwards towards the perimeter, eight pilots pushing against its wings and tailplane, rolling the sagging tires over the hard ground towards the blast-pens.

Airmen jogged arduously in the other direction, their arms braced against the full petrol can that hung from each hand, their teeth clenched and chests tightened against the effort of getting fuel across to the depleted aircraft.

Minutes slipped by and sweat slid from Bryan's brow, stinging his eyes closed as he heaved against the aircraft's bulk, planting boot in front of boot in a slow and strenuous mission to save the plane.

'Whoa!'

The shout came from a man at the tailplane and Bryan wiped his eyes to see the solid walls of an ochre limestone pen embracing the machine in its sanctuary. He pushed himself upright, away from the wing, swaying slightly with the dizziness of exertion.

'Someone put the brakes on,' he called. 'Let's go and get another one.'

As the group trotted back to the runway, isolated engines coughed into life and a couple of Spitfires taxied slowly away, heading for the other side of the field.

The men gathered around another fighter and heaved it into motion. Bryan's ragged breathing dragged the corrosive vapour of spilt aviation fuel into his lungs and he choked, spitting stringy phlegm from his dried-out mouth. The strain on his thighs lessened; he glanced along the wing, more airmen had joined the effort, the Spitfire was rolling easily, backwards away from its dangerous exposure.

Behind him, Bryan heard the bark of a starter battery as another engine kicked into life. Then another sound rolled in to join it; the rising moan of air raid sirens washed over the aerodrome like a flowing tide.

'Shit!' Bryan staggered away from the wing and looked around; the Spitfire was less than halfway to the relative safety of the blast-pens. Over the harbour, away to the east, a garden of anti-aircraft shells bloomed in a tightly-packed bouquet, tiny and silent in the distance. A dread certainty rose in Bryan's throat; Grand Harbour was not the bombers' target on this morning.

'Take cover!' he shouted. 'Get away from the aircraft!'

The men bolted towards the slit-trenches outside the perimeter track. Bryan dodged away from the slashing wingtip as the abandoned Spitfire rolled backwards, slewed sideways and half-pirouetted to a halt.

The bursts over the harbour ceased, leaving the smoke from their violence to drift northwards on the breeze. Against the clearing backdrop, the bombing force eased into visibility.

'Shit.' Bryan spun on his heel and sprinted after the others as the rumble of massed engines overtook the diminishing wail of the air raid klaxon, its hand crank deserted and left to wind away its own momentum. Finally, the airfield's defences opened up with a sudden, brutal concussion.

Bryan ran by a trench crammed with cowering bodies as the first strikes hit the runway, licking waves of blast across the ground that buffeted his back. The next trench was similarly packed. With the cold finger of exposed vulnerability tickling the nape of his neck, Bryan dived behind the pile of spoil that stretched along the back of the trench line. Landing heavily on the hard ground, he fought for long seconds to suck air back into his winded lungs, then, panting against the pain in his side, he edged up the heap of sandy soil and squinted over its crest.

Explosions stitched a pattern of mayhem along the runway, disgorging the shallow earth into dun plumes and flipping aircraft to somersault into the air around their broken wings. Petrol splashed from ruptured tanks, igniting in lurid flashes of yellow and orange, balling flame around its burning vapour and rolling acrid black smoke into the air.

As the formation progressed the pattern of cascading ordnance widened, washing out from the main target, gouging holes in the perimeter track and tossing aircraft against the walls of the stone enclosure in which they'd hunkered for safety. Men, caught in the open, scampered to-and-fro like rodents on a hot plate. Some dived to the ground to squirm their bodies flat against the dry soil, others dropped with the gangly demeanour of rag-dolls, blown diagonally to earth by the vicious, flashing momentum of hot, spinning shrapnel.

The bombs ceased, giving way to the insistent boom of the AA that stuttered to a halt as the raiders processed out of range. Bryan's ears popped as the air decompressed to stillness, his eyes watering with the sharp sting of cordite that drifted across from smouldering craters.

Moments after the guns fell silent, four men, newly arrived pilots by the crispness of their uniforms, climbed out of a trench and walked slowly down the slope towards the smoking destruction on the runways, drawn on by the morbid fascination of the inexperienced. Bryan cocked his head as a menacing rasp vibrated into his ear.

'Get down!' he howled into the void between the men and the sanctuary they'd left too early.

One of them turned to look at Bryan, his pale face blank with confusion, clean, white and unsuspecting. Then the vibration swelled to a roar and the face jerked to the direction of the terrible noise. Cannon shells cascaded through the group, cartwheeling two bodies away in curling fountains of red and purple viscera. The third man ran from the carnage, stumbling over a leg that was shattered midway down his shin, his booted foot flapping behind him as he loped across the ground. The pale-faced man watched him fall as three Messerschmitt 109s slammed over at fifty feet. He dropped in terror to his knees and pressed a fist to his mouth as urine spurted and trickled through the crotch of his trousers.

Another trio of fighters raked their fire along the lines of wrecked and burning Spitfires while three more worked over the gun positions around the airfield. Wave after wave, they strafed, circled and returned to strafe again, until, with a final waggle of wings, they climbed away, formed up and headed north.

The snarl of their engines faded, leaving only the screams of the injured pilot and the sobbing of a frightened boy.

****

The candle's flame guttered and swayed, sending a thin line of greasy black smoke up to the ceiling. Wax dribbled from its wilting shoulder, glistening in the dancing light like a tear, then spreading out on the saucer and glazing to the pearlescence of a dying eye. The candlelight danced to a sudden air movement, jolting Bryan's hunched shadow around on the dining room wall. He lifted his gaze from the flame and blinked against its drifting phantom at the dark figure that entered the room.

'I was saving this for a special occasion.' Copeland sat down opposite Bryan and placed a bottle of whisky and two glasses on the table. 'And I found these in the bottom of my kitbag.' He pulled a pack of twenty from his top pocket. Bryan lit a cigarette from the candle flame while the squadron leader poured two shots of whisky.

'How many Spitfires do we have left?' Bryan asked through a haze of tobacco smoke.

'Seven,' Copeland said quietly, taking a sip from his drink. 'The Germans must've known they were coming.'

'You can probably thank the Spanish for that.' Bryan reached for his glass. 'In any case, they're close enough to see everything we do and it only takes them fifteen minutes to get here.' He shook his head in dismay. 'So, we lost forty brand new fighters, on the ground.'

'It might not matter soon,' Copeland said. 'The reconnaissance types have photographed glider strips being built in Sicily. Invasion may not be too far off.'

Bryan drained his glass and shook his head, grimacing against the liquor's harsh burn in his throat. 'Invasion is a summer sport, they won't come yet,' he said. 'I reckon we've still got a month or two to save Egypt.'

Copeland refilled their glasses. 'To do that we need supplies,' he said. 'Those Spitfires were sent to give us the air cover to bring in a convoy and keep it safe while it unloads.' He looked down into his glass. 'And we fucked it up.'

Bryan hunched forward, stubbing his cigarette into the soft wax pooling in the saucer. 'But we *know* how to do it,' he hissed. 'I was on Kenley aerodrome through the summer of '40. When we landed, they had us turned around and ready to go again in twenty minutes or less. Flying in from an aircraft carrier is no different from coming back after a patrol over the channel.'

'As long as the planes are shipped with harmonised guns and tuned radios, and if the ground crews are organised and ready, we could get the first squadron of new arrivals back up to intercept the bombers that are sent to destroy them. Get the army in to do the lifting and carrying for each crew of armourers and fitters. Assign one team for every fighter that we're expecting.' He leaned back and smiled. 'We only have to get it right once.'

Monday, 27 April 1942

The ropes thrummed with tension as the men pulled hard against the lump of stubborn metal. The charred engine rocked, shifted reluctantly and then relented. It carved a shallow furrow of ochre through the blackened patch of earth in which it sat as the team of men hauled it away towards the pile of scrap in the scrubland beyond the perimeter. Bryan and Ben sweated alongside six other pilots, dragging the weight up the incline. The engine slid in against the edge of the scrappage pile and they dropped the ropes, stretching their spines back into vertical with hands on their hips.

'I would kill my favourite aunty for a beer right now,' Ben said, wiping the sheen of perspiration from his forehead.

'That's shocking,' Bryan said. 'You have a *favourite* aunty?'

'Flight Lieutenant Hale?' The two pilots turned to see an airman hurrying towards them.

'Yes,' Bryan said, 'that's me.'

'The squadron leader wants to see you, sir, together with' – the airman checked a slip of paper in his hand – 'Pilot Officer Stevens. He's over at the readiness tent.'

Bryan and Ben walked the short distance to readiness, ignoring the protesting cat calls from the working party they left behind.

The dappled shade under the camouflage netting offered a welcome relief from the strengthening spring sunshine. Copeland sat behind the trestle desk and greeted them with a smile.

'I want you two to get back to Xara, sort out your kit and standby. You're flying out on the next available transport.'

Bryan's face flushed at the news. 'Flying out?'

Copeland nodded. 'To Gibraltar,' he said. 'You're part of a team of six pioneer pilots. You'll meet an American aircraft carrier there. She'll be loaded with sixty-odd Spitfires. You two will lead the first wave back here' – he raised his eyebrows at Bryan – 'where we shall have ample ground crews standing by for a thirty-minute turnaround to get the aircraft back in the air to protect the second and third waves.' He looked from one to the other. 'This could be our last throw of the dice. Let's see if we can make it a winner.'

PART 3

SOPRAVVIVENZA

Chapter 19

Thursday, 30 April 1942

Bryan eyed the full moon warily as it embroidered the wavelets on Marsaxlokk Bay with silver edges, and it returned his gaze with baleful disdain. Behind him, the outboard motor rattled a staccato rhythm against its own rolling echo as the small launch pulled away from the dock.

Their journey was a short one; the prow swung out towards a squat dark shape resting no more that seventy yards out in the bay. The Sunderland rocked sedately on its mooring. Its tall, narrow fuselage suggested it was a boat, but its four engines and outreaching wings proved it was a plane. The stabilising floats near the end of each wing testified to the marriage of the two.

As the launch approached, a door opened in the flying-boat's port side, close to the water. A man at the prow secured the boat to a cleat, and Bryan, Ben and four other pilots threw their kitbags through the door and clambered in after them. A man in flying gear watched as the launch pulled clear, then closed the door. He indicated the fold-down seats arranged under the portholes that punctuated the side of the fuselage, then ducked away to climb a short ladder into the cockpit.

Bryan sat down and pulled the lap-strap tight. His seat vibrated as the engines swelled into life one after the other. The Sunderland drifted away from its moorings for a few minutes and then surged forward with urgent intent as the throttles opened up.

Bryan craned his neck to peer through the porthole above his shoulder. A foaming wake streamed past, gradually diminishing, together with the battering noise against the hull, as the speed increased and the giant aeroplane lifted away from the water.

Bryan kept his eyes locked on the moonlit silhouette of the receding island until he could no longer distinguish it from the sea's black mass.

Friday, 1 May 1942

A Wellington bomber taxied slowly along the runway where it extended into the bay, like a walrus walking the plank. At the end, it swung through a ponderous semi-circle and sat vibrating under its own idling engines, as if steeling itself for its run along a strip that ended with the waters of the Mediterranean Sea. The engines' grumbling rose to a roar and the boxy fuselage strained against its brakes for a moment, then rolled ever faster along the tarmac, finally wallowing into the air and banking away to starboard across the sea.

Ben pointed across to the dusty terrain that rose away from the barbed wire entanglements on the other side of the runway. 'Where's that?' he asked.

Bryan sniffed. 'Spain.'

'Are they at war with us?'

'Not officially. But I suspect they wouldn't be happy if we win.'

Ben scratched his head. 'Surely they could simply walk across and take over if they wanted to.'

'They could,' Bryan mused, 'but then we'd take their Moroccan possessions, and they don't want that to happen.' He smiled at Ben. 'Diplomacy,' he announced, 'is the delicate balance of back-scratching and arse-kicking. Come on, let's go for a drink.'

They turned their backs on the border, the barbed wire, the gun emplacements and the Spanish, and walked through the North District towards the town of Gibraltar. Military vehicles plied the narrow thoroughfare to and from the docks, so they diverted up a side road in search of their refreshment.

A small group of laughing sailors bundled out of a door and weaved their back-slapping way up the road. Bryan and Ben watched them go, then stepped into the dim interior the party had just vacated. Tables filled the room and a bar lined one wall. People at the tables had plates of food before them that swathed their faces with sweet steam as they chewed and chatted with contentment.

Ben nudged Bryan and nodded at the diners. 'They've got food,' he whispered. 'It looks like real food, too.'

Bryan nodded, the saliva prickling at the base of his gums. 'Follow me,' he said and walked to the bar.

The barman paused in his glass polishing. 'Yes, sir?'

Bryan raised his eyebrows. 'Beer?' he asked.

The barman mirrored his questioning expression. 'Pints?' he countered.

'Yes.' Bryan nodded, pursing his lips in appreciation. 'Pints.'

The barman vanished into the tap room and returned with two large, straight glasses filled with amber liquid. Bryan picked one up and took an exploratory swig.

'Good grief,' he muttered. 'English beer.'

****

An hour later, the two pilots sat picking over the sea bass skeletons on their plates, searching for any remaining shreds of the smoky flesh and mopping up the buttery juices with crisp white bread.

'I'd forgotten,' Ben murmured as he laid his knife and fork on the table and leaned back in his chair. 'I had truly forgotten.'

'We won't be here long; we need to make hay while the sun shines.' Bryan swilled the last of his ale and caught the eye of a waitress. The girl came over and began clearing the table.

'Where's the best hotel in town?' he asked her. 'One where they serve cocktails.'

'That will be The Rock, sir,' she said. 'It's not far, but it is mostly uphill.'

****

They paused for a moment in the sun's strengthening warmth. Above them, the long, whitewashed frontage of The Rock Hotel nestled against its backdrop of weathered limestone. The pale expanse of stone was shot through with scrubby bushes that softened its rough visage.

'Now I'm thirsty,' Bryan muttered as they stepped off the road and resumed their slog up the hotel's parallel and precipitous driveway. Breathing heavily, they pushed through the hotel doors into the lobby, revelling in the wash of cooler air across their foreheads.

Hand-painted wooden signs pointed their way through the building to the bar. The barman took their order for Manhattans and mixed them in a gleaming chrome cocktail shaker. Bryan paid, they stepped out onto a covered balcony and found an empty table in the shade. A copper-coloured cat roused itself from a doze in the corner, stretched first its front and then its rear limbs, and padded across to sit by Bryan's foot, turning its green eyes to watch his face in hopeful speculation.

Set out below the high-perched balcony, hugging the waters nearest the isthmus, dozens of naval vessels, transport and combat ships, lay on their moorings. A wide expanse of empty water separated the furthermost boat from the Spanish coast nearly five miles away.

'That's why the Krauts know about every bloody thing we send to Malta.' Bryan nodded at the hazy strip of land on the horizon. 'The bloody Spaniards with their German binoculars-'

'Hello, Bryan.'

The female voice derailed his monologue and he felt a cable of tension tighten across his shoulders.

'I thought it looked like you,' the voice concluded.

Bryan glanced at Ben's startled visage and turned to find a petite blonde figure standing behind him.

'Hello, Katie,' he breathed. 'Well, this is certainly a surprise.'

The cat wrapped itself around the newcomer's calf, rubbing its chin backwards and forwards while its throat rattled with a rough, bronchial purr.

Ben stood up and stepped away from his seat. 'Would you like to sit down?' He held the chair for Katie, then picked up his drink. He winked at Bryan and wandered off inside to explore the bar.

'May I get you a drink?' Bryan asked.

'No, thank you.' She reached out and picked the cocktail stick from Bryan's glass, sliding it between her teeth to liberate its cherry. 'Glad to see you got off Malta alive. Where are you heading?'

Bryan lit two cigarettes and handed one to Katie. 'We're going back in a few days. There's still a lot of work that needs doing.'

A mischievous smile creased her face. 'How's the love life?'

Bryan's eyes narrowed. 'Less frantic, it has to be said.'

'What about your mystery woman?' Katie picked up his drink and took a sip. 'Is she still holding out?'

'That's different,' he said, noticing with self-conscious surprise the hardening of his tone, 'it's not like we met at a dance.' A pang of regret at the implicit slur crossed his face and he softened his voice. 'It's far more complicated than that.'

Katie took another sip of his drink, pursed her lips and appraised his face. 'I think of you sometimes,' she confessed. 'We were damn good at being lovers.' She smiled at a private flash of recollection. 'More so because I didn't need you to actually love me – and you were never in any danger of doing so.' She caught the look that flashed in his eyes. 'Oh, there's a lot about me you liked, but there was something missing, something I simply didn't have.' She took another sip of the ruddy-hued cocktail. 'You're a charming man, Bryan. I'm tempted to say that you're a beautiful man. But I've only seen you from the position of a plaything. I imagine you're a very different proposition when you're trawling for real love.'

'Have you heard from you husband?' Another pang. He looked away from her and stubbed his cigarette into the ashtray.

'Yes.' Her voice was level, unperturbed by the goad. 'He's been wounded and shipped home.'

'Well, you can be proud that he's done his bit.'

'Not really.' She crushed her cigarette onto the smouldering remains of his. 'It was an accident during transit. Someone dropped their rifle and it went off. Blew his kneecap across the room.' She sighed. 'At least I know he'll be there when I get home.'

Bryan looked back into her face and her eyes sparkled with affection.

'Listen to some advice,' she said. 'It's not possible to change the way somebody else feels; you simply cannot move the mountain to Mohammed. If this woman doesn't love you now, she probably never will. That's a shame… for both of you.'

'Katie!' A British naval officer stood at the doorway leading to the bar.

Katie held up her hand to acknowledge him and Bryan noticed her ring was missing. She pushed his drink back across the table.

'I think I *could've* fallen in love with you. At another time… in another place,' she whispered. 'But I'm fairly certain I would never have moved your mountain.' She stood and smiled down at him. 'Good luck, Bryan. I hope you make it through.'

Saturday, 2 May 1942

At the top of the rock the breeze scudded in from the Mediterranean and looped over the hard ridge of limestone to run down the slope into the town. Ben stood with his eyes closed, facing out to sea, the cooling current caressing his forehead.

'Maybe we should slow down on the drinking,' he said. 'We'll be asked to fly a plane sooner or later.'

Bryan stood off the path with his back to the wind. His urine splashed onto the stone sending a whirl of acrid steam rolling up over the rough surface. He gripped a cigarette between his teeth and his gaze was locked on a macaque that perched on a ledge, scratching its sandy-grey fur and watching him with intense curiosity.

'No need to worry just yet.' He buttoned up his fly and joined Ben on the path. 'Look.'

He pointed downwind to the bay far below them. Floating breakwaters with invisible skirts of chain-linked metal netting corralled the mass of vessels moored along the floating pontoons that pushed outwards from the shore. 'They haven't made space for an aircraft carrier yet. We're safe for a day or two.'

The two pilots started down the steep path, stepping gingerly over its treacherous, jagged surface.

'Are you going to see Katie again?' Ben asked over his shoulder.

'She didn't ask,' Bryan said. 'Anyway, it looks like she's found another dancing partner.'

'Shame,' Ben intoned. 'She's sweet.'

They lurched on down the slope.

'You never speak about a girlfriend,' Bryan said.

'That's because I haven't had one.'

'What, not ever?'

'There was a girl at school. We held hands a few times, nothing more than that.'

'Ha!' Bryan's shout of triumph echoed off the rock face. 'I think we've just decided on the target for tonight.'

****

They descended to street level, arriving sober and thirsty. Bryan led the way, peering down side streets and alleys strewn with litter. From one alley, a laughing woman emerged flanked by two matelots. Bryan stopped at the alley's entrance and scanned the buildings; one had a rough sign suspended over a door that swung open as another couple emerged.

'Down here,' he urged, 'there's a bar down here.'

They walked to the door through the gathering dusk and pushed through into the bar beyond. Scattered tables filled two connecting rooms with a bar set against the back wall of the furthest. Tobacco smoke roiled in thick coils around the exposed beams, condensing onto the beaded amber stain of nicotine that streaked the painted ceiling between.

Bryan and Ben body-swerved between the tables, zig-zagging towards the bar where they ordered two beers, lit cigarettes and surveyed the room. Most tables were filled, their occupants' chatter churning in competition with the general clamour in the room. In the far corner, two girls sat alone. One was engrossed in cleaning under her nails with a cocktail stick, the other was looking directly at Bryan.

185

'Come on,' Bryan said, 'let's socialise.'

As they crossed the room, the woman held the eye-contact, pushing her red ringlets behind her ear. Her companion continued her manicure and didn't look up until they arrived at the table.

'Good evening, ladies. My name's Bryan, this is Ben. May we join you?'

The redhead flashed a broad smile. 'Of course. Monique' – she touched her breastbone with her fingertips – 'and Charlotte.'

Bryan reached for the bottle on the table, twisting it so the label faced him. He raised his eyebrows to Monique, she smiled and shrugged. Bryan flagged down a passing waitress and ordered another bottle of the same.

****

Two hours later the group emerged from the bar into the darkened alley, Ben leaning on Charlotte's shoulder, the girl holding another bottle of wine.

'It's not far from here,' Monique said, 'just a couple of streets across.'

The pavements were busier now the evening was older and the sounds of music and shouted altercations drifted through the air. Bryan walked side-by-side with Monique behind the other couple.

'Are you here for long?' Monique asked.

'No,' Bryan said.

'No-one ever is.' She sighed.

'Isn't that good for business?'

'Yes, but it would be nice to make some friends.'

They reached a terrace of whitewashed houses and Monique unlocked a front door that opened directly into a small room. The space held a wooden table with four chairs, a leather sofa, creased and stained with age and a chipped oak dresser. In the far corner, behind the sofa, was a gas hob and a steel sink. In the opposite corner, an opening led to a short corridor lined with three doors.

Bryan and Ben sat down at the table, Monique retrieved four wine glasses and a corkscrew from a cupboard under the sink and Charlotte vanished down the corridor. Bryan took the corkscrew and squeaked it into the cork.

'Cosy little place you have,' he said, pulling the cork and pouring wine into the glasses.

Monique sat down opposite him. 'It's not the best part of town,' she said, 'but it's... convenient.'

The sound of a toilet flush drifted from the corridor and moments later Charlotte sauntered, shoeless into the room. She picked up a glass of wine and started back towards the corridor, plucking at Ben's jacket sleeve as she passed.

Bryan pretended not to notice his friend's wide-eyed surprise, instead he studied the wine in his glass as Ben stood up with exaggerated carefulness and slipped from the room.

Bryan looked up into a face that might've been quite beautiful only a few short years ago. 'Monique isn't your real name, is it?' He lit two cigarettes and passed one to her.

She took a delicate draw on the smoke. 'Why would I use my real name?'

A metallic thump and a creak of springs sounded from down the corridor.

'Would you mind me asking what it is?'

She smiled and her eyelids fluttered down for a moment. 'Giselle,' she said. 'My real name is Giselle.'

Bryan leaned forward on the table. 'That's far prettier,' he said.

She mirrored his movement, bringing their faces close together. 'My mother hoped I might one day be a dancer.'

The creak of the springs returned, slight and slowly rhythmic.

'Perhaps, one day, you will be.'

She smiled again, studying his face. Her hand moved over his and she rubbed the soft pad of her thumb into the junction between his ring and middle finger. 'So,' she murmured, 'what would you like?'

'Coffee.'

She frowned and drew her face back. 'Coffee?'

'Yes. Do you have any?'

She stood, pulled a percolator and a battered tin from the dresser and crossed to the hob. The squeaking springs increased in tempo.

'It's not often a man involved in this war displays such restraint in my company,' she said. The burner coughed into flame at the touch of her lighted match.

'The war's an all-round beastly business,' he said. 'Sometimes it's just nice to make friends.'

The smell of coffee spread through the room and the creaks grew marginally in volume.

'How many men have you killed?' The question's simplicity belied its layers of sorrowful resignation.

Bryan swivelled in his chair to watch her setting two cups and saucers on a tray. 'I've actually never worked it out… two dozen maybe.' He scratched his cheek absently. 'I've only ever seen one body close up.'

She returned to the table with the tray and sat down. 'How did that make you feel?'

He swivelled back and hunched on his elbows. 'Well, there was a dog eating his face at the time, so I think that might've spoiled the moment.'

The squeaking redoubled in volume and tempo, ran away with itself then shuddered into silence.

'How much?' Bryan nodded towards the corridor.

Giselle poured the coffee and handed him a cup. 'I'm afraid I'll have to charge for me as well, even though you haven't used it.'

Bryan nodded, pulling out his wallet. 'Don't let on that we've had to pay,' he said. 'He thinks we're having fun. It would spoil it for him if he knew we're in a knocking shop.'

****

The two pilots walked back towards the RAF barracks through streets dotted with groups of servicemen moving from bar to bar under the jaded surveillance of patrolling MPs. Ben wobbled slightly and Bryan handicapped his pace to compensate.

'Beautiful night,' Ben announced as they walked. 'Stars.'

'That's the one good thing about a blackout,' Bryan said.

'Yes, but… romance,' Ben continued earnestly, 'romance is a very beautiful thing as well.'

Bryan gave his companion a sideways glance. 'I'm sure it is.'

They walked in silence for a few moments, Ben's face creased into a grin.

'Is this what it feels like to be in love?' Ben clutched his right hand to his heart like a bad thespian.

'Almost certainly not.'

Ben regarded his companion, eyes narrowed with scepticism. 'How *does* it feel, then?'

'It hurts, Ben,' Bryan said. 'It bloody well hurts.'

Chapter 20

Thursday, 7 May 1942

Bryan stood next to his kit-bag, Ben and the other lead pilots gathered around him. The pontoon beneath them undulated in resonance to the restrained swell diffracting past the breakwaters. Beyond those barriers, backlit by the westering sun, the ponderous bulk of a monstrous ship slid into the bay with the sluggish momentum of a grounding iceberg. Offset at the vessel's centre, a tall superstructure bristled with aerials. From a short, angled mast the Stars and Stripes swayed in the breeze. Below the flag, figures moved to and fro along elevated walkways. The carrier's long flight deck held ranks of sand-coloured Spitfires, gathered like roosting gulls on its the rear half.

'Well, well,' Bryan muttered. 'The Americans have woken up at last.'

Two massive anchors dropped away from the hull, dragging heavy chains behind them. They plunged into the water and splashed huge plumes up the grey-painted prow. Halfway along the vessel, close below its flight deck, a large hatch opened and a stairway lowered on cables, its last treads dipping into the water's surface.

A small navy launch scudded across the bay, slowing down and curving around to come alongside the pontoon.

'Six passengers for the *USS Wasp*,' a naval rating called out from the boat. 'Step aboard please.'

Friday, 8 May 1942

The pilots filed into the large briefing room, some picking fibres of their breakfast bacon from between their teeth. Bryan waited for the commotion to ease as the men settled into the rows of chairs that faced the dais. When silence was close, he stood and surveyed the faces before him.

'Good morning, gentlemen,' he began, and hush descended with his words. 'I can confirm that we are headed for Malta, where it is hoped this force will make a decisive difference to the air defence of the harbours and the people that live and work around them.

'For the protection of this very valuable American vessel, your Spitfires are fitted with extra fuel tanks so the captain can get rid of us as soon as possible and get back to safety. When it comes to it, you must obey every instruction you are given by the crew on the flight deck. They know more about getting something airborne from a carrier than you do. Test your fuel taps as soon as you get to a safe altitude. If they're faulty, turn back and ditch. They'll lower a boat to pick you out of the sea.

'We'll form into six squadron-strength flights, each led by one of us.' He gestured to the five men sitting behind him on the dais. 'There'll be three waves. The first flies to Ta'Qali, second to Luqa, third to Hal Far. Upon arrival, you will each be met by a dedicated ground crew. Taxi according to their instructions. When they are happy, you will hand over your plane to the fresh pilot who will be waiting at your dispersal point.

'The Germans already know we're coming, how many of us there are, and how vital it is to their interests to kill as many of us as they can in the shortest time possible. So, there will, in all probability, be packs of 109s waiting for us when we arrive. Remember, the need to carry extra fuel means you are not carrying any ammunition. We'll have to rely on the Royal Artillery, and however many aircraft Malta's fighter control can put up, to keep them away from us.

'Some of you will find yourselves on the general flying roster the day after you arrive. Nothing you've learned during interceptions over England or sweeps over France will help you in Malta. We are not expecting to win the battle we are fighting; we always have far too little and our enemy always has far too much. Rather, it is our task to hold the Germans at bay while using and losing as few of our resources as possible.

'In Malta we are forced to fly defensively rather than offensively. We can't afford the fuel to run regular patrols, so you'll be scrambled when you're needed. Once airborne, your only targets are the bombers, so ignore the fighters as much as you can. If you do get into a scrap, get low and circle an airfield. You never know, the Bofors gunners might spare some ammo to help you out.

'Do not force land anywhere on the island. There are too many stone walls waiting to kill you. And do not chase anything out to sea; you're likely to meet the next lot on their way in. There are no boats to pick you up if you are not in sight of the island, and sometimes not even if you are.'

Bryan cast another look around the upturned faces, some brows carried furrows of concern.

'It gets worse,' he continued. 'Ordinary standards of living no longer mean anything on Malta. You will eat food that tastes like shit, it will very likely give you the shits, and once you have the shits, you will keep them for a long time. You will go to sleep with flies on your face, you will wake up with flies on your face, and the only place to wash properly will be the sea. You will piss into the last man's urine because water is too precious to waste on a toilet flush. You will spend your days covered in dust that will turn your clothes into sandpaper. There's no booze, no cigarettes and the girls are all Catholics. Within days you will wish you'd never boarded this ship.

'You've taken on the most difficult job of the war so far, and it starts tomorrow at dawn. I suggest you enjoy what the galley has to offer for dinner and get a good night's rest. Pick up your flight maps on the way out, and good luck.'

The scraping of chairs and the sudden eruption of chatter filled the room. Ben appeared at Bryan's shoulder.

'You could've told me,' he said, 'about Charlotte. She was a prostitute, wasn't she?'

'I would've thought the clue was in the name.'

'It's not funny. I made a fool of myself.'

Bryan smiled. 'The only fool in that house was me. You have no idea how much I paid for a bad cup of coffee.'

Saturday, 9 May 1942

The sun's disc incised its flaring arc on the horizon ahead of the aircraft carrier. Bryan and Ben climbed the stairs to the flight deck ahead of the pilots assigned to the first two squadrons heading for Ta'Qali. The deck bustled with American crewmen, moving with restrained urgency for the task ahead which they knew, once completed, would allow their ship to turn away from these increasingly dangerous waters.

Bryan winked at his companion. 'Good luck,' he said.

Ben smiled in reply. 'I'll see you at home.'

Ben walked back through the gaggle of fighters standing on the deck. Bryan went the other way to seek out the one at the front, painfully conscious of the runway length the other parked machines had stolen from him.

His aircraft sat on tyres that flattened noticeably under the gross weight of the overloaded fighter. Stretching the full width between the wing-roots, a squared-off fuel tank nestled against the fuselage with the word *'Gassed'* chalked on its side. Bryan handed his kit-bag to a sailor who ducked under the wing and squeezed it into an ammunition compartment, deftly reattaching the wing-panel with a couple of tweaks from a screwdriver.

Bryan swung the parachute pack onto his back and clambered onto the wing. A sailor helped him into the cockpit and pulled his straps tight.

Bryan looked into the man's young face. 'Thank you,' he said.

'You're welcome, sir.' He tapped his fingers against his temple in salute. 'Good luck.'

Bryan felt the massive ship wallow beneath him as the helm adjusted to run directly into the wind. The sailor clambered down and joined the others gathered around the aeroplane. Two men wheeled a starter battery alongside and Bryan fired up the engine, checking the gauges as they twitched into life. Ahead of him, to his right-hand side, the yellow-shirted controller made winding motions with his hands. Bryan eased the throttle forward and noticed three men gather in front of each wingtip, pushing backwards against the leading edge, bracing their feet against the deck, helping to hold the vibrating aircraft motionless against the propeller's thrust.

The controller abruptly stopped his flurry of movement and slashed his arm horizontally to point to the prow. The men at the wings let go their grip, dropping flat onto the deck and Bryan released the squealing brakes. The Spitfire lurched forward and picked up speed, racing along the fore-shortened deck towards the water-filled chasm at its end.

The tail lifted easily and the baleful eye of the rising sun filled the windshield. Abruptly the rumbling of wheels ceased and the Spitfire's corpulent belly dragged at its fragile buoyancy, drooping its body towards the wavetops. Bryan eased back on the stick, flattening the craft's trajectory, waiting for the dragging undercarriage to retract. The wheels clunked home and Bryan flew straight and low to build his air speed before curving up into a shallow climb to circle the carrier.

As he climbed, he watched the second fighter heave away from its standing-start and make its dash for flight. It sagged into the air, expending lift against weight for long seconds of floundering uncertainty before the trade was lost. The nose dipped sharply into a catastrophic stall and the Spitfire dropped into the water. The tail and starboard wing rose vertically, like the desperate hands of a drowning man, before the carrier's bow wave broke over the doomed fighter and it sunk from sight.

The next fledgling fought the same battle, but won.

Every plane that followed bestowed a few extra feet of flight deck to the one that came after, and within thirty minutes the first two squadrons were formed-up and cruising east over the featureless sea.

****

The long flight finally brought Sicily onto the horizon, its coast imposing a dark line into the blue-to-blue division of sea and sky, and Bryan eased their course to south-easterly. As the profile of that island thickened and slid by into his port quarter, Bryan detected aircraft dotting the sky between the distant coast and his formation. He strained his eyes to count them. There were at least eight fighters, probably 109s, maintaining a shadowing course, unwilling to engage three times their number, evidently unaware that their enemy flew unarmed.

The strange off-set formation flew on, stable in its stalemate of perceived dangers; the hunters content to wait for the odds, as they understood them, to change in their favour. Ahead, the twin islands of Malta and Gozo rolled out of the sea, like bronze flotsam floating on a placid blue lake.

Bryan kept the land mass on his starboard side; Gozo slid past, followed by the rocky north end of Malta. He eased the formation into a shallow descent, noting that the hyena pack on his flank chose to maintain their height advantage.

'Wasp Leader to Fighter Control.' Bryan broke the long radio silence. 'We are approaching base with unwelcome company.'

'Hello, Wasp Leader. We've been tracking them. We've sent up a reception party.'

Bryan banked westwards, making landfall over the bay between Sliema and Valletta. Down to his left, all along the edges of Grand Harbour, puffs of gun smoke dotted the quaysides. Bryan glanced into his rear-view mirror and smiled with satisfaction as a densely knit concentration of shells burst in and around the German fighters, causing them to bank away from the harbour. A small gaggle of Hurricanes sliced across from the south of the island, scything over the harbour to engage the intruders. Bryan relaxed, winding his formation into a circuit around Ta'Qali and leading the first few machines in to land.

He bumped down and taxied to the end of the landing strip where an airman waved him down. The man had a placard hanging around his neck which bore the number '1' thickly scratched onto the card with charcoal.

The man caught his eye and mouthed *'Follow me.'* Two more airmen ran to his aircraft, each one grabbing a wingtip, and guided him off the runway.

As he snaked his Spitfire away along the perimeter, Bryan noticed many new protective pens had been thrown together from blocks of yellow limestone, crude but imposing. Each had a number similarly scribed in charcoal on its back wall.

The airmen led Bryan into a stone pen. He cut the engine and clambered out onto the wing, sliding down to the ground on stiff legs. He unhooked his parachute and laid it on the wing-root as armourers pounced on both sides of the aircraft, stripping off the panels and slotting in ammunition boxes. Bryan's kitbag was dragged out and he placed it in the corner of the pen. A pile of two-dozen petrol cans stood along the back wall and a team of four manhandled them across to the Spitfire, passing them up to an airman on a stepladder who tipped the fuel through a funnel into the aircraft's depleted tank. A crew chief supervised the operation, walking round the fighter with a critical glare.

'Where's the new pilot?' Bryan asked the man. 'Who am I handing over to?'

The crew chief scanned the blast-pen. 'Is he still not back?'

'Back from where?'

'The shitter.' The man grimaced. 'He's got The Dog, apparently.'

The armourers clanked the wing panels shut and moved to help with the petrol cans. Bryan glanced towards the latrines and sidled back to the parachute on the wing. The sharp scent of aviation fuel filled the air as the tank topped out and the spillage evaporated on the warm cowling. The airman descended, handed on the half-empty can and dragged his stepladder away from the fuselage.

'Starter battery!' the crew chief bawled at the sky. Two men careened around the wall of the pen dragging a trolley between them. They ducked under the fuselage and attached the apparatus.

Stillness descended around the aircraft. The crew chief swivelled his head towards the latrines, the airmen who stood amongst a scattering of empty fuel cans followed his gaze. No pilot appeared.

'I'll take it,' Bryan said, hoisting the parachute pack onto his shoulders.

The crew chief looked from Bryan to the latrines, to his clipboard and back to Bryan. Shaking his head, he walked away, relinquishing responsibility for the change of plan.

Bryan clambered back into the cockpit and started the engine. The airmen guided him back to the runway where two more of the new Spitfires were lining up for take-off. Bryan waved away the airmen, squeezed the throttle forward and followed the other two fighters down the runway and into the air.

Bryan's face split with a fierce grin of triumph; it was barely twenty minutes since they'd left behind the Luftwaffe in the barrage over Grand Harbour. Now fully armed, they'd meet the raiding bombers that must surely be on their way.

The trio of fighters circled Ta'Qali. Below them, more Spitfires trundled out of blast-pens, powered down the runway and clawed into the air.

'Falcon Leader to Fighter Control. Newly arrived wasps are now airborne.' Bryan recognised Copeland's voice on the wireless.

'Hello Falcon Leader. Visitors are arriving as expected, due north, angels twelve. Watch out for more wasps in the vicinity. Good luck.'

The formation swept around the last curve of its circuit and climbed away north, along the island's spine. The terrain roughened and settlements grew sparse, then the rugged northern headlands loomed into view, softened by sea-haze rolling through the channel between the islands.

'Falcon Leader to Falcon aircraft. That looks like our bandits at two o'clock.'

Bryan scanned that patch of sky. Two formations approached; a dozen or more bombers in a tight cluster, and maybe twice that number of fighters flying high escort above them.

'Twenty-plus aircraft at eleven o'clock.' A voice Bryan didn't recognise. 'Must be the second wave from the carrier.'

'Alright' – Copeland's voice was level and assured – 'let's break up those bombers. Avoid the 109s as long as possible. Tally-ho!'

The Spitfires drifted into a looser formation as they curved towards the bomber formation, intent on slashing through them on a near head-on course. Bryan flipped his safety to 'Fire' and ballooned upwards to avoid the Spitfires ahead of him.

As the indistinct jumble of silhouettes grew larger, he saw they were Junkers 88s. He flicked a glance at the 109s still flying straight and level high above him, then jabbed the firing button, squirting an un-aimed burst into the mass of German raiders before pulling up to zoom above their ranks.

The two formations flashed through each other above the foam-crested waves of the rocky northern shore. Bryan held his course for a second to allow the air to clear around him, then pulled into a tight turn to port, circling back over the bay that cut a chunk from the ridged headland. Bryan levelled out, his nose pointing south.

Trails of smoke marked the fiery dives of two raiders. Others flared away in steep banks, dumping bombs and deserting the battle. But half of the bomber crews pressed on; their progress trailed by the whips of tracer fire they lashed back at their gathering tormentors.

Bryan squinted up to the escort, still unmoved by their comrades' plight. Then he saw the reason for their discretion; the *USS Wasp's* second incoming wave flew a near parallel course to the raid. The attackers had never seen the Maltese sky so full of British aircraft.

Bryan picked his target amongst the persisting bombers, pushed his throttle fully forward and wallowed left and right to avoid return fire. No gunner found his mark, and the Junkers swelled to fill his windscreen like a fattened calf. The pounding of his two cannons rattled his teeth as detonations peppered the bomber's starboard wing, tearing chunks from the cowling and throwing its propeller into a juddering elliptical spin.

As his guns spat their last shells and dropped to silence, the German aircraft lurched into a steep left bank, spikes of flame flashing from its engine. Bryan banked the other way, diving away from battle to run for home against the mottled mantle of Malta's rocky hide.

****

Bryan joined several other returning Spitfires in the circuit over Ta'Qali. When he landed, he was met by a capering airman with a number around his neck who led him to a blast-pen where another ground crew swarmed over his machine.

Bryan climbed down from the wing, flexing stiff muscles and rubbing buttocks numbed by long hours sitting on a hard parachute pack in a cramped cockpit. A Spitfire taxied past behind its numbered chaperone. Copeland pointed at him from the opened cockpit and mouthed '*Wait there.*'

Bryan pulled off his leather helmet and scratched at the stubble on his cheek. His skin was greasy with old sweat and grime, his tongue felt dry behind his teeth and his shoulders ached from the tensions of combat.

The noise of chatter distracted him and he turned to regard the armourers, one kneeling on the wing, the other crouching on the ground below. Their faces sparkled with smiles as they joked with each other over their task. The men heaving the heavy fuel cans up the side of the fuselage expressed the strain of their physical effort with a grim visage and gritted teeth, but they worked swiftly with an efficiency of movement borne out of enthusiasm for their task. Bryan cast his gaze over the wider field which bustled with activity, all carried out with a new sense of purpose. If it wasn't overtaken by some new calamity, it might blossom into optimism.

'What are you doing, Hale?' Copeland's voice broke into his thoughts.

'There was no-one ready to take over.' Bryan turned to face his squadron leader. 'So, I got it off the ground.'

Copeland glanced at the armourers lifting fresh ammunition into the wing. 'Were you in that combat?' he asked.

'Yes. I was right behind you.'

Copeland mirrored the grin on Bryan's face. 'Right, you can stand down now. You've done enough work for one day and I think the rush is over.' He cast a glance across the field. 'It's worked, hasn't it? We've cracked it.'

Bryan followed his gaze. 'Until the fuel runs out.'

'Now, about that.' Copeland's eyes flashed with a conspiratorial glint. 'They're running in a minelayer loaded with stores from Gibraltar. The cheeky bastards have disguised it as a Vichy French destroyer. If all goes well, it should be here tomorrow.' He surveyed Bryan's wearied face. 'I'm sending a couple of trucks down in the morning to join the queue. Why don't you hitch a lift? I'm sure you're keen to catch up on your church attendance.'

Copeland strode off, shouting at an airman to find a fresh pilot for Bryan's aircraft. Bryan wandered along the perimeter until he found pen number one. He retrieved his kit-bag and walked slowly towards the aerodrome gate in search of transport to Mdina. The defiant roar of Merlin engines reverberated in his ears as half-a-dozen Spitfires rose from the runway and climbed away to the north.

Sunday, 10 May 1942

The truck dropped Bryan off on the western root of Valletta's peninsula before heading south to skirt the rump of Grand Harbour and seek out the docked minelayer. It was a fair walk into the city, but it was still early, so he set out at an easy pace. He stayed as close to the water as the road allowed, stopping every now and then to survey the battered docklands on the opposite bank. After thirty minutes walking along the waterfront the view down one of the main docks opened up. There sat the minelayer, her superstructure backed with a row of three funnels, her decks and the adjacent quayside thronged with figures working to unload her precious cargo.

A flight of six Spitfires droned in a lazy curve to the south of the docks. Abruptly their engine note raised and they climbed away northwards, out to sea. The song of their motors blended in with the rising wail of sirens, droning their warning across the capital and its harbours. The civilians sharing Bryan's vigil on the waterfront scurried away to seek refuge. He crossed the road, found a doorway to give him rudimentary shelter and lifted his gaze to the skies over the harbour mouth.

Sprinkles of glittering tracer and the arcing contrails of whirling aircraft witnessed the outbreak of desperate combats far away over the water. More engines roared across Valletta, out of Bryan's sight, blocked by the building against which he huddled, a squadron at least, maybe more. The sirens wound down through a grinding moan to dwindle into silence, their warning delivered, their soldier-operators scampered back to stations with their gun-crews.

Below the skirmishing fighters, a legion of aircraft squirmed into view from the haze. Bryan squinted into the bleary brightness and the vanguard sharpened in contrast against the blue. With inverted gull wings and fixed undercarriage, the strangely demonic silhouettes of Stuka dive bombers advanced on the harbour with the slow menace of medieval siege engines.

The air boomed with shuddering reverberations as the heavy anti-aircraft emplacements at the harbour mouth coughed shells into the sky. Explosions rent the air ahead of the bomber formation, stitching a box of jagged shrapnel between the attackers and their target. One Stuka sagged from the formation with flames flaring from its wing root as it curved away from its fellows. Abruptly its wing folded up against the fuselage, throwing the bomber into a spiralling dive. It tumbled like a broken bird over and over itself to hit the surf and disintegrate into cascading shards as the bomb held snug against its belly erupted in a cascade of soiled water.

The German formation pressed on into the air above the harbour, processing with eery slowness, seemingly indifferent to the barrage as they hunted for their prey. A lethargic coil of smoke belched from the minelayer's funnels, too late to fully screen it from the circling vultures.

The foremost group of Stukas rolled onto their backs with lazy menace, then pulled their noses into near vertical dives towards the docked vessel. The dive-bombers' howling was joined by a new chattering counterpoint as the lighter Bofors guns welcomed the attackers into their range. Tracers stitched a canopy over the water from both sides of the harbour and the Stukas zoomed into parabolic climbs, leaving plumes of water and shattered concrete as testament to several near misses. The dockside teemed with figures fleeing the ship, running between abandoned trucks and crouching against walls as the blast waves buffeted their bodies.

Another section of Spitfires curved in from the south, higher than the attackers. Flipping one-by-one onto their backs, they pulled into dives that mimicked their enemy and chased the boxy tails of their adversaries through the thick interweave of ground fire.

Six more concussions pulsed across the harbour as bomb loads struck. Two Stukas slammed into the water followed by a flaming Spitfire, all three falling victim to the Bofors crews. Four more dive-bombers clawed out of their dives, tracers spitting backwards at the defending fighters that harried them as they jinked away towards the sea, seeking the protection of their sorely pre-occupied escorts.

Bryan pressed his back against the warm, dry wood of the door as shrapnel dropped from the barrage with a metallic tinkle on the smooth stones of the waterfront road. The breeze changed, peeling the smokescreen away from the water and rolling it in the wake of the fleeing raiders. The minelayer emerged into clear view, upright and undamaged. The harbour guns fell silent and the angry buzz of aero engines receded.

Bryan slipped from the doorway and ducked up the nearest side street that led him northwards into Valletta. The city's narrow streets, congested in better times by people and commerce, were now truncated by piles of dislocated stone blocks piled high against walls that sagged and threatened the reckless passer-by.

Bryan zig-zagged northwards like a child in a maze as the all-clear droned out from the harbour. Few people moved through the lanes and alleys, those that did skittered with a crouching gait, like alley-cats unexpectedly caught in the open.

With relief, Bryan found himself emerging onto Bakery Street, its length mercifully clear of debris, and headed towards St Augustine Church. As he approached, he saw the main doors were closed, but a priest stood on the pavement at a side door. As his congregation filed out, he crossed himself and touched each passing forehead in blessing. Bryan took up station across the road and watched the outflow of worshippers.

Jacobella emerged and responded to the cleric's blessing with downcast eyes and a slight curtsy. The priest placed a hand on her shoulder and said something further. Jacobella regarded the man and a flicker of surprise flashed across her features. Then she glanced over the priest's shoulder and caught Bryan's eye. Her jaw dropped and her face reddened with embarrassment. She cast her eyes down again and nodded as the preacher finished his piece, a faint smile tickled across her lips to displace her discomfiture.

The priest turned to the next person emerging from the small door. Thus released, Jacobella crossed the road with Lučija clutching her hand.

'Bryan!' Jacobella reached out and hugged him, kissing his cheek and squeezing him to her. 'What a surprise. What a lovely surprise.'

Bryan blushed in his turn, reaching down to ruffle Lučija's hair to hide his awkwardness. He nodded towards the clergyman. 'Your priest is doing open-air services on the pavement?'

'No.' The trio walked away from the church, Lučija in the middle. 'We had the service in the crypt today because of the air raid; the father thinks the German pilots are targeting churches. Many have been hit, some destroyed. It's cramped down there, no room to give proper communion, so he gives us his blessings at the top of the steps as we leave.'

'It seems he had a lot to say to you.' Bryan winced inwardly at his childish jealousy.

'He did,' she said. 'Sometimes, even a man of God can be – there is an English saying – a bull in a china shop?'

Bryan stayed silent, unwilling to press further.

Jacobella cast him a long sideways glance, chewing her lip. 'He told me my daughter needs a father-figure and that his flock will need plenty of new sheep when this war is over.'

Bryan whistled through his teeth. 'There's nothing quite like the direct righteousness of a celibate clergyman.' Bryan kept his gaze on the paving stones in front of his footsteps. 'It's hardly a very decent thing for anyone to say, let alone a man of God.'

A smile spread across Jacobella's face. 'I've already forgiven him,' she said. 'Now, tell me where you have been all this time so I can decide if I should forgive you.'

Chapter 21

Saturday, 6 June 1942

Flies danced in front of his nose, flying in tight figures-of-eight, waiting for the opportunity to dart at the corner of his eye, or settle unnoticed on his forehead and sup at the salty sweat that beaded on his face. The flat, earthy smell of entrails hung heavy on the sultry breeze, thick and glutinous in his nostrils, roiling the acid in his empty stomach. Three emaciated goats huddled together against the rough stone wall in one corner of the field, staring with blank, uncomprehending eyes as their owner heaved the cleaned carcass of one of their fellows away from the fly-swarmed pile of its steaming guts and onto a low wooden hand-cart. Their flanks quivered in the face of a danger they couldn't fathom as the man wiped the blood and gristle from his blade and advanced towards them.

Bryan turned away from the wall and crossed the road, back to where Ben held the barbed wire apart with his boot.

'What is he doing?' Ben asked.

Bryan ducked through the gap. 'Killing his goats.'

'Why?'

'It's that or let them starve to death.'

The two men started back down the gentle slope towards the airfield.

'Is there nothing we can do to help?' Ben asked.

'Yes,' Bryan said. 'We could defeat Rommel in Africa and then invade Sicily and Italy with overwhelming force.'

Ben glanced at him in exasperation. 'I meant something we could *actually* do.'

Bryan shrugged. 'More convoys. More sinkings. More drownings. More Air Raids. More dead. More homeless.'

'Come on,' Ben admonished. 'The raids have all but dried up. That has to be a good thing.'

Bryan stopped in his tracks. 'There's fuck all left for them to bomb,' he said, 'until some more ships arrive and the whole bloody dance starts all over again.'

A flurry of distressed bleating behind them ended in abrupt silence.

Bryan looked back towards the field. 'It can't be long before *people* reach that condition' – he clasped his hand to his bony jawline – 'including us. Then all the Germans have to do is wait for the most convenient full moon and send across their paratroopers.' Bryan strode off down the slope with Ben hurrying to catch up. 'If that happens,' he continued, 'Malta is the least of what we'll lose.'

Saturday, 13 June 1942

Eleven pilots sat in the dining room in Xara Palace waiting. A murmur of conversation lapped around their heads, laced through with speculation and rumour. Heavy footsteps rang from the stone-flagged lobby outside and the squadron leader strode in with an older, high-ranking officer. A military policeman swept his gaze across the assembly as he closed the door and leaned his broad back against it. The pilots stood to attention amidst the scraping of their chairs.

A thrill of recognition resonated through Bryan as he looked into the old man's face.

'As you were,' Copeland waved them back to their seats and waited for them to settle. 'I'm honoured to introduce Air Vice Marshal Lloyd. I'll let him explain why we've been gathered here.' Copeland sat down amongst his men.

Lloyd cleared his throat. 'Gentlemen,' – strain chiselled the old officer's features and he swept the upturned faces with an edge of beseeching in his eyes – 'you all know that practically every resource we need to keep our grip on this island is getting low, and you're all clever enough to know exactly what will become of us as soon as things run out. So, I'm sure you'll be pleased to hear that two convoys have recently sailed for our relief. One is coming from the west and one from the east. There'll be half-a-dozen merchant ships and a tanker from Gibraltar and eleven merchantmen from Alexandria. Each convoy is protected by around thirty escort vessels.

'Obviously we can expect the navy to do a sterling job in keeping the merchant boys safe, but we're anxious to get air cover over them as soon as we can. Normally, as you know, this happens when the ships are about seventy miles out.' He paused and smiled. 'Your Spitfires arrived here with extra fuel carried in slipper tanks. We stored those tanks and they are being refitted as we speak. The larger fuel capacity will allow this squadron to fly top cover over the Alexandria convoy throughout daylight hours on Monday.

'Three flights of four aircraft will fly in relays, keeping one flight over the convoy at all times. The first sortie will take off shortly before dawn.' He looked around the now stony faces before him. 'Any questions?'

Copeland drew himself upright. 'What if an attack develops as a flight is about to return to base?' he asked.

Lloyd's features stiffened in proxy resolve and his beady eyes glittered. 'It's imperative that enemy action is met with opposition. In those circumstances you'll be expected to stay and fight. If fuel limitations preclude your safe return, you will ditch ahead of the convoy and await rescue by an escort vessel.'

'I see,' Copeland said quietly and lowered himself slowly back into his chair.

Sunday, 14 June 1942

The darkness throbbed around Bryan's head drawing the unseen walls closer to hold him as helpless hostage on his sweat begrimed mattress. He stared with sleepless eyes at the ceiling and listened to a tiny whistling rasp that creaked from his lung on every in-breath. Reaching a decision, he groped for his watch and fastened its strap around his wrist. He climbed out of the bed and dressed in the dark, sitting finally on the mattress edge to push his stockinged feet into boots still damp with yesterday's perspiration.

Slipping from his room, he felt his way down the corridor, descended the stairs and left Xara Palace by the front door. The sudden liberty from the enclosed space lightened his mood, but his compulsion remained. He walked past the ancient slumbering churches, through the gate and across the wide stone bridge to take the road heading east to Valletta.

The tramping rhythm of his footsteps drained the clutter from his mind and he surrendered to the pull that sat in his chest, planting each step on the rough road like a delivered promise.

An hour later, with Ta'Qali airfield receding on his left and the road rising on its way out of the basin, spongy aches spread across his thighs. He paused and swept his gaze across the star peppered dome, lightening at its eastern horizon with the first grey smudges of dawn.

A rattle vibrated behind him, strengthening to a clanking growl. Bryan turned to see the hooded headlights of a truck cruising up the road towards him. He stepped to the edge of the road and waited. The truck slowed and juddered to a halt next to him.

A soldier leaned out of his open passenger window. 'Crikey. Where are you off to, Napoleon?'

'Valletta,' Bryan said. 'Anywhere in Valletta.'

'We're off to St Gregory, out by the harbour mouth. Any good to ya'?'

Bryan nodded.

'Jump in then.' He craned his neck to the rear of the vehicle. 'Hoi!' he shouted. 'Make room in there. We're giving Biggles a lift.'

Bryan climbed into the canvas-covered truck and sat by the tailgate. The gloom inside afforded him the opportunity to stay silent and, once the novelty of his arrival passed, the soldiers continued their mumbled conversations.

Dawn split the Mediterranean sky as the vehicle rumbled through Floriana and lurched northwards under the towering bastion walls that held Hastings Gardens behind their parapets. Bryan's anxiety softened, but his restlessness remained. The truck snaked along the road that hugged the edge of Marsamxett Harbour and wheezed to a halt at the city's seaward tip.

Bryan left the gunners taking over their new station while the transport growled away into the gloom with the relieved crew. He took the nearest alley that climbed away from the harbour and broached this unfamiliar quarter of the city.

The early morning light draped its golden gentleness onto the blocky piles of shattered masonry like an ethereal altar cloth bestowed by the angels of the dawn. Valletta lay around him like a mortally wounded giant, slumped in ruins and bleeding out its precious hope. Nothing moved along its broken thoroughfares except Bryan's gaunt figure, stalking like a wraith through the ancient bones of the decimated capital.

Emerging from a narrow side road, he walked into an open square. A classical Romanesque building squatted along one side of this courtyard, complete with Corinthian columns standing like rigid sentries beneath its triangular portico. An incongruous steeple nestled behind this grand frontage, lofting its delicately pointed spire some two hundred feet into the morning sky. A man hurried down the street next to the building, his plain black robe flapping behind him. He climbed the steps and unlocked a door near the end of the wall. The door creaked open and the man vanished inside.

Bryan walked across to the steps. Next to the door, a small plaque bore the words '*St Paul's – Anglican Cathedral*'. Bryan smiled at the gentle irony of stumbling upon another St Paul's Cathedral and stepped through the doorway.

The atmosphere in the cavernous stone space was several degrees cooler than the warming morning air and a shiver ran down Bryan's back. In front of him, raised on a circular stepped dais in the semi-circular apse, a marble font stood like an ossified flower, its receptacle covered with a polished wooden lid that bore a tall yellowing candle, unlit. Milky white columns, echoing those outside, marched down the flanks of the nave and supported a pale stone ceiling.

Weariness from his walking gripped his thighs. He moved to the pews that serried the floor between the columns, sat down and stared with unfocussed gaze towards the altar and its elaborate columned altarpiece at the other end of the church.

Bryan sensed a movement from behind and someone sat on the pew opposite him across the aisle.

'It's a beautiful church, isn't it?'

Bryan turned to see the robed man, his black cassock now augmented by priestly vestments. He looked the clergyman in the eye. '*Oh, how amiable are thy dwellings, thou Lord of hosts,*' he drawled.

The older man smiled with child-like pleasure. '*My soul hath a desire and longing to enter into the courts of the Lord,*' he intoned and clasped his hands before him. 'Would you like to pray with me, my son?'

Bryan shook his head. 'I've looked for God everywhere,' he said, 'and always failed to find any trace.' He returned his gaze to the western end and the empty altar. 'I'm afraid I don't believe.'

'So, what brings you here?' The priest's voice held no reproach.

'I have an interest in architecture,' Bryan said. 'Of course, not enough to actually *be* an architect.' He turned back to the priest. 'You're very lucky it hasn't been damaged yet.'

The older man smiled. 'No bombs will ever hit my church.'

'What makes you so sure?'

The priest tipped his head to one side, as if he were speaking to a minor. 'God protects us here. He will not allow evil to enter this place.'

Bryan regarded him for a moment with a level gaze. 'You remind me of my father,' he said.

The priest's face suffused with pleasure. 'Thank you. I am most flattered.'

Bryan turned back to face the altar. 'You shouldn't be.'

The clergyman stood and walked a couple of yards down the aisle and then re-seated himself, looking back diagonally across the walkway into Bryan's face. Despite himself, Bryan swivelled his eyes to meet the direct scrutiny.

'I can only repeat my question,' the cleric said.

'I can leave, if it bothers you.'

The priest pursed his lips. 'If you came only to insult an old man, then you have finished that task and indeed, you may go.'

Bryan dropped his gaze. 'I'm sorry,' he said.

The clergyman smiled. 'That, at least, is a start.' He swivelled back towards the altar, turning his face away from Bryan. 'Why don't you pretend that I'm your friend.'

Bryan looked at the back of the old man's head, his eyes resting on the green silk stole that draped over the priest's shoulders, reflecting the morning light with a faint sheen of incongruous luxury. 'It's a woman,' Bryan said. 'A Maltese widow.'

The other man nodded, staying silent.

'She lives in Valletta,' Bryan continued. 'I'm here simply to be close to her. Your church is somewhere to sit, that's all. If she lived in a field, I'd sit in a ditch under the hedge' – Bryan swallowed against a constriction in his throat – 'even though she won't... can't ever...'

The priest turned to look again into Bryan's face. 'Love does not need to be returned to make it real. It does not need to be believed to make it strong; it flourishes as its own reward. Carry it in your heart and ask nothing more than it stays there and grows. Perhaps that's the trace of God that you've been searching for.'

The priest lowered himself onto a kneeler and muttered quietly in personal prayer. Bryan, for reasons he did not understand, bowed his head and listened to the murmuring rhythm of the old man's invocation.

Monday, 15 June 1942

Bryan glanced into his rear-view mirror. Behind him, three Spitfires straggled out into a loose V formation, rocking and wallowing gently through the warm Mediterranean air. He looked at his watch, checked his speed, and consulted the scribbled calculations on the notepad taped to his thigh. Tensing his stiffened buttock muscles against the hard bulk of his parachute pack, he craned his neck and scanned the vast, empty azure plain ahead.

'They should be here,' he muttered to himself. Squinting once more at the hazy horizon, he thumbed his wireless to transmit. 'Falcon Leader to Falcon aircraft. We've reached our calculated rendezvous. Keep your eyes peeled for the convoy.'

He scratched the time and fuel gauge reading on the pad with the pencil he had tied onto his wrist and returned to scanning the blank blue canvas through the spinning disc of his propeller.

'Falcon Two here,' Ben's voice. 'Something's happening over on the starboard quarter, bearing east-south-east.'

Bryan polished the right side of his canopy with the back of his hand and peered at that section of the sky. Barely discernible in the haze, a cyclic pattern of white spots appeared and vanished in the distance.

'I see it,' Bryan answered. 'Looks like AA. Follow me.'

He pulled his nose around and eased the throttle forward gingerly; conscious of his own mortal dependence on the contents of his fuel tank, he resisted the urge to push to full speed. The motes of smoke, growing more distinct as the distance closed, ceased abruptly. Bryan checked his compass so he could hold the course to the still-invisible convoy.

'Aircraft at 10 o'clock,' Ben's voice again. 'Looks like they're heading north.'

Bryan looked to the left of his cowling and strained to pick out the swarm of black specks shuffling across their path. 'Strewth,' he muttered to himself, 'the boy's got good eyesight.' Then he thumbed transmit. 'Looks like they're going home. Let them go. There'll be more on the way, no doubt. We need to be over the convoy before they arrive.'

Moments later, the stick-like silhouettes of sea-going vessels formed out of the amorphous haze and multiplied to scatter the sea's surface. Bryan led his flight in a wide circle around the flotilla, tilting their aircraft to allow the antagonised gunners below to recognise them as friendly. Ending up over the hindmost vessel, Bryan flattened out and overflew the convoy along its direction of travel.

Something snagged at his subconscious; something wasn't right. He surveyed the ships that slid away below his wings, carving white lines through the water with quiet serenity; nothing unusual there. He pulled his gaze back to his control panel; fuel good, oil pressure normal, compass...

'Falcon Leader to Falcon Two,' he called, 'I think my compass is playing up. What is yours reading?'

'Hello Falcon Leader,' Ben sounded bemused. 'Due east. This convoy is heading in the wrong direction.'

****

Bryan taxied off the end of the runway in the failing light. Groundcrew guided him back to his blast-pen and swivelled the aircraft around on the hard pad of dried earth. Bryan killed the engine and pulled out his wireless and oxygen connections. As he unhooked his harness, he glanced across to see Copeland standing, hands in pockets, waiting for him.

Bryan regarded the other man with a steady gaze for a moment, then stood, clambered out of the cockpit and slid down the wing. He shrugged off his parachute and strode across to the squadron leader.

'What the bloody hell is going on? Bryan hissed. 'I've just been nigh-on halfway to bloody Crete flying aerial cover for what turned out to be a naval retreat.'

'I know – we've received word from HQ. It seems the commander had concerns about some of his ships running short of ammunition.' Copeland kept his voice low. 'They lost one destroyer earlier in the day and another was badly damaged. He obviously decided it was safer to turn back for Alexandria.'

'What?' Bryan's eyes bulged with outrage. 'They were three-quarters of the way here! Do they think the Krauts will leave them alone just because they're running away?'

'Come on, Hale.' Copeland laid a hand on Bryan's shoulder. 'You can see why they didn't want to get stuck in Grand Harbour without sufficient ammunition.'

Bryan shrugged his leader's hand away. '*They* didn't want to get stuck here without ammunition?' He stretched out his arms in cruciform supplication. 'What about us?'

'I'm sure the commander is acting in the best interests of his men,' Copeland's voice took on an exasperated edge. 'That's his job.'

Bryan's arms flopped back to his sides. 'So he's just doing his job, is he? There are housewives on this island with more moral courage than that man.'

'That's enough, Hale!' Copeland stepped aside and pointed up the slope to the waiting transport. 'The operation is over. Get back to Xara.'

Tuesday, 16 June 1942

A number of pilots sat at the tables in Xara's dining room. Each nursed a mug of weak tea. Some used the tepid liquid to soften their hardtack biscuit, stoically coaxing it towards edibility. The radio in the corner dribbled out anaemic orchestral music; tinny violins ascending and descending in aimless sonic sweeps, like flocks of emaciated birds scratching forlorn murmurations against a blank, grey sky.

Bryan stared at the fawn coloured liquid in his mug and tapped his biscuit on the table, swivelling it between his fingers, end on end, between each impact. Ben hunched opposite him, elbows on the table, watching the dark slab of hardtack spin and tap, spin and tap.

'They say two merchant ships got through from the Gibraltar run,' Ben offered.

Bryan looked up and the biscuit stilled. 'Two out of eighteen,' he said. 'Even Winston would struggle to call that a victory.'

The music stopped abruptly and a man's voice filled the silence.

'*We interrupt this programme to bring you an address from Lord Gort, Governor of Malta.*'

All heads swivelled towards the radio and one man leaned across to turn up the volume. There was a moment of rasping static, followed by the measured tones of the governor's voice.

'*This evening I intend to speak to you with complete frankness, because I believe the truth never hurts and we are always at our best when we know the worst.*'

Bryan closed his eyes and groaned.

'*Some days ago, two convoys set out, one from the west and one from the east, to bring supplies which we need to restore our situation. The western convoy had to endure severe and prolonged attacks, and only two merchant ships survived the ordeal. They are now in Grand Harbour. The eastern convoy, after suffering from prolonged and intense attacks by the Luftwaffe, was ordered to turn back.*

'*I must break to you what the arrival of only two ships means to us. For some time, we have been short of supplies, and further privations lie ahead of us. But every effort will be made to replenish our stocks when a favourable opportunity presents itself. Meanwhile, every one of us must do everything in his or her power to conserve our stocks and to ensure that the best use is made of all the available resources that remain to us. We must make all possible savings in every commodity.*

'We have the sure conviction that our cause is just. We have trust in ourselves and we have a still greater belief – our faith in Almighty God. Strong in that faith, let us all go forward together to victory.'

'And there it is,' Bryan muttered. 'Victory.' He dropped the hardtack biscuit into his tea, stood up and left the room.

Chapter 22

Monday, 22 June 1942

The pearl-white moon hung in its first quarter, its disc bisected between lambent light and frigid darkness, each state holding equal sway over its pitted, silent surface. Bryan and Ben sat on Xara's roof terrace in the gloom, sipping mugs of tea and staring out across the blackened landscape. Bryan's pelvis poked at his denuded flesh and he shifted his weight on the unyielding wooden chair.

'I walked past the main storehouse today,' Ben said. 'Some wag has built a gallows outside the main entrance. There's a sign that says 'Pilferers Beware' and a little skull-and-crossbones.'

Bryan shook his head in slow disbelief. 'You can always trust the British Army to lead the way in tact and diplomacy. Have we been reduced to hanging hungry men for stealing food?'

'It's not a real gallows,' Ben said. 'It's symbolic, it's meant to be a warning.' He frowned. 'At least I don't *think* it's a real gallows.'

A lethargic silence fell over the pair.

Then Ben slurped noisily from his mug. 'Do you remember that fish on Gibraltar?' he said.

'I actually try not to think about it,' Bryan answered. Then he tilted his head. 'Listen,' he whispered.

The low rumble of engines vibrated through the night, high up and numerous, growing steadily in timbre. Flashes of light scratched at the height of the sky's black dome, sputtering uncertainly for a few moments, then blooming into sudden blinding brightness, each stellar distillation swaying gently to and fro in a slow, scintillating descent.

'Marker flares,' Bryan muttered. 'What the hell are they up to?'

The drifting motes of dazzling illumination overlapped, reinforcing one another and knitting an eery umbrella of flickering radiance over the landscape. Beneath them, in ghostly counterpoint, waves of flashing sparkles sprung into being on the ground, lapping across the fields like the white foam of an alien tide. These in turn guttered, then rallied and swelled, intermingled and finally threw tongues of leaping flame back towards the sky.

Bryan stood up, drawn erect by his disbelief. 'Incendiaries,' he said, his voice stretched with incredulity. 'The evil bastards are setting fire to the crops.'

Sunday, 28 June 1942

Bryan arrived in Valletta late. Transport waned scarce in tandem with the dwindling fuel stocks. It was only his pilot's wings that gained him any traction at all in negotiating lifts. He climbed down carefully from the army truck onto the hard cobbles of the wharf and locked his knees against the insidious tremor in his legs as the truck pulled away. He glanced over the harbour at the ravaged shambles of the docks, then swept his gaze over the city's profile. Its tumbled walls and broken casements lay quiet under the throbbing sun like the ruined vestige of an ancient civilisation.

He set off into the silent wreckage, skirting around, and sometimes forced to climb over, the tumbled stones of annihilated tenements; piles of blocks too heavy and numerous to be moved without machines.

Working his way up the side streets, he encountered no-one. But when he emerged onto a main thoroughfare, he stumbled upon a long queue of citizens lined up perpendicular to his route. Each person carried a bowl or a jug clutched to their chest. Most wore what had once been their Sunday best, now stained and grimed through lack of water for washing. Some wore little more than rags, evidently the only clothing they still possessed.

The closest faces turned towards him as he approached. Their eyes held a mixture of shame and desperation, the combination creating an air of passive hostility. Their self-esteem lay dying in the gaping maw of chronic hunger, but their anger lacked the luxury of energy. No-one talked, no-one smiled. Children stood listless next to parents who could only stare in sorrow at their gaunt, vacant faces.

Bryan muttered his 'excuse-me' as he cut through the line and crossed the road. He looked towards the head of the queue where two large pots stood on a trestle. Women ladled steaming liquid as the shabby procession shuffled past. Above the servers' heads, a canvas banner announced it to be a *Victory Kitchen*. He blinked at the dichotomy and went on his way.

Reaching familiar territory, Bryan walked along Bakery Street and then Mint Street. He paused, looking at the stepped pavement climbing away from him to the gardens. The sweat already prickling his brow had attracted a number of flies. He wiped away the glistening beads and flicked them

213

from his fingers onto the smooth stone steps. Bending his back into the effort, he started the climb, ignoring the insects that careened around his face.

At the top, the breeze from the northern harbour stripped the flies from his head and caressed away the moisture. He strolled the last hundred yards at a leisurely pace, allowing his breathing to settle and relax.

Arriving at Jacobella's door he stopped, a frown creasing his forehead. Across the peeling blue paint someone had daubed the word 'PACE'. He reached out and touched the white painted letters as if to check they were dry, then pushed through the entrance into the hallway.

He knocked on Jacobella's door and footsteps clattered down the stairs. Lučija opened the door and greeted him with a delighted giggle before pounding her way back up to the apartment. Bryan climbed the stairs to find the little girl sitting at the kitchen table clutching the knitted doll and waving it at him, stiff-armed, like a priest sprinkling holy water.

Jacobella bent over her sink, kneading wet clothes under her knuckles in shallow, dirt-fouled water. She paused in her work and smiled over her shoulder; her eyes underlined with gaunt darkness yet still full of sparkle.

'Someone has painted a word on the door,' Bryan said.

She returned to her washing, shoulders bunching with the effort. 'It means 'Peace'', she said, 'but I think it implies surrender.'

'Who would do that?' he asked.

'There are many who listen to Sicilian radio. The Italians speak a lot about their Maltese brethren and some people here believe they are sincere. But it's simply the pain in their empty bellies confusing the loyalty in their hearts.'

Bryan frowned. 'Did they target your door because of me?' he asked.

Jacobella lifted a garment from the sink and twisted it tightly in front of her breast, wringing the water out in a cascade of murky grey.

'Yes,' she said. 'Also, because I work at the newspaper. But don't worry. They will take it no further.' She put the damp bundle of cloth on the draining board, folded her arms and looked him up and down. 'Perhaps if you English looked fat and healthy, there might be a revolution.' She smiled. 'But it's obvious that we're all starving together.'

Bryan unslung his rucksack and pulled out a small tin of fruit.

'I brought this for Lučija,' he said, handing her the tin. 'You should have some too.'

She turned the tin over in her hands. 'I hope you didn't steal this,' she said. 'I understand that's a very dangerous crime, these days.'

'No,' he said. 'I saved my ration for a week and they let me take it in one go.'

'You're a kind man.' She placed the tin on the side and went back to kneading the washing. 'At the newspaper, they say those two ships brought enough for us to last until the end of September.'

Bryan lowered himself onto a stool by the wall. 'Tobruk is lost,' he said. 'If Alexandria falls as well, it will all be over long before then.'

She paused in her work and her shoulders sagged. 'God watches over us, Bryan. We should trust in that, always.'

Wednesday, 15 July 1942

The four escort fighters had vanished northwards some time ago and a hushed stillness still muffled the activity across Ta'Qali. Airmen sat twiddling their thumbs and looking skyward, squinting into the summer glare and straining to hear beyond the passive silence that pressed into their ears.

'What do you know about Keith Park?' Copeland asked.

Bryan pursed his lips. 'He was group commander when I was flying out of Kenley. He made a decent fist of things.

'He's the new AOC for Malta,' Copeland said. 'He arrived yesterday.'

Bryan glanced at Copeland briefly, then returned his gaze to the sky. 'Is that why we're getting reinforcements?'

The four escorts roared out of the distance, buzzed the airfield and banked away to the east. Behind them, the sky gradually filled with the new arrivals; three squadrons of factory-fresh Spitfires curved into the circuit, the vanguard easing down towards the landing strip.

'I do believe things are looking up, Hale,' Copeland said. 'They're sending a fast minesweeper from Gibraltar and a submarine from Alexandria, both loaded with fuel and ammunition. And there's some talk of a convoy for August. A big convoy, properly defended this time. The army are holding the Germans at El-Alamein, so if the navy and our torpedo bombers can disrupt the shipping on its way to Tobruk and Tripoli, there's an outside chance the Germans can be beaten.'

Bryan raised his voice against the swelling din of the landing aircraft. 'One more last chance at the Last Chance Saloon.'

Thursday, 23 July 1942

'Have you got any cigarettes?' Bryan whispered.

'No,' Ben answered. 'No-one has.'

'Damn it!' Bryan hissed in frustration. 'The bastards make us get up before the crack of dawn and they don't even have the decency to pass round some gaspers.'

Copeland's chair scraped the floor as he rose to his feet. All heads turned to listen.

'Good morning, gentlemen. Today we are going to do something different. Our new AOC has authorised forward interception sorties.'

'About time,' Bryan muttered.

Copeland shot him a warning glance and continued. 'We'll be held at readiness until RDF detects activity building up over Sicily. Then we'll be scrambled to fly north and intercept the raid over the sea. We're to support a Hurricane squadron from Luqa. Our job will be to engage the fighter escort while the Hurricanes take the bombers head-on. Just like the good old days.' He swept his smile across the upturned faces. 'Transport is outside. Let's go.'

****

The mid-morning sun hung suspended on the starboard beam as Copeland levelled out at 20,000 feet, cruising due north. The squadron spread across the sky behind him like a peacock's tail. They flew in pairs, ranging out at last as free hunters rather than reacting like tethered guard dogs.

Bryan glanced into his mirror to see Ben's machine tucked snugly on his starboard quarter, then dropped his gaze to the thickening band of the Sicilian coast dead ahead.

'Falcon Leader to Falcon Aircraft.' Copeland's voice resonated with steady authority. 'Bomber formation ahead and below. Ignore them.'

Two stepped squadrons of Junkers 88s streamed in the opposite direction on the left of the British fighters. A ripple of disorder ran through the enemy formation as the pilots recognised the shapes that overpassed them and craned their necks to follow the danger. Their escorts, far faster through the air, were some way behind, chasing them across the sea to rendezvous closer to landfall.

'Steady,' Copeland drawled. 'Keep your eyes open.'

They flew on for less than a minute.

'Bandits, 12 o'clock high.' This time Copeland's words were stretched with tension. 'Let's give them hell. Tally ho!' His Spitfire curved up into a shallow banking zoom towards the onrushing German force. He opened fire as the tightly knit gaggle of 109s flashed overhead.

Bryan held his fire, banked to keep the escort force in view and screwed his head around to watch their next move. Most broke to port, three broke to starboard. Bryan slewed his fighter to the right, following the smaller group. Two of the German fighters formed into a tight pair, the third had broken a few moments late and floundered away from the others on a wider bank.

Bryan eased back on the stick and forward on the throttle, drawing the wayward 109 down his windshield. As the wallowing fighter threatened to vanish beneath his nose, Bryan stabbed the firing button with his thumb. His cannons juddered the airframe with percussive violence, sending smoke trails curving out and downwards to ensnare the Messerschmitt in a pattern of exploding strikes that danced back along its engine and through its cockpit. White smoke belched into its slipstream and the burning fighter pirouetted into a dive towards the sea.

Bryan pulled tighter into his turn, clenching his teeth against the grey mist that crept into the edge of his vision. The other two 109s drifted into view above the top of his windshield, then darted away as they reversed their turn to port. Bryan kicked his rudder to follow and pulled hard on the stick to cut inside his quarry.

A tortured glance in the mirror showed Ben hanging on behind his right wing. Ahead of him, the Messerschmitts split; the leader banked precipitously to starboard, leaving his wingman pulling the port turn. Bryan slashed his Spitfire back to the right, hoping Ben would stay in the opposite turn to occupy the other escort.

Fighting against the tightness in his chest and the pain in his temples, Bryan wrestled the controls to drag his enemy into his gunsights. Abruptly the 109 barrelled onto its back. The canopy flopped open and a figure jumped into the void, arms and legs flailing in space. Bryan throttled back and dipped his wing, watching. A parachute blossomed like salvation, jerked into buoyancy and tore the harness away from its owner. The pilot flipped end over end, tumbling through space, plummeting seawards in a hopeless, helpless drop as the parachute flopped and rolled away on the wind.

Bryan gritted his teeth and swallowed back a sudden wave of nausea. Then self-preservation reasserted its cold imperative and he reversed his turn and scanned the sky.

Fire flared in the middle distance, curving like a burning arrow through the blue. He squinted against the glare to identify the victor, and breathed a sigh of relief when it banked away from the combat showing the wide elliptical wings of a Spitfire.

He circled, waiting for Ben to join him. The rest of the squadron were nowhere to be seen, but far below, at wavetop height, black silhouettes of bombers raced towards Sicily, one or two streaming banners of dirty white smoke.

Chapter 23

Saturday, 1 August 1942

The heat did not build; it arrived, like the opening of a vast oven door. The sirocco's febrile exhalation carried dust from the African deserts and draped it like a patina of rust across everything in its path. The fine, orange silt infiltrated clothes, scratched at eyelids and transformed skin to wrinkling parchment. The dry rocks of Malta wavered in the haze of reradiated heat beneath a sky bereft of cloud.

'I thought 'hungry' was bad,' Ben muttered, 'but now I realise 'thirsty' is worse.'

'Try thinking of your favourite fruit,' Bryan suggested. 'Sometimes you can trick your mouth into watering.'

Ben's face dropped into studious concentration and he clicked his tongue against his dry palate.

The distant crackle of anti-aircraft fire drifted through the sullen air and threads of tracer lashed in low curves over Grand Harbour. The pilots at readiness tensed, leaning forward in their chairs, shifting their gravity, anticipating a shouted order to scramble. Copeland stood and scanned the eastern horizon, shading his eyes with hands cupped on his forehead.

A sudden swell of engine noise was drowned by the thumping tattoo of Bofors guns opening up along Ta'Qali's perimeter. Two pairs of 109s banked across the sky, flashing their pale blue undersides, the black shape of a single bomb nestled between their wing roots. They darted away from the aerodrome, then banked to bypass its western edge, flying south in search of a softer target.

Copeland walked back to his chair. 'Relax,' he called to his pilots. 'They're trying to make us waste our fuel.'

The pilots settled back in their seats, a tense uneasiness persisting on their faces.

'We haven't seen a proper bomber in daylight for at least three days,' Ben mused. 'What do you think they're up to?'

Bryan patted at empty pockets, the last expression of his nicotine addiction. 'They don't *need* to be up to anything,' he said. 'They know we're starving; they only have to count down the clock.'

The suffocating blanket of heat held them immobile and silent for long moments. Fresh beads of sweat prickled through dust-blocked pores and flies arrived to patrol their heads.

'I intend to have a word with the squadron leader.' Bryan swatted at a fly manoeuvring to land on his nose. 'You have great eyesight and you know what to do in a fight; you should be leading your own section.'

'No, thank you,' Ben said. 'I'm *your* wingman.' He squinted at the barren blue sky like a matelot surveying familiar waters. 'That's the way I like it.'

Sunday, 9 August 1942

Bryan remained seated while the congregation stood, sang, chanted and prayed around him. Their words washed over his head without meaning or effect. Only the relative coolness of the stone interior connected with his senses, and he revelled in the relief it brought to his body and mind. Lučija was on the other side of her mother and, through half-closed eyes, he caught her admonishing glances, heavy with child-like outrage that he could abdicate his part in the bewildering ritual in which she was forced to participate.

Jacobella stood and joined the queue down the aisle to receive communion and Bryan smiled an apology at the little girl. 'It's too hot,' he whispered, drawing a hand across his forehead, 'and I'm very tired.' He mimed sleeping on the pillow of his hands.

Lučija pursed her lips as she considered this explanation. Seemingly satisfied, she swung her gaze to watch Jacobella's progress in the shuffling line of the faithful.

****

At the end of the service they sat waiting for the crush through the door to lessen. Lučija knelt on the pew with her chin resting atop the backrest, watching the departing congregation. Her demeanour attracted the occasional hair ruffle or cheek-pinch from older worshippers as they passed. When the crowd thinned, the trio followed them out onto the pavement, back into the fetid, broiling breath of the steady southerly wind.

'Are you hungry?' Jacobella asked as they plodded up Mint Street towards the gardens.

'I could eat my own shoes,' Bryan answered.

Jacobella laughed. 'I have some potato soup, if you'd rather.'

Lućija walked between them holding her mother's hand. She reached up and wormed her other hand into Bryan's.

The front door bore a thick blue bar of new paint that expunged the graffiti. They pushed through into the hallway and climbed the stairs to the apartment.

Bryan sat down at the table and watched Jacobella set the pot on the hob and strike a match to the burner. He looked around at the stone walls and listened to the sound of his own breathing. His gaze dropped back to his hands resting on the stained wood, examining the dust ingrained in the wrinkles of his tanned, leathery skin.

Lućija climbed onto the chair next to him and sat the knitted doll on the table between them. Bryan looked down at her tangled, black hair and bent to untease the knots. He worked carefully for a minute or two before he felt eyes upon him and glanced up. Jacobella leaned against the sink, watching him with a half-smile softening her features.

'I'm afraid the soup will be warm rather than hot,' she said. 'I have so little kerosene left.'

She resumed her preparation and Bryan ruffled Lućija's hair with his fingertips.

'There's a fair chance that things will get better soon,' he said. 'There's talk of another convoy. A big one.'

Jacobella walked over and placed a tray with three bowls onto the table. 'There was the same rumour at the newspaper,' she said as she handed out the soup. 'But there are always mutterings of food amongst the hungry.'

Bryan took a spoonful of the pale liquid, savouring its salty warmth and the liquorice undertone of basil leaves. 'I think it's definite,' he said. 'I'm expected back at the airfield by mid-afternoon. I suspect this week will be rather busy.'

They finished their soup, eating with the carefully deliberate concentration of hungry people consuming inadequate portions. Lućija wandered off to play in her bedroom and Jacobella cleared the table.

'I'm sorry,' Bryan said.

'About what?' Jacobella's asked as she rinsed the bowls under the dribbling tap.

Bryan stood up and moved to stand behind her. 'I shouldn't say things will get better. No amount of food or kerosene will change what you've been through; nothing will make that better.'

Jacobella turned to look at him, scanning his face for long, silent moments.

Bryan shrugged. 'I ought to go. They'll put me on a charge if I'm late.'

'I can't change the things that have happened,' Jacobella said, wiping her wet hands on her apron. 'I just have to care for Lučija. I have to make sure *she* is alright.' Sudden moisture glistened in her eyes. 'It's strange,' she continued, 'Lučija hasn't asked for her father at all.' Jacobella forced a smile that mutated to a grimace as she set her jaw against the onset of tears. She paused until she had won her battle for control. 'But she loves seeing you,' she continued quietly.

'It's not my place...' Bryan mumbled.

'And so do I.' Jacobella placed her palms on Bryan's chest. 'Will you come to see me next Sunday?'

Bryan nodded.

'Will you arrange things so you can stay with me? Stay the night?'

Bryan nodded again. 'Yes.' His voice sounded strange inside his own skull.

She reached one hand behind his head and pulled him down onto her kiss - soft, warm and light. She released him and stepped back, licking his taste from her lips.

'Go and do your work.'

Monday, 10 August 1942

Ben scratched at his greasy hair and yawned as he placed his bowl of porridge on the table and sat down. He prodded experimentally at the grey sludge with his spoon.

'You could hang wallpaper with this muck,' he said. 'I'm sure they put sawdust in it.' He looked up into Bryan's face. 'Are you alright?' he asked. 'You don't look well.'

Bryan raised his eyebrows. 'Oh? Tired, I suppose,' he said.

Ben carved out a glutinous lump of porridge and examined it closely before spooning it into his mouth. He chewed in silence for a few moments, swallowed with a visible effort and licked the greasy residue off his front teeth. 'If this convoy is another cock-up and it all goes tits up, I suppose we'll get flown off before there's a surrender,' he said.

'Almost certainly,' Bryan answered. 'But that's not really the point, is it?' He frowned in sudden annoyance. 'Do you have any cigarettes?'

Ben shook his head, muted by his second mouthful of porridge.

Copeland walked into the mess and waved down the pilots' moves to come to attention.

'It's begun,' he said. 'Early this morning, a large convoy sailed through the Straits of Gibraltar into the Med. The escort includes several aircraft carriers to provide air cover on the first stages of the journey. We are to take over that responsibility as soon as the convoy comes into range. The best estimate of that happening is late on Wednesday or early on Thursday.'

A speculative murmur rippled around the room.

'From now on, all pilots are to be held at readiness on the airfield until the convoy is safely docked. I don't need to remind you how important this is. Transport leaves in twenty minutes.'

Chapter 24

Thursday, 13 August 1942

The bronchial bark of a Merlin engine clattered around the blast-pen walls as a small group of mechanics tuned and tested another Spitfire for operational flight. The sound drifted through the sultry, early morning air to the pilots gathered at readiness. Copeland sat behind the trestle desk under the heavily dappled shade of the camouflage netting, talking quietly into the telephone. He replaced the handset and stared with unfocussed gaze into the middle distance, chewing on his lower lip. Bryan had been watching his squadron leader's conversation and wandered over to the table.

'What news?' he asked.

Copeland looked up. 'Nothing hopeful.' He sighed. 'One aircraft carrier sunk, another one crippled. At least four merchant ships are sunk and the oil tanker has been under heavy attack. The main escorts and the other carriers turned back last night.'

'Not good,' Bryan muttered.

Copeland shook his head. 'It's the tanker that worries me most. We simply can't afford to lose that.'

Both men jumped as the telephone jangled into life. Copeland grabbed the handset and pressed it to his ear. He listened for a few moments then dropped it back into its cradle.

'The convoy is coming into range,' he shouted. 'Falcon Squadron scramble!'

****

Twelve Spitfires climbed away from the Maltese shoreline, clawing for combat altitude on a due west heading. The convoy had steamed south overnight between the island of Pantelleria and the Tunisian coast to stay as far from Sicily as possible. Now they expected to find it sailing east on the final run to Malta.

Bryan shifted his weight on the hard parachute pack and wheezed in a lungful of oxygen through his mask. He glanced down behind his wing at the faceless sea, its blue expanse slashed through with delicate white lines delineating the wind-ripped crests of the endless swell. He dragged his gaze back to his instruments, checked his compass, fuel gauge and oil pressure, then swept the sky above and behind before dropping his attention back to the horizon and the expectation of many vessels.

Smoke heralded the convoy's approach before a single ship became visible. Thick coils of curling smokescreen from careering escorts swathed around thinner columns bannering away from fires on damaged decks.

'Falcon Leader to Falcon aircraft.' Copeland's voice crackled over the wireless. 'Let's take it a bit higher until we're sure about what we're up against.'

Bryan tilted his nose up, holding his place in the climbing formation, and craned his neck to the side to watch the convoy appearing below his port wing. The ships straggled across the horizon, void of any defensive organisation. One merchant ship drifted without a wake, flames licked up the outside of its superstructure and smoke drifted from two ragged holes in its deck. Another steamed slowly in a wide circle, apparently unable to steer any other course. Destroyers dashed through and around the scattered vessels like panicking sheep-dogs, cutting curving swathes through the swell. Each one trailed plumes of thick, obfuscating smoke in a vain attempt to shield the merchantmen from the dangerous sky.

Copeland's voice broke over the wireless. 'Bandits, two o'clock, high. Tally ho!'

Bryan scanned the sky on the forward starboard quarter and picked out a gaggle of fat, black Heinkel bombers crawling south, sullying the dazzling blue vault with their lazy, menacing resolve. He glanced in his mirror to ensure Ben was in position, then swung into the starboard bank with the rest of the squadron.

Copeland led them north on a contra parallel course and Bryan gazed out the port side at the multi-faceted cockpit canopies of the approaching bomber force glittering in the sunshine.

'Attacking now!' G-forces compressed his words as Copeland threw his fighter into a tight left bank to strike the enemy formation on their beam.

Bryan hesitated a second to declutter his space of friendly aircraft, then he too pulled hard to port. The procession of corpulent German airframes swung diagonally across his windscreen, then straightened out as he levelled up. The bulk of Ben's Spitfire teased the edge of his vision as his wingman drifted out to fly next to him, and they both opened fire at the bomber stream, allowing the enemy pilots to fly their machines through the slashing flail of their explosive ordnance.

Bryan flashed over the wallowing aircraft into a clear, empty sky. A detonation in the bomber formation slapped his tail with an unseen wave of pressure and he jinked tightly to put off any return fire. Once clear, he pulled into a left bank to pursue the attackers.

A smudge of oily black smoke hung unmoving in the bomber stream's wake, shattered debris cartwheeled and fluttered through the space below it, testament to the explosive end of one the raiders. A trail of white smoke curving away from the formation led to another burning Heinkel arcing downwards to the sea. Two parachute canopies spiralled in its wake, like stark white carnations blooming into abandonment in an alien summer sky.

Lines of tracer spiralled away from the bombers, lashing through the air like sparkling whips, seeking to fend off the pursuing fighters. Bryan pushed his throttle forward and drifted further from the enemy formation, biding time as he overhauled the lumbering bombers.

The bellies of the Heinkels fell open and black shapes dropped out. Emerging fins first, the bombs flipped to nose-down and wobbled through the air before stabilising and curving down towards the ships strung out below. Unable to look away, Bryan watched the ordnance lance into the spaces between the merchant men, erupting fountains of water through which the vessels ploughed.

Bryan banked left for another attack just as the bombers banked right for home. The lead planes tipped their wings up, presenting their flat, mottled green topsides from which dorsal gunners chopped out bursts of tracer that whipped over his canopy. Bryan squeezed the firing button and held it firm. Two or three explosive hits tore fluttering debris from an upturned wingtip before he flashed over the formation and zoomed away from their desperate gunnery.

Way below, a canopy of shell bursts knitted itself above the water. Bryan scanned high and behind for danger, then looked back to the AA barrage. A second formation of smaller, faster Junkers 88s were running in at low-level in the opposite direction to the high-level force.

Bryan pressed transmit. 'More bombers below. Going down now.'

He barrelled his Spitfire onto its back and pulled into the dive, glancing in his mirror to make sure Ben was following.

The AA barrage intensified; each explosion looking larger than the last as Bryan dropped away his altitude. The Junkers, a dozen or more in number, pressed on. One sprouted fire from its wing and sagged out of formation. Its propellers chopped into the waves and it flipped, splashing into the water with cascading white plumes of foam laced with flame.

The enemy overflew the convoy, stitching a pattern of bomb explosions behind them. Most hit the water, one or two ripped into cargo-crowded decks and shuddered metal hulls with sudden concussive violence.

Bryan dove into the chaos. Bright flashes peppered the space through which he flew and streams of un-aimed tracer zipped up from warships and merchantman alike, undiscerning in a sky filled with targets. Instinct made him weave where the logic was absent as he flattened out into a tail-chase over, and then beyond, the ships. His straining engine rattled the cockpit, but the distance closed too slowly. Wailing with frustration, Bryan jabbed the firing button, streaming out ribbons of cannon fire that curved away below his target, scattering splashes across an uncaring sea.

****

Bryan walked slowly around the Spitfire, looking for bullet strikes and flak holes, while groundcrew dodged past him with ammunition belts and petrol cans. Unable to find any damage, he walked towards the readiness tent.

'Well done, Hale.'

The voice from behind stopped him mid-stride. He allowed Copeland to catch up with him.

'I saw you and Stevens taking a pop at the low-level stream,' Copeland continued. 'I couldn't get down quick enough.'

'Nor could we,' Bryan said as the pair walked on towards readiness. 'We squirted at them as they were leaving but I don't think we hit anything. Are we going out again?'

'Not sure,' Copeland answered. 'The ships that are still capable of making way are coming around the southern end of the island, so RDF can keep an eye out and scramble us if needed.' He glanced at his watch. 'They should reach Grand Harbour this evening. Whatever's left behind is already sinking or will have to be scuttled, unfortunately.'

'It did look like an almighty mess out there,' Bryan said.

'Well, it's only natural that they throw everything they've got at it,' Copeland said. 'It's just a shame that everything they've got is always so much more than everything we've got. Still, we got two of the bastards at least, and a couple more were limping when they left.'

'What about the tanker?' Bryan asked. 'I didn't see anything out there that looked like a tanker.'

'I'll try to find out,' Copeland answered. 'I pray we haven't lost that.'

Bryan nodded silently as he trudged along.

'Are you alright, Hale?' Copeland asked. 'You seem… preoccupied.'

Bryan pulled a thin smile. 'Oh,' he said absently, 'things happen.' He forced a smile. 'Maybe I'm starting to feel my age.'

Copeland cocked his head. 'How old *are* you?'

'Thirty.' Bryan grimaced. 'Perhaps it's time I settled down and took up cribbage.'

'Ha!' Copeland slapped his back. 'Once this convoy situation is put to bed, I'll sign you off for a fortnight's leave. How does that sound?'

'That would be welcome,' Bryan answered. 'Yes, that would be most welcome.'

Friday, 14 August 1942

The bedroom door rattled on its hinges under the enthusiastic knocking of an orderly. Footsteps clomped away down the corridor and the banging on the next door along vibrated down the wall.

'Christ,' Bryan muttered, groping for his watch on the bedside table. It showed a few minutes after four o'clock. 'This is not a good sign.'

He climbed out of bed and pulled on the clothes that lay scattered across the floor. He gave his teeth a perfunctory scrub, scraped the slime from his tongue and rinsed his mouth with stale, lukewarm water from the glass by his bed.

He stepped out into the corridor and followed other emerging pilots down the stairs to the dining room. He spotted Ben and took a seat next to him. An intriguing aroma of frying meat seeped into the room from the adjoining kitchens.

Copeland stood at the end of the room. 'Good morning,' he began. 'I know it's an early start, but we have an important job to do as soon as the sun comes up. The oil tanker is still afloat but has been severely damaged and is unable to make way on its own. The navy have taken it under tow and it's now making slow progress in our direction.

'We've been tasked, together with fighters from Luqa, to maintain constant air cover of at least squadron strength over the tanker and its escort throughout daylight hours today.

'The good news is, three supply ships docked yesterday and unloading has gone on through the night. The really good news is we've had an early delivery from the docks, which I suspect you can already smell. Enjoy your breakfast, it will be a long day.'

****

Bryan swung his Spitfire onto the runway and trundled twenty yards along its length. He squeezed on the brakes and dropped the throttle to idle. Thin streamers of dust swirled back from the fighters waiting ahead of him, coruscating under his wings and spiralling away, accelerated by his own prop-wash.

He looked into his mirror to check progress behind him. A Spitfire stood stationary on the perimeter, its propeller windmilling to a halt. It looked like Ben's aircraft. As groundcrew moved to drag the fighter out of the way, Ben stood up in the cockpit, waving at him and making slashing motions across his throat. Bryan waved an arm from his open cockpit in acknowledgement.

'Fighter Control to Falcon Squadron, you're clear for take-off. Once airborne, take heading two-four-zero. Good luck.'

Bryan glanced once more into the mirror, then banged his canopy shut, released the brakes and followed the rest of Falcon Squadron along the dust-plumed runway into the air.

Copeland banked the squadron into the south-westerly heading and powered into a steady climb as the Dingli Cliffs dropped away to the empty sea below them. At their backs, the sun's disc escaped the horizon, rising with languid serenity and flushing the soft, golden dawn with a brighter luminance.

'Fighter Control to Falcon Squadron, we're tracking two formations of bandits. You are on a converging course. Maintain angels.'

The squadron levelled out and Bryan scanned the horizon through the blur of his spinning propeller. Dead ahead, a dark anomaly appeared through the glare on the sparkling water; four large ships, grouped dangerously close and seemingly stationary, sat exposed in the flat blue wilderness.

'Falcon Leader to Falcon Aircraft,' Copeland called. 'Bandits at two o'clock. Tally-ho!'

The squadron banked gently to starboard and Bryan spotted the enemy formations. The foremost moved with the stodgy pace of bombers, their fixed undercarriage and deep, creased wings identified them as Stuka dive-bombers. Behind, and a good deal above them, a gaggle of 109 fighters shadowed them to their target.

Falcon Squadron lanced towards the bombers. Bryan edged out to starboard, loosening up space to manoeuvre as the squat, ugly silhouettes of the dive-bombers grew larger. A wave of panic infected the enemy formation and it split apart, breaking in all directions. Bryan squeezed off a one-second burst at a huge gull-winged shape that barrelled across his vision before he broke through the melee and banked left to seek another target.

'Look out!' An unrecognisable voice. '109s coming down now!'

Bryan reversed his bank to gain clear sky and looked upwards for the danger. Bright orange motes of tracer streamed down towards him followed by two huge black shapes that flashed past either side of his fuselage. Bryan hauled his turn into the opposite direction to throw them off. A Stuka wallowed into view in front of him. He throttled back, lined up and fired. Hits peppered the enemy's tail cascading tiny shards backwards into its slipstream. The Stuka's rear gunner fired back, squirting a spiral of tracer that looped and swung dangerously close to Bryan's canopy. The dive-bomber lurched into a violent side-slip and Bryan dived away to regain airspeed.

Ahead, a Spitfire dropped through the air in a slow, flat spin, like a monstrous maple seed. The letters on the side flashed clearly into view as it rotated; they were Copeland's. Above the stricken aircraft, a parachute opened, pristine white against the blue.

Bryan pulled into a wide bank and scanned the sky. A German fighter levelled out from a diving turn and flew towards the parachutist. Gun flash sparkled along it wings and cowling. Bryan craned his neck back in time to see the figure in the harness jerk from many impacts. Something hose-like draped away from the man, looping and glistening in the sunlight. The 109 barrelled past a few feet above the canopy. Propeller wash folded the fabric into itself and the parachute collapsed and twisted, streaming behind the plummeting pilot like a tangled shroud.

Bryan howled with impotent rage and kicked his Spitfire into pursuit of the diving Messerschmitt, pushing his throttle hard against the gate. His quarry sped north for home, trading altitude for speed. The German levelled out a few hundred feet above the sea and weaved gently back and forth as he fled, keeping a wary mirror-eye on his pursuer. Bryan levelled out behind him, growling under his breath and rocking against his straps, willing the gap to close.

A detonation against the armour behind Bryan's seat punched the air out of his chest and jolted his head forward. Gasping against his empty lungs he screwed his face around in confusion. A hammer blow shattered his canopy and three concussions smashed into the nose ahead of the windshield. The engine rattled in mechanical agonies for a few seconds, then seized with a sickening jolt that jerked through the airframe.

A disconnected roar filled the sudden silence and Bryan looked up as the sky-blue underside of a 109 slid into place above him. Oil streaks feathered down its length and the malevolent white-edged crosses of the black knights filled its wings. It hung there for a moment, then wallowed over to the right, dropping down to fly alongside him. Mesmerised, Bryan watched its manoeuvre and found himself looking across at the pilot. The man lifted his goggles, as if removing a mask, and met Bryan's gaze. The German blinked impassively then turned his head away, surging his aircraft forward towards home.

Smoke feathered out of the crippled engine and seeped into the cockpit. Bryan watched the German pulling away as his Spitfire slowed and dipped into a silent, shallow dive.

'Shit.'

****

Ben sat on the roof balcony as the evening darkened into night. The low buzzing of insects added a droning undertone to the sedate orchestra which breathed its melodies from the radio set on the bar. The music drifted to a close and the plummy tones of a presenter broke into Ben's reverie. He tilted his head to listen.

'This is the BBC Home and Forces Programme. Here is the news. The Admiralty have announced the arrival of another convoy in Malta. This is the second convoy to reach the beleaguered George Cross island since June last.

'It is understood that some losses in merchantmen and naval craft were suffered in the operation. Enemy losses were two U-boats sunk, two E-boats destroyed, and at least sixty-six aircraft shot down. All ships are unloading without delay.'

Ben bowed his head and the first hot tear trickled down his cheek.

Chapter 25

Engines ripped through the air above her house, vibrating her bedroom window with their passing. Jacobella smiled; she'd learnt the difference in the timbre. These were friendly planes tearing across Valletta; defenders, not destroyers.

She swung her legs out of the bed and padded across the polished wooden floor. At her dressing table she sat, let her hair down and pulled her brush through its dark length, wincing as the odd tangle tripped her progress. She caught her own smile in the mirror and blushed at the happy, wanton glitter that sparkled in her eyes.

She dressed quickly, woke Lučija and went into the kitchen to boil a small pot of water for mint tea. She cut the last of the bread ration in two and spread a thin film of anchovy paste over each piece. Lučija entered the room and she bent to hug her.

'It's the feast of Santa Maria today.' She kissed her daughter's forehead. 'After breakfast, we'll go to the harbour and see what God has blessed us with.'

They finished their meagre breakfast quickly. Jacobella pinned up her hair while Lučija went to retrieve the knitted doll from her room. Together they walked down the stairs and out into the clear early morning air.

They hugged the edge of the gardens and dropped down onto Ordnance Street, traversing the face of the city that looked back over Floriana. They walked across Castille Place and ducked down St Paul Street past the newspaper offices. Turning right off St Paul, they descended a steep alley down to the wharf at the harbourside. The general flow ran with them; citizens drifted in the same direction, drawn by the hope of good news.

On the wharf, Jacobella pushed through the jostling crowds and found a space against some railings next to the water. She stood Lučija in front of her, resting her hands on the little girl's shoulders, and surveyed the docks opposite. Four large merchant vessels nestled against their moorings, stevedores still busy on their decks, unloading the last of the treasures they had delivered.

A flight of six Spitfires roared down the harbour, curving away over the breakwaters and out to sea. Their passing clamour was greeted by a blast of a ship's horn as a huge vessel loomed into view outside the harbour.

Surrounded by tug-boats and low in the water, the battered grey tanker edged between the breakwaters like the majestic arrival of a fat, drunken pharaoh into a newly conquered land.

Cheers rippled through the crowds lining the harbour walls and somewhere a brass band kicked up a dance tune. Jacobella bit her lip to contain the swell of emotion that filled her throat. Then she laughed. For joy and relief, she laughed.

'Ommi!'

Lučija's voice penetrated the noise of the crowd and she bent to her daughter. 'What's wrong?' she asked.

Lučija heaved a sob from her chest and pointed through the railings, down to the water. There, bobbing in the languid swell several yards below them, her dropped doll floated face-up. The knitted blue figure spun slowly in the current that moved it away from the harbour wall. As it became sodden, its legs sunk, tilting its torso upwards, lifting one arm into the air. Then it succumbed to the weight of water and slid below the surface, out of sight.

Sunday, 16 August 1942

Jacobella smiled at her daughter across the table. Lučija's features were still crumpled with sadness at her loss.

'Will he be angry I've lost the doll?' she asked quietly.

'No, I'm sure he won't.' Jacobella reached across and stroked her daughter's cheek. 'Now stop worrying. Go and put on your shoes, or we'll be late for church.'

The pair hurried down the stairs and walked hand-in-hand along the edge of the gardens. On Mint Street, they mingled with the small flow of parishioners heading towards St Augustine.

They dog-legged up the alley onto Bakery Street where the crowd grew denser. Jacobella looked ahead through the bobbing heads. There he was, waiting outside the church doors, his faded RAF cap visible above the milling throng. An electric jolt of visceral excitement clutched her breast and she caught her breath around it. She hurried the last few yards.

The man half-turned and she lurched to a halt. His hair was too dark, his nose was too stubby. He took off his cap and scratched his head, then turned to look into her eyes. His face was drawn and his eyes were shadowed with sorrow.

'Hello,' he said, 'are you Jacobella?'

Her stomach twisted like acid and her heart thumped in a single shocked contortion. She blinked once.

'Yes.' She breathed the word through trembling lips.

'My name is Ben,' the young man said. 'I flew with Bryan.'

The past tense clanged in Jacobella's ears and she shook her head slowly.

'I'm sorry.' The man's eyes glistened with the beginnings of his tears. 'He was posted as missing on Friday. I don't believe there's much hope.'

Jacobella clamped her jaw against the cry that fought for release from her throat. She pushed past the young pilot, jostled through the crowd at the door and escaped into the cavernous, coolness of the church. She guided Lučija onto the rearmost pew and sat next to her. She tensed every muscle of her body to choke the spasms of nauseous grief that clutched at her stomach, the effort genuflecting her torso forward as if in prayer, rocking her body around the pain.

The priest entered and the congregation stood, flowing into the sombre cadence of the first hymn. Lučija jumped to her feet, then noticed her mother had remained seated. Slowly, fearing rebuke, she sat down again.

The service rumbled on. Jacobella remained silent and seated. Each time the multitude rose without her, Lučija huddled closer to her still form.

The congregation sat once more and settled themselves to receive the reading. The priest advanced to his lectern, a smile beaming from his weathered face.

'On this glorious day of salvation, I offer you a reading from Corinthians Chapter 15.'

He paused and straightened his back. The silence in the nave deepened with attentive expectation.

'But when this corruptible shall have put on incorruption, and this mortal shall have put on immortality, then shall come to pass the saying that is written: death is swallowed up in victory.'

The priest raised his arms and lifted his face to the heavens in benediction.

'Oh death, where is thy victory? Oh death, where is thy sting? The sting of death is sin; and the power of sin is the law. But thanks be to God, who giveth us this victory through our Lord Jesus Christ.' He swept his gaze across the assembly. 'Let us pray.'

Jacobella rose to her feet amongst the sea of bowed heads.

'Enough!'

Her cry echoed around the gilt-edged archways and marble columns. It reverberated around the painted domes, the fine paintings and the alabaster statues. It died at last in the folds of gold-stitched silk on the altar. A sea of faces screwed around to stare at her, mouths open in surprise, eyes uncertain with fear. Jacobella ignored them, her gaze fixed on the priest's shocked face as she drew another breath past the constriction in her throat.

'I have had enough of God and Victory!'

Jacobella bent and picked up her daughter. She turned her back on the murmuring congregation and walked out of the church door, away from the cluttered, muttering gloom and into the fresh, clean sunlight.

Epilogue

Thursday, 20 August 1942

Ben walked down the staircase in Xara Palace with butterflies dancing in his stomach. He crossed the lobby and paused to take a steadying breath before he walked into the dining room. Chairs scraped the floor as the assembled pilots drew themselves to attention.

'Sit down, gentleman,' he said, aware of the blush that was creeping across his cheeks. 'I know most of you have carried out offensive fighter sweeps in France at one time or another. Today's operation will not be much different. We're on the look-out for similar things - invasion barges, railheads, airfields and transport on the move. They're not used to seeing Spitfires over their patch, so we'll definitely have the element of surprise on our side.

'For the first time in *my* memory, we'll be flying with guns fully loaded and our tanks brim-full.' He looked around the seventeen pilots seated before him. 'The transport is waiting outside.' He smiled. 'Let's go to Sicily.'

I hope you have enjoyed Falcons and will consider leaving an honest review on Amazon.

Visit my website at www.melvynfickling.com and sign up for the Bluebirds Newsletter for updates on my forthcoming work.

Like my page at Facebook.com/MelvynFicklingAuthor and follow me on Twitter @MelvynFickling

Pronunciation of Place Names

Valletta – As read;

Sliema – *Sleema*;

Lazzaretto – As read;

Marsamxett – *Marsam-shett*;

Manoel – *Man-o-el*;

Ta'Qali – *Tah-Arli* – Anglicised as *Takali*;

Mdina – *Em-dina* – Anglicised as *Madina*;

Mtarfa – *Em-tarfa*;

Hal Far – As read;

Kalafrana – As read;

Marsaxlokk – *Marsa-schlock*;

Xara – *Shara* – Anglicised as *Zara*.

Glossary of Terms

Airframe – Structural skeleton of an aircraft

Aileron – Movable surface usually near the trailing edge of a wing; controls the roll of the aircraft

Angels – Code word for altitude; Angels ten means 10,000 feet

AOC – Air Officer Commanding

Bandits – RAF slang for enemy aircraft

Blast-Pen – Stone enclosure built to protect individual aircraft

Blenheim – British twin-engine light bomber aircraft

Bounced – RAF slang for being attacked from above

Brylcreem Boys – Gently mocking nickname for RAF fighter pilots

Buster – Running a fighter engine on full boost; not recommended for long periods due to likelihood of damage and/or fire

Contrail – Condensation left by high-flying aircraft

Cowling – Curved panel covering the engine of an aircraft

Depth Charge – Specialist mine used against submarines

Dispersal – Area where planes are scattered widely to reduce potential damage if attacked

Dogfight – RAF slang for fighter versus fighter combat

Dorsal – Machine-gun position on upper side or back of a bomber

Elevator – Movable surface on the tail, controls pitch of the aircraft

Erks – RAF nickname for airmen

Flaps – Movable surface on an aircraft, usually near the trailing edge of a wing; increases lift and decreases speed

Flap – RAF slang for emergency

Flight – A fighting unit usually consisting of six aircraft

Fuselage – Main body of an aeroplane

G-force – Force acting on a body as a result of acceleration or gravity

Gaspers – Slang for cigarettes

Heinkel – (111) German twin-engine bomber

Heath Robinson – Cobbled together from available materials

HMS – His Majesty's Ship

HQ – Headquarters

Hurricane – Single-seat British fighter; slightly poorer performance than the Spitfire

Incendiary – Ammunition designed to encourage fire

Jink – To fly erratically to put off an attacker's aim

Junkers 88 – German twin-engine bomber

Kite – RAF slang for aeroplane

Mae West – British pilots' inflatable life preserver

Malta Dog – A virulent form of dysentery rife on Malta during the siege

Matelot – Sailor

Messerschmitt 109 – German single-seat fighter

Merlin – The celebrated engine used in many British aircraft, most famously the Spitfire

MNFU – Malta Night Fighting Unit

MP – Military Police

Orbit – To fly in a circle

O'clock – Used to locate the enemy in relation to line of flight; 12 o'clock is straight ahead, 6 o'clock is directly behind

Orderly – Officer in charge of administration of a unit or establishment for a day at a time

Perdition – A state of eternal punishment and damnation for the unrepentant sinner

Plots – Radar contacts translated to markers on a map

Port – Left-hand side of an aircraft; a port turn is to the left

Prop-wash – Blast of air caused by a propeller

Purgatory – A place of suffering inhabited by the souls of sinners who are expiating their sins in order to attain heaven

RAF – Royal Air Force

RDF – Radio Direction Finding; early form of radar

RFC – Royal Flying Corps (predecessor of the RAF)

Roundel – Concentric red white and blue circles used as identification for British planes

Rudder – Movable surface on an aircraft, usually on the tail; controls yaw of the aircraft

Section – Fighting unit of aircraft usually consisting of two or three aircraft, normally codenamed with a colour

Shrapnel – Broken pieces of bomb cases

Side-slip – Where an aircraft moves somewhat sideways as well as forward relative to the oncoming airflow

Slipstream – Flow of air around an airborne aircraft

Spitfire – Single-seat British fighter; slightly better performance than the Hurricane

Squadron – Fighting unit of aircraft usually consisting of 12 aircraft with six in reserve and 24 pilots

Starboard – Right-hand side of an aircraft; a starboard turn is to the right

Stick – Control column

Strafe – Rake the ground with gunfire from an aircraft

Stuka – Junkers 87; German dive-bomber

Swastika – Ancient crooked cross symbol adopted by the Nazis

Tail-plane – Also known as a horizontal stabiliser; a small lifting surface located on the tail

Tally-ho – Huntsman's cry to the hounds on sighting a fox; adopted by fighter pilots and used on sighting enemy aeroplanes

Tracer – Ordnance that glows in flight to show path of bullet-stream

Undercarriage – Wheels of an aircraft; can be fixed or retractable

Vector – Code word for heading

Vic – An arrowhead formation of aircraft

Vichy French – Collaborationist government of occupied France

Wellington – British twin-engine, long range medium bomber

Yaw – Twist or oscillate about a vertical axis

Author's notes

This is a historical novel based on real events. It is not a history of those events or of the people who found themselves entangled in those events.

Some major historical characters are named for authenticity. All the main characters are entirely fictional. Any similarity these characters may bear to persons living or dead is coincidental.

Locations are real, although the details of real locations have been fictionalised in a sympathetic manner.

The backdrop of events against which the novel is set is well documented elsewhere, although curiously little known even amongst those who have a keen interest in other theatres of this war. I have kept as close as possible to the actual timeline, but some events may have been shifted slightly to accommodate plot requirements. No disrespect is implied or intended to the people who were involved in those events.

Sources

Malta 1940 to 1942 – Ryan K Noppen

Night Fighter Navigator – Dennis Gosling DFC

One Man's Window – Denis Barnham

Tattered Battlements, A Malta Diary – Tim Johnston DFC

Torpedo Leader on Malta – Patrick Gibbs DSO DFC and Bar

Fortress Malta, an Island Under Siege – James Holland

Faithful Through Hard Times – Jean Gill

War Beneath the Sea – Peter Padfield

Spitfire, A Very British Love Story – John Nichol

Malta: War Diary - Story of a George Cross – Internet resource

FlyPast – October 2017 issue – Heroes of Malta

Psalm 84, Quam Dilecta – Thomas Weelkes

Printed in Great Britain
by Amazon

20783962R10139